Elemental Attraction

A Myth World Novel

By

K. Aten

©2021 by K. Aten

First publication 2021
Flashpoint Publications

ISBN 978-1-61929-463-9

Cover Design by AcornGraphics

Editors Micheala Lynn and Nann Dunne

Publisher's Note:

Acknowledgments

This book has been a new beginning of sorts for me. It was a new year, a new publishing company, and new beta readers. My first high fantasy novel was a wild ride for sure and there are a few people I need to thank that helped me make it happen. First I'd like to give big digital hugs and major praise to my betas for Elemental Attraction, Lex and Erle. You two came along when I needed you most and I admire your dedication and attention to detail. Next I'd like to thank May Dawney for stepping up last minute and creating a cover that superbly fit the characters, genre, and overall humor of my novel. May is a miracle worker when it comes to speculative fiction.

Finally, I'd like to thank my Flashpoint team. First is my editor, Micheala, who always knows what to expect from me (good and bad) and guides me with a gentle hand when my terrible grasp of the English language shines brightly in the manuscript. Yes, English *is* my only language but it's *hard*, okay?

Next, I'd like to thank Nann, who has taught me more about point of view one manuscript than I've learned in the twelve previous. POV is also hard and I'd never been properly instructed. Nann, you're amazing and it was a privilege working with you.

Last, but not least, I'd like to give another digital hug to Patty. It's a great feeling when your publisher has faith in you and respects your opinion, it's even better when they can be a sounding board and talk you through your writing block.

Dedication

This book is dedicated to my cats. They contributed to its creation nearly as much as I did. If you call staring for long periods of time, attempting to sit in my lap while I write, inspiring me with gifts of vomit, sneezing in my face from the window bed over my desk, and shedding incessantly across my entire workspace "contribution."

Maya, 8lbs, aka Maya Bean, My-My, or Butterscotch Baby
Clark, 16lbs, aka Clarky, Clarkles, Pink Nose, or Fatty-Fats

Credits

The map for Myth World was created using Azgaar's Fantasy Map Generator v1.61

Website: https://azgaar.github.io/Fantasy-Map-Generator/

Chapter One

I'm tired of sleeping outside.

Ellys spoke aloud in answer to the telepathic whine. "You're an animal, and animals sleep outside."

Roccotári gave a little hop that ended in a stiff-legged, bone-jarring stop in the middle of the road. Her mental voice was as indignant as only she could muster. *I am a nine-hundred-and-forty-two-cycle-old elven mount with intelligence and wisdom greater than that of half this Moder-forsaken country. I...am...not...an...animal.*

There was no arguing with Rocc when she was in this kind of mood. Ellys tried one last tactic. "We're low on coin right now, *cara.* You know that."

Roccotári blew out a breath and began walking again. *And just whose fault is that? I believe you used the words, 'she promises to show me Aphora and all the stars in the sky,' right before you went off with that tavern wench. Then shortly after that, she went off with our coin pouch. And it wasn't the first time that has happened! I sure hope you fight better than you fuck, because falling asleep like that was a pure disgrace.*

Ellys adjusted the leather headband that circled her short, black hair. Half elf, as proclaimed by her pointy ears, silver eyes, and pale skin, she was taller and stronger than most humans. "If I've told you once, I've told you a dozen times, I'm certain she used sleep magic on me."

The towering steed snorted and blew out a good bit of steam in the cool air. *The only magic she used on you was her magical mouth—*

"Enough! We're nearly to Longoria. We have enough coin to book you a stable and a hot rubdown, and if Toroc wills it, I'll pick up some work."

As usual, Rocc got in the last dig. *As long as it's only work you're picking up.*

They traveled in silence for more than a candle mark, heading east around the bay. The road got a lot busier as they traversed the surrounding region outside the capital. Eventually, they found themselves amongst a throng of people and Ellys grew progressively more agitated as they approached the wall that surrounded the city of the Carthunian king.

"Why's it so mage-blasted busy? For that matter, why are people coming into the city so late in the day instead of heading out into the countryside to their homes?"

Luckily, Rocc was significantly larger than a normal horse and most people gave them a wide berth on the bustling main road that led into the capital of Carthune. The rapidly falling sun cast an orange glow around the spires of the castle in the distance. Ellys took note of the brightly-colored, woven banners that flapped from the buildings and poles beyond the gate ahead of them.

You could try asking someone.

"Fine." Ellys raised her voice and called to the soldier on duty at the gatehouse. "Ho there, what's with all the people and what are the banners about?"

The woman motioned for her compatriot, "Watch the incoming crowd." For what, Ellys wasn't sure. Then she moved closer to be heard over the sound of horses and wagons going by. "It's the Sprin-grise Festival. We've got five days of tournaments starting tomor-row. But many people come into the city each night to see the performers that are paid for by the crown." She paused to eye the swords on Ellys's back. "You should enter the tourney if you're any good with those. There's a coin purse for the winner of each event."

"Tomorrow, you say?"

The soldier nodded.

"Is that all events? And where do I sign up?"

"Just sword tomorrow. The other four days will be"—the guard ticked off the rest on her fingers—"jousting, unarmed combat, archery, and mage craft. Sign up tomorrow morning in the field across the river. Take the bridge closest to the castle, and you can't miss it."

I think that sounds like our best bet to score some coin until you find a contract.

Ellys muttered, "Says the one who won't be risking her furry ass against a score of sword fighters."

"Excuse me?"

Ellys gave an embarrassed cough. "Sorry, talking to my horse."

I'm not a horse!

"Anyway, is there an inn you recommend for a night or two?"

The soldier frowned and shook her head. "If you wanted a room in the city, you'd have had to arrive days ago. The only bed you're likely to find will either be full of vermin or rented by the candle mark. Possibly both if you know what I mean."

Ellys slapped her thigh. "Fenwith's balls!" She blew out a frustrated breath then gave a nod to the other woman. "What about a stable?"

The soldier gave her a confused look. "You'd rent a place for your beast and not yourself?" She got laughter and an indignant whinny for her words.

"I owe her one."

"Very well. There's a livery called The Noble Steed. It's across from Gul's Tavern and The Sleepy Sheep. Tell Berg that Moli sent you. He's my mate's cousin and may let you sleep in the stall with your horse if you slip him an extra copper."

Still not a horse.

"Thank you kindly for the information, friend. I hope Toroc's balance flows through your blade with every swing."

Moli's mouth dropped open at the mention of the mysterious Binary Goz of War, but she didn't get a chance to say more. Rocc had already moved them back into the crowd pushing through the gates.

Ellys and Rocc made their way toward the center of Longoria. Ellys had learned to trust the people who manned the gates since they usually knew what was what. She heard bells toll in the distance, signaling that the sun had dropped below the horizon.

The Noble Steed appeared well kept from the outside. Luckily, Ellys had enough silver to cover the cost of Rocc's stabling for two nights, and Berg did indeed let her bed down in the stall for an extra copper. Unfortunately, that took the remainder of their coin and she was forced to eat travel rations for her evening meal. She wasn't looking forward to sleeping in the cold. Even if the stall was inside and sheltered from the elements, it was still early spring and Ellys hated to spend the night chilled to the bone.

As expected, her sleep suffered and the next morning, she woke early and stiff. But it couldn't be helped; she needed activity. She discovered a courtyard behind the livery, and since there were no others up in the predawn light, she used the space to perform *secaeli*, a fixed sequence of moves used in sword training. It was sometimes called the "Sword Dance" by followers of Toroc. Ellys drew both blades and began the complicated warming exercise she had learned as a youngling while growing up in the monastery. Her body flowed fluidly as she touched on the five fundamental stances with each blade moving independently.

By the time Ellys was finished with the sword dance, sunrise had passed and her muscles were sufficiently warm. She reentered the stable and quickly made her way to Rocc's stall. The large elven steed leaned over the gate to lip at Ellys's hair, so the swordswoman rubbed her companion's velvety muzzle. "I'm off to enter the day's tournament. Any requests for me?"

Win.

"I may not, you know. This is no backwoods city. Longoria is the largest in Carthune. They're sure to have swords from all around competing. And if we don't win that coin purse…" She grimaced. Their wealth had always been precarious as each new day challenged her sense of balance, but she tried to take care of Roccotári before herself when a choice needed to be made.

Rocc gave her a nudge. *I have faith in you,* caritas. *I trust your blades to be true and balanced.*

"Thanks, old friend." She turned on her heel and started for the livery door but stopped when Rocc called out to her.

Ellys!

"Yes?"

Bring me an apple after you win.

"Once a horse, always a—"

If you finish that statement, I'll leave the biggest shit pile in my stall right where you plan to sleep.

Ellys laughed all the way out the door. Rocc had done what she always did and brought her out of her sour mood.

It wasn't hard to find the bridge and the field described by Moli. Ellys signed up for the tournament's sword event and moved off to the side to take in her fellow competitors. She had a large pouch slung across her chest that rested at her hip and contained a whetstone, bandages, and rations for the day. Ellys was sick of dried meat and hard travel bread, but it would have to do until she could buy herself a hot meal. She also had a water skin slung over her shoulder. Despite the day's cold start, she would get quite warm and thirsty while fighting.

The day was exactly as long as she had feared as the fighters grew fewer and fewer with each round of advance. At first, Ellys worried that the tournament would be melee style with everyone fighting at once but that proved not to be the case. It wasn't that she questioned her own skill, but rather melee fighting was significantly more chaotic and made one prone to serious injury. It didn't encourage the balance that was important to a follower of Toroc.

The sun neared the horizon as Ellys stood on the edge of the large fighting circle where the last round would begin in mere candle drops. She did a few deep-breathing exercises and purposely didn't look at the sword-wielding behemoth on the opposite side. She'd seen him fight earlier and knew he'd be a difficult challenge. Not only due to his size and the fact that he carried a massive broadsword that was nearly as long as she was tall. Her half-elven heritage gave her strength and stamina beyond most humans, or "gaugins" as elves called them. Her height was also enough to eliminate some of the brute's size advantage. Ellys's worry was that the man most likely wasn't a man, at all, but another half-breed like her. In all the fights she'd seen him in, he never appeared to tire. Her speed was faster, but it had been a long day and she'd quickly slow the longer they fought.

She glanced off to the center of the observation stand where the king and his retinue sat watching the festivities. Ellys had heard rumors of his failing health and even from a distance could see the pallor of the slumped figure on the makeshift throne. She'd also heard whispers that his illness wasn't natural. There was much talk amongst the sword fighters that someone high up in the king's council was making a play for power.

Fortunately, it was none of her concern. Most situations of similar nature eventually balanced themselves, though the southern aggression against Muniers and the magical barrier between the two countries she'd heard talk of was disconcerting. It could potentially affect any contract she received while in the city.

Ellys shook the thoughts away when she realized her mind was wandering. Camen Dru, the abbez of her home monastery and her first sword master, would have taken her to task cycles ago if they'd seen her lack of focus. She pushed down all speculation of war and regicide to focus on the coming sword match. Ellys narrowed her thoughts to just two things: winning the prize purse, and the hope that she wouldn't have to spend another cold night in the stable.

A cacophony of horns cut through the murmuring of the spectators, and the loud speech of the tournament announcer followed in its wake. He had a deep, bellowing voice that easily carried across the gathering. "With the king's blessing, we will get this last battle underway!" The king raised one shaky hand and gave a nod, and the announcer shouted, "We are down to the final round. Guznir the Great has come to Longoria from the vast expanse of the Northern Reach just to participate in this cycle's Springrise Tournament. He is a devout follower of Bron." The crowd cheered and Ellys thought that perhaps some local folks had heard of the man, or they were devout followers of the brutal god themselves.

They quieted again when the announcer raised his hands. "And on the opposite side of the circle we find a follower of Toroc, Ellys DeEnsis. Which one of these war god elites will prevail in the end?"

Ellys sneered at the hulking man across from her and spat on the ground. Followers of Bron were not known to respect the balance. After all, the primitive god of war was called Bron the Brutal for a reason. Unfortunately, Bron was the better known of the two. Toroc, the Binary Goz of War, was a mysterious deity of indeterminate gender who inspired balance. Followers were masters in warring arts but didn't encourage battle unless it promoted equity or resulted in eventual harmony. Hotheaded fighters didn't always appreciate such a view.

Her rumination was interrupted by a roar from Guznir. "Everybody knows that Toroc isn't a real god! Only Bron the Brutal is worthy of the mantle of war!" The crowd cheered with his words, and Ellys let it wash over her. She didn't follow Toroc for their popularity; she followed the Binary Goz for their truth.

She gave the big man a disarming smile and raised her voice. "War is not a state of being. War is the means to an end, and if that end does not promote balance, then truth is lost."

The announcer quickly stepped back from the circle and yelled, "Fighters, you may now raise your blades!" As soon as the last word echoed off the wooden spectator section, Guznir roared again and charged.

Ellys was allowed to use both swords, just as Guznir could use his massive blade. She shed his first swing without taking any real force from the hit and spun out of the way. Ellys did this three times, and each one further provoked the big man's anger. He finally snapped. "Are you a fighter or a fairy? Engage me, you fucking elf trash."

"Hey, some of my closest friends are fae, so watch that bog hole you call a mouth." Ellys was hoping his fury would make him sloppy and imprecise, but unfortunately that proved not to be the case. He yelled again and came at her in a flurry of hard-hitting strokes, which she just barely parried with both her blades. She scored first blood with her speed, but one of his heavy downward strokes was so hard it numbed her hand and one of her swords flew away. She threw herself sideways into a tumble, careful to avoid cutting off one of her own limbs on the remaining sword.

"Ha! Not so confident without one of your little pointed toys, are you? Perhaps I should lop off both ears instead of just one, so you'll be properly balanced when I send you off to your binary god, hmm?"

Ellys drew herself up, took a deep breath, and rapidly moved through her five forms in an abbreviated version of the sword dance. Despite having only one blade, she gave an impressive show, and the crowd ate it up. Even Guznir seemed mesmerized by the spinning metal, or perhaps he was awaiting his opportunity to strike. When she came to a stop again, on the fifth and final form, she gestured with her free hand for him to come to her.

Guznir scowled and lowered his voice for her to hear alone. "What are you playing at, elf?" Then he laughed and spoke louder for the crowd. "You look like a first-cycle fighter trying to intimidate someone who is their obvious superior."

Ellys smiled back. "You look like your mother fucked a tree, and you were naught more than an infected splinter that fell from her getch moons later." Immediately, her words had their intended effect.

Enraged, Guznir attacked again.

With only one sword, Ellys couldn't take the full force of his swings. But she had other plans. Guznir had the greater reach, but he was overconfident. His furious blows hammered down upon her remaining blade, and she was forced to use both hands to receive and shed them away. What Guznir and many other fighters didn't know, was that followers of Toroc weren't simply taught the use of weapons and naught else. Ellys had spent decades learning every weak part, every susceptible joint, on hundreds of different species' bodies. Truthfully, she was a master of more than sword discipline. As a dual student of both the Order of Sword and the Order of Fist, she had been taught to analyze any situation and come up with a counter many steps in advance.

Ellys was prepared for his next sword swipe from his right side. It left Guznir slightly tilted with his right shoulder dropped and his left side open. Using just one hand to hold his blade with her own, she focused all her energy on a forward punch to his ribs and listened with satisfaction as at least one snapped beneath the half-elven strength of her blow. He howled and spun away, grasping his side. Ellys decided it was the perfect opportunity for a teaching moment and raised her voice to address Guznir and the crowd. "War is about more than steel."

He charged again, clearly in pain. His downward blow would have surely cost her the second blade had she been there to take it. But she collapsed beneath his swing and dove between Guznir's legs. When she came up behind him, she gave a kick to his off-balance leg and Guznir fell hard to one knee. Her voice remained loud enough for all to hear. "War is about more than strength."

Guznir flipped onto his back, away from having her behind him, then gave a kick with his massive leg. Ellys avoided the leg and parried a swipe from the big blade. His prone position on the ground made it difficult for him to bring the broadsword around to bear from the opposite direction while one-handed. As events unfolded, Ellys made instant calculations about possible actions. She used his body as a springboard and purposely stepped on the area near his broken ribs. She flipped to the spot just beyond his head and whirled to face his body.

A drop of sweat trickled down from the center of Guznir's forehead, and a look of resignation filled the giant man's face. Ellys brought her sword straight down to his throat, stopping as the magical blade drew the smallest drop of blood. Ellys could have killed him; it was within her right as dictated by the rules of the tournament. She chose not to.

Even the crowd grew quiet at the speed and precision of her actions. In the silence that followed, she called out one last time. "War is about more than speed. The true art of war is about skill, about knowing what to do and when to do it."

The announcer signaled her win, and she removed her sword and stepped away in case Guznir had ideas of furthering their match beyond its intended end. She expected to see a look of rage on his face after her opponent used his sword to pull himself back to his feet. Instead, he narrowed his eyes, tilted his head, and gave her a look of contemplation.

When she spoke again, it was while meeting his serious gaze. Ellys repeated her earlier statement before the match began. "War is not a state of being. War is the means to an end, and if that end does not promote balance, then truth is lost. I've shown you my truth today, Guznir. Do you accept it?" She wiped and sheathed her sword then held out a hand.

Guznir the Great moved his gaze from her face down to the offered hand. With slow movements that couldn't be misconstrued as an attack, he sheathed his own massive weapon upon his back and clasped her forearm. He raised his voice as well, but with admiration instead of ire. "I will respect your truth if you respect my honor."

Ellys smiled. "Your honor was never in question. It was a privilege to fight against another student of war. Good day to you, Guznir." Ellys bowed to him. She was satisfied that she'd brought him back to the balance.

The brawny man smiled back and gave a nod before turning away.

Ellys was rewarded with a jingling pouch and a small golden idol. She could have done without the latter, which was most likely painted smelt metal, but she looked forward to getting a room with the coins. She tucked the idol into her satchel and opened the coin purse to count her winnings. Ellys was unable to hold her tongue once she'd seen what a full day of fighting and a sore body had earned her. "Five copper?"

The announcer was the one who handed over the winning prize. He smiled and jutted out his chest at her exclamation, mistaking it for one of happy surprise. "Yes, one for each day of the tournament. And of course you have the idol to display in your dwelling to remind you of the day's momentous win. Congratulations again, noble fighter."

She merely growled and stalked away from him. Ellys was more than a bit dejected as she made her way back to the Noble Steed. She tried to ignore her rumbling belly as the smells of roast meats wafted out of various taverns. Instead, she paused at a fruit vendor and used one of the coppers to purchase a few apples for Rocc. Everything was more expensive in the city. Back in the livery, she made her way to Rocc's stall.

Roccotári gave a little whinny of pleasure when she scented the apples. *You won.*

Ellys held an apple in the palm of her hand so her companion could take a bite. The fruit made a delightful crunch, and Ellys listened to the wet chewing for a candle drop before answering. "I did."

But you're disappointed.

"I am. The prize for a day of sword fighting was five coppers and some cheap trinket. You're eating one of the coppers now."

Rocc momentarily stopped chewing and nuzzled Ellys's cheek with her soft muzzle. *I'm sorry, cara. If it makes you feel any better, I didn't spoil your sleeping spot.*

"By Toroc, you're too considerate."

The steed gave a bray of laughter. *I know. If it helps, I heard the people in the livery talking about the tavern across the street. You should be able to pick up a contract over there. Use the rest of your coppers to get a good meal. You've certainly earned it.*

Ellys felt a wash of healing energy and welcomed the sudden disappearance of her various aches and pains. She rubbed Rocc's muzzle and set another apple on the post of the stall, within easy reach should her friend want it. "Thanks. You didn't happen to hear anything about a certain king's illness, did you?"

I heard a lot about a lot actually. It seems that Berg is quite the gossipmonger, and many stop in to hear what he has to say. He gets a lot of out-of-town customers and as such has a trough of information to sell, gleaned from friends who work at the palace.

"And?"

Sounds like Chancellor Temet has got his sights set on a higher station than the one he currently holds. He speaks out against the king's failing health in many side councils and pushes for the old man to be replaced by a temporary regent.

"Let me guess, next in line for power is the chancellor?"

Rocc pawed the ground. *Actually, it's the king's daughter, Princess Ameelia. Rumor has it that she's very intelligent and known to be as fair and just as her father.*

"And why hasn't she gotten wind of the king's illness or the chancellor's intentions?"

She's gone off to study at the Mage University of Indenes, over in Saccerid. The king wanted her to have supplemental training to prepare her for the day she is to take over rule here in Carthune.

"If she doesn't return soon, there will likely be no ruling at all in her future." Ellys shook her head. "Speculation is all well and good, but the balance of Carthune isn't part of my path and none of this talk fills an empty stomach. I'm going to head to the trough around back and get cleaned up, then I'll check out Gul's Tavern. I'll do my best to score a contract. After all, I promised before we arrived at Longoria and I won't let you down."

Rocc nuzzled her again. *You've never let me down, caritas.*

Chapter Two

The tavern was busy, but Ellys could tell she was being watched nearly as soon as she entered. Despite the quick healing in the livery, the swordswoman was tired, cranky from sleeping out in the cold the night before, and unbearably hungry. She purposely chose a bench seat with her back to the wall as far from the door as possible. It was good practice to be on guard in a foreign city, especially when she had very publicly beaten a follower of Bron the Brutal earlier. Even if she won Guznir's honor, there were ten who would seek her out and pick a fight on their god's behalf. It was another reason why she was leery about being watched.

Ellys's itchy thoughts were interrupted as a mug and bowl thumped onto the table in front of her. She handed the serving man three coppers without so much as a flirt on her part. The man moved away to help someone else. She promised Roccotári that she'd be all business until their coin purse was full again. But before she could consider any promises or jobs, she needed food in her yowling belly. It had been a long day.

Ellys liked Gul's Tavern immediately upon entering because of the diversity of its clientele and servers. Berg had even mentioned as much when she spoke with him in the rear courtyard of the stables while she was cleaning up. He said that neither the management nor the clientele cared what or whom you were into, as long as you paid for your food, your companions were willing adults, and you didn't start trouble. Ellys lifted a spoon of stew into her mouth just as the cloaked figure in the corner made their move toward her table.

"I saw you fighting earlier today, and I have to say I'm highly impressed. What's your fee?" The voice was low and quiet, with a feminine lilt, though it was impossible to be sure of gender with their face hidden in the dark depths of the cloak hood.

Ellys swallowed. She was already in a foul mood after a poor night's sleep and the disappointing day's winnings. There was a single copper in her pouch after paying for the meal and drink with a little extra for the server. So, the fact that the person sitting across from her chose to make their move now rather than wait until she was done eating only served to irritate her further. "I think you have me mistaken for someone else." Ellys glanced around the tavern and figured she could still score a contract if she sent this one away.

"There's been no mistake. You are Ellys DeEnsis, worshiper of Toroc and winner of the Springrise Tournament day of swords. Right now, you are wearing both swords on your back, and your guild patch is on your arm for anyone to see. If you weren't available, you'd have it covered. So how much?"

The spoon made a dull sound as it dropped into the wooden bowl, and Ellys sat back with both hands flat on the table in front of her. Her hunger had moved to the angry stage. Good humor gone, she squinted at the unwanted guest in front of her. Sure, she needed coin, but the person's know-it-all attitude rubbed her the wrong way. With slow and precise movements, Ellys moved her right arm across her body and carefully rolled her left sleeve to hide the patch. "For you, I'm not available. Shove off."

The body on the other side of the table jerked, and the voice became more intense. "I won't take no for an answer."

"Don't care what you do or don't take. Nothing you say at this point will change my mind."

Rather than answer, the figure reached into the depths of the black cloak. Ellys tensed at first, suspicious of mage work or a weapon. But rather than a blade, the cloaked figure removed a gold coin and placed in on the table next to Ellys's bowl. "This is but the first of three. I need an escort."

In a world like theirs, gold softened hunger pangs and changed a lot of attitudes. Ellys didn't take her eyes off the coin. "Where?"

"Muniers."

They were currently in the city of Longoria, in Carthune. The country itself had decent roads and as such they were only a dozen days from the border. Unfortunately, they wouldn't be able to take the quick route. Ellys grunted. "You're aware that the border is closed, right? Magically, I believe. So…nigh on impossible to get through without an official charm."

"It is closed, but neither Carthune nor Muniers would dare close their border to the Kuwyth Empire. It would be no great feat to detour through Cat's Head so that we can enter Muniers legally."

Ellys envisioned the map in her head and followed the trade road south from Longoria to the split that would take them into the southeastern corner of Kuwyth. "Where in Muniers?"

She could just make out the shadow of pursed lips visible within the hood, and by that alone, she knew it would be no quick jaunt should she take the job. The mysterious patron's words confirmed it.

"Clan Dracona is a handful of days south of Noth, along the coast."

Only Clan went into Clan lands without an escort, which told a lot about the person across from her. The mention of a Clan gave Ellys pause, but a job was a job. She debated the good and bad of it in her head. The destination requested meant they were looking at more than a moon of travel time, possibly two if they were slowed down on the journey. Even so, three gold was triple her normal escort guard rate for that amount of time.

"What's the catch? For that matter, I need a name and a face before I make any kind of decision."

Strong-looking, long-fingered hands came up and pulled the hood down from an unlined and youthful face. The woman's hair was a fiery mix of deep reds and golds, and she had full lips, a strong chin, and high cheekbones. Her skin was dark, nearly black. If Ellys hadn't deduced that the potential patron was a shifter based on their destination, she would have suspected the woman to be one of her own Drow cousins. The stranger looked young, but that wasn't an indicator of anything in a city as large as Longoria, especially for Clan.

"My name is Aderri, and I wouldn't call it a catch exactly. The task merely has two parts."

"Exactly?"

"Yes, I need an escort. That much is certainly true. But I'm also going home to see my Clan after being gone for many cycles."

Ellys's eyes widened. Clans were formed when lone shifters and other magical creatures bonded to create their own family. Often, they would grow for decades until they formed their own mixed shifter community, either taking over a town or creating a new one within Clan lands. They were typically insulated to outside society, and while Ellys had met and interacted with many shifters, she'd never personally met a Clan member in all her cycles of travel. "How long?"

"I was last home sixty-eight cycles ago."

"Hmm, that's a long time to be gone. Will any of the members remember you?"

Aderri glanced up to Ellys's pointed ears. "Not long for some." Ellys nodded in acknowledgement of her own race, half though it was, and Aderri continued. "Most will remember me, but they'll also have…expectations."

Ellys still felt mostly in the dark. And triple fee or no, she wanted details before she made her decision, Rocc's opinion of their finances be damned. "Tell me plain. I'm in no mood for dancing around while my food grows cold."

The flame-haired woman reached out and held her hand over the bowl. Heartbeats later, the stew inside was steaming again. Aderri smiled sweetly and Ellys's gaze was drawn to the tiny fangs digging into her full bottom lip, every bit as alluring as her bold features. Aderri was beautiful and certainly eye-catching to say the least. "Better?"

"And why exactly do you need an escort?"

Aderri pulled her hand back and tucked it into her cloak again. "I told you, the job is two-fold. The first part is to see me across the two borders. While I may have a few tricks up my sleeve—"

Ellys snorted. "Literally."

"My magic is mostly limited to defensive spells and such in this form, and right now the land between here and Muniers is rife with brigands. Not to mention, the strife at the border has tensions running high in both places. It's dangerous for a strapping warrior, let alone for someone who appears unarmed and significantly more delicate."

"I suppose shifting to protect yourself is out of the question?"

Aderri leveled a worried look at her. "It wouldn't be wise." Ellys raised a black eyebrow and Aderri elaborated. "People may panic. Worse yet, the king's mages would be alerted to my presence."

Her answer only served to pique Ellys's curiosity even more, but she didn't press for Aderri's shifter identity. "Fair enough."

"Anyway, safety is of course my primary concern. However, if you should agree to the second part of the deal, I will guarantee one more gold in addition to the ones promised for the escort."

Heartbeats went by while Ellys considered Aderri's words. Then, to buy herself more time, she took a bite of the re-warmed stew. She washed it down with a swig of mead before answering. "And the second part of the task, the one that takes me outside my guard duties and is worth a gold coin all on its own?"

"Cyvrus Dracona has announced his first hatchling, and a summoning was given for the entire Clan to return for the naming ceremony. That includes wanderlings like me. It is imperative that I attend. Tradition says that, unless exiled, a Clan member only ventures outside their home territory to find a mate. It would bring shame upon me to return alone, with no romantic interest at all to show for my decades of travel."

Ellys looked at the woman curiously. "Well, you're certainly fairer that most I've met. Why don't you have a romantic interest if that's why you left?"

Aderri scowled. "Because I didn't leave to find something as inconsequential and mundane as romance. I went out into the world to explore, learn, and gather knowledge. Tying myself to one person for the rest of my life seems like an agonizing bore. Not to mention, if I don't match my race, I'll most likely love then lose any potential mate to old age long before I myself shed the mortal coil, which would be traumatic in its own right."

Aderri's gaze moved away, and Ellys did her best to school the flash of pain from her face. "Hmm."

"What's that supposed to mean?"

Ellys took another bite of her stew and spoke with a full mouth. She had no desire to share her own past trauma. "It means *hmm*, nothing more. I'm contemplating my options. While the idea of your gold sits nicely in my head, I'm not sure it's worth the potential drama. I'm no whore to be prostituting myself out for coin." She paused and quickly amended her statement. "Not that I've anything against whores. Noble profession and all to put up with the lonely and lustful. But that's not my guild, I earn my way with the blades on my back."

"Three gold for the second task."

Ellys dropped the spoon back into the bowl. "Why me?"

Aderri's eyes darted away, and she suddenly looked shy. "Because you're fit and fair of face, and you match my usual type so well, they'd be sure to believe that I chose you as a potential mate."

"Usual type?"

"I do prefer androgyny. And I am especially fond of warriors with swords."

Ellys raised a single dark brow. "Oh really? And why is that?"

Aderri smiled and Ellys was once again drawn to those tiny, pointed canines. "Because warriors can usually keep up."

"No gender preference?"

"Gender is irrelevant to my kind, but I prefer balance, hence the androgyny that elves are known for."

Ellys left the comment alone and told her curiosity to take a long walk down the trade road to Dovahn. Work was work. She mentally rued her promise to Rocc. "How long?"

"It's hard to say, exactly. The naming ceremony itself is an evening-long at most. However, it is tradition to have gatherings and revelry leading up to the event. After that, we'll be free to leave again."

A calloused hand slid toward the coin until Ellys's index finger rested atop it. "And you give your word there will be no sex involved, merely guarding your body from brigands, and guarding your runaway secret from your family with a little romantic play-acting?"

Aderri held up her hand, palm facing Ellys. "On my honor, that is my only intention for your hiring. I'll also pay for any food or lodging costs incurred on the way there."

The additional promises sealed the deal for Ellys, and she pressed her palm flat against Aderri's. A flash of warmth washed between them and flowed up their arms. Ellys's skin prickled from the energy, but Aderri acted as though it didn't affect her at all. Once the pact was sealed, Ellys picked up the coin and tucked it away into her tunic. Aderri pulled back. "I'll give you two more when we reach my Clan lands, and the other three at the end of the ceremony, after we leave."

Ellys scooped another mouthful of stew and spoke again while she chewed. "What now?" Aderri wrinkled her nose as a piece of meat fell from Ellys's mouth back into her bowl. Ellys continued chewing and ignored the reaction. She got enough grief about her manners from Rocc and didn't need another person lecturing her.

"Do you have a room?"

"I only just arrived in Longoria yesterday evening. I've got my steed in the livery across the street, which is where I slept last night. Berg, the livery owner, warned me that with the festival going this quarter moon, I'd be hard pressed to find a place."

"Leave it to me. I've got one more task to complete, and then I'll procure two rooms at the inn next door. Meet me there after you've finished with your stew."

"The Sleepy Sheep?"

"Yes." Then as quickly as Aderri had moved in to sit at Ellys's table, her hood was pulled up and Ellys's new patron was gone without a backward glance.

Ellys spoke aloud, though no one was paying attention to her in the busy tavern. "These jobs get stranger and stranger." She paused. "At least Rocc will stop pestering me."

****

A short while after finishing her meal and drink, Ellys strode up the steps to the inn and pushed through the door. It was chilly outside with the setting sun and spring barely begun, so the warmth felt nice even after such a short walk. She immediately caught sight of Aderri speaking with the innkeeper. Aderri's voice rose with displeasure.

"What do you mean you only have one room?"

The rotund innkeeper looked apologetic enough. He stroked his beard as he answered. "Apologies, miss, but we've been filled for the past quarter moon and will most likely remain so until the festival is over. You're lucky that one person left unexpectedly, freeing up the single room."

Cold air washed through the main room as the door opened behind Ellys and another potential customer pushed in. The innkeeper looked at Ellys, then the man behind her, and turned back to Aderri. "Look, do you want the room or not? I'll have no problems filling it if you don't."

With a quick glance at Ellys, she answered. "I'll take it."

He smiled congenially. "That will be two silver."

"Two silv—" Aderri's voice cut off when the innkeeper looked pointedly at the two people by the door. Rather than protest any longer, Aderri reached into her cloak and pulled out two silver. She handed it over and looked the man straight in the eye. "I expect breakfast for two in the morning."

He dropped the coins into his own pouch and gave a short bow. "As you say, miss." Then he looked toward the door. "Apologies to you both, but we're full. You might try the Rusty Swan down the road."

Ellys nodded toward Aderri. "Oh, I'm with her." The other man grumbled, turned on his heels, and pushed outside.

Aderri asked, "Do you have your pack?"

"It's across the road with Rocc."

Dark red brows drew together. "You didn't mention a companion."

"Roccotári is my steed."

Aderri tilted her head. "And you trust your pack at the livery?"

"I trust Rocc. She won't let anyone near it. What about you? Do you have a mount?"

"No. Horses and I don't get along."

"Really?"

"Yes. I think they're afraid." The innkeeper appeared startled by her answer but didn't speak up.

Ellys gave her a long look up and down and repeated herself. "Really?"

"You can see for yourself tomorrow morning. And before you become concerned, I can easily run at a horse's pace, therefore I don't actually need a mount. I can keep up just fine."

The innkeeper looked back and forth between the two bickering women. "No wonder you wanted two rooms." Then he held out a key. "Number six, up the stairs and at the end of the hall. There's a wash basin and brazier in your room. If you need more fuel for heating, it's in the shed just off the kitchen, over there." He waved toward a door to the left of the stairs.

"Well enough." Aderri grabbed the key and spoke to Ellys. "Go get your pack. I'll wait here for you to return before going up to the room."

Ellys grumbled at being ordered about, but she figured for six gold she'd put up with a few imperious commands from an attractive woman. It took less than five candle drops to jog to the livery, briefly explain the job to Roccotári, and jog back.

Upstairs, the room was clean, if small. Ellys glanced at the long bed that would fit both of them easily, if they weren't complete strangers. "So how do you want to do this?"

Aderri turned to look at her. "How do *you* want to do this? The answer seems quite obvious to me. We have two people that need to sleep and a bed that will fit two."

"I don't appreciate your sarcasm."

Aderri huffed and walked over to the brazier. "And I don't appreciate your persistent ignorance and lack of common sense."

Ellys scowled. "I have plenty of common sense. A person doesn't make their way with sword alone without being somewhat capable. Not to mention I'm half elf," she said haughtily.

"Yes, well you're half human, too, and they're not exactly known for their brilliance."

Ellys cut her off before Aderri could disparage her or her lineage further. "You hired me, remember?"

Full lips twisted as if Aderri had bitten into something sour. "So I did."

"You're a bit of a pilgarlic. Can we call a truce now? I'd like to get through this night and all the rest until I'm absolved from this contract. After which we can go our separate ways."

"Fine." Aderri turned her back on Ellys and held her hand over the brazier. Within a matter of heartbeats, the coals inside glowed bright red. "That should hold us for a while."

Ellys looked around the room, noticed a distinct lack of tinder or other material, then raised a dark brow. "And after?"

Aderri sniffed and walked to the bed. She removed a large, empty-looking satchel from beneath her cloak that Ellys swore wasn't there before. "We'll be sharing a bed, and I'm plenty warm. I'd wager you won't need an extra heat source with me next to you."

Ellys opened her mouth to respond then shut it. It would do no good to rile up the woman who promised so much gold for a finished job. It was best to hold her tongue and hope to start anew in the morning. Her mind made up, she removed her harness and swords, pulled one from the sheath, and laid it across the stand next to the bed. "I'll take door side."

Aderri waved her hand and draped her cloak over the back of the chair. "Fine, I trust your judgment in these things."

Ellys had a feeling Aderri was humoring her but wisely didn't press the issue. It was still early in the evening, though darkness was fast falling outside. They were barely out of winter. The temperature dropped low each night, but the spring rains were mostly finished for the season, a fact that those who made their living traveling the land greatly appreciated.

While Aderri lit a candle the same way she had the brazier, Ellys pulled her pack near the small table and took a seat in the rickety wooden chair. Then she unfastened the top flap and removed a cup and a carefully wrapped bottle. She unwound the spare shirt from the bottle and tossed the garment back in the pack before placing the bottle on the table. It wasn't full size, but then it didn't need to be. She motioned toward the bottle and met Aderri's gaze. "Care for a dram?" Despite her irritation for her patron, balance dictated that she offer hospitality to back up her words of truce.

A single flame-colored brow rose. "Is that… elven wine?"

Ellys poured a few mouthfuls into the cup. "Absolutely."

"I thought elves didn't allow their special wine to flow beyond the veil. Do you have connections with your brethren within the great Ethereal Forest?"

"Absolutely not. But I have other connections that are a bit more trustworthy." She held up the bottle and gave it a waggle.

Ellys's comment drew a curious look from Aderri, but the patron didn't question her. "Not that it will affect me in the slightest, but I'm amenable to the sharing. Thank you."

"You'd be surprised who elven wine can affect."

Aderri walked over to her magical satchel and withdrew a small, ornately carved cup. Then she made the three steps back to the table and took a seat across from Ellys. Less than a candle drop later, they were both sipping the fabled elven wine.

"Well, what do you think?"

Aderri closed her eyes and rolled a small amount around in her mouth. "It's…rather indescribable. It is to ordinary wine as ordinary wine is to water."

"You like it?"

"What kind of question is that? It's the best wine I've ever tasted. Why ever would elves cross the veil when they have such fare?"

Ellys took another sip, enjoying curious Aderri much more than judgmental Aderri. "Because after a millennia in the forest, even the most sublime things begin to lose their flavor. Or so I've been told."

"Hmm, I understand." Aderri paused for a few heartbeats and studied the carvings around the edge of her cup. She traced her fingers across the grooves and patterns then looked up to meet Ellys's gaze.

Ellys was no stranger to the pull of attraction felt by others. She'd been told many times that her silver eyes contrasted nicely with her short black hair. Aderri's interest was plain to see, but Ellys never mixed guild business with pleasure. In fact, relations with a patron were against guild law.

Aderri said, "Since we have candle marks of the evening left, we may as well get to know each other so we can make our romance more believable later."

"As a general rule, I prefer not getting to know people too well."

Aderri took another small sip. "This is part of the job."

The two women stared at each other, as if in a duel, then a sigh filled the quiet room. Ellys's voice held the flat tone of disgruntled resignation. "So it is. How about Elemental Bones instead?"

Aderri stared a little too long, and Ellys feared that her words had done naught more than provoke further curiosity. Surprisingly though, Aderri agreed. "If that is what you wish. But I must warn you, my mind is such that numbers and prediction are fairly easy to me."

Ellys gave her a feral smile. "And I have to warn you that I am uncommonly lucky with games of chance, despite the odds." Before Aderri could ask, Ellys said, "That's without using any magic. I'm fairly lucky all around actually."

"I guess we'll see how the bones fall for us then."

Ellys unstopped the wine. "Care for another dram?"

Aderri held up her cup. "Yes. And thank you."

The laugh sounded loud in the small room. "Don't thank me yet. We still haven't shaken the bones." Once she had their wine replenished, Ellys pulled out a pouch from a side pocket in her pack. The pouch was dyed deep red and appeared supple to the touch. Ellys unwound the string keeping it fastened and dumped ten etched, cube-shaped bones onto the table. The bones were bleached bright white and had darkened runes carved into each of their six sides.

"What animal?" Aderri was referring to the origin of the bones. Sometimes the creature's element gave the bones an affinity for that roll.

"Dragon."

Aderri's eyes narrowed, and the anger was obvious on her face.

Ellys held up her hand and quickly explained, "I fought for a number of cycles in a mercenary company. Some shield mates turned into good friends. Others were quite the opposite. One of the worst was a man named Jonti Coldsteel. As you can guess, we didn't get along. He loved bragging about how many of the elder races he'd personally killed. Dragon, elf, dwarf, even a unicorn."

"Blasphemy!"

Ellys shrugged. "Eh, I met a unicorn once…he was an asshole. At least Rocc got what she wanted out of the meeting. But anyway, the company caught Coldsteel thieving from the stores. The punishment was harsh. All his belongings were stripped from him, and he was expelled with nothing but a grain sack to retain his modesty and a small eating knife. The rest of his belongings were split up between those he'd wronged the most. Needless to say, I got first grab. I chose his gold, which I donated to the local Temple of Toroc. I also chose the bones, and a priest at the temple blessed them to clear away any negative energy and return equity."

"Do you know what happened to him after he was forced out?"

Ellys scooped up the dice. "I neither know nor do I care. His punishment was well-balanced as far as I'm concerned. I've rarely met such a vile individual. Do you prefer to roll by hand or use a cup?"

"It doesn't matter either way for the tumble, but I admit a preference to feeling them in my hands as they rattle around."

Ellys raised an eyebrow in question. "Stakes?" Being highly competitive, Ellys enjoyed the idea of playing for stakes.

Aderri gave a cocky smile back. "What is a game of bones without stakes? I propose that the winner of each round gets an answer to any question they wish. Or they can save the question and use it to deny the question of the other. Sound fair enough?"

Ellys's dark brows drew together. "Suspiciously so."

Aderri won the right of first toss. She shook the cubes within her cupped hands then let them scatter to the table below. She began sorting the various bones in the destiny, which was the proper name of a full grouping of rolled cubes. She sorted them into smaller groups, separated by rune type. Water, air, wind, fire, life, and death were the six runes carved into each cube. She moved aside the two water and two fire as they were elemental enemies and cancelled each other out. She did the same for a single earth and wind. That left four bones: two life and two earth. Each life rune doubled an element so her final tally was four earth.

Ellys tilted her head in acknowledgement. "Nice shake."

"Thank you."

Ellys scooped up the bones and shook them vigorously within her hand. The results of her throw would be pitted against Aderri's four earth runes. The bones scattered across the small wood table, one bouncing off Aderri's carved cup. Right away it became obvious that it was another good shake. Like Aderri, she had no death runes up, but she also only had one life. At the end of the tally, Ellys had four fire sitting in front of her. Unfortunately, Aderri's earth runes were the enemy of fire, but fire was an ally of earth. Enemies always beat allies at the end. Therefore, Aderri took the round.

Not used to losing, Ellys gathered the bones and shoved them across the table with a grumble. "Your round." After a pause she added, "I never lose. How are you so good at this?"

Aderri wagged a dark finger at her. "You don't get to ask the question this time." She scooped up the bones and gently cupped them within her hand, much the way one would cradle a baby chick. Ellys waited patiently while Aderri moved her gaze up to the nearly shaved sides of Ellys's black hair, then farther up to the fringe that flopped over her leather headband and fell near her left eye. She had a feeling about what Aderri would ask, an instinct proven out by her patron's next comment.

"I've never seen an elf with short hair before."

Ellys took a slow sip of her wine and met Aderri's gaze with her silver eyes. "I'm only half elf."

"Even so, why do you keep your hair short? Is there a story behind it, or is it merely practical?"

"A little of both and rather embarrassing."

"You agreed to the terms of the wager."

"Yes, yes." Ellys waved off Aderri's reminder. "To answer your question, I severed my long braid the very first time I sheathed a sword on my back."

Aderri's mouth dropped open, and her pointed incisors on the top and bottom gleamed in the candlelight. Ellys thought they were cute.

Aderri laughed outright. "You did not!"

"I did."

Aderri got her laughter under control, though a small smile remained. "And how long had you been growing it at that point?"

"Nearly forty cycles."

The bones clacked as Aderri placed them onto the table and picked up her cup for a drink. "And why didn't you grow it again after?"

Ellys's face darkened, which essentially shut down further questions on the topic. "I was angry." She inclined her head toward Aderri. "It's your go."

They each played another shake, and Ellys narrowly won out to take the second round. She pulled the bones triumphantly to her side and threw out her own question. "Why is it imperative that you attend this naming event? You make it sound more important than most."

Aderri frowned. "Cyvrus is kin."

"I thought all Clan are kin."

"He is blood kin, my sib."

Ellys suddenly remembered the details of Aderri's job request. Aderri had stated that it was a hatchling ceremony, and she also mentioned that her shifter form may cause panic and that horses were afraid of her. She sat back at the sudden revelation. "You! You're a dragon shifter."

Aderri appeared wary. "I am."

Many reacted negatively to the larger shifter races, especially dragons. And it was clear by the expression on Aderri's face that she feared Ellys would do the same and sever their agreement. Rather than express repugnance or fear, Ellys laughed loudly in the small room. "That's how you had such a blasted good shake in the first round. You've an affinity to the bones themselves."

Relief washed across Aderri's face, but she quickly schooled it. "Mayhap. But don't forget you won the second round."

"True enough." Rather than drag out the game any longer, Ellys picked up the bones and gave them a shake in her cupped hands. They bounced and scattered on the table, and she watched as each cube came to a rest. She grinned at the spread. After tallying the different runes, she had a fortuitous five winds. "Good to see my luck is still with me." She shoved the bones across the table, and Aderri smiled back. Between Aderri's visible canines and her verbal response, Ellys felt a little tendril of worry flame to life.

Aderri said, "Dragons rarely lose. You'd be wise to remember that." Then with a casual toss, she proved her point. The final tally of her shake was six fire. While wind had fire as an ally, fire runes consumed wind as an enemy. The third round was Aderri's.

"Fenwith's balls—"

"Are not as rumored."

Ellys looked startled. "I'm not even going to ask."

"No, but I will."

"Huh?"

"Ask. It's my turn to ask the next question."

"Fine."

"Where did you receive your sword training?"

Ellys carefully put her bones back in the red pouch and slowly wound the string to close it. She took the time to drop it in her pack again before speaking. "I was born in a Toroc monastery."

Aderri's eyes widened. "The Binary Goz of War?"

"Yes."

"How is that possible?"

"My mother was rumored to be quite beautiful. As such, she caught the attention of an elf warrior passing through while on a mission. Rather than continue the assignment for his queen, he dallied in the wood for nearly a half-moon outside my mother's steading. As you know, elves run on their own particular time, which varies depending on the season. Eventually he had to complete his journey, but he promised my mother he'd come back for her."

"Cad."

Ellys shook her head, sadly. "No. From what I was told, they really were in love. Anyway, before he could return, my mother discovered she was pregnant. Babes were revered in their small community, but folks were also very discriminatory of other races. When my grandmother found out, my mother was exiled with only the clothes on her back and one day's rations. She wandered for moons, foraging for food to stay alive, asking all the time for directions to the Ethereal Forest. Eventually, she grew weak with hunger and was delirious when she fell upon the doorstep of a Temple of Toroc. Seeing her condition, she was brought around to the monastery for aid."

Aderri looked skeptical. "They let a pregnant woman inside the monastery? I thought only followers were allowed in, and even then, they had to take a vow of gender balance."

"The vow of gender balance isn't mandatory unless you want to live within the monastery and become a Battling Monk. Toroc would never demand such. But it is common for masters to take the vow once they've been written into the Book of Orders, whether they live on the grounds or not. As for letting nonfollowers inside the monastery walls, they have been known to make the rare exception, as they did with my mother." She took a sip of her wine. "The followers of the Binary Goz are not cruel, and there were no other places nearby that could help. Once she was healthy, her pregnancy was fairly far along. The monks told her there was no physical way to the Ethereal Forest, and she grew forlorn. She…"

Ellys's voice faltered and Aderri placed a warm hand on her forearm. After a cleansing breath, Ellys continued. "She must have languished at the news that she'd never see her love again. She asked the monks to let her stay so she could raise me and promised them a lifetime of service between the two of us. They readily agreed, but she died in childbirth. That left me to pay the debt. I began training when I was fourteen and displayed an affinity for blades. Once I turned twenty, I was required to serve out my mother's promise."

"What happened after that?"

"I left on my fortieth birthday and never looked back." Ellys glanced out the window to the dark sky and pulled her hand away. "The game is over. I'm going to sleep now."

Ellys could see that Aderri had more questions. She could imagine what they were. The few others that she'd told her story to in the past had asked what happened to her father. Ellys had even been asked the reason why she was angry at her father's kin. But she wasn't about to explain herself to a patron who was naught more than a stranger.

Ellys's pain was easy enough to read in her expression alone, but it would have throbbed painfully for a dragon shifter with the gift of empathy. It didn't seem to matter how much time had passed since she left the monastery, the story of her mother and father always left her with an emotional ache. She was glad Aderri didn't push for an explanation.

With a quick nod, Aderri stood and walked to the door. "I need to step out to get rid of this wine then I think I'll do the same. Thank you for your history, Ellys."

Ellys didn't speak, but she let her eyes flash with gratitude.

Chapter Three

Ellys woke in the early light of morning, much too early to actually leave the bed. She fully expected to be cold given the way previous nights had dropped low on their way to Longoria. There was no glow from the brazier, but even so, the room was warm enough for even Ellys's preference. All the heat felt as though it emanated from next to her.

She suddenly froze as Aderri shifted on the bed behind her and a warm arm snaked around her waist. At first, Ellys was going to move it away because she didn't want to be any closer to the person providing her coin than necessary. It seemed unprofessional, and she prided herself in never breaking guild rules to dally with patrons. But as the warmth of Aderri's arm seeped through her sleep shirt, she decided to let it stay. She was tired and had no want nor will to move. Between the comfort of the bed and the heat of her companion, Ellys drifted off to sleep once again.

Later that morning, they broke their fast in the main room of the inn with a few other travelers. Aderri pulled a map from her seemingly bottomless bag and spread it out on the table. Ellys quickly moved it out of the way of her own food. "Must you do that here?"

A chunk of semi-masticated bread fell from Ellys's mouth into her bowl while she spoke. Aderri said, "Must you be so uncouth? And yes, we are getting ready to embark on a journey back to my Clan. It stands to reason that at least one of us should check the route." She narrowed her eyes as Ellys took another large bite and washed it down with a healthy amount of water, which dripped from her chin and onto the table.

"All I'm saying is that you won't need that map. If there's a place in the six nations I haven't trod, I'd be surprised."

Aderri's brow rose as she dipped a bit of bread into her morning stew. "Oh? And how exactly do you propose we get there?"

Ellys held up her eating knife and waggled it back and forth to animate her thought process, as if she traced an invisible map midair. "The trade road to Dovahn runs south from Longoria. It crosses the

Savetch River at the confluence where the Savenza joins. From there, the road continues a handful of days to the crossroads city of Pata. Then it's a half-moon to the border near Cat's Head. A handful of days to cross that region, then on into Muniers along the Northern Trail." She picked at her teeth with the knife as she paused to think.

A look of disgust washed across Aderri's face, and she opened her mouth as if to remark, but Ellys spoke again before any potential words of censure could slip free.

"If I remember right, it's another half-moon to Noth from the border, then from there we'll head south along the coast until we reach Clan Dracona. All in total, we're looking at probably a moon and a half, closer to two if there's trouble."

Aderri tilted her head and spoke respectfully. "You're uncommonly good with memorizing maps."

"I told you, I've walked the land for much too long. I've been to Noth plenty of times, though never south along the coast to your Clan. I know the way just fine. My biggest concerns are the people we'll meet between here and there. At one point, the trade road skirts along the Muniers border. Normally that would be where we'd cross. With the border closed, however, I expect that city to be tense and full of trouble."

"Can we somehow avoid that portion of the road and take a shortcut?"

The wood bowl came up as Ellys scraped the last of the stew into her mouth. She was still chewing as she answered. "Nope. Between the terrain of the area and the territorial tribes around there, the safest thing to do is stay on the trade road."

"You really think the conflict will cause problems on the way?"

Ellys circled her knife in the air. "Look around you."

Aderri glanced around the room and her lips wrinkled with disgust.

Ellys followed Aderri's gaze and noticed a surly-looking dwarf in the corner. He grinned when she made eye contact, emphasizing the rocks in his mouth that replaced his missing teeth. Aderri made a sound next to her and Ellys could only imagine she was put off by the dwarvish practice. Most were. Rather than comment on it, she stuck her eating knife into the tabletop. "Not this room. I meant the country in general. In the past six moons alone, Carthune has closed its borders and put up a naval blockade along the coast."

Aderri responded in a quiet voice, "I still don't understand why they would close the borders. Doesn't the king have a cousin at the royal court in Muniers? They've always enjoyed good relations before. It makes no sense."

Ellys leaned closer and lowered her voice. "There are rumors that the king of Carthune is dying. Much of the running of the country has been left to advisors while his daughter, the heir, is off studying magecraft over in Saccerid."

"At Indenes, the capital?" Ellys nodded and Aderri was aghast. "Has no one sent for her?"

Ellys shrugged. "Supposedly. But between me and you, gossip coming out of the castle says that someone is making a play for power. I'd wager that no one sent for the princess at all."

"That's not right!"

Ellys quickly shushed her and glanced around furtively. "Keep your voice down, will you? I bet there are spies all over Longoria with the castle a stone's throw away. And royal politics is none of my concern, certainly not worth getting thrown into the gaol."

Aderri frowned. "I suppose you're right. It's just that I like the old king. He's always ruled with a fair and just hand. He was the originator of the education network in place throughout Carthune."

"I suspect it will get worse before it gets better. Either way, it's not my business."

Aderri pushed her dish away. Her body language made it obvious that she didn't care for her hired sword's attitude. "How can you be so insouciant? This is an entire country that could fall into chaos without a proper leader. For that matter, what of Princess Ameelia? This is her father."

Ellys pulled her last bit of bread through the empty bowl to sop up the remaining gravy then shoved the dripping hunk into her mouth all at once. "What of it? I've seen the rise and fall of kings and queens before. Power leaves a void that begs to be filled. I'm not sure if you've noticed, but I don't exactly make my living tending to sheep."

Indifference to world affairs aside, even the most naïve would have to admit that Ellys was right about the easy rise and fall of leaders. But Aderri wasn't naïve. "If you don't mind my asking, how old are you?"

"I was born in twenty-four fifty, an auspicious cycle according to some."

Aderri gaped at her. "No! Are you playing the fool with me?"

"How do you mean? About it being auspicious? I don't really know if it was, only what I was told—"

Aderri cut Ellys off with a horizontal chop of her hand. "No, no, of course it's auspicious. Every Sky Tome across the six nations says so. I wondered if you were playing the jester when you said you were born in twenty-four fifty."

Perplexed, Ellys answered her question. "Well, I wouldn't lie about my cycle of birth. It seems pointless."

"Moon?"

"Gando. What about you?"

Aderri shook her head. "Vendi…in the cycle, twenty-four fifty. What are the odds that two randomly-met travelers of disparate races would be nearly the same age, almost to the moon? Only one between us."

Surprise lifted Ellys's dark brows. She'd rarely met someone so long lived. "Wait…we're both one hundred and forty-eight?"

"Yes, that's exactly what I'm saying. Strange coincidence, right?"

Ellys's face twisted with dismay. "No, it cannot be." She considered her mate's prediction from nearly a half century before, and the words fell from her lips in a whisper, completely disregarding their previous discussion, "You'll find love again when you lie with one the same age."

Ellys had always assumed that Gwyneth's prophesy referred to a dalliance of some sort, and since Ellys was significantly older than anyone she'd ever met, there was never a concern. Even now, while on a job, Ellys wasn't worried that she'd have relations with a patron, but the wording suddenly struck her. She repeated the phrase. "Gwyneth clearly said I'd lie with someone the same age." Suddenly she slapped the table and looked up at Aderri. "Son of a wyvern! I can't take this job."

Aderri looked dismayed. "You must. I've already paid you gold, and you sealed the contract." She quickly said, "By your own guild rules, you must follow through with the agreement or pay double the exchanged fee in return and risk guild expulsion. So, you'll owe me six coins."

"You only gave me a single gold."

A challenging eyebrow rose. "And? Do you have two gold to return?"

Just as fast as Ellys had puffed up her chest in certainty, she deflated again. "No."

"Who is Gwyneth?"

Ellys's brows drew down in emotional pain. "She's none of your concern."

Aderri leaned forward. "She is of my concern if something she said affects you taking this job. Is it worth risking guild expulsion and winding up in the gaol for unpaid contract cancellation?"

Torn, Ellys thought hard about the question before flagging down the innkeeper. "Can I get a dram of your strongest stuff?"

He disappeared behind the kitchen and reappeared a candle drop later with a small bottle and a smaller glass. "It's called Fenwyth's Fire. Also, I won't pay for an apothecary so drink it at your own risk." He poured the drink and held the small glass out to Ellys but pulled it back when she reached for it. "That will be a silver."

Ellys pointed at Aderri. "She's paying."

The look Aderri directed at Ellys appeared more curious than annoyed. She slapped a silver on the table, and the innkeeper snatched it up before placing the glass in front of Ellys.

"Enjoy." The innkeeper turned toward Aderri. "You may want to sit back when they down that. It has…explosive results on some people."

"Noted." Aderri turned her gaze back to Ellys. "Now—"

Ellys held up her left hand to stay Aderri's words while she picked up the small glass with the other. She quickly drank down the dram and immediately realized she had turned red as heat washed down her face and neck. A strange shade on one normally so pale.

Aderri had clearly seen the effects of Fenwyth's Fire before and was quick to lift her own hand to catch the small fireball that burst from Ellys's mouth. Ellys gave a little cough and sat back in her seat.

Aderri said, "Soot," and reached out and gently wiped the corner of Ellys's lips.

"Thanks."

"Was that your first time with the fire?"

Ellys grimaced and gave another cough. "And last."

"Who is Gwyneth?"

A long sigh slipped from Ellys's lips, and she slumped against the heavy table. "Gwyneth was my mate for forty-seven cycles. We met shortly after I left the monastery and joined the personal guard cadre for Empress Hecc'la din Tosche."

Both Aderri's eyebrows lifted, causing little wrinkles to form on her forehead. "You joined the palace guard in the Kuwyth Empire? How did you attain that coveted position? I've read about the Elite Guard. Only the best are chosen, and they're usually from established fighters already serving."

"Camen Dru was my sponsor in Toroc's Order of Blade, and they wrote a personal recommendation that was guaranteed to open most doors for me. They are renowned in certain circles for their skill with a sword. I still had to pass a test, but that was easy enough for me. Anyway, I met Gwyneth while I lived in Anza, and we had many cycles together."

"What happened?"

Ellys rubbed the back of her neck, and refused to meet Aderri's eyes for so sensitive a subject. She hated talking about her past. "Gwyn was getting older, and after thirty or so cycles with the guard, I decided it was time to retire and spend all of my days with her. We moved away from the city where we wouldn't be bothered." Ellys glanced away in reminiscence. "It was just Rocc, Gwyn, and me for a long time. I had saved plenty of coin over the cycles, plus we had my bonuses while working for Empress Hecc'la. Between that and Gwyn's minor magics, we lived well enough. At least until she fell ill."

Aderri placed a dark hand atop of Ellys's pale one. "I'm sorry. Was there no one nearby that could help?"

Ellys avoided the question. "Humans, gnomes…some of the races are so fragile, you know?"

"They are."

"Every so often Gwyn would make a prediction about the weather, or a visitor we'd have that day. She had her own magic and was always right." Ellys looked up to gaze into Aderri's dark eyes and swore she could see the flickering of flames within their depths. "I don't want her to be right this time. It's too painful to consider."

Aderri had spent her entire adult life studying at every major educational institution across the six nations. She was intelligent and driven toward problem-solving. In the face of Ellys's grief, it became obvious that their partnership was no longer about simply fulfilling Aderri's duty to return home and save her honor. Ellys needed coin and was afraid of her long-dead mate's prophesy.

Aderri's gaze grew unfocused as she contemplated the problem. "How about this? Rather than lie outright, we don't say anything. Let my Clan assume that if you're coming home with me, you must be a romantic interest."

"But won't they ask?"

Aderri held up a finger. "That's where we'll have to get creative. By answering with the truth in a way that satisfies the false narrative."

"And how exactly would we do that?"

"Ask me a question that you think my Clan would ask."

Playing along, Ellys humored her. "All right, how long have you two been together?"

"Why, it feels like barely any time at all given the span of our lives."

"Hmm, tricky."

"Yes, but not a lie."

"True."

Aderri raised a brow in challenge. "What say you?"

Ellys sat back again, contemplating the new plan. She and Rocc were very short on coin, the stable fee plus her own evening meal having taken pretty much everything that was left.

Ellys looked at Aderri objectively. Her patron was certainly beautiful in a unique way. There was a strength and intelligence to her that reminded Ellys strongly of her past love, though the two women couldn't have been more physically different.

Gwyneth had been the daughter of bakers, pale as Aderri was dark, and short to Aderri's much greater height. The height difference between Ellys and Gwyn had always been something Gwyn complained about. But being half gnome, she was never going to match even humans around her, let alone someone who was half elf.

Ellys considered the plan for what it was, including the risks and rewards involved with it. Finally, she gave a single nod. "I agree to continue provided we keep up the ruse as you suggested, without lying. When would you like to leave?"

"Right away. We can stop for supplies on the way out."

"And fetch Rocc from the stable across the way."

Aderri dismissed the comment, clearly not caring much about Ellys's horse. "Yes, yes, and we'll get your beast." Ellys laughed outright, and Aderri asked, "What is so funny?"

"You'll see when you meet her."

The first meeting between Aderri and Roccotári was certainly interesting. Aderri looked from Ellys, to the steed, and back again. "You have an elven mount? You could have said something earlier. No wonder you trusted the beast with your pack."

Beast? Rocc gave a great snort, and her large head swung around to knock into Ellys's shoulder. *Did she just call me a beast?*

Ellys grinned at her. "I believe she did, Rocc."

I'll have you know that I am Roccotári of Everbloom, kin to Benephrie. I am no simple beast.

It became apparent that even without the steed making her voice heard within Aderri's head, the dragon shifter understood her perfectly well due to her species' innate magic with languages. "Oh!" She stepped back and gave a flourishing bow. "My apologies, Lady Roccotári. I had no idea you were as much a higher race as your elven associate."

Immediately charmed, Rocc leaned forward and wuffed into Aderri's thick hair. It was an affectionate gesture that Ellys recognized immediately. She was a little put out that her long-time companion was so easily won over by a woman who still vexed her with every other sentence spoken. The irritation in Ellys's voice expressed her feelings to both. "If you two are quite finished, I believe we have supplies to gather and a trip to begin." She tied her pack behind Rocc's deep saddle and mounted.

It didn't take long to procure what they needed for the initial leg of the trip. Ellys noted that armed patrols had increased throughout the city and along the trade road south. They couldn't move fast while the way was still so crowded with other travelers. Aderri walked a dozen paces in front of them while she read from a large tome. Ellys split her time between keeping watch for ne'er-do-wells and giving Rocc the silent treatment. Her normally loquacious mount wasn't immune.

Oh, don't be bitter!

Ellys rolled her eyes petulantly, though only travelers coming at them on the trade road could see. And for their part, they probably already thought she was touched in the head for talking to someone they couldn't hear. "I'm not bitter."

Rocc whinnied. *No? So, what's with your mental shield and the silence?*

It didn't take long for Ellys to let out what was bothering her. She had never been good at prolonged shows of anger. She heatedly whispered her response, not wanting her patron to hear. "You only just met her. Yet you act like she's the finest thing out of the forest."

She seems intelligent and perfectly nice to me. What's got you in a tither, hmm?

"She's annoying, bossy, and…and…never mind."

Rocc gave a little shake. *I still like you better, if it helps. Even though you insist on eating goat cheese when you know it doesn't agree with you.* She tilted her giant head and craned her neck around to look at Ellys with one dark eye. *Come to think of it, it's a wonder I travel with you at all.*

Ellys burst out laughing. "Like your horse—" Rocc gave a jarring hop and Ellys quickly amended her words. "Like your elven mount emissions are any more pleasant."

Rocc snorted again, softer. *Perhaps we were meant for each other then.*

"Rocc, half-elven though I am, we share a lineal bond. You can't get more connected than that."

True enough. Rocc took a few more steps. *Are we in balance again?*

"Yeah, sorry. She just rubs me the wrong way."

I can tell. Perhaps things will get better as you get to know each other.

Suddenly remembering that there was an important detail left out of the brief rundown on their new contract, Ellys lowered her voice further. "Uh, Rocc…I may have left something out of the job description for this trip."

The steed seemed instantly curious. *We're not escorting the nice dragon shifter across two borders to her Clan?*

"We are, but…wait, how did you know she was a dragon shifter?"

They'd been traveling together for so long that Ellys could read the body language of every one of Rocc's snorts and shakes. The snort emitted was her companion's version of an eye roll. *She smells like a dragon, and we're escorting her to Clan Dracona. Surely you know who they are?*

Ellys wracked her brain and came up empty. "No, should I?"

Rocc ignored the question. *So, what is the rest of the job?*

"Uh…" Ellys rubbed the back of her neck, a clear sign of her own nerves. "She also hired me to act as a suitor in order to convince her family that she's upheld their expectations of leaving the Clan to find a mate."

Her words proved too much for Rocc. The steed stopped dead in the road and gave out a loud wheeze followed by a bray, even as laughter peeled through Ellys's head.

The sound drew Aderri's attention, and she quit walking ahead of them. "Is she okay?"

Embarrassed at the looks they were drawing, Ellys gave a little kick to Rocc's side while answering Aderri. "She's fine. Probably just swallowed a fly or something." She leaned closer to the wheezing mount's head and whispered, "For the love of Zeledron, knock it off and catch up already."

Sure thing...Moz Dracona.

Ellys slumped in the saddle. "You're an ass."

And so went their first day of travel.

****

The trade road traffic eventually thinned the farther from Longoria they traveled, and they were able to proceed at a fast jog for a few candle marks. Aderri hadn't lied when she said she could keep up. By the end of the first day, they'd gone nearly ten leagues, which almost made up for the late start in the city that morning.

They were lucky enough to find an inn with a stable along the way. Once Rocc was settled with grain and fresh water in a stall, Ellys joined Aderri at the inn.

As fates would have it, this inn also had only a single room available. The innkeeper proclaimed as much. "One room only. There was an unfortunate incident with a werewolf couple in the other during the last full moon." He paused and added, "You're not a wolf shifter, are you? Total mess they leave behind. Poor serving girl is still scrubbing the floorboards, and it's been a quarter moon." He hocked a spit next to his own foot, and Aderri cringed, doubting very much the innkeeper truly cared for the state of the floors.

The shifters probably destroyed the bed. There were at least two bonded pairs of wolf shifters in Clan Dracona the last time she'd been home, and they were infamous for their sexual destruction during the full moon. Rumor had it that was the reason both sets of mates became woodworkers.

"We're not wolf shifters, and we'll take the room." When the innkeeper noticed Ellys near the door, his expression took on a calculating look. Aderri shut him down right away. "Don't even think about upping the cost, you already stated two copper."

He spat again. "Fine. But you both pay for morning meal if you want it."

Aderri shuddered at the thought of eating anything the spitting man would serve. "Fair enough."

Ellys huffed as they made their way up the stairs. "One room again?"

Aderri unlocked the simple latch and pushed her way in. At least the room looked clean. She walked over to the small bed, placed her hand on it, and cast a quick anti-vermin spell under her breath. Usually, her presence alone was enough to scare most critters away, but bugs were surprisingly tenacious. "Mmm hmm." She was only half listening to Ellys's complaints. Despite her braggadocious words about her running stamina, it had been awhile since she'd traveled so far in one day and she was glad to see the bed, cramped though it would be.

"That sleeping surface is barely half the size of last night's," Ellys lamented. "By Toroc, it's as if my luck has completely left me."

Once she was sure her magic had worked, Aderri removed her pack and placed it on the bed, then turned to face the ranting woman. "You're awfully dramatic for a fighter."

Ellys waved her hand toward the bed. "You have to admit that one is smaller than the last."

"What's your worry? It's not as if I'll take advantage of you while you're sleeping."

"What? That's not, I'm…"

Aderri peered closer at the attractive half elf and frowned. "Do you really find my presence so repulsive?" She had a sudden thought that caused a pang in her gut. It wasn't the first time she'd faced judgment for her race. Unfortunately, her telepathy only worked when it involved speaking to those with the same talent. For all other creatures and people, she was forced to rely on her empathy, which told her nothing in this instance. "Is it because I'm a dragon? If so, I'll understand. You wouldn't be the first."

Ellys's mouth dropped open. "Of course it's not because you're a dragon. I have no problems with any other races. As a matter of fact, I've bedded—" Her words cut off, and her face flushed a bright pink, something Aderri had never seen an elf do.

Aderri ignored the blush and Ellys's truncated sentence to the best of her ability. "So, it's just me then?"

"Yes. I mean…no. No, not at all. I'm just…" Ellys trailed off then pulled herself up straight and met Aderri's eyes. "I'm sorry. I've never been comfortable being so casually close to anyone but Rocc, and now I've done the unthinkable and been horribly rude to a patron. It is within your right to halve my fee for this job or report me to the guild."

Rather than answer, Aderri turned back to her empty looking pack and rustled around until she withdrew a good-sized bottle and her cup from the night before. Then she took her find over to the table against the wall near the window. They only had one candle, and it was nearly half gone, so she figured they should utilize the natural light as long as possible. "I'm not doing either of those things. Why don't you have a seat and share my drink for a change? Perhaps we can shake the bones and continue our questions."

It was obvious that Aderri was giving Ellys a way out, and she retrieved her bones and cup from the pack by the door and took her own seat. She nodded toward the bottle. "Just so you know, I have pretty high standards when it comes to drink."

Aderri laughed. "I literally watched you order something you'd never had before then belch fire. You can't be that discerning."

Ellys rubbed along the tip of her right ear, right where it had turned a delightful shade of pink. "You have a point."

"And you have two points, quite cute ones if I may add." Aderri nodded her head toward Ellys's ears, which only served to make them flush darker.

"Erm…" Ellys shoved her cup toward Aderri and didn't respond to her flirting. "You promised a drink."

"So I did." Aderri unstopped the bottle and poured a good-sized dram in each one of their cups as Ellys unwound the cord from the small red bag.

Chapter Four

The next few days continued much the same way. Luckily for the trio of travelers, the trade road was busy enough to warrant an inn or way station every few leagues, especially along the current stretch between Longoria and Savo. Ellys was happy the first night she got a room of her own, though she would never admit aloud that she missed having her own personal bed warmer while traveling so early in spring.

By the time they made it to the large town of Savo, where the Savetch and Savenza rivers merged into one, all three had learned a fair amount about each other. The nightly routine of shaking the bones and drinking wine continued throughout the trip. Between Aderri's affinity with the carved cubes' true nature and Ellys's inborn luck, the two women found themselves well matched.

The morning they were set to depart Savo, Ellys made it down to the common room of the inn first. Their rooms included a morning fare of thick porridge seasoned with sweet spice and honey. She remembered Rocc's words from the beginning of the trip concerning digestive agreeability and avoided the small pitcher of goat's milk. Ellys glanced to her right where the shutters had been thrown open to let in the rising sun, despite the chilly air. She grew impatient at Aderri's tardiness. The other woman was the one who insisted on an early departure every morning, and yet the sun was up and she'd hadn't even come downstairs.

A young sprite took Ellys's empty bowl away as she finished a mug of chava and contemplated heading upstairs to pound on her patron's door. Her mental plan came to a halt when Aderri breezed into the common room from outside. "There you are. Aren't you ready to go yet?"

Ellys twisted her mouth. "I was waiting on you."

"Looks to me as though you were waiting on your own meal."

Ellys opened her mouth to respond but realized it was much too early to verbally spar with her patron. Instead, she downed the rest of the lukewarm drink, rose from the bench, and grabbed her pack from the floor next to her. "Whatever you say. Let's go. We still need to purchase supplies—"

"I've already completed that. I was up earlier than normal, so I thought I'd get that out of the way first thing. All we need to do is collect Lady Roccotári, then we can head out."

"Lady Roccotári…" Ellys muttered under her breath while following Aderri to the stable.

About a league outside the city, Ellys noticed that Aderri wasn't reading from her ever-present tome. Not only that, but she seemed to be walking a bit stiffly. They'd been making steady progress down the trade road and had just started their sixth day of travel. Ellys leaned over Rocc's neck and whispered to her, "Does Aderri look like she's walking strange?"

Any idiot can see she's clearly in pain. Rocc was straight and to the point as always.

"What do you mean? She hasn't said anything to me."

Rocc wuffed steam out her nostrils into the cold morning air. *Well, of course she wouldn't. She has her pride, and you've done nothing but pick at her since we started this contract.* Ellys didn't respond. Rocc gave her a gentle suggestion. *Unless you want to slow the trip considerably when she becomes too lame to continue, I suggest you offer her a ride.*

Ellys groaned, but she knew it was the right thing to do. She slowed Rocc to a stop and called out to the woman in front of them. "Aderri, are you feeling well?"

Aderri also stopped and glanced back, lines of pain etched into her forehead. "I'm fine."

"You're not fine. I can see you limping from here. Won't you join me atop Rocc? She doesn't mind, truly. And she can carry significantly more than the two of us."

"I don't need your pity. I'm fully capable of walking on my own."

Rocc tried convincing her as well. *I believe that you are, but there is no shame in letting someone help.* She gave a little shake and Ellys got the hint.

"Please?" Ellys held out her hand.

Finally, Aderri gave in and limped back to where Roccotári stood in all her glory. "Fine, I'll admit I haven't traveled so far or so fast afoot in many cycles. I appreciate your assistance." Aderri stopped next to Rocc and stared up at the immense height of the mount's withers. She cringed, making her thoughts on climbing so high with sore legs obvious to anyone watching. "On second thought, I'd rather not ride where I can't see what's ahead of me. Perhaps I should keep walking."

"No, please," Ellys said. "I'll dismount and let you have the front of the saddle, while I take the rear. You're not so tall that I can't see around you if the need arises. Besides, you wouldn't find it comfortable with my sword harness in your face." With that offer made, Aderri accepted and Ellys helped her into the saddle. She assumed a creature that never rode horses wouldn't exactly be adept in the art of mounting.

Unfortunately, Rocc carrying both women solved one of their problems but added an entirely new and uncomfortable one for Ellys. Aderri was quite warm, and they were pressed together as tight as you could get while sharing a saddle meant for one kitted-out warrior. The motion of Rocc's gait meant that Aderri's backside rubbed most deliciously against Ellys's groin. She developed a sweat before they'd gone more than a league, and Ellys was afraid she'd embarrass herself if they began a trot farther down the road.

What's the matter, lover? Getting a little warm in the breeches, are we?

Rocc made sure that only Ellys could hear her and Ellys's ears burned with embarrassment and arousal. "Shut up, Rocc."

Ready for a canter?

"Don't you dare."

Aderri turned in her seat to look at Ellys, sliding even harder against the poor swordswoman. "Is something wrong?"

Ellys sucked in a sharp breath and tried to remember that her body had more than just one part. "Nope. Everything is great." Her false cheer was, well, false.

Dark eyes narrowed. "Are you sure?"

Sensing she was about to be found out, and sick of Rocc's wheezing laughter, Ellys did a little hop up using the stirrups so she was balancing on the rear riser of the saddle. Then she did a backflip off Rocc. She called out from the ground behind them. "Now that you mention it, perhaps I should find a bush to take care of some business. Be back in a few candle drops." Ellys waved her hand. "Keep walking, I'll catch up." Then she entered into the underbrush along the trade road.

The last thing she heard was more of Rocc's wheezing laughter and Aderri's confused response. "What in the six nations was that all about?"

****

Spring was slow to warm in Carthune, and once again Ellys's luck proved faulty days later when the sun began to set with them nowhere near a town or inn. The place Ellys counted on to overnight had apparently shuttered since her last stay. "Fenwith's balls!"

"You fling that curse around so much I'm starting to think you have a fixation on the Sun God's sacks."

Ellys twisted her lips in revulsion. "Must you keep bringing it up? While some parts of a creature's anatomy hold plenty of fascination for me, those two do not."

Aderri grinned, showing her little pointed fangs. "Noted."

"This was the place I was hoping to stay."

Ellys, Aderri, and Roccotári looked at the dilapidated two-story building. Half the wooden shutters had rotted and fallen off, and weeds had sprung up throughout the courtyard. Aderri raised a flame-red eyebrow. "When were you last here? This place appears to have been shuttered quite a while now."

Ellys scratched at her temple below the leather headband. "Seems like just last cycle."

It was actually six cycles ago.

Ellys turned to stare at her friend and steed. "No, certainly not that long."

The owner, the elderly gaugin you met at the door, was the very same one that took care of me in the stable. Stands to reason he had no one to leave the inn to when he died. Given the way he wheezed while he lugged my water, I'd wager his death wasn't long after we last visited.

Ellys cursed again under her breath. "There is nowhere else for leagues around, which means we'll have to camp outside tonight." Aderri and Rocc looked on as she muttered and ranted whilst pacing in a circle. "No inn, no shelter, this is why I never take jobs so early in the season. What was I thinking? Gah!"

Aderri whispered to the elven steed when Ellys finally straightened her path and stalked around the side of the building toward a grassy area that lay between the collapsed inn and the forest behind it. "It's not really that big a deal. I've slept outside in plenty of weather. Doesn't she have a bedroll somewhere within her pack?"

Oh, she's got a bedroll. Ellys simply hates being cold.

"Is there a particular reason why? As far as I'm aware, elves aren't bothered by temperature extremes as much as most folk. I'm assuming it has to do with their affinity to nature and living things. I know she's only half elf, but still."

Ellys came back into view, and Rocc spoke quickly but directed her thoughts only to Aderri. *I suspect it has to do with the fact that her mate died in the coldest part of winter. She's never cared to be cold since. It reminds her of Gwyneth's death.*

Aderri's response was a mere whisper since her hired protector was nearly upon them. "Oh. Thank you for telling me."

Ellys pointed with her thumb behind her. "There's a patch of lush grass behind the inn and plenty of deadfall for a fire within the tree line. We should do well enough tonight." She looked upward at the rapidly darkening sky, then toward Aderri. "Would you prefer to gather fire material or organize a space where we won't burn down the forest?"

"I'll make the pit. Fire is an ally to earth."

Ellys cocked her head at the curious statement. "Like playing bones?"

Aderri gave a melodious *hmm*. "Something like that. I told you I'm capable of minor magics, and my element is fire. The game of bones originated from elemental truths. So, while I don't have any talents with water, because it's an elemental enemy of my kind, I do have some minor skills with wind, as well as earth and stone."

"I understand wind because it is an ally of fire. But Earth is an enemy of fire. How does your affinity work exactly?"

"Think of the old enemy rhyme."

Ellys recited the poem from heart, as most people who play the game are intimately familiar with all the rules and sayings that originated from it. "'Fire eats wind to burn and grow stronger. Wind pushes water wherever it may. Water soaks earth so it's solid no longer. Earth smothers fire and holds heat at bay.' So how does that explain your magic?"

"As you know, while earth is an enemy of fire, fire is an ally of earth. So, the affinity still holds, just not as strong. To break it down for you, fire holds the greatest affinity for me as it's my natural element. From there, the rest would be lesser affinities, such as wind, which aids fire much of the time. Then I have an even smaller amount of earth magic, and no magic at all with water. Minor magics get tricky."

"That makes sense as much as it's able I suppose. Magics *are* tricky." Tasks sorted, Ellys came around Rocc and retrieved the thick coil of rope that was tied behind the saddle. She abruptly turned on her heel and made her way behind the inn to the clearing she spoke of. Rocc and Aderri stopped in a flat space that was large enough to make camp. Aderri began calling the earth upward through the grass while Rocc grazed nearby. Ellys continued into the forest.

She returned a short while later dragging a large bundle of dead-wood with the rope. While elves were known for their height, enhanced strength, and speed over that of a normal human, Ellys was only half elven and as such she strained at the weight. She was impressed with the progress Aderri had made setting up the small camp. The large fire circle was bare of any grass and ringed with large kettle-sized stones. Where Aderri had found them, Ellys knew not.

Aderri said, "The well was covered and still in good condition, so I filled our flasks and the cook pot, as well as a trough near the old stable."

Ellys was grateful that the person who hired her was willing to do half the work. Not all patrons had been so helpful. Most expected the hired sword to do everything from saving their skin to purchasing sex for the evening. "Thank you."

It was quick enough work to stack some of the wood within the circle. Ellys waved toward the tinder when she was finished. "Do you think you can, you know…" She trailed off but knew Aderri understood the request for what it was.

Heartbeats later, the wood burst into flames and Ellys shivered at the sudden heat that chased away the night's chill, at least from the front of her. A handful of candle drops later, she turned so she could warm her backside.

Careful, Rocc called out as she approached the warm glow from where she'd been quenching her thirst at the trough. *We wouldn't want a repeat of what you did the last time you stood too near a large fire.* Unless she was speaking to just one person, Rocc always made sure everyone could hear her in their head.

"What happened last time?" Aderri asked.

The steed moved into the firelight, and the flames painted shadows across her dappled silver coat. *It was the dead of winter and Prince Chaveet had hired us—*

"Me. He hired me because you're a horse."

Rocc continued as if she hadn't just been interrupted. *Hired us to take a small chest from his palace in Obita to a fortress in the middle of nowhere.*

Ellys rolled her eyes. "Menia isn't big enough to have any place qualify as the middle of nowhere."

"Technically it's larger than Muniers in landmass size."

Ellys waved off Aderri's correction. "Yes, well all of Muniers is habitable, but Menia has that blasted mountain range that runs through it."

"True. Go on."

"Rocc was kind enough to tramp down snow so we could make a camp just beneath the trees. I made a lean-to for us to shelter in and built a fire between the opening of the lean-to and the field. Wanting to get warm when it was done, I stood on the other side of the fire, much the way I'm doing now."

"What happened?"

Ellys felt her face flush. "While I stood there with only the fire and the weak light of just two moons as my guide, glowing eyes approached in the dark. When the creature leaped at me, I stumbled back in surprise."

"By Cassyn, were you okay?"

Rocc let out a steaming blast of breath. *She fell on her ass right in the fire. Then she rolled out and just kept on rolling through the snow to put out her breeches. Poor Ellys had to stand in the stirrups for most of the next day until the burns healed.*

"Only because you were of no help at all."

Aderri gave Ellys a curious look. "Do you heal faster than a human?"

Ellys glanced at Rocc. "Something like that."

"Still, one day with a burned backside is a day too many. What about the creature, did it hurt you, too?"

That question only made Rocc bray harder, speaking through the cacophony into their minds. *I politely asked the snow fox to move along and not bother my companion further that night.*

Aderri's eyes widened. "A snow fox?" She turned toward Ellys. "Really?"

"Yes, a tiny little snow fox." A snicker followed her words, and she tried to defend her actions of the time. "It startled me."

"Oh yes, I'm sure you must have thought your ankles were in grave danger when it attacked." That caused Rocc to loosen the reins on her laughter, and the wheezing brays began again in counterpoint to the laughter in their heads.

"Ah, fie on you two!" Ellys made a chopping motion with her hand then stalked over to Rocc so she could remove the saddle and pack, hoping the exertion would keep her warm.

The temperature dropped significantly with the setting sun and drove Ellys to her bedroll shortly after they ate their evening meal. The cold air and early darkness meant they were unable to play their usual rounds of bones, which saddened Ellys, though she would never admit it.

Ellys's standard routine was to always face out, away from the fire when she went to sleep under the stars. The common-sense practice was followed by a lot of folk who made their living traveling across the six nations. Rocc did a great job as sentinel, but even so, a traveler never wanted anyone sneaking up on their campsite. Ellys's position meant that her back would be very warm but her front cold as ice.

Cursing came from Ellys's bedroll, and plumes of steam puffed out into the night air as she shivered where she lay. She muttered about buying magical heat stones as soon as they had some extra coin in their purse.

Hearing a noise, Ellys turned to look and saw Aderri as a shadow with the firelight at her back. "What are you doing?"

Aderri opened and spread her own bedroll over top of Ellys. "A wise creature once told me there was no shame in letting someone help."

She's right, you know. I am quite wise.

The cold had made Ellys cranky. "Oh, sh-shut up, R-Rocc." She rolled onto her back to get a better look at her patron. "Where will you sleep?"

"Lift your cover. I'll sleep on the outside, my back to your front so you can still face away from the fire but also stay warm." When Ellys didn't move, Aderri nudged the blankets. "Come on, this is the best way."

Their standoff lasted for more than a candle drop before Ellys lifted the corner of the bedroll. Aderri dropped in a graceful heap to the ground then lay down on her side so Ellys could close the space between them from behind. Ellys's shivering stopped almost immediately.

Aderri reached back behind her, found Ellys's hand, and brought it around to her front so Ellys was holding her from behind. "Better?"

Ellys sighed into the soft hair in front of her face. The tendrils rustled with the passing breath, and Ellys's body relaxed. "Yes. Thank you."

Aderri patted her hand where it rested across her stomach. "Any time, Ellys. You only have to ask."

Ellys tensed, then relaxed again at her words. "I'm not good at asking."

"That's okay, I tend to do what I want anyway." That got a small laugh before Ellys's breathing began to slow into the sweet rhythm of sleep.

A few candle drops later, Aderri whispered, "Goodnight, Ellys."

The only response came from Roccotári, who had witnessed the entire exchange. *Well done, child.*

Aderri wondered just how old the elven mount was.

****

Neither of them spoke of their sleeping arrangement the next morning. Aderri woke as Ellys was leaving the bedroll, but she let the swordswoman have her silence. Ellys elected to walk and let Aderri ride Rocc for the first few candle marks as a way to stay warm until the sun brought a little more heat to the land. She juggled three crunchy red apples she found in an orchard along the way, while giving commentary on the next leg of their journey.

"We have another half-moon to Kuwyth at our current pace. Hopefully, we won't see any delays near the border."

Aderri had pulled a book from her magical sack but it remained closed against Rocc's pommel while she chatted with Ellys. "Why would we see delays at the border? As far as I know, passage between the Kuwyth Empire and all other countries is open. You don't even need proof of destination to pass."

"That was the last I heard as well, but that could change at any time. I haven't seen a war so close to Kuwyth in my lifetime, so who knows how the Empress will respond. I was actually talking about where the trade road splits right at the Muniers border. One way leads directly into Muniers, which obviously we can't take. The other takes us west until we hit Kuwyth."

"That split occurs at the border town of Veniche. From what I remember, the city sits on the bank of the Vendin River with a sister city in Muniers on the other side. It doesn't take a stretch of imagination to realize tensions will be incredibly high there. Not to mention, we're still a quarter moon out, and a lot can change for a traveler."

Little lines of worry appeared between Aderri's brows. "That makes sense. Even with the magical boundary, that entire area is certain to be heavily patrolled."

The crunchy red apple came to a stop one at a time, cradled within Ellys's hands and crook of her arm. "You want one?" Aderri nodded and Ellys tossed her one. She slipped another into the pouch at her hip for Rocc, and took a bite of the third.

She started speaking again while she was mid chew. "So anyway, it's about two or three days across Cat's Head to the Muniers border. Probably three-quarters of a moon from there, based on what you've told me about your Clan lands in relation to the capital."

Aderri made a small noise.

Ellys looked up at her. "What?"

"You amaze me with your directional skill. I, too, have been all over the six nations, and I could never picture the land in my mind the way you do. It's a gift."

Ellys waved off the statement. "It's merely an affinity for the land, inherited through my elven blood, I'm sure. It's no great deal."

"You have skill. Why do you deny it? So what if you were born with it? Isn't that how everything in life works? Sure, you learn some things, but much of our capacity is that which we're born with. Intelligence, common sense, memory, and other things of that nature."

Ellys grew thoughtful as she chewed her fruit. "I suppose when you put it that way, I could consider it a talent much like my innate skill with a blade." She got a smile for her admission, and for a heartbeat Ellys stared hard at Aderri's face.

"See? Now you're getting it."

After another candle mark of walking, Ellys called a halt near a stream so they could refill flasks and take a short break. "Once we get through this stretch, we'll hit the forest proper. It's about a day and a half from one side to the other, with nothing but trees to break the monotony."

You're not going to tell her about the enchantment?

Ellys glared at Rocc. "Well, I am now."

"Enchantment?"

Ellys grumbled about "chatty horses" beneath her breath and took a seat on a nearby log. Aderri sat on a large rock. "There are rumors that the Scir Wudu is haunted, and those who enter are doomed to never leave."

"Surely that's not true. After all, this is the main trade road from the capital to the Kuwyth Empire."

Ellys held up her hands. "I'm not saying yea or nay on the truth of it, though I've personally never had an issue crossing. It was Rocc who brought it up. In all honesty, I think the wood is old and the trees are tall, both things that can make ordinary creatures who are not used to the grandness of the wilderness panic with fright. Probably people getting lost, or brigands taking advantage of the tale, if you ask me."

"That's just ludicrous."

"Maybe, but it's one of the reasons I wanted to stop here to make sure all our gear is good for the passage. A river meanders through, following not far off the road itself. So, we'll have plenty of water. Unfortunately, we'll be spending the evening on the ground again since there are no way stations or shelters."

"I'm not a pampered princess. You know I have no problems sleeping on the ground."

Ellys had taken the opportunity to hone the edge on her hip dagger. She paused in her sharpening and met Aderri's gaze. "I'm aware that it's not a terrible hardship for either of us. I just feel a little guilty that you're paying me so much in coin, yet you still have to sleep on the ground."

Light laughter spilled from Aderri's lips, and Ellys smiled unconsciously at the sound of it. "Ellys, I'm not paying you to find me the softest bed each night. I'm paying you to help me see my way home and make my homecoming a little easier. A scholar of some renown once said that it's better to have a swordswoman at your back and not need her, than to walk alone and be cut down."

Ellys grinned at the obviously fabricated statement. "You just made that up."

"I did, but that doesn't make it less true. So, don't worry. You forget that I've seen you fight, and I'm certain you'll perform above and beyond your hired duties should the need arise."

Ellys felt her ears color once again at her words, and the way she said them.

Aderri pointed at them. "Did I say something interesting?"

Ellys reached up to rub the offending blush away from one of the tips. "Nope, everything is fine. We should probably start off now." She stood and looked around for her mount. "Rocc, get your mangy tail over here."

Hold your tongue, half-breed. I'm not some herd beast you can order about.

"Why don't you hold yours, you horse's ass? The lady needs to mount you."

Rocc wuffed as she drew near and obviously couldn't resist teasing her friend. *Perhaps you're just jealous because you want the lady to mount you—*

Rocc had made sure both of them could hear her comments, and because of this, the blush returned, and not just to Ellys's ears. "Enough!" She turned toward Aderri who seemed barely able to hold in her laughter at that point. "Ignore her. Rocc is as unrefined as a mule and twice as stubborn."

Aderri took to the saddle, and Ellys followed right behind her, putting as much space between them as possible in the tight seat. Aderri shook her head, still full of mirth. "I must say, this trip has been significantly more entertaining than I anticipated."

Roccotári chimed in. *Ellys had dreams of being a court jester at one time, but sadly, her humor is as flat as her feet.*

"I don't have flat feet."

They joked good-naturedly back and forth for a distance down the road, at least until they started into the forest proper. Even though it was midday, the light was halved where it shone through the thick canopy. The way grew darker the farther in they rode, and even the most innocent things along their path took on a menacing tone. Aderri was the first to bring it up.

"I'm starting to understand how the Scir Wudu has garnered its mysterious reputation."

Ellys waved her hand that didn't hold the reins. "Rumors only. This forest is completely safe, I can assure you—"

A loud *crack* cut off the rest of her sentence, and Rocc stopped in the middle of the road. Her ears swiveled and twitched and she snorted nervously. Everything went still and quiet, including the wind. Ellys tensed where she sat behind Aderri, instantly alert. She switched the reins to her left hand and drew one of her swords, holding it out to the side where she wouldn't injure Aderri or Rocc should they be forced into quick motion. When nothing happened for a few heartbeats, Ellys sheathed it again and gave Rocc a little kick with the heel of her boot. "Let's go, Rocc. No sense standing around here waiting for naught to happen."

Rocc took one step forward when a screech echoed through the trees. Aderri called out, "Perhaps now is the time for a slightly faster pace?"

Agreed. I don't feel comfortable going at a full gallop because I don't want to lame myself on a root, but I'm certainly amenable to a trot.

Aderri grabbed the pommel as Ellys wrapped her arms around her from behind to hold the reins fully. They were making good progress until a large branch dropped from above onto the path in front of them. Roccotári leaped the obstacle as the two women held on with all they had.

Ellys called out, "Go, Rocc," and the mare bolted. But she only went about twenty paces down the road before abruptly pulling up short. It took Ellys's increased strength to hold them both on the saddle as Rocc reared and spun in a circle. "Why the blazes did you stop?"

Open your eyes. There's a rope stretched across the path that would have peeled the two of you from the saddle!

When Rocc finally stilled, the rope became obvious just as eight individuals came out of the thick underbrush around them. Ellys immediately slipped from the steed's back and drew both swords. "Rocc, guard her." She stepped a few feet away so she had room to maneuver.

Aderri yelled with worry coloring her voice. "Wait, you can't take them on all by yourself."

Roccotári said, *Rest easy, Ellys is very good at what she does.*

"But there are eight of them."

The steed snorted and moved farther away from where the group of brigands approached Ellys. *So, she'll have a slightly easier time of it than normal.*

Chapter Five

Ellys stood on the balls of her feet, knees slightly bent. She took slow, deep breaths, exactly the way she'd been taught more than a century before. Bringing in extra air to the lungs was essential when preparing for a physical altercation. She watched the approaching brigands, and they watched her. "Is there something I can do for you fine folks?"

A tall, barrel-chested man moved closer and pulled his sword. He spat on the ground next to him. "Sure can. We"—he gestured around him at the rest of the motley group—"are taking up a collection to help see us through the winter."

"That sounds all noble like." Rocc whinnied, but she ignored the steed. "But you see, we're not in the mood to donate. We've also just come out of winter so…you'll have plenty of time to fill your larders before snow flies again."

"Unfortunately for you and the lady over there, this is a mandatory donation."

"I see. Pay to pass?"

The man laughed, and after a beat, the rest of the group followed. "Exactly like that." With a wave of his hand, the laughter cut off. "Now, if you would kindly hand over your coin, we'll let you go without damage."

"And if I say we have no coin?"

The brigand scowled. "Liars get the sword."

Ellys gave him a challenging grin. "That seems rude. I don't even know your name."

"The name's Malik."

"Hmm, Malik No-neck?"

The big man roared. "That is not my name!"

"My apologies. Must have you confused with some other worthless ruffian."

Rather than continue to trade taunts with Ellys, Malik spared a glance at his group and gestured with his sword. "Gan, Zeke, and Fizule, round up that horse. The rest of you are with me. The elf has a big mouth that needs to be silenced."

As she expected, Ellys heard Rocc's indignant voice in her head. *I am not a horse.* She readied herself for the remaining five thieves.

She wasn't surprised to see the Malik hold back while only four approached her. There weren't many fighters who used double swords, and hers made them wary, so there was plenty of space between each one. A few of the men spun their swords in an attempt at intimidation, but Ellys was immune to such tactics. Only two attacked her initially. She begrudgingly admitted that it was a smart move given the circumstance. It was too easy in the heat of battle to be struck by your own mate's sword when closing with a single enemy. She effortlessly parried one blade and used her second sword to catch and shed the blade of the other.

A solid thud sounded nearby. Somewhere behind her, one of the thieves hit the ground and groaned in pain. She assumed it was courtesy of Rocc's hooves. She couldn't think about it long because the two thieves were closing in again. One was sloppy and she quickly rid him of his blade and rapped him on his skull with the pommel of her sword. That left her to bring the full force of her two swords against the remaining man before any of his allies could help him. He took a wild swipe at her head that missed, and she took him to task with a rattling show of speed that divested him, too, of his blade. He tumbled backward and retreated.

Aderri yelled in the short lull that followed. Ellys quickly stuck a sword in the loam at her feet, whirled with a dagger at the ready, and threw on instinct. A man had his hand around Aderri's boot, and Ellys's blade caught him in the back of his left shoulder. He screamed in pain and let go as Rocc whipped around to grab the man by the collar of his shirt. The massive elven mount gave a casual toss and sent him flying away from them to land in a heap.

When Ellys turned again, Malik and two other thieves were nearly upon her. She grabbed the discarded sword and scoffed at them. "You know, if you're going to make a living robbing innocent travelers of their coin, the least you could be is proficient. Unless you've been stealing from grannies and goats, I wonder how you earn anything at all."

Malik's face purpled with anger. She wondered if he had a touch of berserker to him. "You will pay for that, elf scum."

She rolled her eyes. "I'm only half-elf, and my name is Ellys. You should probably learn it, so you know who not to fuck with in the future." Without allowing them a chance to prepare, she simultaneously slashed at Malik and the man to his left. She spun and kicked the knee joint of the third before that one could bring his blade to bear. He dropped to the ground, writhing in pain. The weight of Malik's large sword bore down on her right blade, but she took it easily since he was off balance.

She swiped again at the other thief with her left and sliced a deep cut into his bicep. Luckily for him, it wasn't his sword arm. The move served its purpose, and the man backed off.

Throughout the fight, Ellys had no real worry that Rocc would protect Aderri. Ellys and her bondmate had been through more than a hundred cycles together, and they well knew each other's strengths and weaknesses.

With his lackey hanging back out of fear, Malik was left to attack in earnest. He yelled and swung his blade two-handed for Ellys's midsection. She raised her black brow in surprise at his strength, nearly a match for her own half-elven power. Because of that, she was forced to use both swords to block him, locking them together for a moment.

The lack of sound behind her told her that Rocc had finished her job in dispatching the last of her brigands, and the mental voice in Ellys's head confirmed it. *What is taking you so long? We're wasting daylight while you spar with straw men.*

Ellys laughed aloud and shoved Malik away.

He scowled at her. "What in Abbad is so funny?"

"She"—Ellys gestured toward where Rocc stood placidly with Aderri perched on her back—"just called you a straw man…for your lack of skill."

He looked confused. "The lady?"

"Not the lady. Rocc."

Impossible as it seemed, Malik appeared even more confused. "The horse?"

I am not a horse, you faecal fragment.

Malik quickly shuffled back as his mouth dropped open. "Did she just—"

"Call you a piece of shite? I believe she did."

He growled in anger. "I meant speak into my head!"

"That, too."

Aderri laughed outright and voiced her own opinion as a few men gathered themselves again. "Do you think we can wrap this up and be on our way? I'm not as fond of these woods as you seem to be."

Ellys turned and gave a little bow. "As you wish, Lady." When she turned back to Malik, her face was deadly serious. "I would rethink your current plan. I am a Grand Master of Toroc's Blades. I spared you all today because I hate to shed blood unnecessarily. However, if pressed, I will not hesitate in taking lethal action to restore the balance."

Malik's face lost its ruddy color as quickly as it initially rose. "The Binary Goz?" Ellys nodded and he paled further. There was no one in the six nations who didn't know of the three houses of Toroc. The Goz of War may not be popular, but they were infamous for their Battle Monks. Malik's shoulders slumped in defeat. He was a thief, a brigand, and any number of other unsavory things, but apparently he wasn't stupid.

Ellys gave him time to process while she kept an eye on the others. Obviously, he ordered the attack because he thought a single swordfighter and a lady would be easy victims. He looked around at the remaining men of his band that were standing and those that had yet to rise due to serious injury.

He called out to his fellow rogues. "Let them go, fair passage."

"But, Malik!" One of the men Ellys had wounded held his hand clasped tight to his bicep to staunch the bleeding. Malik cuffed him across the back of the head with the hand that wasn't holding the massive broadsword.

"Look around you, Deetz. Open your drunken ears, you bally-woggle. What part of 'Grand Master' didn't you hear?"

"Still…"

Rolling his eyes, Malik gave the man a hearty shove in Ellys's direction. "Well then, have at it. It's your head that'll roll, not mine."

Deetz staggered and stumbled away from Ellys's dangerous blades, screaming as if she'd already struck him down. He yelled again as he tripped and crawled away. "Fair passage, fair passage! I got it, Malik."

Ellys laughed. "You should find better help."

With the danger clearly past, Rocc walked up behind Ellys. Ever the intellectual, Aderri spoke from her seat in the saddle. "Or find a better way to make a living."

Malik sighed and ran a hand through his greasy hair. His cheeks were gaunt, and his tunic was baggier than it ought to be considering his height and breadth of shoulder. "Perhaps I should."

Seeing a truce of sorts, Ellys wiped and sheathed her swords and swung up into the saddle behind Aderri. She gave the band of rogues one last warning. "I better not see you lot on our way back through." She glanced around at the hungry, young-looking men, surmising that was part of the reason they fought so poorly.

The leader made a gesture toward his group, indicating they should gather up the ones still on the ground. He began to turn away but paused when Ellys called out.

"Malik?"

"Yeah?"

She flipped him the gold coin that Aderri had given her in the tavern as the initial payment for her contract. "I know what it's like to be hungry." He caught it midair with a curious look on his face, and Ellys gave Rocc a little prod to the side with her boot. The steed turned away and continued down the trade road.

As they approached the strung rope, Aderri lifted a familiar looking dagger and sliced through. Then she turned to meet Ellys's gaze and held out the blade, pommel first, so the swordswoman could take it. "I hope you don't mind, but I retrieved your weapon and cleaned it."

Grateful, because she had forgotten about the throw amid all else that had gone on, Ellys slid it back into the empty sheath on her belt. "Thank you."

"No, thank *you*. Indeed, you performed admirably and justified my faith in your skills."

I'm pretty sure she could have done all that without spending our only gold.

Ellys patted Rocc's side. "Clearly you weren't paying attention. Two of those were naught but boys, and all held the hollow cheeks of ones seldom fed. Sometimes the people doing bad things aren't really bad. It's just their circumstances have led them to a place that is less than ideal. It's my hope that sparing them today, helping them, will also help those men achieve balance."

They moved on in silence, until Aderri broke it. "I wasn't aware that followers of the Goz of War pursued peace. Nor that anyone outside the monasteries and temples of Toroc followed the Goz."

"They exist, though are few and far between. And it's not that we pursue peace, specifically. Rather, we strive to achieve balance. War is usually about an imbalance of power, between two lands, two people, or two religions. To achieve the quickest victory, one side must be the most skilled. Once balance has been achieved, the war is over and peace will reign, at least for a time."

"What of the warriors and generals that spend their lives in one battle or another? How does that figure with your teachings?"

"There is another, less discerning, God of War. Most of those that I've met follow him."

Aderri's mouth twisted. "You mean Bron?"

"Yes. Shrines to Bron the Brutal litter the war-torn Western Marches of Legaria." Ellys's face cleared again thinking of her own Goz. "One of the reasons I stayed with the teachings of Toroc, despite leaving the monastery behind, was because of the philosophy of balance. Toroc is a different sort of deity. For instance, there's an entire martial discipline in the House of Fist that centers around the principle of conquer through submission."

"What a fascinating ideology. Do you think you could teach me?"

Ellys considered Aderri's request. "I can teach you some, though the deepest teachings are reserved only for followers of the three houses."

Aderri turned and smiled at Ellys, sharp little points digging into her lower lip. "I would appreciate anything you offer."

It was another loaded statement, and Ellys wondered if Aderri was purposely flirting, or if her words were merely an accident of conversation. She didn't have to wonder long. Aderri gave her a quick wink before turning to face forward once again. Ellys sighed. The woman tested her resolve like no other.

****

Later, they made camp in a tiny clearing just off the trade road. It got dark fast in the tall trees, and the clearing was no different, surrounded on all sides as it was. The river that ran through the forest along their route was the Savenza, the same they'd had to cross earlier via a tall stone bridge. It was significantly smaller upstream from where it joined with the Savetch, but it was still wide enough to give the trio a source of fresh water. And despite the early spring weather, there was plenty of lush grass next to the stream for Rocc to graze.

The two women ate a simple dinner of cattail and fish stew and sat by the fire to stay warm after, Ellys a little closer than was safe.

The temperature had once again dropped with the setting sun, and Aderri's breath fogged as she spoke, flickering and drifting away in the firelight. "May I ask you a question?"

Ellys had warmed up to Aderri over the past nine days of travel. They'd exchanged a surprising amount of information, considering they were relative strangers to one another and that Ellys didn't like to talk about herself much. She tilted her head, staring into Aderri's eyes in the firelight. If she looked too long, she swore that deep within they burned with their own flame. Maybe they did. Ellys had never met a dragon shifter before and as such didn't know much about their person, other than they apparently ran hot.

"You don't have to answer if you don't want. I'm merely curious about something."

Startled out of her observation, Ellys cleared her throat. "Apologies, I was lost in thought. What is it you would like to know?"

"Again, you don't have to speak on the topic if it's too personal. Everyone knows the Monks of Toroc take a vow of gender balance."

"That's correct."

"And you're a follower of Toroc?" Aderri's voice lilted with the question.

"I am, to the best of my ability."

"So why don't you follow the same vow?"

Ellys laughed aloud at the question, and Aderri's tense expression relaxed at the sound. "For starters, I'm not a monk."

"You're not? What's the difference between a follower of Toroc and a monk?"

Ellys spoke as if it were the most obvious answer in the six nations. "Only monks are allowed to take the vow."

Aderri grumbled at Ellys's answer that wasn't an answer. "So, there are followers of Toroc that aren't monks? I've never heard of such a thing."

"Of course there are. Monks choose to live at the monastery their entire lives, leaving only to make a journey of duty or transfer to another monastery. On rare occasions, they are called to battle to preserve the balance and something of that import usually only happens once a generation. But to become a monk, to be offered the vow, you must first make the Quest of Toroc."

Aderri tilted her head. "The what, now?"

"Before your name can be recorded into the Book of Orders, you need to complete a quest, proving your worth to the Goz of War.

Once the quest is complete, you're given the choice to take an oath of gender balance."

"What does the quest entail?"

Ellys shook her finger. "Ah, that's one of the things I can't tell you. Just know that each person's quest is different, and they can take a lifetime to complete. But once done, the seeker may return to the monastery and take the vow of gender balance if they so choose. Only then will they become an actual monk."

"Hmm…" Aderri peered into the fire. She turned back to Ellys with more questions. "But what of you? You've stated that you're not a monk. Didn't you make your quest?"

"I left on my quest but never returned, therefore I cannot become a monk. Some quests can take cycles to complete, so a follower of Toroc may not be a monk and yet still walk the path. Others are gone decades trying to complete their quest until they eventually return."

"Oh." Aderri blinked at the new information. "And have many done that? Never returned?"

The heat of the fire made Ellys feel strangely relaxed. "Just one has never returned that I know of."

Aderri threw a pebble at her companion. "Really? You could have told me that from the beginning." She got an unrepentant shrug for her ire.

Aderri was quiet for a candle drop, at least until she asked another question. "What about masters? You've mentioned before that you are a 'Master of Swords,' yet you tell me that you're not in this Book of Orders, nor are you a monk."

"You don't have to be a monk to become a master, but you do have to be a master to become a monk. The mastery of blade or fist is about skill level. Whereas monkhood is about total life devotion to the way of balance and the monastery."

Ellys could easily read the curiosity on Aderri's face. She'd learned her fair share about her patron during their journey. Aderri had told them that some of her kin were known for hoarding gems, others gold. But for Aderri, her greatest treasure was knowledge. That alone meant Ellys had to be wary that she didn't say too much. There were secrets she kept as a follower of Toroc, and there were her own secrets she didn't wish to share for more personal reasons. No matter how many subjects they touched on while shaking the bones, or sitting around a fire, Ellys didn't speak of her past. It was too painful.

"Do you think you'll return to a monastery someday and become a monk? Or are you content as you are?"

Ellys sighed at the questions she'd long held no answers to. "Truthfully, I don't know. What about you? Have you been traveling the six nations in pursuit of knowledge since you left your Clan?"

"I have. When I first set out, I decided I wanted to visit the largest, most opulent, library ever to exist."

"You went to the capital in Kuwyth?" Aderri nodded. "How old were you?"

Aderri gazed into the fire as if her thoughts traveled back countless cycles and memories. Her answer confirmed Ellys's mental guess. "I left around the same time you left the monastery."

"It's strange to think that we were probably there at the same time but would never have crossed paths due to our disparate disciplines."

"Fate is a strange mistress. Anyway, I'd gone as far as I could go within our own Clan, as well as the southern university of Noth. I decided that the only way to continue my education was to leave the Clan behind."

"And they let you go, just like that?" Ellys snapped her fingers.

"Not exactly. You see, my name carries a lot of weight within Clan Dracona."

"Yours was the founding family, so a lot of expectation, too, I suppose."

A strange look washed over Aderri's face, but she never gave any details about the makeup of her family and Ellys never asked. "Yes, something like that. Our particular Clan is also the official guardian of Muniers's coastline, dictated in a pact signed by the twin regents, Melanai and Molokai, nearly eight hundred cycles ago."

Rocc nickered. *I learned that bit of history when naught more than a foal within the Sacred Grove. It was a grand ceremony and on the auspicious occasion of three full moons.*

Both women turned to look at Roccotári where she stood near the water's edge. Being so far outside the fire light, she was more of a shimmering shadow than solid form. Ellys found herself just as surprised as Aderri. "You knew who Clan Dracona was all along."

I know many things that your feeble gaugin brain is unable to comprehend. I can't be expected to tell you everything. It would take the rest of my considerable life.

"I'm half elf."

Sadly. Which means you'd learn half as fast as I could teach.

Ellys grumbled and tossed the same pebble at Rocc that Aderri had thrown at her but let the argument drop.

Aderri said, "Wait, how old are you?"

Nine hundred and forty-two.

"Well that certainly explains a lot." Then Aderri continued as if her companions hadn't just been bickering over lineage and shared information. "Anyway, because of Dracona's importance to Muniers, I knew I had to come up with a plan. I didn't want to simply leave my family behind and never return. Exile was out of the question. I spent the cycle leading up to my departure researching Clan law. It was then I decided that I'd announce my search for a mate."

Ellys jerked a thumb over her shoulder in the direction they'd come from before making camp. "If you're terribly desperate, I know a few brigands who are down on their luck and wouldn't mind settling in with a warm body—"

She got another pebble thrown at her head for the suggestion, but it didn't stay her laughter.

Ignore the gaugin-trash. Sometimes she can't help the drivel that spews from her mouth. I think it's admirable how you found a way around your Clan's rules that allowed you to pursue your passions in life.

Aderri gazed at the ethereal silver horse that approached them from the stream. "And what is your passion in life, Lady Roccotári?"

Rocc came closer and lipped Aderri's wild red locks affectionately. *My passion is to aid my lineal bondmate in whatever way I'm able. I count myself fortunate that the two-legger mixed-breed I'm stuck with isn't half bad.*

Ellys rolled her eyes. "Well, I am only half elf."

Rocc snorted. *Yes, that's the part that isn't half bad. The rest of you...* She didn't have to finish the sentence for the women to understand.

Ellys waved her hand in the air. "Whatever, nag."

I love you, too, Ellys.

During their conversation, Ellys sensed something deeper in Aderri's motivations that she wasn't saying. While she normally wouldn't delve into someone's personal story, they'd been doing their best to get to know each other over the course of their journey. Not to mention, Aderri had no qualms about prying into Ellys's history. "I sense more than the reasons you gave me as to why you left your Clan. Are you willing to share?"

Aderri gave her an unreadable look, her eyes reflecting the flames of the firelight. Then she sighed and looked away. "You're right, there are other greater motivations than simply not wanting to settle into one place. I—" Aderri swallowed but didn't continue.

There is no judgment here, child. If this is a story you want to share, know that we will not break your balance or trust. Rocc gave Aderri a light nudge.

Aderri turned to rub the soft muzzle. "I don't like to admit it, but I, um, I've never cared for my dragon side. One thing about being a shifter is that when you take the form of your animal, you also take on a lot of their personality and their, uh…I guess wildness would be the best word. I feel out of control when I'm her, and I become anxious. Have you ever seen something the size of a house get anxious? It's not good."

Ellys said, "I've heard other shifters say as much. But you don't have to shift, do you? Or is your familial line tied to something external that provokes such a change?"

"It's not a familial tie, but rather a bond of duty. Clan Dracona is bound to the throne of Muniers, as Rocc pointed out. We were gifted our region with the understanding that we'd always guard the coast from invaders. As such, every member of the Clan, smallest to largest shifter, is expected to spend time patrolling. My kin, the dragons, patrol the coast to watch the waves for invaders. Had I stayed, I would have been forced to become my dragon regularly, over and over again, for the rest of my life."

Every warrior instinct Ellys possessed screamed that Aderri had left something unsaid, but Ellys respected that some things were too private to share so she didn't push. Unfortunately, her distraction over Aderri's secret meant she wasn't as tactful as she should have been with her next statement. "Instead, you chose to run?"

Aderri whipped her head around to stare at Ellys, obviously angry. "I didn't run! But why should I subject myself to something I abhor for the rest of my life when I could explore and follow my calling? I hate the dragon and wish she weren't a part of me. I chafe at the weight of expectation that comes with her. That's not something you can understand."

Ellys held up a placating hand. "My apologies, Aderri. I didn't mean for it to come out that way. And believe me, I do understand what it's like to have the develes of Moder dogging your steps. A life without happiness is only half-lived."

Aderri's shoulders dropped into a more relaxed state. "Apology accepted. And thank you."

"We all have parts of ourselves that we wish didn't exist, issues we refuse to acknowledge for one reason or another. I've found that life seems to be about running away from one problem and to another."

"And?"

Ellys looked at Aderri curiously. "And what?"

"What is your solution?"

The half-elf laughed loudly into the night. "If I had a solution, I wouldn't still be running."

First moon had risen and they'd be bedding down soon. Aderri spoke without looking at Ellys. "It's going to be cold again."

The responding sigh made a fog of breath float between them in the firelight. "I know." Ellys couldn't keep the resignation out of her voice, and Aderri looked her way. She wasn't looking forward to another cold night but refused to ask any boon of her patron. Ellys sensed the other woman's eyes on her and knew Aderri would offer anyway.

"Would you like to share a bedroll again to conserve heat?"

"I'll probably be all r—"

Rocc stood close enough to give Ellys a shove which sent her sprawling dangerously close to the fire. Ellys righted herself and glared at the steed but quickly changed her words. "I meant to say, that would be highly appreciated. Thank you."

Roccotári wuffed into Ellys's hair, causing the swordswoman to gently push her away. But she couldn't shove away her friend's mental voice. *See? That wasn't so hard, was it?*

"Whatever. Don't you have some acorns to count or something?"

If that's your way of asking me to take watch while you sleep, sure.

Ellys stood abruptly and moved to grab her bedroll from where she'd placed the saddle on the ground earlier. She gave Rocc a gentle rub to the softest part of her nose. "You sure you'll be okay for the entire night?"

Rocc snorted. *You know I don't need sleep quite the same as you do. I'll be fine. Go on, get some rest.* She gave Ellys's shoulder another shove, and Ellys smiled at her in the darkness.

"Thank you, old friend."

****

Ellys pressed into the warm body in front of her, one hand around the tavern maid's midsection, the other arm serving as a pillow for them both. They'd gone back to the room where Lorna promised a night of pleasure worthy of Aphora's halls. Ellys moved her hand against Lorna's stomach, feeling the smooth skin she'd only imagined while still downstairs. Ellys's sex tightened when Lorna pushed her ass against her and moaned.

"Soft," she whispered into the attractive woman's thick, curly hair. The rough fabric of Ellys's tunic brushed against her nipples, and she returned Lorna's moan as they hardened. It felt natural to move her mouth deeper into the hair at Lorna's neck so she could nip at the skin there. A gasp and mewling whine was drawn from the woman in front of her, and Ellys practically purred. Her hand moved lower when a voice intruded on their fun.

Ellys.

Ellys whispered again. "Go 'way, Rocc. I'm busy searching for Aphora's halls."

Ellys! The voice was louder, sterner, the second time.

The swordswoman stiffened and woke instantly. Only then did she realize the liberties she was taking with her patron. "Fuck!" She threw herself backward and ended up outside the bedroll in the grass between them and the burned-out fire.

"Not quite, lover. But there's still time," Aderri said drowsily. Clearly, she was amenable to dalliance.

"No! I refuse to touch you in such a way," Ellys yelled. She began pacing in the low light of the moons, muttering curses to herself for nearly breaking her professional oath. Some dallied with clients, but she had a reputation to maintain.

"If you find my body so abhorrent, you're more than welcome to warm yourself in the cold night air." Aderri slid from beneath the bedroll and stood.

Pardon, Lady Aderri. But she's not casting aspersions on the state of your loveliness, or your personality. Rather, most guild members hold themselves to a vow of professionalism. Despite being a cad and a self-professed student of passion, Ellys prides herself on never breaking that particular vow.

Aderri looked from where Rocc stood nearby to the pacing Ellys farther away. "Oh."

When Ellys heard Rocc's explanation, she turned around to pace in the opposite direction. Her sight impaired by the darkness, she nearly ran straight into Aderri. Aderri was quick to grab her to prevent either of them from falling. There was a part of Ellys that was impressed by her strength. Then she realized that her mind was wandering into forbidden territory yet again, and she stumbled back. "You can't touch me."

Aderri gave her a wry smile, and Ellys's vision was well enough in the dark to see it so close. "Well, that's going to make the rest of this job more difficult to complete."

Ellys stilled, realizing that her professionalism was in jeopardy either way. Whether she dallied with the client, or didn't fulfill her part of the binding contract, she would lose her guild membership. Disgruntled, Ellys huffed. "You don't understand."

"Oh, I understand attraction and biological urge just as well as the next person." Aderri took a step closer. "I also understand that things happen that are beyond our control. Nothing went too far, not that I would complain if it did, mind you."

Suspicious, Ellys asked, "What do you mean?"

"Ellys, I believe I told you when we met that you are very much my type. That certainly hasn't changed just because we sealed a contract. My dreams got away from me much the way yours did. It was unintentional, but I'm not ashamed of it and neither should you be."

"But...professionalism..."

Aderri stepped closer and placed a hand on Ellys's tense forearm. "You had a dream, Ellys. Nothing more. You haven't crossed a line. I promise you."

Ellys pulled her leather headband off to run trembling fingers through short black hair. "Even so, I should probably sleep separate for the rest of the journey."

"You'll do no such thing. You're going to follow me over to our shared bed roll and finish the night's sleep. We won't convince anyone of our romance if I arrive with an elf-sized, sleep-deprived, hunk of ice in tow." Rocc snorted from nearby but didn't add anything to the conversation.

Ellys slumped, her headband hanging loose from her fingertips. She contemplated her options. If she pulled away from Aderri now, her failure would be certain. Whereas the attraction and her response to it that led to dalliance was a little easier to control. Finally, she conceded Aderri's point. She was too tired and cold to debate any further on the subject. Instead, she decided she'd consider the situation in depth the next morning. "Fine, you're right. I can't pull away or I risk failing the second portion of the job. Can we just go back to sleep and pretend none of this happened?"

"I think that's a sound idea." Aderri headed back to where they'd bedded down.

Ellys called out a warning. "But if I get too handsy—"

Rocc chose that moment to speak up. *I think that between Lady Aderri and me, we can preserve your virginal honor.*

Ellys rolled her eyes and crawled back inside the bedroll, groaning at the residual heat still beneath the coverlets. She looked over her shoulder in the near-darkness and made a face, mocking Rocc's deference to their patron. *"Lady Aderri...*you're such a donkey sometimes." Aderri slid in the bedroll, back to her original position, and Ellys shivered behind her.

You love me, Ellys.

"Then I must love donkeys." That was all Ellys said before she relaxed and began her slide into slumber. She'd proven many times during their journey that she could fall asleep anywhere almost instantly. Of course, she roused just as fast when danger was afoot. But while her breathing had evened out with the return of physical comfort, Ellys hadn't quite reached Somna's realm. She easily heard Aderri's quiet voice in the night. Oddly enough, she also heard Rocc's, which meant her bondmate knew she was still awake and wanted her to hear.

"Will she be okay?"

She'll be fine. She just needs some time to acclimate and settle in.

"I know this is an unusual job. I can never begin to tell her how much it means to me that she's going outside her normal skill set."

Ellys heard a quiet wuff. *I wasn't referring to the job. But on that note, I think the five more gold coins owed will sufficiently express your gratitude.*

Aderri chuckled quietly and whispered back. "Such a greedy steed. You'd think you were part dragon."

And you're an intelligent and compassionate soul...one would think you were part elven steed.

"Goodnight, Lady Roccotári."

Sweet dreams, Lady Aderri.
Aderri fell silent as her body relaxed in front of Ellys.

Chapter Six

Ellys was cranky the next morning, despite waking warm and well rested. She mumbled beneath her breath and stomped around their small camp as she collected and repacked her gear. There was a reason she kept her distance from patrons and most others. She suspected that sharing so much of her life's story with Aderri over the previous nine evenings had caused her to lower her guard in her sleep. She was going to do her best to not let that happen again. A task that would be extremely difficult when they needed to prove to Aderri's Clan that they were close enough to be romantically inclined toward one another.

"Do you want to talk about it?" Aderri was already up and coaxing the last of their wood into a flame. Their normal routine was to pack, eat, and return to the road just after first light.

Ellys knew Aderri didn't need the fire to heat their meal. It was obvious that Aderri started the fire for her, perhaps as a peace offering. Ellys shivered in the morning air and moved closer to the warming flames as her steaming breath curled and rose in front of her. Even so, she didn't feel like discussing her dishonorable actions from the night before. "Not really."

Aderri paused from flipping the rock cakes and looked at Ellys. "Are you able to do this job? We have a long way to go before we get to Clan lands."

Ellys stood from where she'd perched on a fallen log next to the small, stone-encircled fire. "I am fully capable of seeing you across the borders and into Muniers. You'll find no blades as sharp as mine, no skill as adept. I am a Grand Master in Toroc's Swords—"

Rocc plodded back into the camp from wherever she'd been. *She means your skill at playing the suitor. And you may want to keep your voice down. You're shrill enough to scare the fish from the stream.*

"Shrill? I'll have you know—"

"Ellys."

Ellys paused in what was sure to be another full rant. "Yes?"

Aderri approached her slowly. "I'm going to ask again, can you do this? If you can't, then I need to know now because I'll have to find another to take your place, pretending to be a love interest. All I ask is that you see me to the nearest large city before I cancel your contract."

"I…" Ellys looked at Rocc, whose mind was strangely silent in the wake of Aderri's question. Ellys was all too aware of how empty their coin purse was after paying Rocc's stable fee back in Longoria. She also knew it was probably foolish to give away the single gold that Aderri had already paid for her escort service to Muniers, but it was Ellys's duty to maintain Toroc's balance when needed. And sure as anything, those forest brigands were in need. If Aderri cancelled the contract, she wouldn't get the two remaining gold for the escort to Clan Dracona, nor would she get the three promised for playing the suitor. They'd be well and truly impoverished, which meant no more stables or hot mash for Rocc. It would also make it harder for them to help anyone else maintain the balance.

Ellys scrubbed her face with both hands and made eye contact with her long-time friend and steed. "I won't let you down." She knew Roccotári would understand her deeper meaning. Finally, she straightened, dropped her arms to the side, and faced Aderri.

"I have no choice. This is my profession." She held up a hand to stay the words she could sense on the tip of Aderri's tongue. "Maybe not exactly how we're going about it. But there are plenty of times I've had to play a role as part of my job. In the Elite Guard for the Empress, I had to be a captain though I've never gravitated toward leadership. When behind enemy lines, I was forced to be a spy. Balance clearly states that sometimes we will be forced to make the hard cuts while in service to Toroc, and there are other times when we will make no cuts at all."

Aderri's shoulders sagged. "Thank you. I loathed to find another so close to the ceremony. I was late enough to meet you as it was. Not to mention—"

Curiosity piqued, Ellys tilted her head. "Not to mention?"

"I actually like you. Maybe in another time or place, if there weren't coin and duty between us, we could have been good friends."

Ellys nodded, glad they'd come to some sort of agreement. "I think that's entirely possible. But a warning to you, this sort of thing won't be easy for me."

"How do you mean?"

"I mean that I'm not comfortable being close to another, at least not since I lost my Gwyn. But I am comfortable making a new friend, and that brings a closeness of its own. Luckily, we have an entire moon to develop this friendship. I think that's the best we can do in lieu of the real relationship we will be mimicking."

Aderri gave her a broad smile. Her full lips stretched across those little pointed canines, and dimples shone deep into her cheeks. She was unfairly attractive, and Ellys lamented fate that put them together professionally instead of for a single night at an inn. Aderri broke Ellys from her musings.

"Let's eat and be free from these woods, shall we?" With those words, Aderri grabbed a rock cake in each hand, the heat having no ill effects upon her skin. She placed one on a broad leaf then drizzled a little honey on top. When finished, she recapped the jar and stuffed it back into the depths of her endless travel pack.

Ellys wiped her hands on her breeches. "Okay."

They ate in companionable silence initially, then Ellys voiced the one thing she was looking forward to. "I don't know about you, but I'm ready to sleep in a real bed tonight."

"Are you sure there will be an inn this time?"

Ellys took a swig from her skin of water. "Yes. Once we clear the forest, there's another large trade road that intersects this one, running a more direct route southeast to Muniers. Obviously, we won't be taking that road, but there's also a town at the junction, called Pata. It's grown into a decently-sized city over the past few decades because of the crossroads location."

"Is the other road busier?"

"Well, it crosses this one. I wouldn't say it's necessarily busier heading straight into Muniers closer to the eastern edge of the border, but it does carry people from the heavily populated region along the coastal towns to the Northern Reach, where King Arvol keeps his training grounds for the army."

Aderri nibbled at her cake. "Hmm…I suspect given the amount of unrest across Carthune, the road to the training grounds will be well trod."

"You're probably right. But I'm sure there will be plenty of people heading southwest toward the Kuwythian border as well. Either way, I'd gamble there will be significantly more people on the road once we get past Pata."

****

Later that afternoon, Ellys and Aderri were walking to stretch their legs. To stave off boredom, they began challenging each other with riddles.

Aderri asked the first one. "What word is always pronounced wrong?"

Ellys walked along, brow scrunched in thought. She repeated the question aloud to herself to puzzle it out. "What word is always pronounced wrong?"

Oh ho, that's a good one!

Ellys narrowed her eyes at her steed. "Don't tell me you know the answer."

Okay then, I won't tell you that I know.

"Fine, be that way. Now, it probably has something to do with the wording. I know a lot of these riddles are tricky."

Aderri stifled laughter with a hand over her own mouth. "You're not wrong."

Ellys scowled at her. "Is it…Tizzlebaenalbraeth?"

Female laughter echoed inside and outside Ellys's head, and she kicked a stone on the road in irritation. "Oh, just tell me already. I don't know why I agreed to this game. I'm miserable at these things."

"It's wrong."

Ellys rolled her eyes. "I already know Tizzlebaenalbraeth is wrong."

Aderri reached out and gave Ellys a little shove, causing the half-elf to stumble. "No, the word that's always pronounced wrong *is* wrong."

"What?"

Aderri tried again with different emphasis. "Ellys, the word is *wrong*."

Ellys huffed. "Well, how am I supposed to guess correctly if it's wrong?" Loud braying made Ellys hunch her shoulders in irritation.

How in the abyss of Abbad have you made it so far in life? You're thicker than a bucket of mud, even for a gaugin. Rocc wandered closer until she was able to use her shoulder to push against Ellys's opposite side.

Quick hands pushed her away. "Oh, shove off, you accursed

nag." That only made Rocc bray louder.

Aderri gave her a pitying look and put her hand out to grab Ellys's bicep. "Stop for a moment, please?" Aderri's touch was firm, and Ellys ambled to a stop, unable to deny her request.

"Yes?"

Aderri spelled out the answer to the riddle. "W-R-O-N-G. The word wrong is always pronounced 'wrong.' Understand now?" She stepped back as Ellys threw her hands up in the air.

"Oh, for the love of tuppery! All that for such a simple answer?"

So simple, yet you couldn't even guess it.

Ellys whirled and pointed a finger at Rocc in mock anger. "Not another word, or no more breeding visits for you!"

Rocc gave a snort. *Like I need you to find me a stallion for a night of fun.*

Aderri gave Ellys's shoulder a squeeze as they began walking again. "It's your turn."

Ellys thought for a few candle drops then turned to Aderri. "Okay, I heard this in Parelgar tens of cycles ago. What has an eye but cannot see?"

It took Aderri but a heartbeat to come up with the correct answer. "A needle."

"Wha—how did…oh snake balls!" Ellys looked sideways at Aderri, gifting her patron with a cross look. "You could at least pretend it took effort to come up with an answer."

Aderri gave her a fanged grin. "I stumped you and you didn't stump me. Are you ready to pay the price?"

"I hate this game," Ellys mumbled.

Rules are rules, my pointy-eared friend.

That time Ellys kicked another stone at Rocc, who in turn trotted ahead of them braying. "You have pointed ears, too, Donkey."

Ah, yes, but I'm a superior race and my ears serve a purpose. Unlike you inferior two-leggers.

Ellys rolled her eyes. "That doesn't even make sense."

Aderri added her own two coppers worth of opinion. "Perhaps she's speaking in riddles and that's why you don't understand?"

"Fie on you both. Why must you always join forces against me?"

"Because it's more fun that way."

Ellys gave in. "Fine, what do you want to know?"

"Who was your first love?"

There was no pause, no hesitation between Aderri's question and Ellys's answer. "Gwyneth. She was my first and only. She was…" Ellys smiled and trailed off as she remembered her time with the lost light of her life. "Her smile could warm any room. And although she was no follower of Toroc, she did her best to walk in balance with me. And, by Aphora, she was beautiful inside and out."

Ellys's voice reflected the love she still carried for Gwyn. She caught a brief look of surprise, then Aderri pursed her lips in a manner that looked an awful lot like jealousy. Ellys tried to ignore it, assuming she had misread Aderri's expression.

"She must have been a true light in the sky."

Ellys turned her head to meet Aderri's gaze. "She really was. What about you? Have you ever been in love?"

It took Aderri a lot longer to answer. The only sound between the three travelers was the wind in the trees, bird song, and the plodding of Rocc's hooves. Aderri's voice was soft and wistful. "No, not once."

"Why?"

"I've never really given my lack of deep love much thought." She fell silent for a number of paces before adding to her answer. "I guess I've been completely focused on expanding my knowledge, moving from place to place and practically living in the major libraries across the six nations."

Ellys looked at her curiously. "How do you know when you're done, when you've gleaned all you can from the gathered knowledge available?"

"There is no greater treasure than knowledge, and if done correctly a person will never stop learning."

Spoken like a true dragon. Rocc moved closer again to nibble at Ellys's sleeve. *May I have one of those apples in your pack? I could use a snack.* Ellys paused to dig for one of the extra fruits she'd tucked away, and the other two paused with her.

Aderri said, "Spoken like a true horse."

Rocc snorted and stomped her hoof in displeasure. *I. Am. Not. A. Horse.* Ellys laughed and the nibbling turned into a small bite. *Tell her, Ellys.*

Ellys found what she was looking for, despite the laughter that shook her shoulders. She held the crunchy red apple out in the palm of her hand, and Rocc quickly snatched it. The steed took a large bite and chewed while the rest fell to the ground. Shaking her head at her long-time friend, Ellys did as requested. "Fine, if it will make you happy." She turned to Aderri. "She's not a horse." She waited a beat then added, "Clearly, because she's a donkey." That sent Aderri into a laughing fit, and Ellys secretly thrilled at the sound.

Candle drops later, they'd begun walking again and crested a large hill. All three paused in the middle of the road as they took in the town below. The river that had been pacing the road through the forest left them shortly after they exited the trees. They'd finally found it again, taking note of the way it cut in from the northwest to neatly bisect the town. Half a dozen bridges crossed the water at regular intervals.

While they had occasionally met fellow travelers going in the opposite direction on the trade road, no one had overtaken them from behind since before they had entered Scir Wudu. Even so, the number of travelers met along the southern trade road paled in comparison to what they could see in the distance, heading northwest along the river road.

Aderri was the first to speak. "I don't remember this town from the last time I was down this way. If it were here, it couldn't have been more than an inn and well."

Ellys gave her a strange look. "When was the last time you took the trade road south?"

"Hmm, I can't remember. I spent nearly the past ten cycles in Longoria, and before that I was in an academic stronghold to the far north, on the Emur Peninsula. And to get there, I traversed the entire northern breadth of the Kuwyth Empire. At least fifty cycles."

"So, it's been awhile."

Aderri showed Ellys that little lip bite she was fond of. "You can say that."

Ellys ignored the flirtatious wink that followed a comment that was rife with double meaning. "Come on, let's head down this hill and find a room. I'm tired of sleeping on the ground."

I do just fine standing. You could try that tonight.

"Keep it up and you'll be standing in the street, begging for your evening grain."

Aderri moved to rub Rocc's neck affectionately. "Don't worry, I'll make sure you get a stable and some feed."

Annnnd now dragons are my favorite species. Sorry, Ellys.

Ellys opened her mouth to retort then stopped. "You know what, I don't even care. I just want a warm bed, a hot meal, and a scalding bath." Suddenly she pointed at Rocc. "And not a single word about odor either."

Rocc tossed her head. *We share a lineal bond. I would never disrespect you by saying aloud that you smell like a half-dead ogre.*

"Uh, thank you?"

Because I can't lie, you smell like a fully-dead one. Best you keep clear of other travelers until we can procure you that bath.

Aderri abruptly covered her mouth but a small laugh slipped out. "Come along, companions. The sun will set and moons rise soon. I, too, could use a bath and a hot meal."

Aderri and Ellys opted to ride Rocc to get into Pata sooner than they would have on foot. Even though the steed moved at a fast trot, the two riders still had time to observe the foot traffic in the distance. The tail end of a large column of soldiers had successfully cleared the crossroads just beyond the city, and Aderri pointed at where they marched roughly southeast, obviously having come down from the Northern Reach. "Is that the entirety of the king's army?"

Ellys spoke from behind Aderri, her breath ghosting past her right ear. "Not at all. Armies are massive, and from what I know of Carthune, theirs is especially robust with a large navy and ground force. There's no way they'd send all the troops south to the border."

"Why is that?"

"As I said before, I think someone is making a play for power. I'm fairly positive King Arvol isn't responsible or even aware of the troop movements. If I were trying to usurp power from a popular ruler, I'd be sure to have the right people in charge of the military first. Then I'd keep a few battalions close enough to call, but not so close as to tip my hand or make the people in the capital nervous."

Ellys's lips accidentally brushed Aderri's ear, and she shivered within the circle of Ellys's arms. Aderri's voice was breathy when she spoke again. "That makes sense."

It didn't take long down the main road into the city for them to cross one of the wide bridges that spanned the river, stopping a short way beyond in front of a clean-looking inn. "The Rusty Harp. Wonderful," Ellys said. They dismounted and moved out of the way of foot traffic.

Aderri gave Ellys a questioning look when she spoke so harshly. "Have you been here before? Is there something wrong with the place? We can continue on to the next one if you like."

Ellys waved her off. "No, this was the location recommended by the soldier manning the Trade Road post. He specifically said it was the first inn over the main bridge. I trust a soldier's judgment to know what a fellow soldier needs."

Everyone knows that harps are typically symbols used by elves, though I've rarely seen any outside the Great Ethereal Forest. It certainly has me curious as to what manner of creature would hang that sign.

"I don't want to make small talk. I just want a bath and meal." Ellys walked to the door and stood waiting for Aderri. "Are you coming?"

Rocc's voice was soft within Ellys's head, but she could still easily hear her through the clamoring of her own thoughts. She knew her bondmate's tone was in deference to her feelings about the elder race. *Elves make her testy.*

Aderri turned to look at Ellys where she stood impatiently near the door. "Clearly. I suppose I should come in with you since I'm the one paying."

Ellys was first through the door and mostly expected what they found inside. But Aderri had no such dealings with elves and gave a small gasp of obvious surprise when she looked around the common room of the inn. Much like the magical bag that Aderri carried, the inside of the building was larger than the outside. Not only that, but there was a massive tree growing up from the center that was in no way visible from the outside.

"How—"

"It's veil magic."

Aderri turned in a circle to look upon the magnificent room and finished looking at Ellys who had already seated herself at a nearby table. "Well, at least we know the innkeeper is an elf. I wonder where they are?"

Ellys waved a hand through the air and scowled. "Who knows? Elves run on their own Goz be-damned time."

Aderri took a seat with her and tilted her head. "Why do you hate elves so much?"

"Yes," a lyrical voice called out from the side of the room. "The flaming beast poses an excellent question. Why do you hate elves so much, half-breed? Clearly our race has given the best part of you."

Ellys exploded from her seat in unbalanced rage. "The best parts of me came from Toroc. The rest is nothing but flesh and skin, you insufferable—"

Her words were cut off by a strong hand across her mouth. Aderri said, "Peace, Ellys." Ellys stilled within Aderri's solid embrace, and Aderri lowered her voice. "Don't take them to heart. They can no more stay their judgment than a herd beast can silence their lows at the end of the day. It's in their nature to think themselves above us. You of all people should know this."

Ellys knew Aderri's words were true.

"If I let you go, will you keep your mouth shut?"

Ellys nodded. She didn't keep her promise to Aderri, though she did temper her words. "Do you have so little care for business that you insult potential customers as soon as they walk through the door?"

The tall elf shrugged as they approached the two travelers. Their face was as androgynous as all others of the race, and it was impossible to tell gender without the elf giving a name or pronoun. Even then, things could be subjective. "What if I told you my rudeness is part of a curse, as is the operation of this inn?"

Elves were a slippery bunch, as Ellys knew well. "Is it?"

"Of course not. The lesser races are simply beneath us."

Ellys made to speak again but stilled with a hot hand against her own. "Please," Aderri said, "I don't feel like engaging in a drawn-out philosophical discussion on whether or not elves are a superior race."

"Elves will talk you out of half your life, then walk away as if they hadn't stolen your precious cycles."

Laughter met Ellys's bitter comment. "True enough, mutt. I am Mekke-sen and also the innkeeper of The Rusty Harp. What can I get for the two of you?"

A growl met the innkeeper's words, and Aderri shook her head at the newly-identified male elf. "We need rooms for the night, as well as a meal and a bath."

"Well that certainly explains the smell."

Ellys very nearly drew a blade but stopped just shy of raising her arm over her shoulder. She peered closer at the elf, taking note of the very fine lines of age on his face. She considered the name of the inn and sudden understanding came over her. He had been away from the Ethereal Forest a long time. "You are *en-eledron*!"

"What does that mean?" Aderri asked.

Even as she said the words, Mekke-sen sagged and lost the arrogant rigidity to his posture. "It's true. I was exiled hundreds of cycles ago. It is because I can never return to the veil myself that I brought some of it here. It's just me and my magic now."

"What were you b—"

Ellys cut her off before Aderri could get the question out. "Never, ever ask an elf why they've been banished." Aderri's look was questioning, and Mekke-sen remained unhelpful and silent. "Even hearing of a banish-able veil offence will taint your spirit and may prevent you from entering the veil."

"It also may not, mutt-ling."

Ellys pointed a finger at the innkeeper. "Keep quiet, veil-breaker! Now that I know what you truly are, you will no longer insult me."

"Please," Aderri interrupted again. "Can we please just get rooms, meals, baths, and a stable for our mount?"

The arrogant posture returned to Mekke-sen's stance. "Five gold."

"Five gold! I don't carry that kind of coin. What do you take me for?"

Mekke-sen inspected pristine fingernails. "A dragon, of course."

Aderri huffed, her own irritation becoming obvious. "I'm *adagnitio*, not *opes*! My treasure is knowledge."

The slim, long-fingered hand gave a wave. "Fine, three gold. And we don't have individual baths here. Just the bath house." He glanced from one woman to the other. "But it closes at sundown, so if you want a bath you'll have to go soon."

Ellys cursed at her luck. On one hand, she was going to have a room to herself with a real bed. On the other hand, she would have to share the bath house with her patron, a woman whose body had dominated many dreams over the past few nights. She mumbled beneath her breath. "Toroc, if this is a test, I'll do my best to pass."

Aderri looked at her. "What was that?"

"Nothing." She turned her attention to Mekke-sen. "Will someone come around and take my steed, or should I tell her to make her way to the stable in back?"

A pale eyebrow rose. "Tell her? Your steed?"

Ellys smirked. "Elven mount."

"Impossible."

The smirk softened into a genuine smile. "Lineal bond. Roccotári is the only good thing I ever got from the elves."

Surprise washed across Mekke-sen's face. "Roccotári, you say?"

"Yes."

"Interesting." Mekke-sen held out his hand for payment, and when Aderri provided the gold coins, he reached into his pocket and produced two keys, handing them to Aderri and Ellys. "Once upstairs, follow the pull of the keys to your rooms. Ring the bell on the counter downstairs, and you'll be served the evening meal. I'll personally take Lady Roccotári around to her stall and give her a warm mash, if that pleases you?"

Ellys was disconcerted at the abrupt change of attitude. "Of course, thank you."

Mekke-sen didn't respond. Instead, he gave a flourishing bow and left with a swish of his tunic.

"Well…that was certainly unexpected."

Ellys snorted derisively and headed for the stairs. "You have an unfortunately high opinion of elves. Personally, I expected nothing good of the interaction, therefore I wasn't surprised."

Aderri followed her up. "Lucky you."

Ellys turned to look back over her shoulder and winked at Aderri, unable to help the natural flirt. "Usually."

It didn't take long for the two women to settle into their rooms. Ellys rushed through her perusal of the space, hoping to check on Rocc and get to the bath house before Aderri. Rocc seemed well enough and comfortable in the stable outside.

There is something off about that elf.

Ellys began grooming Rocc's silver hide. "I thought elves were the superior race and all that drivel?"

Rocc hedged. *Well…I mean, most elves are superior among two-leggers, but there are exceptions.*

"Like me."

I was thinking of Aderri actually. But I suppose you can be considered an exception, too.

Ellys gave her a light swat on the rump with the brush. "Nag. But you are correct about Mekke-sen. He's en-eledron."

The steed gave a light kick to the wood wall behind her. *Exiled! Nothing good comes out of the veil and stays.*

The hand holding the brush stilled. "You forget that I myself cannot go back."

Ellys, no. Your case is different. You bargained with Ardruel to never return. In exchange, she didn't sever the forbidden lineal bond between a mere half-elf and steed. She even let you keep your father's gear. That is not the same as committing a crime so terrible that you're banished for thousands of cycles.

"Even so, there's little difference whether they banished me or I banished myself. I am barred from the Ethereal Forest for the rest of my days, and you are banished with me for as long as I live. I will always be sorry for that, my friend. Some days…"

Some days, what?

"I wonder if you should have let her sever the bond. You wouldn't have lost your grove nor your race. Not to mention you'd never have to worry about meals or shelter had you stayed."

Rocc turned her head and lipped at Ellys's hair affectionately. *There is nothing in the six nations or beyond that could be worth the loss of you, caritas. You have honor, and that matters more than any lifetime in the trees.*

Ellys leaned her head against Rocc's shoulder and gave her long-time friend a hug. "Thank you."

I can think of no better person to be bonded to. Now, it's time you made your way to the bath house. You smell worse than the stable cart outside.

"Fine, I'll leave you to your evening." She dropped the brush in a nearby bucket and made her way around the back of the main inn where she'd already sussed out the entrance to the bath house was located.

Ellys stepped inside and counted her luck that Aderri wasn't there yet. She quickly undressed and walked into the large pool of water set down into the stone floor. It was ingenious really, and Ellys assumed more of Mekke-sen's magic went into its creation. Unfortunately, she realized too late that the hearth fire had gone out, probably because it was near sundown. That meant that the chamber and pool were rapidly cooling with the coming night. She'd have to rush her bath and risk getting chilled, or get out of the water and build the fire herself in the nude. "I am such a blooming bally-woggle!"

"Not that I'll disagree, but is there a reason for your sudden castigation?"

Ellys swung her head around to stare at Aderri as she pushed through the door. "Oh, I was just—"

"Isn't it a bit chilly in here for you? Apparently when Mekke-sen said it closes at sundown, he meant they stopped keeping the hearth aflame." She lit two wall torches then walked over to the fireplace and stacked wood inside. With a wave of her hand, fire roared into existence.

Aderri held her hand out for nearly a candle drop, and Ellys assumed it was to be sure the wood caught sufficiently, not that she really knew how Aderri's magic worked. "That's all well and good, but unfortunately, the water has lost much of its warmth as a result." She was taken by a shiver while she said the words, as if to emphasize her point.

"Never fear." Aderri quickly removed her clothing and stacked it on a bench near the wall. Ellys caught a tantalizing glimpse of dark flesh and glorious curves before turning her eyes away in search of soap. Aderri's voice got louder as she approached the stone steps that led down into the pool. "If there is one task I'm always good for, it's heating things up."

Aderri entered the water with a splash, and heartbeats later, it grew noticeably warmer where the currents of her entry swirled around Ellys. "By Goz, that feels amazing."

"How warm do you want it? You mentioned scalding earlier, but my heat tolerance will be significantly higher than yours."

Ellys opened her eyes and met Aderri's gaze. She studiously ignored thinking of the soft wonderland she knew to be just below the surface of the water. "I can definitely stand it hotter."

"Is that right?" Aderri moved closer as the water began to heat further.

Ellys swallowed. "Yes."

"How about now?"

"Warmer."

Aderri moved until she was right next to Ellys, and she made no secret of her perusal of the tall half-elf's smooth, toned flesh. Ellys closed her eyes to the appraisal, and Aderri leaned in to whisper, "How hot do you like it?"

The water temperature increased to near scalding. Ellys's lips parted in pleasure, and her skin tingled at Aderri's nearness. "Right there. That's perfect."

Aderri suddenly moved close enough to brush lips against Ellys's pointed ear. "Good. I aim to please." Then she pulled away, and Ellys watched with slitted eyes as she floated on her back to the opposite side of the pool.

Ellys closed her eyes to the retreating curves floating above the water, but she couldn't scrub the image out of her head. She whispered under her breath, "By Toroc, she's going to kill me."

Aderri called out a candle drop later, "Toss me the soap, please?"

"Sure, I'm done with it." A lathered-up Ellys lazily tossed the soap to the other woman but misjudged the distance in the dim light. Aderri had to rise out of the water to catch it, exposing her breasts. Ellys abruptly closed her eyes and dunked below the surface to rinse. She came up again and pushed the short, dark strands out of her eyes.

"You okay over there?"

"Never better."

"You warm enough?"

"Oh yes, I'm perfect. Hot in fact."

"You certainly are." Aderri winked, and Ellys dropped below the surface again.

She heard the other woman's laughter and gave a scream of sexual frustration beneath the water's surface, eyes shut of course. It wouldn't do to see any more tantalizing bits, thus increasing the uncomfortable throbbing in places she'd rather not think about while bathing with a patron.

Chapter Seven

Despite Ellys's insistence that she liked the water scalding hot, it eventually grew too warm for her enjoyment. Aderri seemed quite content leaning against the side of the pool, her eyes closed and body glistening with water droplets in the combined fire and torchlight. Ellys tried not to think of all the explorable flesh across from her. Rather than risk dizziness by remaining in the pool, she decided it was time to leave. "I think I'm going to head back to my room now."

Aderri's pupils glowed with some internal fire when she opened them. "So soon?"

Ellys was certain those eyes didn't always burn, but she couldn't pinpoint the specific times when they did, or the cause. She filed away the information for thinking about later. Or to use as a question should she win another round of bones the next time they played. "I'm as clean as I'll get, I suppose."

"Not according to Rocc." Even as she said the words, Aderri gave Ellys a smile, apparently to show she was just teasing.

"Yes, well Lady Roccotári is probably shitting in her own stall as we speak, so I hardly think she's any judge of cleanliness. You can take a horse out of the barnyard, but you can't take the barnyard out of the—you know what, scratch that because…"

As one, Ellys and Aderri spoke the familiar words, "She's not a horse," then they burst into laughter.

"I should go." While Ellys's mind was responsible for the words, her body had other ideas.

Adcrri's eyes were slitted, and Ellys could feel the weight of her gaze. "Okay."

Ellys began to stand then grew uncomfortable at being watched so intently and resumed her seat. "Are you going to stare at me like that as I leave?" Aderri's full lips were parted just enough that Ellys could see the tips of her fangs. The look in her eyes alone had Ellys's heart racing. But the teeth, the tongue that poked out to wet those lips, and the water droplet that followed a path into Aderri's cleavage, caused another reaction. Ellys had never felt so much like prey, and she suddenly wondered what Aderri was like in the midst of pleasure. Would she be in control, or let control take her?

"Why wouldn't I? After all, you're the one with the 'look but don't touch' rule. It's certainly not a philosophy I subscribe to."

Ellys had forgotten she'd asked a question during her slow perusal of her patron's body. Patron. Aderri was her patron, a fact she would do best to remember for both their sakes. She raised a hand out of the water and circled her finger in the air to emphasize her words. "Can't you just…turn around, or something?" Aderri threw her head back and laughed. The abrupt action caused her breasts to break the surface of the bathing pool. The sight froze Ellys in place as much as it superheated other parts of her anatomy below the water. She moaned, "By Toroc…"

"And miss this view? I think not."

Ellys squeezed her eyes shut. She drew in a deep breath through her nose and blew it out past her lips. She opened her eyes and leveled a stern gaze at Aderri. It was then that Ellys knew she was being toyed with. She decided two could play at that game, so she quickly rose from her seat. The dark water splashed and cascaded from her body, sounding quite loud in the small bath house. Aderri's gaze grew impossibly intense, as if she watched every rivulet stream from Ellys's skin.

"Fine. I hope you enjoy the back as much as you do the front because I'm leaving now." With that, Ellys waded toward the steps and exited the pool. She moved quickly to the drying cloths then dressed in her clothes just as fast.

"I enjoy it all."

Ellys tried to act as though Aderri's response didn't cause things to clench that had long been left untupped. But her body knew the truth even if her brain refused to admit it. She couldn't get back to her room fast enough.

Unfortunately, her room was cold when she entered, and for a heartbeat, she regretted not sharing with Aderri. She quickly built a fire in the hearth and turned back the bedcovers to allow the stuffed mattress to warm. She reached down to cup the fullness of her sex through her breeches and moaned at the contact. At the rate they were going, she was unsure she'd make it to Aderri's Clan lands without combusting. "Dragon fire." She snorted.

Once she was certain the hearth wood had caught enough to burn for a while, Ellys locked the door and drew one of the swords from her back and placed it within easy reach of the bed. Then she divested herself of the sword harness and the rest of her clothes. Less than two candle drops later, she slid nude between the coverlets and reached down to stroke herself again. The hair of her pubis was the same short, velvety carpet that all elves had. It required no grooming and felt a bit like moss, not at all like others' she'd been with. Her fingers slid through dewy nectar, and Ellys sucked in a breath. She whispered, "*Cuthylani*," an elven word whose rough translation was something like "sweet pleasure."

Out in the bath house, Aderri neither had to make the trip up to her room, nor did she have to build a hearth fire. But the heat was there just the same. She cursed Ellys's name even as she stroked herself with two fingers below the surface of the water. Eventually, Ellys's name whispered from between her lips without cursing at all.

****

Aderri and Ellys left their rooms at nearly the same time the next morning. Ellys was dressed for the road with blades across her back and cloak tied loosely around her shoulders. One side of the cloak was thrown behind her shoulder to make room for the travel pack. She nodded at Aderri but otherwise stayed silent.

Aderri smirked and Ellys knew she was thinking of their time in the bath house the previous evening. "Good morn, Ellys."

Ellys grunted in return. There was a table with basic morning fare, as if Mekke-sen had anticipated their arrival ahead of time. It didn't take long to break their fast, which was a good thing as Ellys had maintained her silence throughout. She was usually cranky in the morning, but her own actions the night before had left her feeling particularly out of balance when it came to Aderri.

They stood when they were finished eating, and Aderri put her hand on Ellys's forearm before they could head for the door. "I'm sorry if I upset you last night."

Ellys gazed upon the dark skin of Aderri's hand resting against the paleness of her own arm. Finally, she looked into those flaming eyes of her patron. "You didn't upset me."

"Don't lie to me, Ellys."

"I swear by Goz that I'm not lying. The truth is—" She paused to collect her thoughts. "The truth is, I upset myself. This attraction between us isn't exactly subtle. And while the flirting is fun, it's a dangerous game we play when the journey's only half over." Aderri removed her hand and Ellys missed the warmth of it.

"I understand. You don't trust me."

"Honestly? I don't trust myself."

"So how do we go from here? I know you want to keep things strictly professional. Do you need me to give you more space? I can attempt to cut back on the flirting but—" Aderri paused. "I'm afraid that's a natural part of my personality. I don't even realize I'm doing it most times."

"I need—"

Whatever it was that Ellys needed was cut off by a loud bang and thud outside, coupled with a mental shout. *Ellys!*

Ellys immediately dropped her pack and ran for the door. Even as she yanked it open with one hand, she was drawing a sword with the other. Aderri was right behind her, despite having no real weapons or offensive magic. What they found in the stable was beyond shocking. Mekke-sen was unconscious against the far wall outside Roccotári's stall, nude from the boots up. There was a rapidly blackening bruise in the center of his chest, and Rocc stood over his prone body pawing at the wooden floorboards. She tossed her head and blew out a harsh breath through her nostrils, radiating fury with each twitch and stomp.

"Whoa, what happened?" Seeing there was no immediate danger, Ellys sheathed her sword and approached the agitated elven steed with an outstretched hand.

Rocc shook her head violently, sending her long mane cascading in all directions. *I refuse to speak of it! But suffice it to say, I know why this vile elf was banished from the Ethereal Forest, and he is deserving of every single day of that thousand cycles.* She swiveled her big head around to gently brush against Ellys's shoulder. *He's going to be out for a bit, and I'd like to leave now.*

Both Ellys and Aderri stood shocked for a moment. Ellys pulled herself together first, knowing her long-time companion was distraught and in need of comfort. "Of course. Let's get out of here."

"Should we just…leave him like that?"

Ellys looked back at the mostly nude elf and saw a line of ants marching near his foot. "Actually, do you still have your jar of honey?"

Aderri gave her a wicked smile, obviously understanding

immediately what Ellys had in mind. She reached into the satchel that had been slung across her shoulders all through morning meal. Aderri opened the jar and handed it to Ellys, watching as the honey flowed in smooth ribbons toward the ground. Ellys drizzled a path starting near the line of ants and continued it up Mekke-sen's boots and legs, finally puddling it all over the mossy hair of his groin. Then she recapped what was left of the jar and handed it back. The trio left the stables laughing, only pausing long enough for Ellys to run into the inn and grab her discarded travel pack.

It wasn't long down the road before Ellys moved closer to Rocc and stroked her neck. "Are you okay?"

Rocc lipped at her hair above the leather band. *I'm fine. He didn't do more than touch my flank, but his intention was easy enough to read, in both thought and deed.* Even though her mental words were proof enough, the affectionate way Rocc rubbed her velvety muzzle against Ellys's cheek convinced her all the more that her friend was indeed fine.

Ellys turned her attention to Aderri. "Sorry about the honey. My temper nearly overtook me for a candle drop back there, and I struggled to find a solution that would allow me to keep the balance."

"I for one thought it was brilliant, and I'll gladly pay for two jars when we restock supplies on the way out of Pata." Aderri wandered closer to Rocc as well. "I'm sorry you had to put up with such unwanted attentions. Is there anything I can do?"

There is nothing that needs done, truly. Though I cherish you for asking. Thank you, cara. Rocc paused for a candle drop then addressed them both. *Can you believe that elf-trash called me a beautiful example of horse flesh? That makes me so angry I could go back and kick him again.* She gave a little stomp, mid-plod, and snorted. *I am not a horse.*

Aderri reached out and stroked her neck. "Of course you're not, darling. You are a beautiful lady, and shame on anyone for not seeing it."

Ellys smiled at the interaction but kept her thoughts and her words to herself. Instead, she worked to dissipate the rage she felt for her best friend's mistreatment. Vengeance was not allowed when you followed Toroc's path.

They took some time to replenish supplies for the next leg of their journey, including two new jars of clover honey. They left Pata a little later than normal, which put them right in the middle of heavy foot-and-wagon traffic heading southwest. As Ellys suspected, the going was significantly busier. They opted to ride double on Rocc for the first half of the day to give them a better vantage point. Aderri pointed out the obvious.

"Half of these people look like families with all their worldly belongings, not traders and regular travelers."

"I'm sure they sense war coming and are heading toward the empire where they think they'll be safe. They're wrong, of course."

Aderri turned her head to peer at Ellys. "Why do you say that?"

Ellys gesticulated with the hand that wasn't holding the reins. "Look, we both know that the Kuwyth Empire is vast. I've traveled the breadth and width of it multiple times. And one certainty is that unless you're in a large city, the rest of the empire tends to be a bit…lawless."

Aderri faced forward again in her seat. "I guess I never realized. All my studies have taken place in cities with large libraries or universities. I haven't spent much time in the rural areas of Kuwyth." She turned again. "Will we be safe cutting through Cat's Head to get into Muniers?"

Ellys took note of the worry lines etched between Aderri's dark red brows. "That depends. How much coin do you have for bribes?"

"Bribes?" Aderri's mouth dropped open, and she sputtered for an answer. "I will not pay bribes for safe passage entitled to us by Kuwythian law."

They were interrupted when Rocc tossed her head and gave a little whinny. *You two are missing the nearer complication.*

Ellys glanced around, suddenly wary. "What do you mean?"

We'll be hard-pressed to find a place at the next inn with this many people on the road west.

"Fenwith's b—" Ellys abruptly cut off her favorite curse, remembering the way Aderri teased her for it. "Uh, by Bron, this is the worst luck. Can you swing us out from the road and pick up speed to overtake the majority of the crowd?"

Aderri tensed where she sat in front of Ellys. "But it would require candle marks of fast riding to get ahead of all the people that left before us. There is no way Rocc can sustain that kind of pace."

Oh really?

Ellys groaned. "Shite! Now you've done it." She gave up guiding her mount at that point because she knew Rocc was going to find her own way.

"What do you mean?"

"Best hold on to something and prepare to finish the day with a sore ass because now she's got something to prove."

Roccotári broke from the crowd and began to pick up her pace a dozen or so steps off the main road. When she sped into a canter, Aderri gripped the pommel while Ellys held her arms tight around Aderri's waist and squeezed Rocc's body with her legs. One good thing about sharing a saddle was that the speed didn't do much to dislodge them. The downside was that Ellys was once again intimately aware of every bit of motion and pressure of Aderri's body against the front of her own. It was delicious torture, and they had candle marks to go.

****

The trio didn't stop until a candle mark after midday. As Ellys predicted, Aderri's bottom was well and truly bruised from the prolonged gait. By that point, they were far ahead of the initial crowd heading out of Pata.

Rather than break out her meal right away, Ellys opted to do a few stretches in order to loosen her muscles after she dismounted. Aderri did her own share of loosening up, mostly because she was afraid to sit down again. After a few candle drops of stretching, Ellys drew both swords and went into a complicated routine that appeared to be just as much art as it was war, at least to Aderri's admiring eyes. Ellys had called it a sword dance when she'd performed it on previous evenings of their journey. She was broken from her reverie by Rocc's mental voice.

I can smell a spring nearby; would you care to join me?

Aderri didn't take her eyes off Ellys, instead shaking her head. "Not just yet, thank you."

Rocc gave a snort. *Suit yourself. But be sure to feed more than your eyes while we're stopped.*

That got Aderri's attention. She whispered, "Are you implying that I'm ogling?"

While the steed couldn't shrug the way a humanoid could, she got her point across just fine with a small shake of the mane and twitch of her shoulder. *I'm implying nothing, just reminding you to keep your strength up. We've a long way to go before we reach your Clan lands.*

If only to prove Rocc wrong, Aderri gave in. "Fine, I'll come along with you. The water skins need filling anyway. And perhaps I can find some tender cattails near the pool."

You're not likely to find more than shoots and stalks this time of cycle, same as when we camped in Scir Wudu.

Aderri winked. "The best part if you ask me."

They picked their way through the trees, following Rocc's nose toward the spring. Even with their nightly talks, Aderri was still very curious with regards to her traveling companions. Unfortunately, their walk through the woods and over fallen logs was a bit painful after the tumultuous ride to the clearing. When the third small gasp escaped from Aderri's lips, Rocc abruptly stopped.

Are you feeling well? Was the ride too rough for you?

Aderri took a moment to stretch the backs of her legs and grimaced. "I'm not going to lie. My nethers haven't felt like this since I spent three days in the Clarendon Wood with a satyr named Donalt."

Rocc gave a little nicker of humor. *What was so special about this Donalt?*

A smile slowly curled upon Aderri's face at the memory. "Well for starters, he was very large—"

"What was large?" Ellys's voice interrupted. "And what is taking so long? I completed a full routine, and you're still not back with the water."

"Uh, largely into music," Aderri said quickly, not having heard Ellys approach through the trees.

Rocc gave a wheezing bray of laughter. *Sounds like you were more interested in the shape of his flute than the skill of his tune.*

Aderri gave a sniff. "Mayhap."

A noble steed indeed.

They both started laughing as Ellys looked on in confusion. "Did I miss something?"

Rocc tossed her head. *Nothing important. I was going to offer a spot of healing to Aderri here since she's sore from our morning ride. It's the least I can do considering I was responsible for her bruised hindquarters.*

"Wait, you can heal?" Aderri asked

Ellys stroked Rocc's neck with affection. "She is a creature of earth, just as you are one of fire. Rocc can be a conduit of living energy if she chooses."

Aderri's mouth dropped open as she turned her incredulous gaze from Ellys to Rocc. "Truly? How does it work?"

You are an adagnitio through and through, aren't you? Rocc gently lipped Aderri's shoulder to show she was only teasing. *But to answer your question, as long as I'm careful, I can pull energy from magical ley lines deep within the earth, or even living things around me, to heal either myself or someone I'm in contact with. I would require your permission though.*

"Permission granted."

Ellys laughed. "That was easy. Where is your pride, woman?"

I'm to understand you don't need a healing then? Rocc's liquid silver eyes stared directly at Ellys, and the swordswoman's laughter cut off immediately.

"Actually, on second thought, Aderri n'all Dracona is a very wise soul. I will gratefully accept a healing after our patron."

Rocc gave a very loud snort. *That's what I thought.*

Aderri said, "So, pulling this energy…do you use it for more than healing?"

Put your hand upon my neck, please.

Aderri complied then snapped the fingers of her free hand. "Wait, is that how you're able to go without sleep, or run for so long without rest? Can you pull energy as you move?"

Yes, yes, and yes. Now quiet please. It only took a few candle drops for Rocc to complete the healing and move away from Aderri's hand. *How is that?*

Aderri did a few stretches, then squatted and straightened. She grinned at Rocc, back in high spirits after being in pain half the morning. "I feel good as new. Thank you."

Rocc wuffed and moved over to stand by Ellys. Aderri asked why it took less time with her, and Ellys said, "I wasn't as bad off. After all, I had the stirrups. When my backside started hurting, I'd stand up a bit to alleviate the pummeling."

The steed stomped a hoof and gave her lineal bondmate a nudge. *Good. Can we get to the spring already?*

"I have so many more questions about your power-pulling ability."

Rocc nuzzled Aderri's shoulder. *I have no problem answering, but wait until we head out again. Running can get boring, and I like conversation when we're going from one place to another.*

Aderri gave her a rub to the muzzle for her request. "Okay."

They reached a small town by evening, one big enough to have an inn and a stable. It was a good thing Rocc had gotten them ahead of the majority of the group departing Pata that morning because they got the last two rooms available. The inn itself was also a busy tavern with a minstrel and full dinner service.

Ellys and Aderri agreed to get settled into their rooms and meet downstairs for evening meal. They found a table near the side of the room where Ellys could have her back to the wall. Then they waited for a serving maid.

The first one to come around was practically spilling out of her corset, and much to Aderri's displeasure, only seemed to have eyes for Ellys. "The name is Zama. What can I get for you, handsome?"

Not immune to the flirting, Ellys grinned. "My patron and I are here for evening meal. Do you just have one thing available, or is there a selection?"

"We have fish for two copper. But I wouldn't order it. It's just bottom-feeder river trash. There's also stew, which is pretty good and also two copper. But we've got a special tonight on a full platter of roast and tubers for only a copper."

Ellys looked at her in surprise. "Why only one copper?"

"One of farmer Dev's cows got loose and had the misfortune of wandering into our back stable yard. So, everything Innkeeper Jebben sells is profit."

Aderri raised a dark red brow at Zama. "And what, this Jebben is allowed to just keep the cow without having to return the beast to its rightful owner or pay for it?"

Zama raked her eyes up and down Aderri's body and gave a disdainful sniff. "Around here, possession is three-quarters of the law."

"But still—"

"And Jebben's axe is the other half."

Aderri held up a finger. "Um, that's not how maths work."

Zama rolled her eyes. "Not everyone is a scholar." She turned her warm gaze back to Ellys. "What would you like? I promise I'll do my best to satisfy you."

"Oh, I'm sure you will—"

Aderri cleared her throat and Ellys quickly amended her statement. "Erm, I mean, I'm sure the meal will. I'd like the special, please." She looked at her patron. "Aderri?"

"I'll have the same and a glass of wine."

Zama gave another sniff and scowled, muttering under her breath. "Fancy folk." Then louder she spoke to Aderri. "No wine here, just honey mead or ale, both a copper."

"Fine, honey mead then," Aderri ground out through clenched teeth. She heard Ellys snicker quietly, which didn't improve her mood in the slightest.

"I'll have the same, Zama. And thank you."

Aderri fished the coins out of her pouch and placed them on the table.

"Your service is my pleasure." Zama gave Ellys a little curtsey and scooped up the coins before making her way across the main room toward the back, presumably to get their food and drinks.

"Well, she was certainly annoying."

Ellys raised a single brow. "Oh really? You're not just saying that because she was pretty and flirtatious?"

"Pretty?" Aderri scoffed. "She isn't exactly my type. Not to mention, did she have no shame practically throwing herself at you?"

"What's the harm? It's not like the two of us are together. We can each seek pleasure where we choose, and she clearly thought I was not with you."

"Something tells me she wouldn't care either way."

"Perhaps you're right. Despite that, it's all harmless fun. You're free to find your own night's entertainment as well."

Before Aderri could answer, two platters were placed in front of them on the table. Another young man circled around a candle drop later with their meads. Aderri was intent on eating her meal and mercifully Ellys didn't comment.

While it was true that they weren't a real couple, the serving maid's flirting rankled Aderri. It wasn't as if she herself hadn't considered letting off a bit of steam, but they'd been traveling close for nearly a half-moon and there hadn't exactly been an opportunity. Not only that, but Aderri had grown fond of her handsome companion. She glanced at Ellys through lowered lashes and realized her problems wouldn't be solved by a quick round of tupping with a stranger.

They finished their meal just as the minstrel started playing quietly in the corner. Zama came back to clear out their platters. Once again, her gaze was for Ellys only. "Are you staying to hear the bard, and would you like another mead?"

"I—"

Before Ellys could finish her statement, Aderri slapped two more coppers on the table and stood. "Get what you want, Ellys. I'm retiring for the evening." She quickly made her way to the back of the room where the door led into the inn proper.

Candle drops later, Aderri paced back and forth in her room. She was in turns annoyed and jealous, then back to being annoyed again because she was jealous. "Of all the—what an insufferable, randy, horse's ass."

She paused in her ranting long enough to build up the fire in her hearth. When she was finished, she turned to head over to the small bed and was interrupted by a knock on the door. Curious as to whom it could be, Aderri walked over and opened it.

Ellys stood in the doorway holding a jug of honey mead, her cup, and her bag of bones. She shook the bag and rattling sounded loud between them. "Care for a couple rounds?"

"What happened to Sama?"

"I told *Zama* that two plus one is zero. She wasn't happy, but I don't know if that was because she couldn't do the maths, or because I walked away to speak with the innkeeper about her rudeness toward you." She shook her cup, which clanked with the two unspent copper coins. "The mead was on him."

Aderri raised her brow. "Oh really?"

"I am a Grand Master of Toroc's Blades. I know how to get my point across when necessary."

Aderri laughed and pushed the door open wide, allowing entry. "What am I to do with you?"

Ellys deposited the mead and cup on the small table by the window, then gave another rattle of the red bag. "Shake my bones?"

"Fine." The candle lit with a wave of Aderri's hand as Ellys settled into a chair and poured the mead. It was another night of learning for both of them, on many levels.

Chapter Eight

Ellys looked around with concern as they rode into the border city of Veniche. Even though the magical barrier was on the other side of the river, they could easily see its shimmering length running east and west. There was no top to be seen, just the wall going up and up until it was out of sight. She whistled. "That's no small undertaking."

Aderri's gaze followed the line in the sky, then she pulled a map from the satchel slung across her chest and studied it. The bottom of the paper crinkled where it rested against the high pommel of the saddle. Ellys peered over her shoulder as Aderri traced the length of the Carthune/Muniers border. "Based on my understanding of the greater defensive magics, they'd need at least a mage per ten leagues or so. What would you say the length of the border is in total?"

"Hmm, ten times that?" Ellys paused as she contemplated the size of the war effort. "By Toroc, the cost for mages per day alone would deplete the nation's coffers in no time at all."

Rocc blew out a loud breath and shuddered beneath them. *Unless the magic is purchased with life instead of coin. Can't you two smell it?*

Ellys took a whiff and recognized the stench of something unsavory that lifted the hairs standing at the back of her scalp. "No. They wouldn't dare. That would break the balance for the entire region."

Aderri made a face, looking as though she, too, could feel the press of darkness the farther they traveled into the city. She slumped in the saddle in front of Ellys. "I'm afraid Lady Roccotári makes a logical point. That's the only way they'd be able to maintain something so immense." She shuddered. "Why…it would take probably one sacrifice a day per mage."

That was my calculation as well.

"Where do you think they get the sacrifices?"

Ellys growled. "My guess is they emptied out the gaol first, whether those imprisoned deserved death or not."

After the gaol, I'd wager they'd next go after travelers and strangers.

Ellys straightened and gazed around warily with Rocc's mental words. "Abbad will take them before I let them take any of us."

With both women tense in the saddle and the smell of death magic in the air, everyone was on edge as they made their way through Veniche in search of a meal and bed for the night. Aderri spoke quietly and Ellys assumed she didn't want to call attention to their passage any more than necessary. "It's late afternoon now. I don't think they'll mess with us. Let's find an inn as soon as possible and get out of here by first light. I don't like being this close to that wall."

"Unfortunately," Ellys said, "the road paces it for a short way when we continue toward Kuwyth. Veniche is the split where the main trade road continues into Muniers toward Noth, and the secondary fork heads west to the empire. I'm hoping it won't be well traveled when we leave so we can make good time tomorrow. As it is, we're still seven days from the next border we need to cross."

"So…first thing tomorrow?"

"Perhaps earlier. How are our supplies? I could go get some after we acquire rooms at the inn."

"No, I don't think it's safe to wander the city once the sun goes down. We have enough to last a few days, I think we'll be fine."

"Okay."

That evening, they sat in Ellys's room shaking the bones. Aderri grinned over her cup of wine. "Five fire takes your four earth. What shall I ask of you next, hmm?"

Ellys snorted. "I'm sure you'll think of something. You've become adept at getting the details of my life out of me over the past seventeen days."

"Admit it, you enjoy these sessions. I know I do."

There was a candle drop of silence while they stared at each other. Finally, Ellys admitted, "I do enjoy our evenings together. It's strange."

"In what way?"

Ellys took a deep breath. "I…I haven't been this close to someone, spent this much time with someone other than Rocc, since Gwyn."

Aderri started to reach for Ellys's hand but pulled back instead. "How does that make you feel? Is this okay?"

A tentative grin crept across Ellys's lips. Her smile had been known to charm quite a few over the cycles, and the softening of Aderri's expression indicated that she was no exception to the lure of Ellys's attractive features. "It is. I feel like you've become a friend in a short period of time. I'm comfortable with you in a way I haven't felt with anyone in ages."

Hearing those words, Aderri reached across and placed her hand over the back of Ellys's. "I feel the same way. I know we have disparate histories and experiences, but I, too, have spent most of my life traveling. You don't make a lot of friends that way, at least not ones you know with certainty that you'll remember for the rest of your life."

Ellys inclined her head slightly. "True."

"And yet, I feel as though we will be such friends. And because of our growing closeness, I think we have a real chance at pulling off this act for my Clan."

"I can only hope…after all, I have gold coins on our success." They both grinned.

That evening, Ellys fell asleep thinking about their conversation. On one hand, her growing closeness to Aderri was frightening. She remembered well the start of her courtship with Gwyn. And while Gwyneth and Aderri were two very different people, there was something about both that set Ellys at ease deep within her soul. She tried to remind herself that Aderri was naught more than a patron and destined to leave her life just as quickly as she came into it. Unfortunately for her, the reminder was chased by an image in her head of Aderri's face and the way those two little canines dug into her bottom lip with each flirt and smirk. That night, Ellys dreamed of dragon fire melting the ice around her heart.

****

The next morning, they were up earlier than normal and didn't bother to break their fast downstairs, opting instead to eat travel bread and apples while in the saddle. The city was still dark and quiet when they made their way down the road, and the great barrier shimmered off in the distance to their left.

"This feels wrong."

Ellys's voice was muffled behind Aderri's right ear. She didn't turn to make eye contact, but instead she pitched her voice loud enough to be heard over the sound of Rocc's hooves hitting the ground in a three-beat pattern. "What feels wrong?"

"Leaving that city behind knowing what we know about the magics involved. It goes against everything I believe to let such a gross imbalance continue. This is not the natural process and is exactly the kind of thing I'm trained to fight against." Ellys waved angrily toward the wall. "I hate it."

Aderri sighed. "I feel the same way, but there's nothing the three of us can do to save this land. The region is crawling with troops, and blood mages are not something you face without a lot of power at your back."

They rode along in silence for over a candle mark. It was still twilight for a good distance, so they came across no other travelers. A few candle marks west of Veniche, the trio rode facing the rising sun. Ellys mentioned that the first few days of travel toward the Kuwyth border would be done through extremely hilly terrain. For the most part, the road wandered through canyons and around what peaks the king's men hadn't leveled off. While Ellys was grateful for Rocc's stamina, she was sick of the brown rock and thick brush that comprised the landscape around them.

The monotony of their morning was broken by the sound of ringing blades echoing from ahead. Ellys picked it up first. "Do you hear that?"

Rocc quietly whinnied and stopped. *Swords. The fighting is close, too, around that next bend.*

Aderri craned her neck to look up and around them. "Is there no other route so we can avoid whatever skirmish is ahead?"

"Not until we get out of these blasted canyons. There's a river about a half league down the road, but that doesn't help us avoid what's around that bend. I suppose I'll have to go see what the trouble is."

After nearly a moon of traveling together, Aderri knew that Ellys didn't usually put her nose into someone else's business, preferring to leave events to balance on their own. But it was obvious that their current circumstances meant Ellys would have to scout ahead. Ellys dismounted and patted Rocc's rump. "Keep her safe, I'll be back." Then she took off at a quiet sprint in the direction of the fighting.

When she disappeared around the tall rock outcropping about one hundred paces in front of them, Aderri expressed her concerns.

"There aren't many places to hide around here. Do you think she'll be discovered?"

The large elven steed let out a great sigh that sounded incredibly human. *I think if Ellys sees something that breaks the balance, it won't matter if she has a place to hide.*

"How likely is that?"

Rocc dug at the ground with a hoof. *The ringing blades are of good quality. I hear loaded horses, and I can smell oil in the air, meaning the gear is well maintained. There are somewhere between two and three swords engaging in the fight. My guess is soldiers, and whoever they are attacking will be far outnumbered.*

"Fenwith's balls!"

Should we investigate, Lady Aderri?

Someone cried out in the distance, and Aderri immediately grabbed the pommel of the saddle. "Go!"

It was a good thing Aderri was stronger than a human or else she would have been thrown backward when Rocc leaped forward into a gallop. They raced up the road, and when the duo rounded the corner, they were met with a most unusual scene. Ellys and another swordswoman stood back-to-back with swords drawn. Ranging around them was what looked to be a troop of soldiers, also with their blades drawn. Two men were on the ground next to a pair of crossbows, either dead or unconscious. Aderri could see familiar throwing knives stuck in one's chest.

Ellys noticed them immediately, but the rest of the group wasn't far behind. In the distraction caused by Rocc's arrival, one man dove for a dropped crossbow and brought it up to bear on Aderri. Ellys immediately broke the circle by lunging at him with both blades in motion. Aderri knew they were sorely outnumbered, a fear confirmed by Ellys's voice, which sounded rough with worry.

"Get her out of here, I'll catch up later." At that point, the other woman, who wore the uniform of a guard captain, was also engaged with multiple people. Rocc moved a short distance away, then hesitated, prancing in place. They both watched as another attacker picked up the second crossbow.

Aderri wasn't so keen on the plan and looked at Rocc from her place in the saddle. "What are you doing? We have to go back and help them."

Ellys gave a muffled shout, and Aderri glanced back at the melee. Despite the pain she must have felt from a crossbow bolt in her leg, Ellys yelled to urge Rocc on. "Go now! Don't come back until you can leave her someplace safe. I'll figure a way out of this. You know I will."

Be safe, caritas. The steed was clearly torn but spun and leaped away, not turning back or stopping again. All Aderri could do was hang on for dear life as Rocc set a breakneck pace away from the fighting.

****

Ellys knew she was in trouble when the bolt buried itself past the barbs into her thigh. She stumbled and only righted herself with the aid of one of her swords. Even injured, she still managed to incapacitate two more fighters before she was forced to turn quickly to the right and her leg gave out completely. She cut a quick glance over to the stranger that had been fighting at her back, only to see the woman unarmed with her hands in the air. Ellys knew they were done.

One of the men stepped forward. "Well, Captain Kessel, looks like your mysterious benefactor wasn't much help after all."

Feigning bravado, Ellys said, "I'd tell you to look around and count the bodies to see how much help I've been, but maths don't seem to be your strong suit. I met just the woman for you a few towns back."

Everyone paused to stare at Ellys. The leader of the troop scowled. "You're a mouthy elf who doesn't seem to realize when you've been beaten. Just who in Abbad are you? This was never your concern, but lucky for us, the mages are always in need of more fuel."

Ellys painfully pulled herself up until she was standing again. Her swords remained on the ground, per the direction of the other two soldiers with loaded crossbows. "My name is Ellys DeEnsis, and I pledge to Toroc that you'll regret your imbalance this day, at least for the rest of your short and miserable lives."

The word "Toroc" whispered between the fighters only caused a ruddy flush on the troop leader's face. "You will not use that false God's name around me. There is only one strength in war and that is Bron!"

"Bron is the god of short sight and shorter temper, as anyone with half a wit about them knows."

Her talking and provocation served their purpose in stalling the group in their current location. She had to give Rocc time to leave Aderri in a safe place before the steed could return. Rocc was fast but not *that* fast. One enterprising young man waggled his crossbow. "Sergeant Gahn, what do you want us to do with her?"

Gahn growled. "Tie the elf up like Kessel. If they make a move to resist, put a bolt in their other leg."

"And the wound, sir?"

"Remove the arrow however you can, then tie up the leg. After all," the troop leader said and gave Ellys an evil grin, "they don't have to live long…just long enough. I believe Mage Conast is the nearest, and we're scheduled to make a drop there next. This saves us the trouble of finding another straggler on the road."

Ellys cursed when she was roughly shoved to the ground and held down. Then she gave a ragged scream when one of the men jerked the barbed head of the arrow from the meatiest part of her thigh. A gush of blood followed as the sharp points tore even more flesh. They made quick work tying it up with a strip of someone's blanket.

One man grabbed her belt pouch and opened it. "What's this? Not even a copper in here."

Ellys gritted her teeth but maintained her bravado, if only for her own peace of mind. "Unlucky for you, I left the full pouch in my other cloak."

He gave her a kick to the wounded leg that made her vision go black for a few heartbeats. "Shut up, fucking elf trash."

Another said, "Hey Deg, maybe the mage will cut out their tongue before they steal the elf's soul."

"Do elves even have souls?"

"Conast is gonna find out!" They all broke into laughter, with the exception of Ellys and the tall woman tightly bound with ropes twenty paces away.

Gahn gave a loud whistle, bringing the group under control again. "Put them both on the wagon. I want to make our deliveries and be back in the city in time for dinner and bones at The Silver Stallion."

One man called out, "The Silver Stallion? Are you shaking the bones, or taking the bone?"

The troop leader laughed. "Perhaps a bit of both, which is why I'm anxious to get underway. It's been too long since I've had a good man to ride."

Another soldier laughed. "Sir, you ride us all the time."

Gahn gave a negligent wave through the air as he sheathed his sword then made his way to where the horses were picketed. "Not in the fun way, I can assure you. Besides, I said a good man."

Groans and laughter echoed off the stone walls of the canyon, a strange sound given the abundance of their dead swordsmen lying around in the rising sun. Ellys gritted her teeth when they slung her into the wagon. As luck would have it, the other woman stopped her roll, otherwise she'd have ended up on her face atop the wooden boards. Unfortunately, it still felt like her leg was going to come off. "Blasted troll-fuckers."

The woman next to her asked, "Tell me, stranger, does your foolish bravado help ease your mind concerning your fate?"

"My fate?" Ellys turned and managed to pull herself upright to sit shoulder to shoulder next to the soldier she had tried to save. Based on the glimpses she had when they were fighting back to back, the stranger was nearly Ellys's height, which was rare for a human. But where Ellys was black-haired and silver-eyed, the stranger had hair and eyes of burnished gold.

"We're both bound to feed the barrier, or at least you are. I'm not sure what will happen to me since I'm not only a deserter, but also a high-ranking officer in the king's army."

"Captain Kessel?"

The captain gave Ellys a wary look. "How did you know who I am?"

Ellys attempted to answer, but abrupt movement of the wagon turned the sound into a pained hiss. After a pause, she said, "Did you take a knock to the head during the fighting? That bit of orc piss masquerading as the sergeant of this troop spoke it earlier."

The woman blushed. "So he did. Perhaps I should introduce myself formally then. My name is Toridae Kessel and I am…I was the captain of the third company overseeing the eastern coast."

Ellys raised a single dark eyebrow and leaned back to take in the fit soldier. "You're a long way from the coast, Captain Kessel."

"Call me Tory, please. It's the least I can do since coming to my aid ultimately signed your death sentence. And I don't know if you've heard, but the old king is dying."

"That's not exactly news. Saw his pasty carcass myself during the tournament in Longoria."

"Yes, well I have trustworthy people in the palace who sent

word that it's not of natural causes. Chancellor Temet is attempting to move up in status and already has many high-ranking military generals in his deep pockets. Not only that, but he's succeeded in cutting off all our allies—"

"In Muniers."

Tory spared a glance toward the wall. "Yes, the king's cousin is a guest of the court there. Temet is the driving force behind troop movements and the sea blockade near our border with Muniers." She shook her head disapprovingly. "He stripped every ship along the western coast to send down. At least he didn't touch the northern fleet that I know of. Even on the brink of war, or perhaps because of it, our small coastal towns still worry about pirates. Anyway, the only one that can possibly wrest control of the military and citizens from Temet's greasy hands is King Arvol Ohtani's daughter."

"I heard as much during my short stay in the capital. I also heard that Princess Ameelia Ohtani is studying at the Mage University of Indenes."

A pained look washed across Tory's face. "Yes, she is. And I've pledged to bring her home with hopes she can stop this war."

Ellys was an expert at reading body language. You had to be to reach the rank of Grand Master within any of the Orders dedicated to Toroc. There was something in the pain of the captain's gaze, and Ellys sensed more story beneath the woman's words. They had the time to talk, and any conversation was better than thinking about the sick throbbing that continued to wet the makeshift bandage around her leg. "Why you?"

"Pardon?"

"I'm sure there are others who are loyal to the throne. And it stands to reason that you'd be well positioned to aid in those seeking to keep the king in power if you stayed in command of the third company. What made you decide to steal away to seek out the princess?"

Tory's voice was quiet, barely heard over the sounds of horses, jingling tack, and the creak of the wagon. "It had to be me. She wouldn't believe anyone else." Ellys simply stared at her until Tory gave in. "We've known each other since we were kids."

Ellys gave a small smile of understanding. "And have you also been in love with her since you were kids?"

"We loved each other."

"What happened?"

Tory sighed as though the weight of the world were on her

shoulders. Or perhaps it was the weight of regret. "Royal protocol, disparate social statuses, and a promise at faster career advancement in the third company."

"I see. You chose a fast promotion in hopes of feeling worthy of the girl, and instead she saw it as abandonment and ran as far away as possible. Am I close?"

Tory growled. "Your words are as much a weapon as those blades of yours."

Ellys gave a bark of laughter. "By Toroc, I suppose you're right. And should you find the princess, how will you both return in time?"

"Ameelia is a fully trained mage, and her main ability is with portals. She primarily went to Indenes for advanced training in magic, but she's also taking regency training with the prince there. Ameelia can make a portal anywhere as long as the other end is within sight, and she can keep doing it over and over. When we were seventeen summers, we once ran all the way to Kuwyth simply by jumping from tall hill to tall hill. So, the getting back won't be a problem. Unfortunately, none of that does any good if I die in this Moder-forsaken canyon, or wind up in a cell below the palace."

Ellys bumped against Tory's shoulder. "Stay strong, my friend. Help is coming."

"You mean the woman?" Tory gave Ellys a skeptical look. "She didn't look like much of a fighter."

"No, Aderri is my patron. I'm referring to the other one, Roccotári."

"The horse?" Tory's voice rose. "Surely you're joking."

Ellys found herself uttering the words that had been driven into her mind for more than a hundred cycles. "She's not a horse."

"Whatever you say, friend."

The ride continued in silence after that.

****

Roccotári wasn't tired when she finally skidded to a halt nearly ten leagues away from where they'd last seen Ellys, but she was lathered and breathing hard. Aderri could feel Rocc's worry, but it didn't lessen her anger any. As soon as they came to a stop, Aderri was off her back in an instant. She spun around to berate the steed. "Just what do you think you were doing? I can't believe you left her there, wounded and outnumbered. We have to go back right now—"

I am going back, but you're staying.

It was the first time Aderri had ever heard Rocc raise her voice, and to do it within one's head was quite unpleasant. "What do you mean I'm staying?"

Ellys's orders were to get you someplace safe and come back for her.

"And do what exactly?" Aderri raised a red brow, challenging with tone and stance. "Are you going to take on twenty-odd men armed with swords and crossbows? Unless you have more tricks up your hoof than what you've shown me over the past eighteen days, I don't exactly see you untying her bonds when no one is looking."

A sigh exhaled from Rocc's lips, and the steed dropped her head. *Ellys said she'd get free. She promised.*

Understanding Rocc's worry for what it was, Aderri approached her and put a soothing hand on Rocc's withers, just in front of the pommel of the saddle. "She's not getting away with that leg injury."

Rocc struck the ground with a hoof. Aderri had been traveling with her long enough for her to recognize the frustration, even if Rocc's words hadn't confirmed it. *I know. But I have to do something!*

Aderri blew out a breath and cast her gaze to the sky analyzing her feelings and motivations. Looking back along the path, every single candle drop spent in search of each little scrap of information, Aderri found her life half-lived. But Ellys and Roccotári had shown her there was another way, that you could learn as much outside the grand libraries and universities as you could from deep within the cities and surrounded by people. Ellys warmed a heart that was already raging with flame, and that was no small feat. She mattered as much as Aderri's precious search for knowledge, perhaps more, and Aderri wasn't going to let her go without a fight. "I'll get her."

Rocc turned her head to look at Aderri with one anxious eye. *I thought we already established that you needed to stay here for your safety.*

Rather than spend a moment more in debate, Aderri simply stripped off her cloak, satchel, and clothing. After stuffing all her belongings into the satchel, she hung it over Rocc's pommel. Nude and standing on the rocky ground, she met the large steed's gaze. "It's not me whose safety you need to worry about."

She glanced at the hills to either side of them and gave Rocc a nod. "You may want to give me some room. After all, dragons aren't known for being small. Also, I can cover a lot of ground quickly so the distance back won't be a problem. Wait for us here to be sure the soldiers won't be as likely to catch up again after I've retrieved Ellys."

Rocc snorted and tossed her head in aquiescence, though her displeasure was obvious to read with Aderri's empathy.

After a moment's hesitation, Rocc trotted away to watch from a safe distance. She was curious what would happen after Aderri's transformation. When the shifter admitted to hating her dragon form days before, she also spoke of the wildness. It was something every shifter faced, from the smallest of foxes up to, well, dragons. Not all shifters were able to control their base urges, hence the safe space between them.

Shimmering surrounded Aderri, and it looked similar to the way heat will make the land ripple and warp in the distance. Then her form wavered and expanded, changing shape and size, all the while maintaining her distinctive coloring. Mere moments later, where Aderri once stood, there was a magnificent dragon in her place. With scales that glimmered between black and brown, and highlights of red along her eye ridges, wings, and the armored plates that ran from crown to tail, she was magnificent.

The dragon's keen gaze narrowed and focused in Rocc's direction. Great nostrils scented the air, perhaps following that age-old instinct to find a meal.

"You sssmell sssweet."

Roccotári called out to her, *Remember your place and your task.*

The massive dragon's head tilted in one direction, then the next, and smoke curled from her nostrils. Her voice held a strange duality, between the guttural verbal speech emanating from between the dragon's curled lips, and a replica of Aderri's own voice within Rocc's head. "Tasssk?"

Save Ellys.

"Ellysss, yesss. She holdsss my bonesss." With those words, Aderri leaped into the air with a succession of powerful strokes and flew off in the direction from which they'd come. All Rocc could do was wait and worry, and hope it wasn't too late to save her bondmate.

Chapter Nine

The farther she flew, the more Aderri came back to herself and reasserted her personality over that of the dragon. She hated the fact that she initially looked upon Rocc as food, but rather than dwell on something she couldn't control, she focused on the task at hand. She had to find Ellys. Even with so serious a quest, she reveled in the freedom of flight that she'd long denied herself.

She spied a flock of geese a short while into the journey. They were heading roughly northeast, honking and flapping in formation. She felt the push of wildness from her dragon self and dove straight through, great maw opening and closing with meaty snaps. Far from being disgusted by her own actions, Aderri crunched at her meal of goose with delight. This time it was harmless and not directed at one of her friends. She'd also forgotten how taxing flying was, or how hungry it made her.

It took less than half of Rocc's running time to cover the ten leagues back to where they last saw Ellys. Aderri squinted as she peered down at the area with her keen dragon eyes. Even if the dead soldier's bodies weren't immediately visible, the scent of death in the air was obvious enough. Logic dictated they'd have to follow the road with their horses and wagons, so she climbed higher into the air and glided slowly along the canyon to watch for movement below.

When Aderri spied her quarry, she let out a great roar and dove toward the ground with terrifying speed. At first no one noticed. They merely looked around in confusion as the dragon's roar echoed through the canyon. Then one of the soldiers looked up, pointed, and yelled. Aderri went into a barrel roll and exhaled a gout of fire as long as her body. The fire itself spun like a twister of flame, and the hardened fighters screamed. Most dismounted from their horses and ran for cover behind rocks and outcroppings. Aderri was too far away to do any damage, but she wanted all the soldiers to scatter away from the wagon.

Both restrained women looked up at the sound of the roar, and Tory's mouth dropped open. "This can't be fucking good."

"Fenwith's bloody left ball!" Ellys knew exactly what plummeted from the sky above, and her heart thrilled with both excitement and fear. "On the contrary, Captain, this is the best."

Everyone watched as the dragon snapped out her wings at the last heartbeat and swooped upward again. Aderri let out another blast of flame toward the rocks where half the soldiers hid, and screams rent the air. Some died instantly while others ran around aflame, desperate to put the fire out. Unfortunately for them, dragon fire was incredibly hard to extinguish. There was a misconception that dragon fire began inside the beast and spread outward with the exhale of breath. Rather, dragons let out a spout of highly flammable stomach acid that ignited as it moved up past their molten heart. The liquid that soaked the bodies, rock, and dirt made the flames nigh impossible to put out.

Ellys watched the chaos around them with glee. It quickly became obvious that their cover was of no real use against a massive dragon. Sergeant Gahn stood and took valuable heartbeats to look around at his remaining soldiers while the dragon climbed higher in the sky. "Nothing we have will penetrate that thing's hide. Round up what horses you can and let's get out of here."

"But, sir, what about the prisoners?"

Gahn snagged the reins of a panicked horse and swung up into the saddle. "Let the dragon have them."

The dragon turned far above to circle around and make another pass, prompting the men below to scramble into action. Some had to double up because many horses were either dead or too skittish to catch. As one, the remaining thirteen bolted down the road toward Veniche. The two women in the wagon watched as the dragon gave another roar and dove after the retreating group. Ellys broke into gales of laughter that quickly turned into a gasp of pain as she jolted her leg while trying to twist around to watch.

Tory scowled. "What is it about our imminent death that you find so funny?"

Ellys waved negligently toward the black-and-red wyrm of flaming destruction and grinned. "Death on the wing, maybe, but certainly not ours. That's my patron."

The former captain's eyes grew wide as she peered at the dragon laying waste to the retreating men. "You mean the gorgeous woman that was on the back of your horse is the very beast that is currently—" Tory turned her head away and swallowed. "Uh, biting the head off Sergeant Gahn?"

Ellys twisted again to witness the head in question drop to the ground. It was a balanced act in her book. "Eh, at least she didn't eat it. And yes."

Candle drops later the screams and roars died down, though the fires continued to burn hotly. The dragon glided in slow circles down to the ground in the widest part of the canyon. She approached the wagon where Ellys and Tory sat tied inside. Despite Ellys's near certainty that the magnificent creature who approached them was Aderri, her heart still raced to be the focus of that disconcerting stare.

Tory whispered next to her, "Are, uh, are there flames within the depths of its eyes?"

"Her eyes, and yes."

When Aderri was five paces away from the pair, a low growl rumbled up from deep within her chest. To Ellys, it sounded a lot like one of the great cats that hunted the northern savannas of Kuwyth, but on a much larger scale. Also, though dangerous, the large, furred beasts weren't covered in impenetrable scales nor did they have smoke curling from their nostrils. They were simply large, striped cats. This was no cat. Ellys whispered under her breath, hoping Tory wouldn't hear her. "Please be Aderri, please be Aderri…"

"What was that?"

"Nothing."

Tory stared wide-eyed. "By Cuon, that beast is twice the size of my family home."

Aderri had moved close enough to rock the wagon when she leaned over to sniff the women. Ellys gave a little shiver at the warmth emanating from the dragon's hide, and her voice came out higher than she liked when she responded to Tory's question. "Everything is fine, I promise. But, uh, we should probably get out of this wagon. Can you stand?"

Tory's hands were tied in front of her, and she nodded. Without waiting for another reply, she struggled to stand in the back of the wagon. Once upright, she held out her tied hands to pull Ellys up as well. "Let me help you."

Ellys raised her own tied hands to grasp Tory's but hesitated when the dragon gave them another low growl. Aderri swung her gaze to Tory and moved a step closer, rolling the wagon forward a pace. The captain nearly lost her balance, and by the look on her face, almost did the same with her bladder control when Aderri's flaming eyes focused on her from a stride away.

The dragon's voice was a menacing low rumble that made the hairs on the back of Ellys's neck stand on end. "Mine."

Tory sucked in a breath. "Uh, I don't think she wants me to touch you."

Ellys lowered her hands and moved her gaze from Tory to the massive dragon that could easily swallow two men whole…or two elves. "Hey, Aderri. I'm kind of injured and, you know, in a lot of pain. It would be great if you let my new friend here help me up."

Aderri stood unmoving for nearly a candle drop, then blew out a massive blast of iron scented breath that washed over the other two. She took an awkward step back, and the rumble of her voice made Ellys and Tory jump slightly. "My apologiesss, Elysss. You are not my posssesssion."

The voice had Aderri's unique inflections and timber, but it was so deep Ellys could feel the vibration of it in her bones. "Uh, okay?" Ellys was confused by her comment.

Aderri took another step away from the wagon. "You may risssse."

Ellys let out a sigh of relief and held her hands up again for assistance. When they were both standing, Tory retrieved their weapons from where they'd been stowed in the front box of the wagon. She managed to cut her bindings with her dagger then held the blade out. "Here."

Ellys sliced her own rope on the outstretched knife. "Thanks."

Once both women had their various blades sheathed, Tory helped Ellys to the edge of the wagon bed. She jumped to the ground and helped Ellys down as well. Ellys's head spun with blood loss, and she cursed her wound as she landed. "Fucking unbalanced bastards."

Tory steadied her. "I don't know, I'd say your dragon friend did a good job of balancing them out with the way she made a point to take two arms or two legs off at a time."

Aderri growled again. The rumbling speech was quieter but still coming from something the size of a large house. "Get control of your dragon, Aderri."

Ellys looked at her with concern. "Is something wrong?"

Aderri gave a sniff as the scent of Ellys's blood became stronger, and her eyes focused on the swordswoman's leg. "The wound ssspreadsss. You need Rocc."

"Why in Abbad does she need a rock?"

Ellys attempted to tie the bandage tighter, fighting a wash of dizziness at the action. Her half-elf stamina could only hold out so long with the amount of blood she'd lost. "She's referring to my steed, Roccotári."

Tory tilted her head. "I see." Clearly, she didn't.

"We mussst go."

Despite the presence of the fearsome beast, a few horses still milled around in the canyon. Even so, Ellys grimaced. "Uh, I don't think I'm going to ride very far or very fast. Is Rocc on her way back?"

Tendrils of smoke curled from Aderri's nostrils. "No. I can take you." She paused and swung her massive head around to look upon the other woman. "Both of you."

Tory's eyes widened as she looked from Aderri to the blue expanse above her. "In the sky?"

"Yesss."

"Uh, I'm perfectly fine making my own way, my lady…er, my dragon?"

Ellys turned to the former captain. "Are you sure? We could get you over the border safely, and I know time is of the essence right now."

"More like over the border as a snack."

Aderri snorted. Ellys found it a strangely undignified sound to come out of a dragon's snout. Rather than respond to Tory's muttered reply, Aderri turned her gaze toward two of the healthier looking horses. "I will call them to help." Ellys and Tory watched in amazement as two mounts approached the trio, and Aderri looked back at the captain. "They will take you asss far asss you need to go, provided you treat them well."

Tory recited a proverb many learned as naught more than children. "I'm not about to look a gift horse in the mouth…erm, I mean dragon."

Ellys shook her head and laughed. "No, you definitely mean horse. I don't think you want to look the dragon in the mouth, I'm pretty sure she's got some bits of armor stuck in her teeth."

Aderri smiled at Ellys's humor, though it appeared more frightening than mirthful. "The black one isss called Sssnow, and the bay isss Benna."

"Snow?" Tory said.

"She didn't sssay the why of the name, jussst told me the name."

"Fascinating. I didn't realize horses were so intelligent."

A hoof struck the ground with obvious irritation, and both horses whinnied. Tory quickly added, "No offense, ma'ams."

Aderri gave a guttural laugh. "Not all are, about the sssame asss people."

Tory sized up the two horses that stood nearby. "Snow?"

Sure enough, the black horse whickered and moved closer. Tory checked the saddlebags, which were well stocked. "Oh look," she said, and lifted out a bag. "The previous owner left his money pouch." She dropped it back into the saddlebag, gave Snow's sleek black neck a friendly rub, and addressed both horses. "You help me find the princess, and I'll guarantee apples all along the trip."

The mention of apples brought the bay near, and Ellys laughed at the predictability of it, which quickly turned into a hiss of pain. "Aderri, we should all be on our way soon. Preferably before I bleed out in this Moder-forsaken canyon." She glanced up at the massive dragon, trying to determine how in the six nations she would stay on while high in the sky. "How do we do this?"

Aderri lowered herself to the ground. "You can sssit sssafely between the firssst and sssecond armored plates behind my neck. You will be sssecure there and find it easssy to hang on. I've been told the shape isss sssimilar to a war sssaddle, very form fitting." She shook her head. "I am sssorry for the sssibilance of my ssspeech. It isss…embarrasssing." She ducked her head slightly, and Ellys resolved to ask her about it later.

Tory helped Ellys limp closer to where Aderri had jutted out the first joint of her front leg. Ellys had to ask, "Do people, uh, ride you often?"

Aderri had clearly forgotten that she was in dragon form and gave her usual coquettish response. "Not asss often asss I'd like." Then a scaled eyelid shut in an obvious attempt at a wink.

Both women stared for a heartbeat, but Tory was the first to respond. "Did a dragon just flirt with you?"

Ellys grinned. "I'm afraid that's Aderri's second nature. I'm sure she has no idea how to turn it off, changed shape or no."

Aderri reared her head back. "My apologiesss, Ellysss. I forgot who I wasss for a moment."

"After nearly a moon traveling together?" Ellys waved off the apology before accepting Tory's help in mounting the spot Aderri mentioned. "I've grown quite used to being regularly propositioned by a beautiful woman. Practically immune by now."

Tory looked from Ellys, to the massive dragon and wisely kept her mouth shut. "Okay then." She gave a little wave at Ellys. "I suppose this is goodbye. I wish you luck tending to your wound, and I thank you for attempting to come to my aid." She turned to Aderri and bowed. "I thank you for actually saving us. Maybe you should be charging her, hmm?"

Aderri craned her head around and gave a rumbling laugh. "Maybe I ssshould."

Ellys was starting to really feel the effects of blood loss, but she couldn't let the insult go without a proper balanced response. She rubbed her smallest finger across her eyebrow, a sign of insult across the six nations. "You're hilarious. But in all seriousness, I hope you find Princess Ameelia in time to prevent Carthune and Muniers from all-out war. Even better if she still loves you."

Tory covered her heart. "From your lips to Aphora's ears. Now, be off with you before you faint from blood loss and fall from the sky like a star." She raised a hand as though to slap the massive rump of the dragon. She gulped when Aderri's gaze swung around to look at her. "Erm, sorry. Habit." Tory quickly lowered the hand and strode back to where her new mounts stood.

Ellys saluted the captain then grabbed the massive armor plate in front of her as Aderri's wings began beating with incredible strength to lift them into the sky. Dust swirled around them, and Tory held her hand up to shield her eyes. Ellys shut her own eyes for a candle drop, and when she opened them, they were far above the ground. Terror thrilled through her for a heartbeat. Then realizing she was indeed wedged in between the massive, armored plates, she took the opportunity to look around. Ellys assumed the queasiness was from blood loss and not a fear of heights. She'd never once been so high and whooped with delight.

The sound of Ellys's obvious joy thrilled Aderri though she refused to dwell on the why of it. She ignored her dragon whispering *"mine"* inside her head. She staunchly refused to give in to the urge to possess and claim Ellys as her own. Instead, Aderri flew along for a bit until she estimated they were about halfway back to where she'd left Rocc. Ellys had been quite vocal at first but eventually quieted, and she feared for her companion's health. "Are you ssstill with me?"

"Barely."

Ellys's voice was faint with the sound of rushing wind past them, though Aderri's superb dragon hearing picked it up. She could also hear Ellys's heartbeat and became concerned when it started to race and the swordswoman's breathing grew shallow. "Hold tight, Ellysss. We will be there sssoon."

A high-altitude wind gust buffeted the dragon and her passenger. In Ellys's weakened state, she was pitched from the makeshift saddle into the blue sky above. Barely conscious, she didn't appear to register the fact that she was free-falling to the ground far below. As Aderri turned to aid Ellys, she heard her swear and call, "Aderri! By Toroc, this is no balanced way to fucking die."

Aderri swooped down and caught the back of Ellys's sword harness with a single, long talon on her left claw. Then she spied a familiar running figure far below. The dragon dove toward the ground with reckless speed, pulled up short with great buffeting beats of her wings, and carefully lowered Ellys's unconscious body to the ground in front of Rocc, who had stopped and waited for her to land. "Quickly, she fadesss."

Rocc immediately pressed her muzzle against Ellys's cheek to begin the healing, standing motionless for countless candle drops. Aderri changed back to her two-legger form, though she didn't leave Ellys's side to retrieve her discarded clothing. She had to be sure her friend was out of danger first. Little by little, Aderri listened to Ellys's heart grow steadier, and through the rent in the unconscious woman's trousers, she observed the flesh that knit itself back together. Eventually, the half-elf's eyes fluttered open, and Aderri breathed a sigh of relief.

Silver eyes widened as Ellys fixed her gaze on Aderri. "Aphora's tits, you're naked."

Really, Ellys? You nearly die, and that's the first thing your stupid gaugin brain can think of? Not 'thanks for saving me, Rocc and Aderri?' Or, even thanking me for healing you when you once again foolishly rushed into danger?

Ellys sat up and reached out to stroke Rocc's soft muzzle. "Thanks, old friend. Of course, I'm grateful to you both. Captain

Toridae Kessel was severely outnumbered. The balance was completely destroyed, and she needed help. What was I to do?"

Oh, I don't know…perhaps come back for your companions so they could assist you?

Roccotári's mental voice was nearly a shout in Ellys's head and she winced as she realized how frightened Rocc had been. Ellys scratched just beneath her head band. Her response was quiet when she met Rocc's liquid gaze. "I'm sorry. I acted impulsively and put us all in danger."

"I was never really in any danger. It takes a lot to actually harm a dragon." Aderri joked about Tory's comment. "Why am I paying you again?"

Ellys turned to look at her. "How was I to know that you'd go all—Fenwith's balls! I, uh…you, erm…" She shut her eyes and gave a vague wave toward Aderri. "Can you please cover yourself?"

Aderri removed her clothing from the satchel that was still slung over Rocc's pommel. "Clearly, I'm paying you for your wit and charm."

And fake marriage potential, don't forget that. Rocc gave a wheezing bray of laughter while Ellys stood and rifled through the saddlebags for fresh clothing. Then she stripped off her own armor and headed resolutely toward a nearby stream.

"While you all are mocking me, I'm going to take a few candle drops to clean off the dried blood and sweat. I hate to put my dirty breeches back on but this pair is lost without a fair bit of mending and a good soak for all the blood."

Fully clothed, Aderri called out, "Too bad you can't fix your personality the same way."

Ellys crossed her first two fingers in a silent but vulgar display of profanity and held up her hand so her companions could see them clearly as she walked away. "Fix this." Laughter followed her all the way to the stream.

Ellys didn't linger long in the water because of the temperature, and when she came back to her companions, she was cleaner if a lot surlier. "We should put some more distance between here and that scorched canyon." She didn't mention the bodies of the Carthune soldiers they'd left behind. Ellys glanced off in the distance and could just make out shimmering sky where they knew the border wall to be. She shivered. "That blasted stream was freezing."

Aderri noticed the shiver from where she stood next to Roccotári. "You're cold."

"I've been worse."

"Nonsense! You can ride in front of me, and you'll be warm in no time."

"You hired me to protect you and…" She trailed off when she caught sight of Aderri's knowing smile. "Just say it. I failed as your hired guard and should have my commission revoked. But despite all that, it wouldn't be comfortable riding behind someone with two swords on their back."

A long sigh met her words, and Aderri swiftly mounted Rocc, moving toward the front of the saddle. "No one is revoking anything, and you've performed your duty admirably so far. You're not a god, goddess, or even a goz, Ellys. There's only so much one person can do, and remember, it's perfectly honorable to accept help when it's offered. As I mentioned when we were setting up camp that first night outside an inn, I have no problems lending a hand when necessary."

"That's different."

Aderri rolled her eyes. "It's no different. Would you think less of a patron that stood by with a sword in hand while you were horribly outnumbered?"

Ellys thought for a heartbeat. "Yes. Under those circumstances, I certainly would. But you hired me precisely because you have no weapons and aren't a trained fighter."

"Trained fighter, no. But when it comes down to it, I am a weapon. While I have my own reasons for not wanting to set the dragon loose, none of them are so dire they prevent me from helping a friend in need."

"Are you my friend?"

Rocc snorted with irritation. *Absolutely. She left patron status more than a quarter moon ago, and if you pulled your head out of your—*

Aderri interrupted. "Of course I am, and I'd like to think you feel the same way."

Ellys met her eyes. "You know I do." She wanted to say more but pressed her lips together instead.

Aderri wondered if Ellys felt the pull between them in the same way, or if her lost love precluded any sort of connection. She greatly admired Ellys's passion and loyalty and knew without a doubt their journey would leave her changed more than the dragon she was born with. "I will never let anything happen to the two of you if I can help it. It's not in my nature to ignore a friend in need. I hope you know that by now."

"You faced your own greatest fear in the form of your dragon to return to the canyon to save me. Not only that, but by changing form and coming alone, you also saved Rocc. Those sorry excuses for soldiers wouldn't have thought twice about shooting her down. I owe you a debt of honor."

Aderri leaned down to rest her hand on Ellys's shoulder. She tried and failed to ignore the delicious muscle beneath her fingertips even during so serious a conversation. "You owe me nothing, though I wouldn't turn away a little friendship."

"That I will gladly provide."

"Good. I'd like to move on now, because according to you, we have days to go until we reach the border, and I've lost my taste for Carthune and its soldiers."

Ellys swiftly mounted behind her and chuckled. "Funny, you weren't complaining about taste when you bit Gahn's head off—oof!" Her words were interrupted by a firm elbow to the ribs, but Aderri noticed that she didn't complain. Instead Ellys relaxed behind her, and she soon realized it was because the swordswoman had begun to warm with Aderri's body heat. Ellys whispered in her ear, "Thank you, Aderri. For everything."

Aderri tried to ignore the butterflies that flitted in her stomach from the brush of Ellys's lips, but the dragon lurked below her subconscious thoughts, whispering *"mine"* within her heart.

Chapter Ten

The next few days passed without any altercations, much to the trio's relief. They arrived at the border between Carthune and the Kuwyth Empire on the afternoon of the twenty-fourth day of their journey. The road they traveled had crossed two others within the last few leagues, and as a result, there were quite a few people ahead of them at the official border crossing.

Well, this can't be good.

"Why are people turning away? Look." Aderri pointed at a family with two donkeys and a horse-drawn wagon heading down the road away from the gate. As they watched, even more were sent away without being let through.

"Hmm, this could be problematic if they're not letting refugees through. Do you have more of those gold pieces stashed away? You may want to have some handy."

Aderri turned her head to look at Ellys. "Nonsense. I'm not some refugee, I'm traveling to my ancestral home."

Ellys said as they neared the front, "I hope you're able to prove it, because these guards don't seem to care." Even as she spoke, one of the Kuwythian border patrol, an orc by the looks of him, narrowed his beady eyes and spat on the ground.

One soldier spoke in heavily accented Carthu before the previous wagon had fully rolled away. "No one goes through today without an official seal from the Empress."

Aderri gaped at the man. "How are we to get a seal from the Empress if we can't get through?"

"Not my problem. Move along." He waved them to the side.

"Now you see here!" Aderri quickly dismounted.

Much to Ellys's dismay, at least five of the border troop drew weapons, and one in the tower raised his crossbow. She rubbed her thigh muscle at the remembered pain from just such a weapon. "Mind the balance, Aderri. I don't think you should—"

"I'm traveling back to my Clan in Muniers, and you lot have no call to stop me at this border."

The one with the captain's insignia on his uniform looked around at his fellow soldiers. "Oh-ho, no call huh?" The rest of the well-armed and armored male and female troopmates in attendance seemed amused. "And who exactly are you?"

"Aderri n'all Dracona."

He raised a single brow and grunted. "I see."

"Good. Now that you understand, we'll be on our way."

"Still don't care. No seal means no pass."

Aderri took a hard step forward and raised her hands. "Why you little runt of a pig—"

Be wary, child. Rocc, too, tried the voice of reason.

Ellys could see by the expression on the guard captain's face that he recognized Aderri's name. She assumed that no one stationed so close to the border would be ignorant to the significance of the ancestral guardians of Muniers coastline. At least that was information that Aderri had passed on the previous evening. But she had also been a soldier once and knew that orders were orders.

The captain would have no way of knowing what manner of threat Aderri posed. He simply knew she was a shifter and immediately raised his sword with threatening intent. He strode forward, apparently to frighten her into backing off.

Ellys quickly hopped up to stand in the saddle and did a forward flip to land in front of Aderri, thus blocking her from potential harm. She didn't draw either of her swords, instead holding up her palms indicating a wish for peace. She addressed the captain in the main language of Kuwyth rather than six nation common. "*Hold, brethren. I have your seal.*" It was luck that she had removed it from Rocc's saddlebags to place in her coin purse earlier in the day.

"*Fetzpah!* "

Ellys switched back to common again. "Not impossible." She slowly moved her left hand to reach into her pouch. From it she withdrew a ring with a flat face featuring the carved seal of Kuwyth. Inside was stamped with the final cycle of her honorable service. She held it out to the guard, who took it warily. "My name is Ellys DeEnsis. I served as captain of the Elite Guard for Empress Hecc'la din Tosche between twenty-five oh six and twenty-five twenty-three."

One of the other guards scowled. "Elf trash."

The captain's demeanor changed instantly, and he spun around to address his goblin lieutenant. "Shut your hairy face, Crug. This warrior speaks truth." The captain handed the ring back to Ellys, then he sheathed his sword and saluted. "My apologies, Captain. My grandfather served with Empress Hecc'la's Elite, and I grew up hearing the tales of his fierce elven commander named Ellys, a warrior who saved his life on multiple occasions. I'm honored to meet you because without you I wouldn't be here today." Ellys tilted her head and raised a single dark brow. "My father was born after you retired."

"Oh." Ellys gazed at him, trying to discern who his grandfather could have been. While the man looked vaguely familiar, she couldn't come up with a name. "May I ask who your grandfather was?"

"Timus Solblee. His troop called him—"

"Timus the Temper. Yes, I remember him now. What he may not have told you was that he saved my life on occasion as well. You come from good stock, Captain."

He held out his hand to Ellys. "It's Captain Tamo Solblee, and I honor you." They clasped forearms, then he turned to the two at the gate. "Let them through. And hurry up, we've got a line as long as a dragon's tail out here."

Aderri turned to look behind her and snickered. "Not quite."

Both Rocc and Aderri started forward, but Ellys approached Tamo instead. "A heartbeat please, Captain."

"What is it?" He gave Ellys a curious look.

She leaned in close so only he could hear. "I have a friend that will arrive in the next day or so. Her name is Toridae Kessel, and she'll have with her two mounts, a black and a bay. She is a former captain herself, fair of hair and face, near my height. Tory is on a quest to bring home the princess of Carthune in hopes to quell the coup and subsequent war that is building. It would honor me if you could let her through as well."

Captain Solblee stepped back and saluted. "Your honor is my honor. I'll consider your seal good for the three of you and leave instructions to let her pass when she arrives, in case I'm not on duty." He glanced at the long line of people hoping to flee over the border and scowled. "It will be worth it if her passage brings order to Carthune and puts a stop to all this."

"Thank you." Ellys saluted him in return and followed her companions through the gate. She could hear Tamo already yelling behind her at the next unfortunate travelers without passage approval.

Ellys and Aderri remounted Rocc after they'd gone through the gate so they could put as much distance between them and the soldiers as possible. Aderri was quiet for a few candle drops, but Ellys could sense the questions building up. She addressed it first. "Go ahead, say what you need to say."

"That was unexpected."

"I suppose."

Aderri glanced back over her shoulder. "Why didn't you say you had a seal in the first place?"

Because her gaugin half is as stubborn as a rock troll, that's why.

"Or perhaps as stubborn as an elf-bred nag," Ellys snarked back.

"Can you two not fight right now? You argue like a…a…an old, bonded pair."

"Well," Ellys said, "we are lineal bondmates, and we've been together for…hmm, one hundred and seventeen cycles, give or take a few moons—"

Aderri interrupted her mental maths. "I meant romantically."

Roccotári snorted and shook them in the saddle. *Definitely not. No gaugin could think of satisfying an elven steed, and from what I've witnessed, Ellys is more likely to fall asleep on the job than not. Losing all our coin in the process.*

"It happened one time."

Rocc turned her head to the right so she could look at her riders with one large judgmental eye.

"Okay, so it happened a few times, but it wasn't my fault." She met Aderri's gaze from a few inches away, and her breath caught at the way the other woman's dark red hair framed her nearly black skin. Ellys had known for at least a half-moon that Aderri possessed a sharp wit and soft heart. But it was in that moment, when they sat so close as to breathe the same air, she realized exactly how beautiful the shifter was. "Some, uh, women use magic to bespell a person in the bedroll."

"Oh really?" Aderri's lips curled into a slow smile, the little points of her canines digging into a full bottom lip. Ellys stared at the lip. Hard. "Well then, I suppose it really wasn't your fault. However, I am disappointed by one thing…"

Ellys was having trouble focusing on anything but the way

Aderri's lips moved to form words and sounds. "Disappointed?"

"Yes. I'm disappointed that you would waste your time tupping someone that needed magic to ensnare you. Clearly their natural charisma and charm were lacking."

"Clearly." Ellys breathed in slowly, enjoying the heat and smell of the woman pressed tightly to the front of her.

Suddenly, Aderri burst into laughter, a sound that was joined by Rocc's own humorous response, both as an equine bray and voice within their minds.

Ellys shook herself, not understanding what was so funny. "Um, what were you saying?"

Aderri reached over her right shoulder with her left hand and patted Ellys gently on the cheek. "Nothing. I'm sure the individuals in question were just maintaining the balance when they made away with your gold."

"Exactly." Ellys gave Rocc a little dig to the flank, not so hard that it would actually hurt her friend. "See. She understands."

Oh yes, she certainly does. Ellys scowled when Rocc swung her head around again and gave Aderri a wink.

****

It took three days to cross the Kuwyth region of Cat's Head and make their way into Muniers proper. It seemed the Kuwyth border guards had no issue with people leaving the Empire; they were only under orders to prevent people from coming in during a time of potential war between neighboring nations.

The first night in Muniers, the three were forced to camp outdoors. Ellys was grumpy but tried to focus on the mission rather than dwell on another cold night outside. She cursed under her breath as she laid out her bedroll.

Rocc moved closer and lipped her hair affectionately. *You should be happy that the nights are warmer this far south and that spring is at last making its presence known.*

Ellys patted her hands along the length of her makeshift bed before moving it to grab a random stone. She tossed it away with a frown and glanced toward where the sun was rapidly sinking over the horizon. "The sun follows its own schedule, and I'm still sleeping in the loam." She felt a tap on her shoulder and turned to see Aderri smiling at her.

"Here, step aside for a heartbeat."

Curious, Ellys stood and moved out of the way. She watched with interest as Aderri closed her eyes and raised her hands. One by one, every stone in the ground beneath them came to the surface and rolled away to the edge of their small camp. Ellys grinned at her. "Heh, I literally watched you move the stones for the fire ring a half candle mark ago and already forgot about your affinity with earth. That's quite handy."

"Oh, it's for me, too." Aderri placed her roll atop Ellys's. "I don't think it's come up, but I fully admit that I hate sleeping on a lumpy surface."

Both dark eyebrows went up in surprise because throughout their entire journey, Aderri had never said a word about sleeping outside on the ground. "Really?"

As a two-legger or as a dragon?

Ellys said, "Leave it to you to make the moment strange."

Aderri walked over to wave a hand above the stone-encircled pile of wood that Ellys had gathered not a quarter candle mark before. Flames burst to life and crackled merrily before Aderri walked back and sank down to the piled bed rolls. "It is a valid question. The sleeping comfort of a dragon varies from individual to individual. I don't happen to like it either way. Just another reason it's easier for me to stay in this form. A comfortable bed doesn't usually stand up to a dragon's weight, nor do they come in a sufficient size to hold me."

Ellys moved to sit next to Aderri, if only to enjoy the warm fire from a relaxed position. At least that's what she told herself. Rocc nickered nearby, her version of a chuckle. Ellys glanced over her shoulder to look at Rocc and muttered, "Get out of my head," before turning back to Aderri. "I would imagine not."

"I did have an uncle who loved sleeping on piles of gold."

Ellys tried to picture enough gold in piles that would hold something as large as a dragon. She couldn't. "Hmm."

It stands to reason that with enough time his body heat and weight would eventually compress the piles into a form-fitting bed.

Aderri laughed. "That's exactly what happened. Still…I'm not willing to wait hundreds of cycles in one place for my bed to soften up. I like learning too much, and that requires travel."

"Wait, *had* an uncle? I thought dragons were long-lived."

"Well yes, when left to their own devices. However, as the protectors of the Muniers coastline, Clan Dracona faces invaders and danger on a semi-regular basis. Srovthlyn was hit by a ship-mounted catapult filled with giant tar balls in the cycle twenty-four seventy-two." At Ellys's curious look she elaborated. "It was enough to partially coat a wing and foul his flight. He crashed into the ocean and drowned. Before they could reload the catapults, my father laid waste to the entire ship in flaming retaliation."

Ellys whispered, "Elemental enemies."

"Pretty much, yes. Dragons tend to panic when in a large body of water. That and he was a shite swimmer, even as a man."

The two women sat shoulder to shoulder, and Ellys pulled her saddlebags closer. First, she brought out a partial wheel of cheese and a small loaf of bread. She broke off large pieces of bread for herself and Aderri. Then she unwrapped the cloth from the cheese, cut it in half with her eating knife, and shared it with Aderri. "This is the last of it. It looks like the rind has gone pretty hard, but the cheese is still good." She cut a small slice from her half and popped it into her mouth before pinching off a piece of her bread to eat with the cheese.

Aderri nibbled at the sharp treat. "You're right about the rind, but I think the flavor is even better now than when you first picked it up. I still have a few bottles of wine left in my bag. Would you care to share one?"

"I'll never turn down good wine."

Rocc thumped the ground with her hoof from a few feet away. *What about bad wine? I've seen you drink that plenty of times.*

"Fine, I'll never turn down any wine. Are you happy?"

Of course. After all, I'm the magical steed, and you're a simple half-breed. Now, how about one of those apples you've got in your pack?

Ellys raised a single dark eyebrow and turned to look at Rocc. "How do you know we still have apples left?"

Magic, of course.

"Minotaur shite—"

Her retort abruptly cut off as Aderri reached around her and into the saddlebag to withdraw an apple. Aderri's words didn't even register when she began speaking because all Ellys could focus on was the press of a soft breast against her forearm. "She can probably smell them. It has nothing to do with magic. I've never met a steed who couldn't smell an apple from yards away." Once she had the fruit in her grasp, Aderri held it out so Rocc could come near and take it from her hand.

See? Someone loves me.

Ellys muttered absent-mindedly, too focused on that brief bit of contact and the memories of their time in the bathhouse that it provoked. "Uh-huh."

Once Rocc had her treat, Aderri twisted in the opposite direction to where she'd left her satchel near the bedroll. She reached deep inside and pulled out a wine bottle. She turned and held it up between them and smiled. "I'm too tired to look for my cup, too. Do we even need them at this point?"

"Probably not. We're going to be a lot closer than drinking from the same bottle of wine in the next half-moon."

"Seems strange to think we've only known each other just under a moon. I—" Aderri flicked her gaze up to look into Ellys's silver eyes then dropped it to the bottle. Rather than speak, Aderri grasped the stopper where it stuck from the top of the bottle and twisted it free.

Ellys could see that Aderri fought to remain silent and wondered what her friend was going to say. "What?"

Aderri took a healthy swig of wine. "It's nothing." She passed the bottle, and Ellys took her own long pull.

"No, what were you going to say? I hope you know by now that you can tell me anything and I won't judge you. We're friends, right?"

Aderri gave her an odd smile. "That's just it. I feel like we've known each other a lot longer than we have. There's this connection…this pull, like if we'd met under other circumstances, we could have been great friends. Perhaps…more?"

Ellys smiled and handed the bottle back. "We are friends now, and I have no want for different circumstances that would only lead us back to the same place. I've found your companionship a lot more pleasant than I expected. Certainly, a world above my usual patrons."

A fiery red brow went up. "Oh?"

"Well yes. For starters, you're a lot nicer."

"Really?"

"And a lot more attractive, er, I mean…bollux!"

Aderri rubbed Ellys's forearm. "Don't worry, I know what you meant. I don't think it's a secret that we're attracted to one another. After all, that's part of the basis for your second contract with me. I couldn't have hired just any sword to guard my person and play the suitor. It had to be someone my Clan would believe."

"I suppose that's true."

"But in that regard…" Aderri faded off, looking unsure again.

"Yes?"

Aderri glanced at Ellys out of the corner of her eye. "I know you probably don't want to hear this, but my Clan will have certain…expectations from a suitor."

Ellys swallowed thickly, knowing exactly what Aderri was referring to. "Oh. And we can't just say I'm shy or something? Is it normal to be outwardly affectionate in your Clan?"

"How many dragons have you met, or shifters in general?"

Ellys considered the question then remembered the inn they'd stayed at days before with the shifter couple that wrecked one of the rooms before their arrival. Then her mind wandered stubbornly back to that gods-be-damned bathhouse. "Ogre spit."

"Exactly. My question for you is, what are you comfortable with? With me being away for so long, they're going to expect a romance that has me thoroughly besotted. That and they know how I am with a romantic partner."

"Did you dally much when you were still living with Clan?"

"A few here and there. My past partners and I may or may not have destroyed some furniture of our own."

That broke some of the tension, and Ellys let out a genuine laugh. "I can only imagine."

"So, what are your thoughts on the topic?"

Ellys gave her a rakish grin. "I mean, I'm not opposed to doing some damage in the course of good tupping. Why, this one time I—"

"I meant the topic of what level of affection you're comfortable displaying in regards to our arrangement."

Ellys turned her wide-eyed silver gaze toward Aderri. "Oh, that. I mean, we discussed it days ago, and I said I'd do whatever was necessary to make your Clan believe I'm a legitimate suitor."

Aderri put her hand back on Ellys's forearm. "Only to your comfort level, Ellys. I don't want you to do anything that compromises your honor or puts you out of balance."

Both fell silent for a candle drop, then Ellys answered. "I don't mind casual touching and cuddling if that's something you would normally do. I suppose kissing is on the table as well, since we're trying to play the part of two people madly in love." Her heart skipped at the thought of feeling that deeply for someone again. Romantically, she never really moved past her life with Gwyn. Though if Rocc was to be believed, Ellys had chosen to never allow herself to move beyond their love.

"And you can do that? Kiss and not act like the world is ending because I'm your patron?"

"Fair point. But that was different. This is part of the job that my patron is asking me to do. It's not a dishonorable bit of tupping that my libido is clamoring for."

"I see." Aderri narrowed her eyes. "If I weren't your patron, would it be so dishonorable?"

"You're purposely muddling the subject and making this hard for me."

"I'm sorry, no more teasing. I'll try not to make it more difficult for you going forward. But I need to know you can do this, that your memory of your past lover won't prevent you from convincing those around us of your implied feelings toward me."

Ellys looked down at her battle-scarred hands. Then she turned and was caught in Aderri's flaming gaze. "I suppose there is only one way to find out, isn't there."

"I suppose there is."

The space between them grew smaller and warmer, illuminated only by the light of their fire and a trio of moons in the sky. Both closed their eyes as their breaths mingled in the night air and their lips met with the softest caress. They pulled back for a heartbeat and met again with more pressure. Aderri ran her fingers through the fine black hair at the nape of Ellys's neck and pulled them together tighter yet. Ellys moaned deep in her throat when she felt tiny pinpricks from Aderri's teeth graze her lower lip. The experience far exceeded what she'd imagined too many times since their journey began. When they pulled apart after long candle drops of kissing, both were breathing hard, and Ellys was more stimulated than she wanted to admit.

That seemed pretty convincing to me. Well done.

Ellys was still trying to regain control of her traitorous body and whirling emotions, but she was aware enough to grab for the last bit of bread forgotten on the bedroll and throw it at Rocc's head. "Stuff it, nag. You really do excel at making things strange."

Aderri laughed. "Strange or no, she's right. I'm satisfied."

A wave of flirtatiousness washed over Ellys, and she turned to lean close again. "Are you though?"

Flaming eyes widened, and Aderri flashed her teeth before playfully shoving Ellys back. "If I'm not allowed to tease, then the rule works both ways."

"So, it's a rule then, set by my patron. Would you even say it's an order?" Ellys grinned and Aderri squirmed in her seat. Ellys noticed the action and figured her friend was equally as aroused. From all the talking they'd done over the past moon, she knew it had been awhile for both of them.

"Yes," Aderri huffed out.

Ellys burst out laughing, but she didn't speak of the fact that the kiss felt a little too real. It made the situation a lot easier for her, but also so much worse. They'd be able to play a convincing couple, but Ellys was certain she'd spontaneously combust from her own sexual frustration by the end of the contract. And that wasn't even considering the persistent way Aderri's kind smile pulled at the loose threads around her heart. She glanced at Aderri and saw those flaming pupils reflect the firelight. Perhaps the fire in her loins wouldn't be so spontaneous after all.

****

Maybe it was the talk of physical closeness, or perhaps the aroused state that both women fell asleep in, but Aderri's dreams that evening were anything but chaste. She dreamed that she and Ellys were mated, and that it wasn't a faux suitor she was bringing home to the Clan, but a real one. The dream jumped forward to them in the bedroll exactly as they'd fallen asleep. Aderri and Ellys were kissing, tangled together in a passionate embrace. Wanting to be closer yet, Aderri pushed Ellys onto her back and moved to straddle her hips before diving down for her lips again.

She moaned as she rolled her hips against Ellys's pelvis, enjoying the strong grip her lover had on her ass. Aderri heard her name whispered in the wind, then heard Ellys's name called the same way. Their kissing went deeper, and she shuddered when Ellys's tongue caressed each of her canines before moving to twine with her own tongue. She slowly pulled back and trailed her mouth lower, first nibbling Ellys's jaw, then moving down to her neck. Ellys's grip tightened, and she whined at the stimulation. Aderri bit the flesh pressed tight against her lips, the points of her teeth denting the skin but not quite breaking it. Ellys moaned and shuddered below her, and that same voice called their names again, only louder and more insistent. Suddenly Aderri woke as if she'd been doused in water.

Ellys looked up into Aderri's surprised eyes, the moonlight illuminating them clearly. Both were panting as if they'd run leagues through the trees. The half-elf reached a hand up to feel the side of her neck. "Did you bite me?"

Incredibly hot and aroused for the second time that night, Aderri struggled not to rock her sex against the woman below her. "That depends," she panted.

"On?"

She smirked at Ellys. "On whether or not you liked it." She leaned closer and enunciated her next words clearly. "I'm a biter."

Ellys sucked in a breath, only to exhale again abruptly at the sound of Rocc's voice in her head. *Welcome to the waking world. I see neither of you is worse for wear. Let me guess, you were…practicing again?*

Aderri rolled off Ellys's hips to lay next to her as they answered. "Yes," Ellys said.

"No."

Ellys gave Aderri a betrayed look. "Why aren't you helping me?"

Aderri attempted to straighten her riotous curls even as she caught her breath. "She's a telepath, a fact which you well know. It's not like she'd believe a lie from our mouths when our thoughts are clear as day."

"Fenwith's great golden balls!"

"Again with that? Wrinkled sun god sacks are the last thing I want to think about in times like these."

Or maybe if you'd both been thinking about them, this little scene would never have played out in your dreams.

Aderri scrunched her nose, and Ellys turned away from the cute look to glare daggers at her long-time companion.

Rocc shuffled a step farther away from their bedrolls. *I'm just trying to preserve your honor, Ellys. You were quite put out the last time this happened.*

Ellys's temper flared. "Gah! I'm not going to be *put out* as you call it! Need I remind you that we're here to do a job?"

Rocc brayed. *Obviously my job is a little different than yours. For example, my duty includes a lot less of this.* Rocc opened her mouth wide and stuck out a thick tongue, one of the most un-romantic actions Ellys had ever seen.

She didn't bother answering. Instead, she scrubbed a hand across her face and shivered in the cool midnight air. "If you're quite finished, I'm tired and I'd like to get some sleep before sunrise." Aderri snickered, and Ellys pointed a finger at her. "And you—"

Aderri settled farther into the bedroll and gave Ellys a curious look. "Yes?"

"Keep those hands and teeth to yourself or, Abbad take me, I'll break the balance and dump you in the stream myself."

Aderri grinned, letting little points dig into her full bottom lip. "We certainly can't have that. I pledge to be good for at least the rest of the night."

"How about for the rest of the journey?" Ellys asked.

"Oh no, that's just not possible."

Dark brows rose in disbelief. "No?"

"No. For the rest of the journey…I'll be better." Then Aderri winked at Ellys and promptly rolled onto her side so all Ellys could see was a mass of dark curls in the moonlight.

Ellys whispered into the night air, "Bollux, but you're going to kill me before we're through."

Aderri whispered back, "Oh, but what a way to go, hmm? Goodnight, Ellys." She closed her eyes to sleep, and so did Ellys.

Chapter Eleven

The thirteen days travel roughly south from the Kuwyth border to Noth were the most uneventful of the entire journey. Despite tensions along the entire northern border of Muniers, most people went on with their daily lives. Aderri pointed out that there was increased troop movement but not to the extent they saw in Carthune. A lifelong student of war, Ellys countered that only half of the soldiers mobilizing in Carthune were doing so because of the aggression between the two countries. The other half were most likely to stage an uprising in conjunction with the impending regicide.

It was late afternoon as they rode through the city gates of the outermost wall into Noth proper. Ellys looked around them curiously. "It's been a long time since we traveled to the capital of Muniers. Other than an obvious population increase, it looks exactly the same."

Did you know that the Nothian stronghold is one of the oldest structures across the six nations? Even the Citadel in Anza isn't so old.

Aderri patted Rocc's neck. "Thank you for that information. I didn't know that, and I've met at least one set of twin regents." She tilted her head in thought. "The previous pair, I believe. Cassyn knows how something made of mere stone and earth could hold up to the ravages of time, wind, and water. It goes against elemental reason."

Ellys considered her statement as she stared far ahead to where the massive stronghold sat upon the cliff. It had proven to be impenetrable for all its existence. "Perhaps it has special magics."

Magics are *involved. You two can't see, because it's not in your nature, but every single brick and stone has been bound with fire and sealed against the enemy elements.*

Aderri stared at the back of Rocc's head then moved her gaze up to the distant fortress. "How is that even possible?"

Rocc gave a little twitch of her withers. *The stronghold sits at a conflux of powerful ley lines. Beyond that, I don't know the actual spells involved. It was standing long before my time and will probably remain long after. Either way, I'd wager the greatest mages of an age had a hand in its construction. It's a true symbol of how much strength can be found when earth and fire ally together.*

Rocc's words gave Ellys much to think about. She considered her own magical nature as well as Aderri's. They, too, were of earth and fire. Ellys wondered if they would be stronger together, or if their natures would prove too dichotomous. While fire was an ally of earth in bones, earth was an enemy of fire. Even the youngest children knew to douse flame with a scoop of dirt. Perhaps because of that simple truth, Aderri would never be interested in anything greater than a passing contract and fleeting friendship.

Ellys briefly closed her eyes as the contradictory thoughts and memory of her own words assailed her. To wish for more went against her own path in life as well as the history of her love. She gave a subtle shake of her head with the hopes of ridding herself of the foolish thoughts.

Aderri glanced back at her. "Do you need anything in the way of supplies while we're in the city?"

"I don't think so. Why?"

"Because I know of an inn where we can stay, but it's on the way out of Noth, right along the coast."

"I'm okay with that. Rocc?"

Rocc whinnied. *I'm as fresh as when we started off this morning. Though I wouldn't object to a nice rubdown and hot mash now that we're only a handful of days from our destination.*

Aderri laughed. "I haven't visited in more than sixty cycles, but I'm pretty sure The Stolen Pelt has everything needed to meet your desires, m'lady."

Ellys was curious. "If you left Muniers decades ago, how do you know the inn even exists, let alone has a spare room or two?"

"The owner, Ailith, is a longtime friend of mine with many cycles left in her. Her inn isn't large, but if she doesn't have any rooms available, she could at least direct us toward another inn of similar quality."

Ellys stiffened in the saddle when she contemplated the familiarity and warmth with which Aderri spoke of her friend. She wondered if this was one of Aderri's dalliances of the past.

She didn't appreciate the churning in her guts that such a thought provoked. Rather than admit to all that, she kept her response neutral. "That's reassuring, at least."

"You're curious and something's bothering you. You can ask whatever you like, Ellys."

Shocked, Ellys tensed in the saddle behind Aderri. "How did you know?"

She's got empathy, and you're as obvious as a goat in a chicken yard.

Aderri said, "You know, if I remember correctly, The Stolen Pelt happens to have a first-rate bathhouse. I certainly hope she's got a room for us because I can't wait to have a long, hot soak after traveling so many days without."

I wasn't going to say anything, but from the smell of her, Ellys could use a soak as well.

Ellys gave Rocc a little dig with her heel. "Are you even listening to yourself right now? I wouldn't tease the person responsible for both your rubdown and the hot mash you're craving."

Aderri laughed at their familiar antics. "No worries, it's a very well-run inn. Ailith has staff for all that."

Ellys muttered from her seat on the back of the saddle. "Of course she does."

It took them another candle mark to make it through the bustling city to where the coastal road followed the water roughly southwest. The size of the capital was obvious by the way businesses, residences, and other establishments spilled along each of the roads out of town. Every so many generations, another protective wall was built. Three rings of varying heights now surrounded the city of Noth, spreading out and away from the stronghold like ripples in a pond. Even so, homes and businesses still expanded well beyond the last wall that had been built a few hundred cycles before.

The Stolen Pelt was one of the grandest inns Ellys had seen since leaving Longoria. "I thought you said her inn wasn't large?"

"The tavern is new."

"And the rest?"

Aderri craned her neck around to take in the expanse of weathered wood and stone. "She seems to have made some other improvements as well."

Both dismounted and Ellys said, "New since when? I thought you hadn't been back in more than sixty cycles.

That's not exactly new by most standards."

Aderri raised an eyebrow but conceded. "You make a good point."

Not all inns had an attached tavern, and both travelers looked forward to a good meal, even if there was no room for them to stay the night. While Ellys felt comfortable enough leaving her packs with Rocc outside, Aderri pointed out that it made more sense to bring their gear in since they were hoping to procure a room. Ellys shouldered her pack and followed Aderri into the tavern, but not without first giving an affectionate rub to Rocc's muzzle.

Don't forget my mash! was the last thing Ellys heard in her head before pushing through the door.

Inside was busy with many of the tables full and a minstrel playing in the corner. It was late afternoon heading into early evening so Ellys assumed it would only get busier from there.

Aderri grabbed the attention of a passing server. "Excuse me, but I'm looking for Ailith."

The server of indeterminate gender's eyes widened when they noticed Aderri, then they moved their gaze to Ellys where she stood with two swords strapped to her back. "She be in the back, but the barmaid won't let ye through. Ye'll have to wait 'til Ailith comes out."

"Can you give her a message for me?"

The server pursed their lips and scowled. "Not sure you've noticed, but I be busy. Ye can order or piss off. Don't care which."

Rather than get offended, Aderri burst into laughter. "I'm glad to see she's got such protective people helping out around here. She'll want to know I'm here. But just to make it worth your time…" Aderri pulled a copper from her waist pouch.

The coin disappeared, and the server gave a quick nod to Aderri and Ellys. "I be heading to the back anyway. Name?"

"Aderri n'all Dracona."

The server took a small step back as their mouth dropped open. Without another word, they spun on their heel and headed for the door at the back of the room, just beyond a scowling, heavily-muscled barmaid.

Ellys asked, "What was that all about?"

A look of pain pulled at Aderri's lips; an expression observed keenly by her companion. "I told you a half-moon ago that Clan Dracona is the ancestral guardian of Muniers's coastline. Our name holds…weight anywhere within the country."

"That looked a lot like fear to me."

Aderri's eyes shuttered with sadness, and she looked away. "Clearly, they figured out what I am. My coloring is pretty distinctive within the Clan, and the name itself would be a direct confirmation."

"Hey…" Ellys gently cupped Aderri's cheek and bought her gaze back around so she could look into those flaming pupils. "What you are is not who you are. You have nothing to be ashamed of, and I would know because I feel like we've come to understand each other pretty well. I've seen all of you at this point of the journey."

Aderri seemed to snap out of her crisis of self-esteem. She winked at Ellys. "You haven't actually seen all of me yet, but we can change that later in the bathhouse, if you like."

The memory of Aderri's curves above and below the water back in Pata, as well as that brief glimpse after Ellys's rescue, was enough to make Ellys sweat. She held her hands up. "I've seen enough of you to know that you're good, erm, I mean a good person." Luckily, she was interrupted from further embarrassment when a voice cut through the din of the tavern.

"By sea and selk, if it isn't Aderri!" Ailith was a small woman with long, grayish-brown hair that was pleated into a braid down her back. She wore a tunic with comfortable trousers and the softest-looking boots Ellys had ever seen. The height difference between them was almost comical when she caught Aderri up in a great hug, complete with spinning around. The pair nearly knocked into multiple chairs. Most folks leaned away, as if they were expecting the exuberant display.

Ellys and Aderri had discussed their contract during their travel out of Noth, and Ellys knew it was time for her to start earning those gold coins. She'd have to choose her words carefully so she didn't lie outright, in order to avoid lending validity to the prophesy foretold by Gwyn so long ago. "You must be Ailith."

The innkeeper stepped back and thoroughly appraised Ellys, then gave Aderri a knowing smirk. "I see no matter how many cycles wash out with the tides, some things never change." The look she aimed at Ellys was almost predatory. "Aren't you just delicious."

"'Lith, you're making her nervous."

The small woman grinned as she peered up at Ellys. There was at least a foot difference in height between them. "Am I though?"

Ellys looked helplessly to Aderri before turning back to Ailith and admitting, "A little."

Aderri looped her arm through Ellys's. "This is Ellys. We're traveling back to the Clan for the naming ceremony."

Ailith nodded. "I heard there was a new hatchling, but we've had a lot of tidbits of news flying around Noth lately so that pearl fell out of my head. Still, I'm surprised you came. I thought you were done with this corner of the six nations."

"The invitation was less a request and more of an order, so I had no choice. And you know the weight of expectation means I can never truly be done. I will have to permanently return eventually."

Ailith stared hard at Ellys. Her eyes were the same grayish-brown as her hair. "And why are you here?" She narrowed her eyes and sniffed. "You're not Clan."

Ellys looked down at her in surprise. "You can tell that from smelling me?"

"Not at all. You have an odor that would best be solved with some soap and water. I can tell because I can tell, no other reason."

Aderri stifled a laugh and answered her friend's question. "I asked her to come with me. Ellys knew how much it meant, so she agreed to make the journey and attend the ceremony."

"You're pretty brave to follow Aderri into the fire."

"Bravery is needed when you face something that makes you afraid. Discomfort and unfamiliarity merely require a healthy dose of loyalty, which Aderri has from me in abundance. Balance prevails." Ellys gave her a benign smile then made the sign of Toroc by briefly touching her chin, then left and right sides of her chest with the first two fingers of her 'chi,' or right hand. The 'doa' hand and entire left arm rested against her stomach, palm facing up.

"Well, well, well. It's not every day you meet a follower of Toroc outside their Goz-be-damned temple."

Aderri laughed. "Still casually blasphemous, I see."

"What's the worst that can happen? Not like I have much else to lose in this life or the next."

While Ailith's mouth smiled, her eyes grew hard and Ellys wondered what the story was behind the words. She glanced around, noting the successful inn and tavern. Surely Ailith had plenty to lose but it wasn't her place to ask. "Since you so politely pointed out my lack of cleanliness, do you happen to have a room available for the two of us? Aderri mentioned your bathhouse, and I'll need a stall for my steed."

Like a flipped coin, Ailith's mood changed. "I've always got a bed for Aderri…and whatever companion is in tow."

Ellys scowled to think about Aderri sharing a bed with any other companions, especially if that person was Ailith. She was mollified somewhat when Aderri didn't release her arm as they followed Ailith through the busy establishment to the same door the innkeeper had come through a mere handful of candle drops before. Rather than taking them into the inn proper, as Ellys originally suspected, Ailith led them through a kitchen to another door which only opened with a key from around her neck.

"The inn is actually full right now, but this is my private residence," She gave Ellys a smile as she led them farther into the building until she came to a stop next to a closed door. With a flourish, she turned the latch and swung it open to reveal a good-sized room with a luxurious bed and its own hearth. "And friends are always welcome to my spare room."

Aderri smiled at her long-time friend. "Thank you. I'd love to catch up, but both of us have been traveling for more than a moon and are in desperate need of a wash. Interested in wine and a warm fire later? You can tell me when you added the tavern and expanded the rest of the inn."

"And you can tell me where you found such a handsome companion to take home to the Clan."

Ellys gave a frown, but Aderri never lost her smile. "Of course. And our steed?"

"Oh, you can take your horse through the yard to the back. You'll find a stable hand ready."

"She's not a horse." The words came out naturally and without a second thought on Ellys's part. After a hundred cycles of companionship, it had become habit to defend her friend, even if Rocc wasn't near to hear.

At Ailith's confused look, Aderri elaborated. "Lady Roccotári is an elven mount and Ellys's lineal bondmate, so she needs to be treated with respect."

A wondrous smile lit Ailith's features. "Fascinating! I always love meeting fellow magical creatures. I'll go introduce myself and get her settled before handing off instruction to my head stable keeper, Josten."

"She likes hot mash." Ellys immediately felt the fool as the words slipped out, but she couldn't reel them back in for all the gold in the world.

Ailith burst into laughter. "I don't know a single horse—steed—that doesn't."

Ellys relaxed and joined her. "True enough." She didn't bring up the comment about Rocc being a fellow creature of magic. She'd simply ask Aderri about it later. "And about that bath?"

"I can certainly accommodate you both." The words came out flirtatious, and Ellys wasn't sure how serious to take the innkeeper. "Now, if you want a little adventure, you can go back into the main tavern and through the other door. From there you'll see a plaque designating the location of the bathhouse. It's larger, but you're sure to have company due to the full inn. However, if you would like a little privacy, I've got my own bathing room here. Continue down this hall to the far door. It's not spacious like the other, but it will easily hold the two of you. Especially if you're friendly." She winked.

Friendliness was the last thing Ellys wanted, but she couldn't say anything in front of Ailith without raising suspicion. She glanced to Aderri and found the woman already smirking at her. Aderri answered for both of them. "I think the private bath is more to our preference."

"I assumed as much. There are drying cloths stacked in the room as well as kindling for the hearth. And if there is one certainty across the six nations, it's that Aderri n'all Dracona is well versed in lighting fires."

"What can I say? It's a talent."

Ellys stepped into their room and dropped her pack on the floor near a small table. "Thank you for your hospitality, Ailith." She glanced between them. "If you'd like, I could bathe now and let you two catch up."

By the look in Aderri's eyes alone, Ellys knew she wasn't going to get away with avoiding her friend's nudity so easily. "And let the sight of that body"—she raked her gaze from the tips of Ellys's pointy ears all the way to her travel-worn boots—"go to waste? Not a chance in six will I."

Ailith laughed again and clapped Aderri on the shoulder. "I don't blame you. I wouldn't either. And on that note, I'll let you two clean up. We can take evening meal in the tavern if that's acceptable?"

"That's fine with me. Ellys?"

Ellys gave them a wan smile. "I'm amenable to whatever place has the quickest spirit."

Ailith pointed at her and winked. "I had a feeling you'd say that. Live by the sword, drink by the handle." Then she turned and made her way down the hall to the tavern door.

"Well?"

Ellys met her companion's eyes from less than an arm's length away, and her breath hitched as she was caught in the flaming depths of Aderri's gaze. "Well, what?"

"What do you think?"

Ellys glanced around the room she'd stepped into. "Seems nice enough for a night."

"I meant Ailith."

"Oh, well she's fairly…forward, isn't she?"

"Ailith is fairly a lot of things, forward being the tamest."

Ellys harrumphed and crouched down to dig into her pack for the spare shirt and trousers she'd washed two nights before in a stream and mended the night after. She gave the shirt a good sniff then stood again. "I suppose they'll have to do. I was hoping to have something a little cleaner to wear to meet your Clan." Ellys paused to look at the surprisingly refreshed clothing that Aderri was wearing. "How is it you're always so blasted speck-less? We've traveled the same distance together, and yet you've nary a stain or poor smell." Ellys narrowed her eyes suspiciously.

"You know I have low-level magic."

"And?"

"As well as an affinity for earth."

Ellys rolled her eyes. "Are you telling me you just"—she waved her hand about—"spell it away?"

"It's not as simple as you're indicating. I discovered the amalgam spell my second cycle of traveling outside Clan lands."

"Amalgam spell?" Ellys had half a mind that Aderri was putting her on. After all, why would she let Ellys travel in dirty clothes after they'd come so far together, rather than share such a miraculous spell?

"Come on, I'll tell you in the bath." Aderri led the way down the hall indicated by Ailith, and against Ellys's better judgment, she followed. Aderri pushed through the door and, despite not being in use, the room was quite warm. She used her magic to light the wall sconce, then looked around and smiled. "Looks like she filled the pool earlier, and we're probably stealing the very soak that Ailith had planned for herself after the tavern closed. I'll give her this, it's a very smart location."

The hearth wasn't lit. Ellys glanced around in confusion, taking note of the bathing pool that was large enough for them to soak without touching, if they were careful. "What do you mean?"

Aderri pointed at the bare wall to their left. "The kitchen hearth is just on the other side. Building the bathing room here guaranteed it would be warm most of the time. If my guess is correct, the pipe for filling the tub probably runs through the wall to a cistern on the kitchen side nearest the cooking fire. Fairly brilliant." She made short work of lighting the hearth with her magic before getting ready to bathe.

Seeing Aderri undress, Ellys whirled around so her back was to the center of the small room and began removing her own clothing. "You mean this wasn't here the last time you were in Noth?"

"In the nearly seven decades since I was last home, half this inn is new." Ellys heard sloshing from the tub area and assumed Aderri had entered. She was right and turned around just as Aderri spoke again. "As a matter of fact, she previously only had a handful of rooms and a small area to serve a meal to the patrons. I'd wager it's at least triple the size now."

Luckily, most of Aderri's body was covered by dark water in the dimly lit room. Ellys was grateful for the small things, though she could have done without the unabashed ogling. Rather than call her out, Ellys chose to remind herself that Aderri was a patron and continued the original conversation. "Interesting. Now, tell me how you make the clothes clean, and why you've never bothered to aid me with it." She got a splash for her demand.

"Fine. The amalgam spell is similar to the one that I use to cleanse my sleep space of vermin, but I've merged it with a heat spell and tied it to the earth element. As for why I didn't help you out…" She paused and looked toward the candles flickering in the wall sconce by the door. "In the first half-moon or so that we traveled together, it was simply because I found you incredibly contrary, and you didn't ask."

"And after that?"

Aderri gave her that familiar smirk. "I enjoyed the view of you washing in various streams a little too much. I am a creature who appreciates the androgynous aesthetic which you have in abundance." Her hands came out of the water and she shrugged, unrepentantly.

"I should have expected an answer of that sort. Would you be obliged to help me out going forward?"

"Of course. I'll do whatever my lover wishes."

Ellys rolled her eyes, but rather than respond, she grabbed a cake of soap from the shelf near the tub, an action mirrored by Aderri. Both women were silent for a while as they washed thoroughly then sat to soak up the heat of the water that had been supplemented by Aderri's fire magic.

It had been a long two-score days of traveling, and Ellys was happy for the chance to relax and unwind. If truth be told, she had a wee bit of anxiety at the thought of posing to be someone's suitor, especially given the fact that she would be doing so in the midst of a Clan full of magical shifters. Surely at least one of them would be able to smell a lie from truth. She tried to remember how she was with Gwyn, thinking maybe she could mimic some of those actions and reactions in the situation to come.

Almost as if Aderri could read her mind, she said, "I have concerns about our visit to my Clan."

"I was just pondering similar thoughts. When do we need to meet Ailith in the tavern?"

Aderri grinned, digging the points of her teeth in provocatively. "Oh, given the comments she made before heading back to the inn proper, she's probably not expecting us for a few candle marks."

Ellys swallowed and knew she'd regret asking, yet still she did. "Candle marks?"

Aderri gave her a wink. "Shifters have an abundance of stamina, a fact I thought for sure you'd be aware of at this stage of your life."

Her words only served to make Ellys warmer, and she sputtered. "Well s-sure, uh, I mean I've been with shifters before, but they're not..."

"Not what? Were they too much for you, Ellys?"

Ellys scoffed and displayed the fabled superiority complex of her magical heritage for the first time since they'd been traveling together. "Not at all. I am half elven, and while shifters certainly have stamina and strength aplenty, they still can't keep up."

A smirk met her words. "Are you speaking of battle or bed sports?"

"Both I suppose."

They met each other's eyes across the small pool and both dissolved into laughter. Once they regained control of themselves, Aderri leaned forward in the tub, closing the gap between them. It was close enough that Ellys could feel the caress of Aderri's breath tickling the hairs that fell in a drying tangle across her forehead. "Let me give you a bit of information, in case the topic comes up later. I'm no ordinary shifter."

"What's that supposed to mean?"

"I'm a dragon. If you haven't figured it out from more than a moon of traveling together, let me break it down for you. Basic magical conservation theory states that any creature of magic is born with a certain amount of energy sufficient to carry it around. If that energy is compressed into a smaller form, they will retain their strength and endurance, proportional to that form. So, to repeat…I'm a dragon."

"Uh—"

Aderri reached farther across and gently shut Ellys's mouth, seemingly satisfied that she'd made her point. Ellys found Aderri's smug look annoying, but she also held just a tiny bit more regard for her friend.

Aderri said, "You know…while you continue to vex me with your rigid code of honor, I have to admit it's one of the things I admire most about you."

Ellys wasn't sure how to respond, so she fell upon politeness. "Thank you. Does this mean you'll stop teasing me?"

Aderri's unabashed laughter rang off the walls, and chill bumps washed down Ellys's arms. "Not a chance." Aderri suddenly stood from the water, and Ellys's eyes followed the cascading torrent down her dark skin to where it dropped back into the tub. "Come, we should probably take some time to discuss how we will pull off this ruse. Lying without actually lying. I'm also hungry."

"Uh-huh."

Aderri grinned and snapped her fingers in front of Ellys's face. "Clearly you are, too. My eyes are up here."

Ellys blushed and turned away. "Sorry." Once she sensed that Aderri had enough time to dress, Ellys pulled the plug in the bottom of the bathing tub that she'd felt with her foot when they first got in. Then she stood and grabbed a nearby drying cloth.

"Here."

Ellys looked up from her task to see Aderri holding out her trousers. "I've cleaned all the items you have with you. I'll do the rest in your pack when we get back to our room. I even have a mending spell that should take care of the worst of the rents."

"Thank you again."

Aderri gave her a sly smile. "You can thank me later with a kiss."

"What?"

"That was what I wanted to speak with you about in our room. How are we to convince anyone that we're lovers if we don't play the part? People will notice if things are awkward between us."

"But we've already kissed. Isn't that enough?"

"Ellys, we kissed once. Are you saying you can do it reliably whenever needed, in front of an audience, mind you? How do I know you won't freeze up and forget the basic mechanics? You could be a terrible kisser when under stress, then this entire thing would be naught but an unbelievable chore."

Ellys quickly finished dressing as she attempted to defend her skills. "I have it on good authority that I'm an excellent kisser at any given time."

"Whose authority? From what I hear, you're always asleep soon into the deed."

Ellys growled at the infuriating woman. "Toroc take me, but you're impossible."

"I'm pretty sure they won't take you, but I will if you ask nicely enough."

Rather than answer that last jibe, Ellys stalked out of the chamber toward the room they were to share for the night.

Chapter Twelve

Back in their room, Ellys demanded, "Explain what you meant in the bathing room."

"You've said that you spied before when in service of the Empire. Did you have to play many different roles to do so?"

"Of course."

Aderri walked over and sat upon their bed. "And I'd wager you needed to study and prepare to play those roles, much like an actor before a performance."

"Yes, but—"

"This is a role, Ellys. It may be a mix of those two types of performance, but it's still a role. You can't pretend to sword fight if you've never held a blade."

"I've held all blades."

"You're being purposely difficult. Fine then, you can't pull off a convincing performance as a master of a particular discipline if it involves an unfamiliar weapon."

"Are you calling yourself an unfamiliar weapon?" Ellys smirked.

Rather than take affront, Aderri winked at her. "Oh, absolutely."

Knowing she was beaten, Ellys gave in. "I hate that you're right on this. What do we need to do?"

"Obviously, we need to practice together."

"Practice what exactly. Holding each other, more physical displays of affection?" She lowered her voice and grinned. "Whispering sweet bits of romance to each other?"

Aderri patted the bed next to her. "All of those, yes, but I'm also talking about kissing." Ellys's smile disappeared. "Not to bring up a potentially painful subject, though my empathy tells me you're remarkably well adjusted on the issue, but how were you with Gwyneth?"

Ellys thought back to her past life and how she and Gwyn

behaved together. Even near the end when her love was significantly aged, they still behaved like randy youths. She collapsed backward onto the bed next to Aderri. "Fenwith's balls…you're right."

"I think you secretly love when I am."

Ellys sat up and met Aderri's gaze that had gone strangely fiery again. "Says you. How should we do this?"

"How do you normally kiss someone with whom you've been tupping?"

"Well, I mean…this isn't a normal situation."

"That's certainly the truth. And I don't know what to tell you other than you just do it. Make it feel natural like the first time we kissed."

"Easy for you to say. Just talking about this and plotting it out feels anything but natural."

"Are you this timid with all your bed partners? Is that why they charge you for the honor of tupping and subsequently make off with your coin?"

Finally pushed to her limit, Ellys leaned forward abruptly. She grasped the sides of Aderri's face and pulled the other woman toward her, if only to stop the flow of teasing words. The kiss was full of frustration at first, but it quickly turned to a mix of curiosity and thrill. There was a scent about Aderri that had nothing to do with their recent bath or the soap used. Aderri's hair was a curly mass, dry because she hadn't washed it. Her curls held a musky, smoky smell that Ellys found pleasant. If anything, their second kiss eclipsed the first by far, despite all their talk. Perhaps it was because Ellys was trying to prove a point, using the only weapon at her disposal in that moment: passion.

Aderri moaned into the kiss, and Ellys knew exactly how she felt. Despite Ellys's code of honor and insistence on professionalism, it was everything she'd been wanting for more than a half-moon. It wasn't the tender and somewhat shy exploration in front of a camp-fire. The passion between them was an explosion of sensation and emotion. Ellys's lips were firm and her tongue teased the entrance of Aderri's mouth. Both women moaned when Aderri finally opened her lips and met the questing organ with her own.

Ellys's will was nearly undone when she felt the sharp little points of Aderri's canines and pictured what it would be like to feel them on other parts of her body. Then she remembered that fading dream from earlier in the trip and grew warm.

They pulled apart abruptly, both panting despite their much-touted stamina. Ellys was the first to speak as she ran a hand through her nearly dry hair. "By Toroc!"

"I'd have to agree with you there. Cassyn has nothing on the heat of that kiss. Suffice it to say, I don't think we'll have a problem making the attraction believable."

Ellys leaned away with a feeling of trepidation. "We'll have to do that again?"

Aderri nodded. "That was the point of this practice, Ellys, to show that we could both perform instantly when necessary and look natural while doing it."

"But…how often do you snog in front of your family, er, I mean the Clan?"

"We need to do it enough to be believable, no more, no less. This is something we can't plan out, Ellys. We'll just have to watch the situation and act accordingly. Okay?"

Ellys worried that more than her honor would go up in flames if they continued this heart-dangerous game. Unfortunately, she was under contract and really did need the gold. She had promised Rocc and would not go back on it because of a little discomfort on her part. And there was no need to make her companion's life any harder by perpetually wandering the land in an impoverished state.

Her blossoming emotions where Aderri was concerned left Ellys feeling as if she were betraying her lost love's memory, and she mentally begged Gwyn for forgiveness even as she gave in to the inevitable. "Yes, we'll figure it out as we go."

Aderri seemed to sense Ellys's vulnerability. "If you'd like, I can clean and mend the rest of the garments in your pack before we meet up with Ailith."

Ellys stood from the bed and gave herself a mental shake to eliminate some of her internal conflict mixed with a good bit of arousal. "I would, thank you." She walked across the room to her pack, and Aderri followed.

"You should bring your bones with you to the tavern. Ailith is always up for a good shake."

"What about you?" Elemental Bones was a two-person game, and Ellys didn't want Aderri to feel left out.

"I'll be fine, I enjoy watching as much as playing."

A black brow rose and Ellys smiled. "Do you now?"

Sharp white teeth dug into Aderri's lower lip before she

answered with a humorous twinkle in her eyes. "I can play the winner."

Ellys pulled her spare garments out of her pack one by one for Aderri to work her magic on. Once they were all clean and repaired, she rolled them up and returned them then grabbed the familiar red pouch from a side pocket. "I'm ready when you are."

When they got to the door, Aderri pulled it open and looked back over her shoulder at Ellys. "I highly doubt that."

Still somewhat reeling from the kiss and the emotions it brought forth candle drops before, Ellys thought it best not to encourage Aderri's flirting and chose to change the subject. "If I'm to throw bones with Ailith, what is her element?"

"You couldn't figure it out?"

"No…wait, she said something like, 'by the selk,' and she's a magical creature…she's a selkie! That means she's got water magic."

They walked through the door leading into the main tavern, and Aderri gave her one last wink. "Who knew that not all swords were as dull as iron?"

Ellys scowled. "Can you cut the teasing until I've at least had a meal and some mead? It makes your brand of humor a little easier to swallow."

"If you want easy, you'd have had to pay *me*." Aderri turned away before Ellys could retort and greeted her friend who had seen them enter. "Ailith, we're ready for that promised meal, and Ellys here brought her bone set. I'm curious to see how the two of you match up."

Once they had a meal in their bellies and mead all around, Ellys felt a lot more relaxed. It also helped that Aderri had turned conversation toward Ailith as they caught up with events of the region over the past handful of decades. Ellys would chime in when asked about one thing or another, but for the most part, she was content to listen to various exploits of the two women when they studied together.

Finally, after one of the more contentious tales, she spoke. "So, your magics are elemental enemies. How did that work for, you know, when you were together? How was it?"

"Volatile."

"Too much."

The second answer was from Aderri, and she elaborated with a curious look from Ellys. "We tried early on to make a romance of it but…" She trailed off and Ailith finished for her.

"Alas, it was naught to be. Friendship was entirely possible, as was the occasional night of tupping, but any kind of long-term relationship would have never worked. Our temperaments are not well suited in that regard."

Aderri nodded. "Our love leaned more toward philia than eros in the end. But for friendship…I'm glad to count her among the closest."

Ailith leaned forward onto the round table. They'd chosen one at the edge of the room out of respect for Ellys's need to have a solid wall at her back. Her keen gaze moved from Aderri to Ellys and back again. "Now you two though…any clam can see you've got destiny written all over you."

Ellys glanced nervously at Aderri before asking the obvious. "How do you mean?"

"For starts, you've both got this roiling sexual tension about you that one would think would have been sufficiently worked out by now. But clearly, your passion is great enough that it burns just below the surface at all times."

Ellys flushed but Aderri laughed and confirmed Ailith's statement. "It certainly does."

"Then, there are the mingling magics all around you." Ailith motioned with her hands, mimicking swirling waves from one woman to the other. "As you know, just as with Elemental Bones, earth is fully capable of smothering fire as an enemy if not careful. However, fire has known to harden the resolve of earth, thus becoming an ally. I think the success of this romance will depend highly on who is stronger of will and want."

Ellys grunted. "Interesting observation."

"Speaking of the bones…" Aderri had clearly picked up on Ellys's discomfort and sought to change the subject. "Ellys brought hers to play."

Ailith made a motion over the table. "Let's see them. Aderri knows I like to guess the source."

Forgetting who her companion was for a moment, Ellys opened the pouch and let the set of rune-carved bones spill onto the wooden table. Each cube made a dull *clacking* sound as it bounced until coming to a rest. Curiously, they all gravitated toward Aderri's third of the table. "I have to warn you, I've had fairly good luck with them."

Ailith plucked one of the ten from its resting place and immediately dropped it again with a look of fury upon her face. "*Cablu*! I cannot believe you'd carry these in her presence." She began to rise but was quickly stilled when Aderri grabbed her forearm.

"Peace, Ailith. She wasn't responsible for the death of the source. Not only that, but she returned dignity by giving temple donations and having them blessed. I trust in Ellys's honor, as you trust in mine."

Ellys was grateful for Aderri's defense and gazed at her fondly. "Thank you." Aderri responded with a caress across the back of her hand.

Ailith settled again, still simmering with anger. "Where did you get them?"

"A treacherous turnout from an old mercenary group I served with. He eventually wronged one too many, and fate caught up to him."

"Hmm, interesting. Do you believe in fate then?" Ailith looked around the table at the women, opening the question up for more than Ellys.

Both spoke at the same time with surety of expression and voice, "No." Then they glanced at each other, obviously startled by the identical response.

Ailith threw her head back and gave a hearty laugh, garnering the attention of her companions and nearby tavern customers alike. Once she was in control of herself again, she explained. "I've often found that those who least believe in fate are usually the ones most guided by it."

Ellys considered Gwyn's prophesy and shuddered. "By Toroc, I hope not."

Aderri said, "I've read the Sky Tome numerous times, in a variety of languages, and each mentions the auspicious cycle of our birth. Other than that, I can't say I've seen proof of anything."

Ailith rolled her eyes. "You and your adagnitio brain, always needing proof!"

"Are you two going to play or what? I told Ellys I will take on the winner."

"You want *me* to play against *you*, my elemental enemy, on a bone set forged in the fires of your very kin? I think not. You can play with your elf after we finish." She winked at Aderri.

Ellys protested, "Hey, I win my share against her, despite Aderri's affinity with my set."

"That's because fire loses to earth, being an enemy. I suspect that is the only thing keeping her from sweeping all your matches."

"What will that say about our match then? Earth loses to water."

"I guess we'll just have to see how the bones fall, won't we? Stakes?"

"How about a dram of your strongest spirit?" Ailith nodded and Ellys asked, "And for you?"

She got a mischievous smile for her question. "You have to tell me your favorite part about sharing a bedroll with Aderri."

Ellys blushed furiously to the tips of her pointed ears even as Aderri burst out into laughter. "Some things never change, do they?"

"And others live in ever-rolling motion like the tide." Ailith nodded toward Ellys. "Toss for start."

Ellys won the right of first roll, and soon enough, the bones were bouncing across the table, inexplicably staying away from the area around Ailith. It was an excellent throw. Ellys had five earth runes. She also had one of each: life, death, water, fire, and wind. Seeing five of one element, she declared, "Elemental miracle!" and Ailith groaned as Ellys removed the lone death bone from the destiny.

After that, she grouped the remaining bones by type then began pushing them off to the side in correct order of elimination. She called out as she tallied them. "Earth will be my primary, so I'll flip the life rune to another earth and remove it and the wind since they are elemental enemies. That means I can remove the water and fire for the same reason. Let's see…" She cleared all from the table but the remaining five earth.

Annoyed at the good roll, Ailith snapped, "Yes, yes, we all see."

"Don't mind her, she's always been a sore loser."

Ailith kicked Aderri's chair leg. "It's only because you've always been a smug winner." She looked back at Ellys. "So final tally is five earth."

"Yes." Ellys grinned, knowing she had a good score to beat.

The tavern owner quickly scooped up all ten bones and rolled, groaning as she saw how many death runes were showing. "What is this bucket of chum-fuckery?" Both Aderri and Ellys began laughing when Ailith pulled all four death runes from the destiny.

"Looks like your luck has abandoned you, old friend."

Ailith crossed the first two fingers of her left hand and held them up in front of Aderri's face, then she scowled at Ellys. "Your bones hate me."

"Impossible. My set isn't enchanted, nor is it sentient. You've just had an off throw is all. Now, are you going to tally, or do you simply concede defeat on the round?"

Ailith mumbled something beneath her breath and shoved the entire group toward Ellys. "That's pointless since the four death cancel out two elements per on their own, meaning there is nothing left to tally. Take your next roll."

"Ah-ah-ah, not so fast." Ellys waggled a finger at her. "You agreed to the stakes. It's on you to deliver."

Ailith's mouth dropped open. "I was agreeing to the entire match, not per round."

"Funny, but you always bet per round with me when we used to play." Aderri got a scowl for her memory.

"Betrayer! Fine." Ailith circled a finger in the air, catching the attention of the server who originally greeted Ellys and Aderri when they arrived at the inn.

They hustled over to their table and looked nervously toward Aderri then back to Ailith. In an instant their face transformed completely. The server gazed at Ailith in nothing short of adoration then quick as it appeared, the expression shifted to something more neutral. "Another round of mead, 'Lith?"

"Not just yet, love. I'd like you to meet my long-time friend, Aderri. She's taking her companion, Ellys, home to her Clan." She turned to her guests. "This fine selk is Doonie."

Doonie scowled. "Ye know that's not my name."

They got a wink for their admonishment. "True, but ye know I like saying it just to see that handsome scowl. Could you bring Ellys here a pip of Cuon's Tears?"

"You sure?" They looked Ellys up and down. "I see the ears, but that tells me naught about their constitution."

"She'll be fine."

Doonie nodded and rushed to comply while one of Ellys's dark brows rose with skepticism. "You're giving me a pip's worth? How is that your strongest?"

Doonie returned less than a candle drop later to leave the pip then rushed away again at the call of their name from across the tavern. Ailith shoved the tiny container, no bigger than the size of her thumb, across the table. "Just because I've lost doesn't mean I want to kill ye."

Ellys looked to Aderri for confirmation of Ailith's words and was met with those flaming pupils that both disconcerted and intrigued her.

Aderri asked, "Have you never heard of Cuon's Tears before?"

"No. Is this a local brew then, and what does the Goddess of the Oceans have to do with it?"

"About as local as you can get." Aderri turned to look at Ailith, and they both burst into laughter at what seemed to be a private joke. Ailith shoved the pip closer. "Just drink it. And remember—"

"Yes?"

"You asked for the strongest."

Ellys delicately lifted the pip between her thumb and forefinger, looking at the cloudy brew within. "Nothing can be as bad as Fenwith's Fire." Then before either woman could disagree with her, she opened wide and tossed the liquid into her mouth.

Aderri and Ailith both leaned closer to observe Ellys's reaction. They waited a full ten heartbeats without Ellys moving a muscle. Finally, Ailith broke. "Well?"

Ellys opened her mouth to speak then abruptly fell face down onto the table, luckily slumping in such a way that she landed with her forehead on the bones, thus saving her from a broken nose. More than just their little trio witnessed the reaction, and laughter sounded throughout the tavern.

While Ellys couldn't move or feel anything, with her body gone oddly numb, she could still hear. All the voices sounded much louder than normal.

"Do you think she'll be okay?"

Ailith gave a hum of assent. "If it were most, I'd say this was the end of the evening for her. But a half-elf? Give her a few candle drops, and she'll be back up and ready to play the next round."

As predicted, after a short time, Ellys was able to move again. She groaned and stirred. When she lifted her head, Ailith burst out laughing to see it, but Aderri looked startled.

Ellys looked back and forth between them, then at the table where her head had been. She reached up and felt two indentations on her head where it had landed on the bones. She fingered the two marks, made out that they were of earth and fire, and thought perhaps there was some credence to fate after all.

After more than a moon of traveling together with Aderri, Ellys felt just as branded on the inside as she appeared on the outside. When she glanced at Aderri, her friend looked shaken, and Ellys wondered if perhaps she felt the same. Rather than bring it up in front of a much-too-curious innkeeper, Ellys asked the other question at the forefront of her mind. "By Toroc, what was in that?"

Ailith didn't answer right away. Instead, she lifted her own mug for Doonie to see and motioned to all three of them so the server would bring another round of mead. "Did you know that when a selk has lost her skin, she weeps the entire night of every full moon?"

Ellys looked at her curiously, wondering about the topic change. "I've heard that legend, yes."

"The tears are no legend. Some have speculated that they have healing properties, but nothing with so sad an origin can be helpful. No, they are only good for a temporary disruption to your system, much like a dozen strong drinks will feel like a knock to the head."

Ellys's lips thinned as she pressed them together in realization. She gave Ailith a grave look. "Is there no hope for the skin's return?"

"It was stolen ages ago by my husband, who is by now long dead. It is unlikely I'll ever find where he hid it."

"I'm sorry, Ailith. If it were within my power to find and return it to you, I would. No creature should be cut off from a part of their true self." She looked at Aderri, thinking about how the dragon shifter spent her life denying part of her own magic and makeup because of fear and the expectations of Clan and history. Aderri frowned but didn't speak.

Ailith's hand slapped the table, startling Ellys from her heavy gaze. "Enough. Let's get on with our match, shall we?"

Respecting Ailith's wishes to let the subject die, Ellys grabbed the bones and tossed again. That time she had a much less fortuitous roll. When all her runes were tallied, she was left with three water. Not bad, but not great either, especially if Ailith ended with an elemental enemy, or the false ally of water. "Bah! Apparently, they hate me now, too." She shoved the ten carved cubes across the table in annoyance.

Ailith scooped them up and let them rattle between her cupped hands before rolling them onto the wood with a flourish. She smiled with delight. "Oh, that's much better."

Once everything was tallied, Ailith was left with three earth runes, enough to beat out and remove each one of Ellys's waters. Since earth was a false ally to water and not an elemental enemy, it got to stay while the other rune was removed from the destiny. Ellys threw up her hands in defeat. "I can't believe you beat me with my own element."

The other two laughed at her dismay, but Ailith quickly reminded her of the stakes. "Don't be sore. Just tell me what I want to know, and we can move on to the final round."

Ellys drained her mug and started on the newly deposited one. "Remind me again. That was a full mead ago, plus a knock to the head against your table."

"What is your favorite part about sharing a bedroll with Aderri?"

Ellys contemplated the wording and was reassured that she could answer without outright lying because they'd indeed shared a bedroll many times. Aderri, for her part, appeared extremely curious about what Ellys would say. Full of her own mischief, Ellys cut a quick glance to Aderri and grinned, then turned to answer Ailith's question. "I like that she's a biter."

Ailith pounded the table in merriment. "Yet another thing still the same with you." She chucked a fist against Aderri's shoulder and continued to laugh even as she snatched up the bones to begin the last round.

The third and final round went much the way the second did, though neither won by rolling their natural elements. They both finished with wind, but it came down to Ailith having one more rune than Ellys.

She rubbed her hands together with apparent glee. "Final question. When did you first realize you wanted to be with Aderri?"

Silence reigned at the table for nearly a candle drop and Aderri rested her hand against the back of Ellys's. "You don't have to answer if it makes you uncomfortable. She can pick another less intrusive question."

Ellys met Aderri's eyes and considered the question in all its merit. The first answer that came to mind was true if a little personal. Because of Gwyn's foretelling that she'd find love again if she were to lie with one of the same age, falsehood was too much of a risk. Ellys also knew her first thought would work well in Ailith's expectation as well as what Aderri's knowledge was of their little ruse. She peered at Aderri out of the corner of her eye, noticing how the other woman was on the edge of her seat. Then she turned to Ailith. "The first night she warmed me by the fire."

At first Aderri looked shocked, but Ellys could practically see the wheels turning. She knew that her friend would contemplate both the question and the answer, then realize the fine line Ellys walked with her wording. Ailith's question was vague and could be miscon-strued to mean nothing more than being in someone's presence. Expressions flickered across Aderri's face, and Ellys found it curious to note that when Aderri's gaze settled on her, it was filled with long-ing. Then quick as it appeared, the emotion washed away.

Before Aderri could say anything, Ellys leaned over and gave her a quick kiss on the cheek. She winked at her pretend lover and grinned at Ailith. "How could I not want to be with her? She's the hottest woman I've met."

Aderri groaned at the bad joke, but Ailith laughed and immedi-ately lifted her glass. "Let us drink to Aderri, then, and the heat of her perpetual flame."

Aderri shook her head but lifted her glass with the other two. As one, the trio intoned the traditional wish for good health that had originated somewhere in the distant past of the Kuwyth Empire. "*Te Zah!*" Then they finished their drinks and slammed the cups to the table. All around them, stragglers in the tavern did the same when they heard the women, and cries of "Te Zah!" echoed through the room.

Aderri snorted at her long-time friend. "Was the cheer really necessary?"

"What? It's good for business. People will finish one drink and order another." All three laughed, and Aderri rolled her eyes.

✳✳✳✳

In the end, they caroused in the tavern for many candle marks, some of which were taken by Aderri and Ailith catching up on the cycles that had been missed between the two. Ellys was content to watch the women, though the more she drank, the less her gaze moved away from Aderri's smiling face.

Despite Ellys's metabolism, she'd imbibed so much mead that she was completely in her cups by the time the tavern was set to close. Ailith returned to their table after seeing the last person out of the public room. She took one look at the tipsy warrior and said to Aderri, "Good luck."

Aderri smiled. "I won't need it."

Ellys stood from the table abruptly. "Will it disrupt your stable if I go visit my steed?"

"It shouldn't, why?"

"I like to say goodnight to Rocc when we're separated for too long." She felt an embarrassed flush spread across her cheekbones.

Ailith shrugged. "It should cause no problems."

Aderri rose as well. "Would you like me to come with?"

"I'll be fine." Ellys was still looking at them when she turned away and promptly tripped over a chair leg, stumbling. Ellys turned the stumble into a forward roll and popped to her feet as if she'd meant to do it all along. She spun back and grinned at Aderri. "See? Fine!" Then she strode a dozen paces to the door and exited before anyone could say a word.

Ailith watched as the door shut behind her then looked back at Aderri, who continued to stare after Ellys. Her words were quiet, for Aderri alone. "How long into this romantic farce before you fell in love with her?"

Caught out, Aderri schooled her expression before responding. "Whatever do you mean? You know she's coming with me to meet my Clan."

A hand settled over Aderri's atop the scarred wood table. "What I know is *you*. I'm well aware that her coming home with you is nothing but a sham. You've stated too many times your need to remain untethered, to see the world and collect as much knowledge as your dragon brain could hold. Not only that, but her guild patch is turned inside out, meaning she's taken on a mission."

Aderri frowned and attempted to maintain the ruse. "It could also mean that she's merely not open to a patron right now. And perhaps I've finally grown tired of wandering."

"Never."

"Then maybe I've collected all I can hold, and Ellys and I crossed paths at the right time."

Ailith shook her head. "Closer, but still not the full truth."

Aderri sighed and slumped in her chair. After nearly one hundred and fifty cycles of friendship, even with a decades-long absence from each other's lives, Ailith knew her too well. "Fine. She's a hired guild sword that I paid to see me here from Longoria."

"And?"

"And for the promise of extra gold, she's agreed to play my suitor to explain to the Clan my long absence."

Her friend crowed in triumph. "I knew it! Aderri n'all Dracona would never simply settle in to Clan expectation so easily."

Aderri glanced wistfully toward the door that Ellys had gone through candle drops before. "Of course not." When she looked back at Ailith, Aderri was well and truly caught out. Ailith knew.

"You never answered my original question though."

Aderri propped her chin against her fist, peering at Ailith through lowered lashes. "I wouldn't call it love, more like…extreme interest."

"Infatuation maybe?" Aderri looked thoughtful then nodded. "And her?"

"I know she's attracted, but from what I've observed, the woman can be as randy as a stag in spring. I'm sure she's wanted to bed plenty along her path. And unfortunately for me, I'm merely a patron to her, a means to more coin. Besides, she is a widow and has shown no indication that she's open to romance after losing the love of her life."

"Hmm. Much about her makes sense now. You know I always recognize buried grief when I see it. And I wouldn't be too sure about lack of feeling on her part. The two of you have fate stamped upon your souls, much the way a coin is stamped on both sides. I think you're more intertwined than you realize."

"You know I don't believe in fate, 'Lith."

"Neither does Ellys apparently, yet here you are."

Aderri glanced toward the door. "Yes. Here we are."

Ailith reached across the table and squeezed both of Aderri's hands in a familiar gesture from long ago. "Your elf is stubborn. Clearly, Ellys is so blinded to all but her past that she refuses to see that love is everywhere. It's not a finite thing to be had and lost. Her understanding of such things will come upon her slower because it has to wade through a history of grief."

"What are you saying?"

"Give her time. She'll show you soon enough how she feels."

Aderri inclined her head. "I'll heed your words as your insight has never steered me wrong before. And time is one thing we both have aplenty."

Chapter Thirteen

The stable at the rear of the inn was dark, but two of the three moons had risen, and that was enough for Ellys to see her way to Rocc's stall. Evidence of Rocc's favorite game lay on a table close by. Fearing the steed was asleep, she whispered into the near darkness, though in her state of inebriation it wasn't so much a whisper as a quiet shout. "Rocc."

Keep your voice down, do you want to wake Josten?

Ellys honed in on Rocc's familiar exhale of breath and made her way to the steed's side. The door had been left open, as was usual when Rocc made her voice, and thereby her intelligence, known. Ellys embraced her friend's neck, lovingly running her hands through Rocc's silky mane. "Sorry. I've missed you, old friend."

You're bung-soaked. Have you spent the entire evening in the tavern? She wuffed against Ellys's shirt. *At least you smell better than when we arrived.*

"Aderri and I had a soak in Ailith's private bathing room. It was—" She abruptly pulled back and met Rocc's large liquid gaze. "Did you know Aderri is an amazing kisser?"

Roccotári wheezed in her own brand of laughter. *Not intimately, no. But I gathered that from your encounter a few days ago. I take it you've been 'practicing' again?* Ellys nodded and felt a dopey grin on her face. *You've had more to drink than I thought. It wasn't that Fenwith's Fire, was it?*

Ellys stroked the top of Rocc's soft muzzle with her left hand. "No. Cuon's Tears."

Oh?

"Ailith is a selkie who has lost her pelt."

Oh. The name of the inn makes sense now. Sadness and more poured from the elven steed straight to Ellys's heart. If anyone understood what it meant for a magical creature to lose a part of themselves, to lose connection to the place they felt most at home, it would be Rocc. After all, because of her bond to Ellys, it would be a very long time before she could return to the Sacred Grove within the Ethereal Forest, the place of origin for her kind.

"Yes. There is great imbalance there, but I don't know how one would help her with it stolen away so long ago. Not to mention this contract remains hanging over my head. I can right no wrongs so long as I have this last task to perform. Barring the gold we'll receive, the rest seems like a wasteful few moons." Even as Ellys said the words aloud, a deeper part of her knew they were false. She wondered if the prophesy would still come true if she was only lying to herself.

But we've both made a new friend and a dragon shifter is a very good friend indeed.

"True."

And have you considered that completing your contract is creating balance of a sort?

Ellys gave her a curious look. "How do you mean?"

Rocc nudged Ellys's breastbone with her nose. *Think on it. Aderri's purpose in this life is to accumulate knowledge. She's as much a dragon in that regard as any I've met before. But due to the unique circumstances tied to her Clan and this land, she could not leave and fulfill her destiny. By giving her an alibi, you are maintaining the balance.*

"I don't believe in destiny."

Laughter sounded in Ellys's mind. *That doesn't make it less true.*

Ellys sighed. "I don't like the way this contract makes me feel."

I think you do. The steed got a light shove for her mental response.

"You know what I mean! Aderri…she…I'm just so twisted inside. Maybe I need a good tupping to clear my head."

Another snort with an added hoof to the wooden stable floor as emphasis met Ellys's denial. *You don't need a minx in the moss. You need to stop acting the ass and look at the situation objectively. You like her.*

"So? Of course I like her. It's been more than a moon of traveling together, and I'd like to think we've become friends. And stop calling me a donkey. I'm not stubborn."

Not stubborn? Ellys, if you were water, you'd flow uphill just to prove a point.

Ellys grinned but conceded as some of the mead began to fade from her system. "Perhaps. But that doesn't mean anything when it comes to my friendship with Aderri."

What I'm trying to say, and don't take my head off with one of those blasted swords for it because you know I'm only saying this out of love, but I think your heart is moving on whether or not your head agrees.

A loud gasp sounded through the stable, causing more than one horse to whicker. Ellys stepped back from Rocc, losing contact with her bondmate completely. "Move on? Gwyn was the love of my life."

Rocc closed the distance between them again. *Ellys, love is not finite. A creature isn't born with a limited amount to be doled out to one person or another. Love is boundless, and whether or not any of us wish to admit it, we are capable of a multitude of life's loves. Take it from someone who is many times your age. Yes, each of our great loves will be unique in their own way, but they are all connected to your heart just the same.*

"I…uh…but I don't love her though?"

Are you asking me or telling me? Much like Aderri, I've read various Sky Tomes across the six nations, and your cycle of birth was auspicious for many reasons. Fate is not done with you. Your destiny didn't end with Gwyneth. It was only beginning.

Ellys sucked in a breath as grief momentarily crashed over her in a wave like the ocean. Then she let the breath out slowly, and the feeling ebbed away. "I wanted it to end with her."

Rocc lipped at Ellys's hair affectionately. *I know you did, cara. I was there to help you heal after. But you were meant to do many great things. You've helped maintain the balance for nearly one hundred cycles, not to mention you still have your Quest of Toroc, assigned long ago and left unfinished.*

The warrior grumbled. "You know I've searched everywhere for this blasted 'Phrenic Flame' and have yet to find it let alone warm myself by it. Besides, that was another impossible dream I gave up on since it was worthless to me."

It was never worthless if it meant connecting with your true self. Do you still want to be one of Toroc's Battling Monks?

"It's been so long since my training, I'm really not sure."

What do you want, Ellys? If you can't say the words, then close your eyes and think it for me.

"Fine." Ellys closed her eyes and the image of Aderri, head thrown back in laughter came to her first. Joy radiated around the other woman in the memory from one of their evenings spent tossing the bones. The image was quickly replaced by one of Aderri nude in the tub across from her just a few candle marks before. Then the kiss took over all other thoughts.

Rocc wuffed and leaned her shoulder into Ellys's side. *Looks like you know well enough to me. Perhaps you should do something about it.*

"I'm under contract, and you know guild law as well as I."

Rules can be broken.

Ellys snorted quietly, conscious of the stable hand that was most likely sleeping nearby. "And you're supposed to be a creature of orderly, magical nature."

Even the laws of magic can be bent to the wills and whims of fate. Good night, Ellys, you should get some rest for the journey tomorrow. There's still much to prepare for in your role as Aderri's suitor. Rocc's parting comment left Ellys with a lot to think about.

"Oh, we did plenty of preparation tonight. I think we're good."

I'm sure you did. Even so, you need your sleep. Go on now— She gave a little shove with her head. *Off with you, and leave this poor, noble steed to her rest.*

"Noble steed my ass—ouch!" She got a light bite to the shoulder and rubbed it indignantly. "Fine, I'm going. I'll see you in the morning, old friend."

We're halfway there already.

Ellys glanced out the stable window nearest to them and saw the third moon breaking the horizon over the ocean. "So we are." She quietly made her way back to the inn and to the room she shared with Aderri, her head and heart stuffed full of emotions and fears of both the future and the past. Heartfelt discussions with Rocc often left her in such a state. The mead and spirits certainly didn't help.

A well-trained warrior, Ellys entered the room silently with the barest *snick* as the door latched shut. Even so, she found Aderri gazing at her in the moons' light of the open shutters. "Hi."

Aderri's voice was equally as quiet. "Hi. Did you have a nice visit with Rocc?"

Ellys began stripping down to don her sleep shift. "It was fine. She seems well cared for, and I saw a Knights and Knaves board near her stall, so I suspect she was schooling poor Josten while we were in the tavern."

"Does she play well then?"

Ellys turned her back to the bed as she undressed the rest of the way and slipped the sleep shirt on. Even though she knew Aderri could easily view her nudity in the low light, it made Ellys feel better if she couldn't see those flaming eyes watching her with desire. Rocc had brought too many things to the surface, and Ellys was afraid of another improper night whilst sharing a bed. She turned back when she was dressed and slipped under the coverlets. "She's nearly a thousand cycles old and a fiend with strategy. What do you think?"

"Are you okay?"

"I'm fine."

"I could make a joke about how fine you are, as you've used the word twice in a handful of candle drops, or I could ask you not to lie to me."

Ellys turned so she was facing Aderri on the bed. It was a decent enough size at least, better than most of the inns they'd stayed at until that point. And of course it was deliciously warm since Aderri must have gone to bed shortly after Ellys went to visit Rocc. "Lie to you?"

"You know what I am, Ellys. There are at least ten ways I can tell you're lying to me right now—"

With inhibitions lowered due to an evening filled with drinks, as well as her deepest emotions roiling near the surface, the truth spilled from Ellys's lips without a second thought. "No, I know *who* you are. What you are doesn't matter to me because you're my friend and one of the most amazing people I've met in generations."

Aderri closed her eyes. "Thank you."

Her face was awash with hope, and Ellys tried her best to ignore it. "And because of that, I do owe you honesty. I'm not completely fine. Rocc brought up some unfinished things from my past tonight, some emotions I thought I'd long conquered. Being so deep in the cups upset my emotional balance for the unexpectedly heavy discussion."

Aderri responded, "Despite your self-proclaimed stamina and half-elven heritage, you did seem particularly affected tonight."

"I drank a dozen mugs of mead if I drank one."

Aderri laughed quietly. "And a pip of tears."

"Yes, and that blasted pip. I can safely add that to my list of things I never want to drink again."

More laughter. "Do you want to talk about it? Whatever unfinished business Rocc brought up that has you so melancholy, I mean. I can feel it, you know. Your sadness."

"I assumed. And the subject was my unfinished quest, along with a few other things. Rocc asked if I still wanted to be a Battling Monk."

"Do you?"

Ellys closed her eyes. "I don't know. I thought I did for many cycles, then I met Gwyn and lost her. After that, not a lot mattered other than maintaining the balance and taking care of Rocc."

"And now?"

Ellys opened her eyes and could see little sparks of flame dancing in each of Aderri's pupils. Emotion filled her chest once again, and she swallowed. "More things matter, as I suspect you know, but I'm afraid my quest is a mystery I'll never solve."

"What if you did?"

What was left unsaid between them was that deeper connections didn't matter if Ellys were to dedicate the rest of her life to the Binary Goz and tie her soul to a monastery.

"I suppose I probably would return to the place I grew up for induction."

"Would anyone from your youth still be alive? What about the master that trained you, Camen Dru was it?"

"No one there at the time I left for my quest would still be alive, but they would have written it down in the Book of Orders, to be checked off upon my return."

"You said yourself that you've dedicated your life to maintaining the balance. With no one there who is familiar, is there a reason for you to complete this quest and return for induction? And would you take the Oath of Gender Balance if you do?"

"I suppose I could go to any temple to be added to their tome. There's really nothing left for me in Llofgroon. And truthfully?" Aderri nodded. "I have served Toroc just as well over the cycles on my own as I would within any monastery. My Goz knows my heart better than any other. It's not forbidden to refuse one's Quest of Toroc, just frowned upon."

"And the vow?"

"At one time, I would gladly have taken it in service to Toroc. But it's been too many cycles, and I am what I am. I've never felt a particular pull to label and declare it, and I've grown comfortable within this identity. Even so, I'd probably still do it."

Aderri asked, "Why does induction pull you so?"

"Roccotári."

"Ellys…I don't understand."

She tried to explain. "I would do it for Rocc. If I took the oath and became one of Toroc's Battling Monks, we could live at any monastery. I could maintain the same level of service to Toroc, but Rocc would have a more stable life." Aderri laughed louder than she should have, and it took a heartbeat for Ellys to get the pun she herself had made. "Cute, but you know what I mean. She gave up a lot to bond to me."

"Wasn't the bond sealed the moment your father died? It's not like she had a choice."

"That doesn't make it less of a sacrifice. And the bond was never intended for a half-breed like me. Roccotári begged Queen Ardruel not to sever it. She pleaded out of love and respect, and in memory of my father. I will always do what I can to make sure she knows her worth in my life."

Aderri reached down, tangled their hands together, and gently squeezed Ellys's fingers. "It shows."

Ellys's gaze softened in appreciation of the gesture. "What about you? Are you anxious to get this visit finished so you can go back to traveling the land in search of knowledge?"

"I suppose."

"You don't sound sure."

Aderri looked away toward the open window where one moon slowly sank from view within the frame. "Much like you, I, too, have done some soul-searching tonight. It's just…I didn't realize how lonely I was until I began traveling with you and Rocc. Despite how insufferable you are at times…it's been nice."

"Thank you, I think. And I know what you mean. I want you to believe, contract or no, I count you as a true friend now. Whatever you need, just send word and I'll come help to the best of my ability. And perhaps sometime down the road, we'll find our paths align again for another adventure."

Aderri smiled. "I may just hold you to that." She leaned over and deposited a kiss to Ellys's cheek much the way Ellys had done to her earlier, then closed her eyes. "Goodnight, Ellys. I hope Somna sees you sweetly through the night."

"The same to you." Ellys gazed at Aderri long after she heard the other woman's breathing settle into the gentle rhythm of slumber.

Her head and heart were a confusing roil of emotions that prevented her own dreams until the first moon dropped below the horizon.

****

The next morning dawned much too early for Ellys's sleep-deprived mind, but confusing dreams and racing thoughts woke her before she was ready. Her head ached, probably from the pip of tears the night before. It was certainly a potent brew. Aderri was still asleep so Ellys quietly slipped from the bed and dressed. Aderri finally stirred when Ellys was sliding her second sword into its sheath.

"Ellys?"

"Everything is fine. It's early still. You should get more sleep. We have a few candle marks until we were planning to leave."

Aderri opened her eyes a mere slit to peer at Ellys in the dim light of the room. "Where are you going?"

"To clear my head." Aderri's gaze remained unwavering, so Ellys elaborated. "There's an area in the courtyard behind the inn that's large enough for secaeli. I noticed it last night." Aderri didn't relax from where she'd sat upright slightly and gripped the coverlets. She had mentioned often enough how much she enjoyed watching the sword dance.

"Are you sure?"

"Stay and enjoy Ailith's hospitality a bit longer. We both went to bed late, so there's no harm in getting a little more rest. Besides," she said and winked at Aderri, "you can watch me perform the warmup some other morning."

Aderri looked confused at Ellys's insistence but nodded. "Okay."

"Good. To make it up to you, on one of the nights between Noth and Dracona, I'll show you the full dance we reserve for festivals." She'd hoped Aderri would give it a pass so she could work through her emotions. Having the subject of those confusing thoughts so near would do little to give her peace.

"You're so sure that's why I want to get out of bed, to watch some sweaty warrior swing around her swords?"

Ellys laughed at her indignation, feeling lighter already than she had in the past day. "You're not exactly subtle with your attraction."

Aderri smirked. "Neither are you."

"Fair enough. I'll come back here for my pack, let's say a candle mark after sunrise? I want time to go through the routine and do a quick rinse after. We can take first meal in the tavern. I'm sure the food will be just as good as it was last night."

"I'm sure it will be. Fine then." Aderri snuggled into the covers. "Balanced thoughts, Ellys."

All Ellys could see above the coverlets was a mass of flaming red curls. The darkness of Aderri's skin was lost to the shadows of the room. Ellys gave the other woman a fond smile. "Balanced dreams, Aderri." Then she strode from the room.

Morning activity had already begun as Ellys made her way through the kitchen. She exited a side door she'd discovered the evening before when she came back in after her talk with Rocc. It offered a quicker route to the stables and storage shed behind the inn. The silence across the open area nearest to the stalls was broken only by the occasional shifting horse or soft nicker in the fading twilight. She unsheathed both swords and caught a glimpse of the androgynous server, Doonie, watching from the shadows.

The warm-up exercise was as much an art form of the soul as it was a principle of war. As her blades flashed and spun in increasingly faster arcs, Ellys felt her heart open and mind empty of all unbalanced thoughts. Her speed increased as she sought enlightenment, and before she knew it, the exercise had come to an end. Blades flashed in a flurry of crisscrossing strokes until she finished in a lunge with one sword raised into the air and the other pointing straight in front of her in a forward thrust. It was the opposite placement as the first fundamental stance of secaeli, to show that all things come full circle in the end. What she discovered was nothing more than Rocc's truth from the night before.

Ellys stood breathing heavily for a few heartbeats, mute with resignation at the demands of her heart. She didn't move again until the sound of soft boots crunching on the stones of the courtyard caught her attention. She whirled around and assumed a defensive position, startling the approaching selkie.

"Where did ye learn all that?" Doonie asked.

Ellys was surprised that Ailith hadn't mentioned anything about her fealty to Toroc. They seemed...close. At least Doonie appeared as though they wanted to be close to Ailith. The innkeeper herself was harder to read. Ellys said, "I grew up in a monastery of Toroc and spent thirty cycles training, twenty of that in direct service to the binary Goz, before setting off on my own." She glanced at Doonie's short but muscular build. "Why do you ask? Are you a sword fighter?"

"I have rudimentary knowledge only, but I be needing more training."

Sensing something deeper than the mere itch to pick up a new skill, Ellys pressed them. "Why is that?"

"I...I want to find Ailith's pelt and bring it home to her."

Ellys's eyes widened at the immense undertaking. "Uh, that's...do you at least have an idea about where her late husband could have hidden it away?"

Doonie nodded. "I have some thoughts, and I plan to visit the sea oracle for advice. But if the quest takes me overland, I'm not sufficiently trained to defend meself if I'm caught by brigands."

"And you're prepared to travel what could be thousands of leagues away from the sea, looking for something that may be impossible to find?"

They gave a resolute nod. Ellys considered her options with such a limited amount of time left in Noth. She knew there was a local monastery in the city, though she'd never visited. Every capital across the six nations had monasteries dedicated to the Binary Goz of War. Making a decision, Ellys sheathed her swords and stepped forward. "If you find me a piece of parchment, a quill, and some wax, I'll write a sponsorship letter to the abbez of the Nothian monastery. With the letter, they will test your aptitude, then train you up to two cycles in whatever battle form you show mastery, be it blade or fist."

"I'd have to become one of yer Battlin' Monks then?"

"No, you don't have to become an acolyte. You'd be a guest, training at the temple for the allotted time under my sponsorship."

They looked shocked by the news. "Ye...ye would do that for me?"

"I would. I trust Aderri, she trusts Ailith, and Ailith trusts you. We've come full circle in a cycle of credence, and trust promotes Toroc's way, so I'm happy to oblige. Especially if you're actively seeking to right a wrong and bring balance into both your lives. That's a noble cause, and it's my lot in life to support such pursuits."

Doonie was quiet for a few heartbeats and more sounds filtered into the space behind the inn as people began waking for their day. "Thank ye." Doonie looked away from Ellys for a moment then spoke again. "I was afraid of her, ye know. Yesterday."

A dark brow rose in surprise. "Afraid of Aderri?"

"Yes. Our nation be one that's especially mixed, and the Clans er powerful. But in Muniers, that one in particular holds the most. They were given land many generations ago as a reward for defending the stronghold. In exchange, they must live in service to guard our coastline."

"That tells me you know who they are, but not why you're afraid."

They only whispered, "Clan Dracona is full of *dragons*. Dragons swallow us smaller creatures whole."

"You mean ocean creatures?"

"I mean all. Parents tell their young to behave or Dracona will get them. They say that the buffeting winds along the shore at night be naught more than the beat of their massive wings."

"You've met Aderri now. Do you still feel the same fear?"

Doonie laughed. "Now I think boggles hold more danger than the dragon shifters, at least if they all be like Ailith's friend."

Ellys chuckled with them. "Don't be too certain. I've seen that particular dragon bite the heads off men and roast them alive with flaming breath. They are dangerous, sure, but then so is any well-trained sword or poorly trained mage." Ellys let her words sink in then glanced to the sky and rising sun. "We'll most likely leave within the candle mark but will take first meal in the tavern. If you bring what I asked for, I'll write out the letter before we go."

For the first time since Ellys had met them, they had a fire of determination in their dark brown eyes. "I will, and thank ye again."

"Maintain the balance, and no thanks will be necessary."

Doonie nodded and slipped through the door that Ellys had exited earlier, leaving Ellys to dunk and rinse her head from the fresh rain barrel near the corner of the inn. At least some of the pain in her head had lessened with the pumping blood, though lack of sleep and lingering effects of that blasted pip kept her from feeling fully battle ready. It was sure to be a long day if food didn't help. She refused to ask Rocc to heal what was due to her own stupidity.

Aderri was already packed and gone from the room when Ellys stepped inside, so she took a few moments to be sure her gear was in order before leaving the space behind. Typically, a good meal and some juice would finish the job of restoring her to full health thanks to her elven heritage, though it was possible that Ailith's magical pip of spirit could cause the ill effects to linger longer than normal.

Ellys made her way through Ailith's private residence and back into the tavern proper. She found Aderri right away, studying a scroll at the same table they'd been gaming at the night before. A large platter of fruit, nuts, and roasted meat sat to her left. Aderri suddenly looked up as if she could sense Ellys's presence in the room, and Ellys thought that perhaps it was one of the many talents possessed by the dragon shifter.

Aderri smirked when Ellys settled into the same seat she'd occupied the night before. "It took you long enough."

"I'd tell you what you could stuff and where, but you'd probably enjoy it. I need food and something sweet to drink. I got caught up in conversation with Doonie outside, but by Toroc, now I'm in need of something to soothe my aching head."

"Feeling your cups, are you?" Aderri waved her hand to garner the attention of a new server while Ellys groaned and lowered her head to the table, abruptly feeling her lack of sleep on top of doing secaeli without any food in her belly.

"I've had significantly more spirit in a single sitting and not felt as poorly. I'm pretty sure it was the pip."

"Or the knock to the head."

Ellys mumbled, "Same difference. I'm sure breaking my fast will take care of all but the exhaustion. I'm fairly knackered."

It didn't take long to request some juice and a bowl of porridge. In the meantime, Aderri shoved her platter toward her companion so they could share. Ellys could feel Aderri's eyes on her as she scooped up a few pom berries and tossed them into her mouth. She gave her companion a grateful smile. "Thank you."

Ellys's own victuals were placed on the table in good time, and she made short work of the meal. Doonie arrived halfway through with the promised supplies, and Ellys took a break to write the letter of sponsorship. She pulled a different ring from her waist pouch and held the wax above the folded crease of the letter.

Aderri watched curiously and raised a brow at Ellys's request. "Can you melt this for me?"

"Sure."

A heartbeat later, the wax dripped enough for her to seal the letter properly, then Ellys returned the ring to her pouch. She held the letter out to Doonie. "Good luck, friend." Doonie glanced at Aderri, gave a nod, and scurried out with the letter tucked into the front of their shirt. Ellys slurped a large spoonful of porridge, ignoring the dribble that ran down her chin and dripped back into the bowl. She addressed Aderri's obvious curiosity mid-chew of her second bite. "They want to learn sword work, so I offered to sponsor them to the local monastery for two cycles of training."

"Did they say why?"

"Apparently, they want to go on a quest to find Ailith's stolen pelt. As it is a task I've already mentioned that needed balance, I had no choice but to lend aid however I was able. I wish them all the luck in the world."

"As do I. It's a good thing you did for Ailith and Doonie, Ellys. I know balance is important to you."

"It is, but…"

"But what?" Aderri prompted.

Ellys gave her a look of open honesty. "But Ailith is also your friend, and I know she means a lot to you. I did it for you, too."

The moment was weighted as the two maintained eye contact, neither admitting to the stirred feelings that had begun to uncurl like swirls of smoke inside them. A slamming door somewhere upstairs disturbed their intent focus on one another. Aderri shook herself physically then reached into her satchel and pulled out her map of Muniers. "We're about five days out from Clan lands."

The food and juice fueled Ellys's physical equilibrium, and her humor returned on its heels. "Faster if neither of us wants to sit for a few days after we arrive."

Aderri groaned. "By Cassyn, don't remind me. At least Rocc healed the pain she created with her fast pace and indomitable stamina."

"It's always a wild ride when she gets like that."

A familiar voice said, "Wild rides, indomitable stamina…I'm surprised you could do more than fall into bed with the state poor Ellys was in last night." Ailith had finally made an appearance, much to Ellys's chagrin.

"I was up long before you lot, thank you very much."

"'Lith," Aderri said in a warning tone.

"Ai, don't be so serious. You know I'm only joking. It's obvious that your elf is feeling my tears. I doubt she would have been capable of tupping had the two of you been in a legit romance."

Ellys abruptly sat up in her chair, startled. She spun her gaze to Aderri. "She knows? Bollux!"

Aderri smoothed her forearm with a caress. "Fear not. Ailith knows when to keep her tongue from wagging."

"And when to let it fly." As if to prove her lascivious point, Ailith wiggled the organ in question at Ellys.

Ellys scrubbed her face with both hands, ignoring the innkeeper's taunt. "It's too early for this."

Both Ailith and Aderri laughed at the put-upon woman, but Aderri said, "She's right. How much do we owe you for your hospitality?"

Ailith gave her an indignant look. "Owe me? Friendship is a coin all on its own, and I've told you before that you'll never have to pay in my place."

Ellys tried to do the honorable thing, even though she wouldn't be the one paying. "But this is your business. Surely you can't just give away free nights to all your friends."

Ailith wagged a finger at her. "Ah, but you didn't stay at the inn. You were guests in my home. And your tales alone were worth a wee bit of soap and some mugs of mead."

"But it was a lot of mead." Ellys tried to reason.

"Bah." Ailith waved her hand around. "The price of nectar is inconsequential when you dwell in the land of honey the way I do. Mead is cheap."

Aderri spoke up. "What about the tears?"

"Those are worthless, paid for by only one. Now if you don't mind, I'd like to leave that sorrowful subject alone until the next sixty-cycle visit."

Aderri pushed the empty platter toward the center of the table and stood, quickly followed by Ellys. The innkeeper rose in a more leisurely fashion.

"Well enough, my friend." Aderri stepped closer to Ailith and gave her a tight embrace before pulling back again. "It was good to see you, 'Lith. I'm glad we got to catch up."

"I feel the same way. Now it's your turn." She stepped toward Ellys and before Ellys could react, pulled her into a quick embrace as well.

"Barring war, conscription, or any other unfortunate circumstance, be sure to stop back here on your way out of Muniers."

Ellys gave her a curious look. "How do you know she's leaving again?"

Ailith jerked a thumb in Aderri's direction while the woman in question looked on. "This one has wings, and ye can no more pin her down than you can a cloud." She turned to Aderri. "Besides, fate has been pulling you away from the Clan for cycles, so who are any of us to say nay?"

Aderri frowned. "You and your talk of fate again. I'd more likely take my chance with the bones than some grand destiny."

Ailith gave them a mysterious smile. "Perhaps they are one and the same, hmm?"

Chapter Fourteen

Rather than going to the stable to retrieve Rocc, they found her just outside the door with her tack and saddlebags in place. *What took you so long? I've been fed, brushed, and dressed for the past candle mark.*

Ellys snickered at the "dressed" comment while Aderri gave her an amused look. "Have you been standing out here the entire time?"

Of course not. Rocc nodded her big head toward the broad expanse of water that they could see a fair distance away across the main southerly road. *I took a walk across to the shoreline and cantered along the beach for a bit.*

"Was there much to sea?" Ellys looked back and forth between both companions. "*Sea*...get it?"

Aderri groaned, a sound that matched the one Rocc made in Ellys's head. "You are the worst. Why do I put up with you again?"

Ellys drew herself up to her full, not inconsiderable height and gave Aderri a flourishing bow. "Because I am a Grand Master of Toroc's Blades, wielding ever-sharp elven swords and riding the most loyal of steeds across all six nations. And we are at your service, Lady Aderri n'all Dracona."

Rocc sent a strong blast of air in Ellys's direction. The exhale was so hard that it flapped the lips in front of her equine teeth. *It's a good thing horses can't throw up because that was a pompous, big-headed, and truly nauseating display.*

Ellys and Aderri froze and slowly turned to stare at Rocc.

What? What did I say?

Ellys burst into uncontrollable laughter. "You...you, Goz—" Aderri joined her though it was a little more restrained. Neither could speak to explain through their mirth.

What in the six nations is so funny?

It took a few candle drops of Rocc fuming, but eventually Ellys was able to bring her laughter under control after wiping away a few tears. She looked to Aderri, who in turn seemed to be trying her best to appear innocent. "Do you want to tell her or should I?"

Rocc stepped closer and rammed her head into Ellys's sternum, causing Ellys to stumble back a few steps. *Abbad take you both. Explain already.*

"You just, uh, called yourself"—Ellys looked around dramatically to make sure no one was close enough to hear then whispered—"a horse."

The prideful elven steed snorted angrily before spinning on her hind hooves and setting off down the road. She left Ellys and Aderri with one parting thought in their heads, clearly directed at Ellys. *You're an ass.* It only made them laugh harder.

They walked along for almost a candle mark with Roccotári far ahead and nearly out of sight. "How long do you think she'll stay angry?"

Ellys shrugged. "Hard to say. I think she's more upset with herself than with us."

Am not!

The half-elf yelled to her steed, "Get out of my head, you nag! You're not supposed to listen to our conversation when you're purposely ignoring us."

Who says?

Ellys yelled again, "It's the rules!"

Rocc stopped on the road where she was and turned around to see them but didn't come any closer. *There are no rules. Ask Aderri.*

Ellys glanced to her right where Aderri paced along next to her then looked toward Roccotári, who grew larger to their sight the closer they drew. "Why ask Aderri?"

Rocc finally trotted toward them, closing the last few strides. *Because she is adagnitio. If there is a gaugin law or knowledge of such a thing in all the land, she has probably stumbled across it by now.*

Aderri snorted. "You certainly have a high opinion of my thirst for, and retention of, knowledge."

Rocc put one hoof out in front and lowered herself into a bow. *I have respect for any master of their craft.*

Ellys rolled her eyes at the display. She was tired of carrying her own pack, so she circled around near the back of the saddle when Rocc straightened again. "I'm a master…where's my respect? Hold still while I tie this on."

Oh yes, Grand Master DeEnsis, your wish is my command.

Aderri handed her own satchel to Ellys for cinching on top of the saddlebags. "Let it be said that one doesn't need an actual voice for a creature to make their sarcasm heard. Now if you two are quite finished, I'd like to put some distance into our day. I want to get this Clan visit over with as soon as possible."

They both mounted and Ellys spoke over Aderri's right shoulder. "Are you anticipating parting ways with us already?" Though she said the words in jest, part of her sorrowed that Aderri would say yes.

Aderri looked at Ellys out of the corner of her eye. "Not at all. I just—" She sighed. "Coming home to Clan Dracona makes me twitchy. I'm always worried that they won't let me leave again after, and there's so much left to learn of life."

"What happens if you go against their wishes?"

"Banishment, of course. Oh, and breaking a millennium of expectation."

Ellys sucked in a breath at the thought of her friend suffering such a fate. "That seems extreme."

Aderri slumped where she sat at the front of the saddle. "Ellys…that's just our way. The Clan can't risk everyone moving away, or even leaving for prolonged periods of time, or we would lose the territory and be no more."

"Surely they can't prevent everyone from leaving. The population would explode beyond what the land could sustain. Every elf knows the value of earth."

It's just the dragons that can't leave, isn't it? Because they are the true guardians of the coastline.

Aderri took a few heartbeats to answer. Her voice sounded sad and wistful. "Yes. Yet another reason to hate my heritage."

Ellys circled both arms around Aderri and gave her a hug from behind. "Don't worry, we'll take care of this so you can maintain your freedom. I promise to do right by you, to keep your situation balanced."

The words, "thank you," came back softly, almost drowned out by the strong breeze and raging waves of the sea where they crashed against the rocky shore near their current location along the road.

They followed the road southwest to Clan lands. Ellys thought about her love and history with Gwyn, as well as her growing feelings for Aderri. Feelings she hadn't fully realized until her conversation with Rocc the evening before.

Meanwhile, Rocc seemed content to swiftly walk along, and Aderri was quieter than usual.

That evening they made camp in a clearing near the road, and Ellys was the first to bring up Aderri's unusually low mood. They sat next to each other on the bedroll, as had become their habit over more than a moon of travel when forced to sleep outdoors. Ellys reached into her pack to pull out the bottle of wine she'd discovered in the saddlebags a few candle marks outside Noth. Aderri had said, "Ailith always enjoyed leaving little gifts and surprises for as long as I've known her."

Ellys removed the stopper to take a swig and passed it to her left. "After so long away from your Clan, will you know many people still?" Aderri was silent for a few heartbeats. She grabbed the wine bottle and drank after Ellys. They'd become so comfortable in each other's presence that neither bothered with their cups anymore unless they were sitting at a table, throwing bones.

"There are quite a few who I'll remember and who will remember me. Obviously, my immediate family, Dracona. My sibs from youngest to oldest are Gessy, Dlemna, Jorl, Bonvi, Wolstahd, and Cyvrus."

Ellys raised a dark brow at so many names. "And where are you in that mix?"

"I'm the second-eldest behind Cyvrus. I have many more Dracona kin, just not so closely related. The abundance of dragon numbers is what helps us patrol and defend the shore."

Despite all her travels, Ellys had never spoken so closely with someone who was a shifter and part of a Clan. And she'd never met a dragon before Aderri. Rocc beat her to the next question.

Who leads Clan Dracona? Is it a council of the various races, or is there just one who has final say? I've only visited single-race shifter communities. Clans seem like they would be…tricky.

Aderri snorted derisively at the question, seemingly to indicate that Rocc's choice of wording was too underwhelming to describe Clan politics. Ellys wondered if that was yet another reason Aderri seemed to hate her heritage.

"That's one word for it. Clan Dracona will always be led by a Dracona."

Ellys and Rocc spoke at the same time.

"Because you're biggest?"

Because you're oldest?

"No, because we hold the land. Centuries ago, Dracona came to the Twin Regents' aid, promising fealty and protection in exchange for land. And on that land, they welcomed all lone shifters who had nowhere else to go. Some obviously were loners for very dark reasons, and they were quickly driven away or dispatched, depending on their nature. But for all those willing to work and dedicate their lives to the Clan, they were given steadings and a family that would be there when they needed it."

Ellys said, "It sounds nice, if a little insulated."

Aderri gave her a rueful smile and took another drink of wine. "And therein lies the problem for a knowledge-seeking dragon with a passion for travel."

Rocc blew out a loud breath from where she stood nearby. Her dappled silver coat looked orange in the firelight. *Tired of seeing the same long stretch of shoreline every day?*

"Yes."

"You never answered who was actually in charge."

Aderri gazed into the fire, and her shoulders slumped. "The Clan leader is called the Drakaina. The current holder of that title is Zevieri Dracona."

"Is that your father?"

Aderri met her gaze, pupils flaming brighter than Ellys had seen any other night. "My mother. Clan Dracona follows maternal lines of succession. My father's name is Koldaht. His only role in Clan leadership is as mother's advisor."

Ellys's eyes widened with shock. "But that means—"

You're next in line to lead the Clan. What happens if you don't return or are banished as you fear could happen?

"My official title is Riki, Inheritor of the Mound. If law dictates that I cannot ascend, then my sister Bonvi would be next on the Mound."

"I—" Ellys shook her head slightly. "There's so much information that I fear I'm not keeping up. What is the Mound? Is that like a throne? Do you want to lead the Clan? Does Bonvi?"

Aderri leaned over to shove Ellys with her shoulder. "You're like a child with your curiosity."

Or an adagnitio dragon.

Aderri pointed at Rocc. "Okay, I'll give you that one. The Mound is what we call the seat of leadership. The Drakaina is aided by a council of shifters so that all the species are represented. My mother will lead until she dies, steps from the Mound, or the council votes for her to descend. In that case, the mantle of Drakaina will pass to the next Dracona in line of succession, which is me."

"What happens if the Drakaina has no, uh, hatchlings? Say they aren't mated, are paired to the same gender, or mate outside their species altogether?"

Very subtle.

Ellys tried her best to be casual and ignore her bondmate. "Would the mantle of Drakaina pass to a sib's hatchlings?"

Aderri shook her head. "Dragons are capable of parthenogenesis."

Ellys scowled. "Speak plain so someone who hasn't spent a hundred cycles on the inside of a library can understand."

"We can produce eggs without the need of another. There are serpents and other creatures with the same ability. As such, no Drakaina has ever failed to produce hatchlings."

Fascinating. Dragon shifters lay eggs in their shifter form rather than live childbirth in their two-legger form?

"Yes. We have to stay in dragon form for upwards of a half-moon until we produce a single egg. Then it takes about two moons until the hatchling breaks through."

Ellys grunted. "Do dragons have to sit on the egg like a bird?"

Aderri scoffed. "No, the egg sits in a padded nest near a constantly tended hearth fire. Where do you get your ideas from? Have you seen me in dragon form? I'd crush an egg!" All three laughed at that. "Shifter offspring don't happen very often and are considered a blessing to the Clan. That's why we have the *Cognoment*, or naming ceremony, that usually occurs two moons after birth. Or in the case of Dracona, two moons after the hatchling emerges."

Suddenly much about Aderri's request for a suitor and her nervousness the closer they got to Clan lands made sense. Ellys gave her a knowing look. "You think you'll be under a lot of pressure to stay, don't you? But the current Drakaina, your mother…she must have centuries left to rule, right?"

"Yes. And while it's true that no one will be needed to take the Mound for a very long time, dragons like certainties."

Ellys handed back the last bit of wine. "But unpredictability is an adventure in and of itself."

"Truer words were never spoken." Aderri finished the wine and gave the bottle to Ellys who replaced the stopper. Then after taking a few candle drops off in the bushes to ready themselves for sleep, they slipped between the layered bedrolls.

Ellys shivered when Aderri's warmth began to seep into her skin. "Thanks for explaining everything tonight. It helps me understand you a little better."

They gazed at each other in the firelight. Two of the three moons had risen. Aderri asked, "And do you want to understand me better?"

"Of course. The more I understand you and where you come from, the better I can help."

"Oh."

She looked disappointed, and Ellys's stomach knotted. "Oh, what?"

"So, it's just about earning your coins then?"

Ellys's voice was firm when she answered. "No. It's not just about earning my coins. It's about doing the right thing, maintaining the balance, and most of all, being your friend. I'm not a complete cad, you know. I feel closer to you than I've felt with anyone else in a very long time." She paused then added, "But yes, I still need the gold. After all, Rocc has to eat and she's kind of a pig about apples."

I heard that.

"Good. Stop eavesdropping."

Aderri laughed and Ellys was glad to see the beautiful smile return. "Thank you."

"You can thank me by turning over and facing the other way to keep me warm. It's still blasted cold at night."

Aderri did as requested and faced away from the fire, relaxing as Ellys moved closer to snuggle in from behind. Her words were whispered into the darkness. "Not nearly as cold as it used to be."

No, it's not. Sweet dreams, Aderri.

Ellys remained relaxed, despite Aderri's words having set loose another wave of emotion to batter at the ragged wall around her heart.

Aderri's quiet voice whispered into the night, "Safe watch, Lady Roccotári."

****

The remaining days of their journey went by in the blink of an eye. Per Aderri's request, they spent their evenings talking about anything but the imminent Clan visit. She was worried for good reason, and Ellys was loath to upset the balance, so she let the topic fade after that first night, though curiosity about Aderri's family still clawed at her.

On a late afternoon, five days after departing Noth, Rocc stopped abruptly and blew out a nervous breath. *I smell a wolf.*

Aderri said, "That's because we crossed into Clan lands about a league back." She took time to pull her hood up, thus hiding her flame-colored red hair, and Ellys didn't question the reason why.

"How could you tell we're on Clan lands?"

"A shifter can tell when in the land of other shifters." Aderri apparently tried to be mysterious but Rocc ruined it.

There was a sign that said 'Dracona' some distance off the road a league behind us.

Ellys huffed in annoyance. "And neither of you thought to tell me?"

Rocc shook her withers and laughed in their heads. *I didn't think I needed to. After all, aren't you a Grand Master of Toroc's Blades, wielding ever-sharp elven swords, and riding the most loyal of steeds across all six nations?*

Aderri burst out laughing. "She's got you there."

A howl split the air, and Ellys made to draw one of her swords but was stopped by Aderri's squeeze to her thigh. "That won't be necessary. If we continue on, whoever is keeping watch will approach and confront us on the road before we get too close to the main shifter town."

"And that's a good thing?" Both Aderri and Rocc ignored Ellys's snarky comment.

A fox has been following us for the past half candle mark or so. Could it possibly be a friend of yours, Aderri?

"They could be. We had only one fox family the last time I was here, Chordata. Some of the smaller shifter species tend to be a little…leery with so many predators."

Ellys remembered Doonie's comment about Dracona—*Dragons swallow us smaller creatures whole.* Wisely, she didn't bring it up to Aderri. "That makes sense."

Aderri's prediction came true another twenty strides down the road as a wolf/person hybrid rushed out from the trees, snarling at them. The creature seemed taken aback when no one reacted with fear or panic. The roughened voice growled at them. "Who are you, and what is your business with Clan Dracona?"

Ignoring the threatening wolf shifter, Ellys spoke to Aderri. "I never realized there was a partial form when shifting. Can all of you do that?"

"The more powerful ones, sure. We can technically stop at any part of the change, though there are varying degrees of pain associated with that. The easiest shift pauses are at human, beast, and the midpoint between."

"I asked you a question!" The wolf-beast stomped.

Rocc stomped a hoof back. *I can do that, too. Now if you please, we're having a private conversation.*

The werewolf's eyes widened as they looked back and forth between the two riders. "Who said that?"

Suddenly, a small fox ran onto the road. Rocc swung her head in its direction. *That's the one I was talking about. I recognize the white blaze on its head.*

Shimmering enveloped the fox, and in a matter of moments, a man stood where there was once a small woodland creature. He was pale with russet-colored hair and very, very nude. Not expecting the dangling show, nor used to the casual nudity of shifters, Ellys wrinkled her lip. She waved her hand up and down, gesturing at the fox-man. "Can you put that away?"

The red-headed man scowled. "You seek out a shifter clan, yet you would disparage our natural state? If you're not comfortable with body parts, you can go back the way you came."

"Oh, I've found pleasure enough with all the body parts. Just give me a bit of candlelight, some wine, and a comfortable bed— oof!" Her words cut off when a sharp elbow connected with her mid-section.

"Bezol Chordata, do you always make assumptions about strange travelers?"

The man took a half step back. "How do you know my name?"

Aderri reached up to her hood and slowly lowered it. If anything, the sight of her familiar face and coloring had the opposite effect of calming the man's nervousness. He quickly lowered his head in a sign of respect before addressing her again. "My apologies, Riki. Are you…they said they were calling home all wanderers for the naming ceremony, but we weren't sure who would arrive in time. Are you stay—"

"Aderri, you came." Ellys hadn't noticed the werewolf change off to the side. But where there once was an upright creature with a dark brown pelt, there now stood a woman of middling cycles.

"By Cassyn, Seli!" Aderri motioned to Ellys that she wanted to get down so they both dismounted as the woman walked over. Ellys tried her hardest not to stare at either of the nude sentries.

The two women hugged and pulled apart again. Aderri turned to her travel companions. "Ellys and Rocc, this fine wolf is a friend from my youth. She even studied with me for a brief time in Noth. The trouble that Ailith, Seli, and I used to get up to…"

"Ailith? How is that old selk anyway? I'm assuming you came down from Noth. Is she still drinking her weight and serving up snark and beds in equal measures?"

Ellys laughed. "That's the most dead-on description I've heard."

Their reunion was interrupted by Bezol's gruff voice. "Seli, we need to get back to patrol. There's still a quarter day to go before we're relieved."

Seli looked back at Aderri. "Duty calls, I'm afraid. But I want to hear all about your adventures and meet these fine folks properly later, *adsequor*?"

Aderri smiled. "We will, I promise." With one last wave, Seli then Bezol changed back into their four-legger forms and took off into the trees, racing and yipping at each other.

"Well," Ellys said, "I'm relieved at the lack of bloodshed. That went better than I anticipated."

You're a donkey.

Aderri continued to stare in the direction her friend had run off. Ellys may have been a donkey, but she was still sensitive to Aderri's moods after traveling more than a moon together. "Do you miss them?"

Aderri turned and gave her a sad smile. "I do but I also know that I had to travel and seek knowledge. It's a feeling I've always had, and I don't regret it." She took a deep breath and let it out before continuing. "We should probably remount and ride. It's not far now, but it's best if we get there as soon as possible so we can settle in before all the questions start."

They retook the saddle, and for speed's sake, Rocc broke into a canter. Ellys didn't bother with reins; she rarely did. But she did wrap her arms around Aderri while the other woman held the pommel to avoid being bounced from the saddle. Ellys thought of the middle-aged woman and pitched her voice loud enough to be heard over Rocc's hoof beats. "Is Seli a lot older than you?"

"Younger." She turned her head and saw Ellys's surprised expression. "You know how it is, Ellys. It is the nature of those of us who are especially long-lived to leave everyone behind."

Her words threw Ellys into a memory from her past life. One night while sitting by the hearth fire, Ellys gazed at Gwyn's smiling, well-lined face and sorrowed to know their time would eventually come to an end long before she was ready. That was when she really understood the sort of loss that came with her half-elven heritage. Ellys kept silent for the rest of the ride, deep in thought. But one thing that whispered in the back of her mind was that she and Aderri were well-matched and could age together if both had an interest to explore real romance.

****

The road they were on continued through the forest for a while, then the surrounding land eventually grew sparser as the terrain turned to rolling hills. They topped one such hill, and Ellys asked Rocc to stop so she could look over the main Clan village. Aderri sat in silence as she took it all in. Eventually, they made their way down into the town proper. Plenty of people walked here and there, children played, and even a few animals wandered about. It looked much like any other village, until a great blast of air buffeted them from above and a massive dragon landed in a clearing at the town center.

Aderri spoke quietly. "Looks like it's time to earn your pay, darling. Are you ready?"

Ellys tightened her arms around Aderri's waist, pulled her into a warm embrace, and whispered in her ear, "It will be my absolute pleasure." Ellys was startled at the truth of her own words. Aderri stiffened for a heartbeat within the circle of her arms, and Ellys wondered if her friend felt that very truth with her empathy. She quickly pushed her feelings down again, aware that she'd been throwing out confusing emotions over the past handful of days, starting the morning they left The Stolen Pelt. Ellys was afraid that if she admitted to that little flame deep within her heart, it would crush the ember that she held for Gwyn.

Before Rocc had come to a full stop, shimmering surrounded the dragon, and the great beast shrank down to a nude woman with dark skin and flaming red hair to match Aderri's. Aderri motioned to dismount, and they climbed from the saddle. The shifter was upon them in a flash, throwing herself toward Aderri with nary a word spoken but plenty of tears. Aderri simply wrapped her arms around the crying woman and held tight. Ellys and Rocc could only look on.

The emotional reunion lasted a few candle drops until the two dragon shifters pulled apart. The stranger looked upon Aderri with unabashed joy. "You came!" Up close, the familial resemblance was obvious in the turn of their noses and shape of each woman's eyes. Ellys assumed she was close kin, probably a sib.

"Of course I came, Gessy. You know I wouldn't miss the chance to tease Cyvrus about a first-born snapping at his wyrm." Aderri pulled back farther to stand next to her sib, her arm loosely wrapped around Gessy's shoulders. "Ellys DeEnsis and Lady Roccotári, I would like you to meet my nestmate, Gestolde n'all Dracona."

"Nestmate? I thought you said—"

Rocc bumped her head against Ellys's shoulder. *She means her sib.* The steed bent her front legs to perform a majestic bow. *It is my pleasure to meet you, Lady Gestolde.*

Obviously hearing the words in her head, Aderri's sister looked delighted. "Oh my, you are magnificent! And you can call me Gessy. No one calls me the other except at formal functions. Can you talk to everyone that way?"

Rocc preened. *Only those intelligent enough to understand.*

Ellys grinned at seeing an exuberant younger version of Aderri. "Ignore her. Rocc is an elven steed and as such lets her superiority go to her head sometimes, a fact that I know quite well as her lineal bondmate." Ellys performed her own bow. "Though it really is a pleasure to meet you, Gessy."

Gessy laughed with unabashed abandon, much the way Aderri was prone to doing. "So handsome and funny." She turned to Aderri. "Are they the reason you've stayed away so long?"

Aderri gave Ellys and Rocc a fond smile. "Some of it. I know you just got off patrol and are probably fit to eat an entire low beast. The three of us still need to settle in and refresh after our journey down from Noth. What do you say we catch up later?"

"Papa will want to have a celebration for your homecoming."

"Isn't the naming ceremony celebration enough? I'd also wager mama wants no such thing."

Gessy waved off the remark. "She's too busy to plan anything, and the Cognoment isn't until next quarter moon. This is important right now."

"Quarter moon?" Ellys swallowed nervously when she realized she'd have to play the suitor so much longer. Yet there was another part of her thrilled at the idea.

"Yes, second full moon of Cervi. That's what the notice said."

Aderri gave Ellys an apologetic look. "They sent notices out with a prediction of timing based on when the egg was laid. Essentially I was given two moons to get back to Dracona in time for the ceremony, and I thought it would take longer to get out of Kuwyth."

Rather than be angry, Ellys was pleased when she realized what a prime opportunity she'd been gifted to gain more information about Aderri. "No worries. This will give me longer to get to know your family. Tell me, Gessy, do you have any good stories from Aderri's youth?"

"Of course I do. Why this one time, when Vizzy's chickens got loose—"

Aderri clapped a hand over her sister's mouth to stop what was sure to be an embarrassing story. "Okay, now that we've settled the timing, I'm taking Ellys and Rocc to my home. Tell papa and mama we'll come to the keep this evening."

"They're going to want to see you as soon as possible."

"A fact I'm well aware of. But we've been riding since early light, and I'd like to at least change into fresh clothes. Plus, Lady Roccotári needs to be taken care of as well. Do you think you could stop by the shop and pick up enough supplies to get us through our stay? I have some things in magical stasis, but we'll need a few fresh items." She looked toward Ellys and Rocc. "Eggs, grain, hmm, what else?"

Apples.

Aderri laughed at Rocc's input. "Of course, how could I forget apples?"

Ellys thought for what she might need in the coming quarter moon. "Mead and chava?"

"I have some chava in stasis, but we'll probably need more before we leave." Aderri turned back to her sister. "Some chava and perhaps a few jugs of mead and bottles of wine."

Gessy nodded. "No problem. I'll have them send a cart in the next couple of candle marks. Now, I've got to get dressed and fetch that meal before my stomach turns inside out. I burned a lot of energy today."

"How is the coastline with the land on the brink of war?"

"A blockade extends a few leagues out to sea from the coastal border. We have to fly farther out to be sure none of the Carthunian ships are trying to circle around and approach from the south. So far all is quiet, but it feels like the land is balanced on a blade's edge."

Aderri frowned. "I'm hoping Princess Ameelia returns to take over for King Arvol in the next few moons so this entire situation can be cleared up before a massive amount of bloodshed begins."

"Unfortunately," Ellys said, "it's already started in Carthune." She was thinking of the fiendish barrier and the blood magic that fueled it.

When Gessy opened her mouth, obviously to question the comment, Aderri shook her head and spoke first. "We'll fill you in later. There's a lot happening outside Muniers, and I may as well tell the story once to you and the rest of Dracona together."

"Fine then, until later." Gessy gave Aderri one last hug and turned to head down a different packed-dirt road. "See you later, Aderri, Ellys, and Lady Rocc."

Ellys looked at Aderri. "She seems fun. Does she live in the town? Where does she sleep?" Ellys was referring to a previous discussion about how some dragons prefer to sleep in their serpent form and others like sleeping as a human.

"Gessy is the town gossip and couldn't bear not to live where all the action is. I highly doubt that's changed much in the decades since I left. As to housing, she and my other sibs are a lot like me and prefer a soft bed inside a smaller home. My parents and one aunt are the opposite, which is why they live out at the keep."

"Is it generational then?"

Aderri considered the question. "In some respects, I suppose it is."

"And speaking of homes, you have a house here? And it's been, what, closed up for the last sixty-something cycles? How is it maintained? Wouldn't the wood rot or be vermin infested?"

Laughter burst from Aderri's lips and Ellys thrilled to see the joy brighten her face. "So many questions. Firstly, I'm a dragon and thus a predator, which means many vermin don't care for the smell of my place. Second, my home is made mostly from stone and magically protected, and my family maintains the land around it for me. But rather than talk about it, let's go see for ourselves."

She turned to Rocc. "I even have a small barn with stalls behind the house, protected the same way. You should be just as comfortable there. Or, if you wish, the house was made for easy accessibility by larger hooved creatures, and you're welcome to stay inside."

"Larger hooved—you let horses stay in your home?"

"No, we have a few centaur families in the village, as well as a variety of other shape shifters and hooved species, so the dimensions are such to accommodate most."

As much as I appreciate the offer, given the choice, I prefer to stay in more of an outside environment where I can feel the natural magic of the land all around me.

"I suspected as much but felt it necessary to offer."

Chapter Fifteen

It took the trio of travelers nearly half a candle mark to make their way to where Aderri lived at the edge of town. On the way there, Ellys observed that most of the homes within the village were built from stone, and she assumed it had something to do with the material's sturdiness, a proven necessity for certain shifter species. Aderri's domicile was larger than some of the others, but that made sense given the size of her other shape, as well as her relative importance within the Clan as Riki.

The home abutted a dense tract of forest, and Aderri led them around to the back where there was a stone and wood barn next to the tree line. It was large enough for a few horses. Rocc and Ellys waited while Aderri made multiple gestures in the air near the door and intoned, "*Vozzi, cuma, des, collahn, szhee!*" The door wavered to Ellys's sight then went back to normal.

Fascinating. Is that a sleeping spell with inorganic components?

Aderri looked pleased when she turned around to face them. "You recognized it then?"

Rocc wuffed. *Not the words, but I could see the lines of magic as they shifted and pulled away. They looked similar to a standard sleeping spell, but there were colors of earth mixed in.*

Ellys grew irritated at her bondmate and looked at her sharply. "I've known you for more than a hundred cycles, and you've never once mentioned that you're so knowledgeable on the subject of magic. Why?"

Would you discuss advanced sword fighting technique with a farmer? I think not. Magic isn't something you're familiar with, so it would do no good to engage you in long discussions on the topic.

Ellys made to retort, then shrugged as her irritation drained away. "Fair point."

Aderri said, "Come along you two. Let's get Rocc set up in a comfortable stall." She opened the large door, and they could see a good-sized space inside. There were two stalls and a hay loft, as well as storage for other equipment and feed. She pointed to each area on their way to the far stall.

"All latches in here are designed so intelligent beings, such as yourself, will be able to open them. The same goes for the inside of the big door." She turned to where Ellys was touching the pristine wood that had stayed solid for nearly seven decades without upkeep. "Can you gather deadfall from the woods and place it in the bin by the back door? Oh, and take the bucket around to the well at the stall side of the barn?" She pointed to where the end of the trough butted up to the external wall of the barn, above which was a small door. "Open that door from the other side to access the trough. It's a lot easier."

Ellys was impressed. "Smart."

"Even with plenty of shifter energy, that doesn't mean I or anyone else wants to make multiple trips around the barn carrying buckets of water enough to fill this." She gestured toward a large trough that ran between the two horse stalls so both could access it. "While you're doing that, I'm going to cast an anti-vermin spell in here, then I'll put some straw in the stall and give Rocc a bit of the stored grain."

Ellys gave Rocc's muzzle an affectionate stroke. "Sure." Then she disappeared with the bucket out the door and out of sight.

Aderri climbed the ladder into the loft and threw a few armfuls of straw down into the left-most stall. Once she was back on the main level, she opened a storage bin. "I'll set you up with some hot mash once I get fresh supplies and leave a few apples within easy reach. Is there anything else you need?"

Rather than answer the question, Rocc changed topics completely. *I'd say we've all grown quite close over the past moon and a half, wouldn't you?*

Aderri paused what she was doing to give her full attention to the steed, unsure where the question was coming from or leading to. "Certainly. I consider both of you close friends after nearly two moons of traveling together. Why do you ask?"

Ellys has become very careful with who she trusts and opens up to since Gwyn. She may seem the rogue when it comes to matters of the heart, but she's really just the opposite.

Aderri smiled fondly. "I've kind of gathered that since getting to know her. She's a little uncouth when it comes to manners but rather sweet most of the time, honorable and selfless. For example, take her dedication to her long-lost love. Even that is admirable."

Rocc stepped closer to Aderri and nibbled her hair, and Aderri felt Rocc's pleasure with her empathy. *Indeed. And she tells anyone who cares to ask that the reason she doesn't search for love is because she found the greatest of her life cycles ago.*

A thought had been sitting at the back of Aderri's mind since hearing Ellys's tale of the day she lost Gwyn. "Something has been bothering me about Gwyn's death. I thought you met Ellys before she left the monastery. If you were there during her golden cycles with Gwyn, why didn't you heal her the way you healed Ellys after the attack in Carthune?" She didn't get a response for a few heartbeats and worried that perhaps it was too sensitive a topic for even Rocc to discuss. Aderri was about to apologize when Rocc's voice sounded softly within her mind.

She refused.

Aderri was shocked by the answer. "What?"

Gwyneth was near the end of her natural life when she fell ill. When I tried to heal her, she refused and her strength of will was great enough to prevent me from giving her life force. While it saddened me, I knew she was at the end of her cycles and within the proper balance of things.

Even if she weren't an empath, feeling Rocc's sadness with just the short telling of events, she would have sorrowed just the same. Aderri considered how Ellys must have felt a bit betrayed that her love didn't want to hold on. "How did Ellys take Gwyn's decision?"

She tried to perform decumora. Aderri didn't want to ask, suspecting the meaning based on context. Rocc explained anyway. *Ritual suicide. Ellys said that she and Gwyn were two halves of a whole and for her to remain alone broke the balance.*

Confusion stole over Aderri's face. "But…she's here now."

She possessed none of Gwyn's magical strength, and I…I couldn't let her go. She was my other half, and I couldn't lose her so relatively soon after losing her father.

Aderri closed the distance between them and wrapped her arms around Roccotári's neck to give comfort through touch. "I'm sorry that either of you had to go through that. It was an incredibly difficult loss compounded by Ellys's grief."

It was, but that's not why I brought up the subject of Ellys's lost love.

Aderri released the steed and stepped back. After hearing the story of her friend's painful past, she was more resigned than ever to give up hope of a romance. "If you're trying to warn me off from pursuing her, there is no need. I know where I stand in relation to her past and heart. Yes, I'm interested but I can't compete with a memory."

No, you can't. But then again, neither can Ellys.

"I don't understand."

The real reason she keeps everyone at arm's length is so she will never have to suffer a loss like the one she had before. She's afraid of love, fearful of finding a new love, that it will somehow displace the memory of Gwyn in her heart. What she doesn't realize is that we are all full of limitless potential and one love doesn't detract from another.

Aderri froze, too afraid to hope. The conversation was eerily similar to the one she had with Ailith days before. She wanted to hear more, yet at the same time, she didn't want to betray Ellys. "It's a completely understandable response, but are you going somewhere with this, Roccotári? It's one thing to tell me the tale of Gwyn's passing that I suspect others also know. But I don't want you to break any confidences with me where Ellys is concerned, I respect her too much."

I would never break her deepest confidences. You know that. But you can feel her emotions shifting, aligning with yours, can't you?

"I—" Aderri was going to deny her feelings but knew it was pointless when Rocc could read her just as well as she could read Ellys. "Yes. I've felt her opening up more over the past handful of days than in the moon previous. I just assumed she was happy that the job was nearly finished. Are you telling me that she's developing romantic feelings?"

I'm telling you nothing. That's something you'll need to ask her yourself. But don't expect full honesty if you're not prepared to give it. Rocc let the subject drop after that and stood patiently waiting for Ellys to return.

As if wishes alone had summoned her, Ellys walked through the door with a jaunty grin. "And done. The wood is stocked, and the trough filled with fresh water. After all, I wouldn't want my poor pony to get parched."

Rocc fake-charged her for a few steps then pulled up short. *Just for that, I'll tell every bard we meet about your moment with the snow fox.*

She shoved at Rocc's shoulder. "Like you don't already."

Fine, I'll tell Aderri's sister.

Ellys's eyes widened comically. "Hey now, I'm trying to make a good impression here." When Rocc kept up the weight of her gaze, Ellys finally relented. "Fine. I take it back. You are a magnificent steed and deserve your weight in apples each day."

That's better. Rocc snorted once then walked back to the stall for a drink. *Thanks, Ellys.*

Good humor returned with the comedic banter, and Aderri laughed at their antics. "You two carry on like a couple of court jesters."

Ellys rested her hands on her hips and grinned. "And you laugh more often than not. Admit it. It's one of the things you like most about our unrivaled companionship."

She got a smile for her declaration. "Perhaps it is. Come along, I'll get you set up with your very own room with a bed fit for a travel-worn half-elf."

Ellys followed Aderri out of the barn. "You certainly know how to entice a person."

With Rocc's previous thoughts in mind, Aderri added a little extra sway to her walk. Then she glanced over her shoulder and smirked. "A simple bed, Ellys? Hardly. You'll know when I'm enticing you because the bed won't be empty when I offer it." With those parting words, she worked more magic, then opened the rear door of the house and pushed inside, leaving Ellys flushed with interest in her wake.

As promised, Aderri's home was larger than average, in both ceiling height and width of the doorways. There was no upper floor, but the single level made more sense if she wanted it accessible by all the different shifter races, including centaurs. They entered the kitchen and Aderri led the way through the house into a great room, complete with a large hearth and an assortment of furniture. It was spacious enough to represent her status within the Clan, but not so large that it was unmanageable for one person.

"Your home is well laid out. I like it. Did you frequently have a lot of guests when you still lived here?"

"Thank you. And it's a tradition to take turns hosting friends and kin for meals and general celebration. Now, if you'll follow me, I'll show you the rest of the house and you can pick out a bed." She gestured toward a few doors leading off the main room. "One is for my private rooms while the other leads to a hall where the guest rooms are located."

Ellys grabbed at Aderri's sleeve and stopped her from walking away. "Wait."

Aderri looked back at her. "Yes?"

"How likely is it that you'll have company here in the quarter moon leading up to the naming ceremony?"

"Pretty likely, why?"

"I can't believe I'm going to be the one to bring it up, but the success of our ruse is hinged on every part going right. Won't shifters be able to tell if my scent is only leading to the guest rooms and not to your door?"

Aderri's eyes widened in shock. "Fenwith's bloody left ball!"

Ellys snickered at the rare curse. "I'm clearly rubbing off on you."

"I didn't even think of that. But you're right. Not only would they be able to tell you hadn't been staying in my room, but they'll also question why I don't have your scent all over me."

"So..." Ellys began.

"So?"

Ellys grinned. "How big is your bed?"

"You seem pretty eager for someone whom I had to beg to share a bedroll so you didn't freeze to death on the way here."

Ellys sniffed haughtily. "Yes, well that same someone has also grown to appreciate a warm bed at night."

Aderri burst into laughter, a sound that echoed in the rafters of the great room. "I've always heard that the quickest way to a warrior's heart is through their stomach. Clearly that's not the case with you."

"The quickest way to any two-legger's heart is through their stomach, but it's a pretty gruesome task if you ask me. Just in and up." She motioned like she was stabbing a sword. "Lots of blood involved."

Aderri shook her head. She should have known she'd get such an answer. "Just keep those bloody swords out of the bed, and we'll be fine. Come along. I guess I'm showing you to my room then."

Ellys's voice was low with a hint of flirtatiousness when they walked through the door into Aderri's room. "Does this mean you're enticing me now?" Aderri whirled around, surprised at the comment. The pause lasted for a few heartbeats then both women began laughing. Perhaps the coming quarter moon would be more entertaining than expected.

****

Candle marks later, the three friends were headed out again toward Dracona Keep. Aderri and Ellys rode Rocc upon her insistence. Ellys was confused by her steed's behavior. "Why are you so eager to get there?"

Rocc spoke as she cantered along. *Being of average mind and composition, you couldn't possibly comprehend what it's like to meet and converse with other intelligent creatures who are outside what our world deems to be 'normal' form. There is a...shared experience to be found amongst others of us living in a two-legger world.*

"Did you just call me average?"

Aderri said, "I understand what she's saying. I lived many cycles with people of other forms and saw the reactions they got from the species who walk upright on two legs. Perhaps it's easier as a shifter because I can take a form that 'passes,' but I know well enough the reaction my dragon receives."

Only you don't have the added agony of seeing hundreds of creatures around you that look like you but are really just dumb beasts of burden.

Ellys gave a little dig into Rocc's flank. "You mean you're not?"

Before she could stop laughing, Rocc did a strange little hop and buck that dislodged Ellys from her perch in the back of the saddle and sent her flying. Thinking fast, Ellys performed a flip in midair and landed on her feet facing away from them. She stumbled a step after landing then spun around and pointed at Rocc where she stood placidly a few feet away. Aderri sat perfectly in the saddle, crying with laughter. "Was that necessary?"

Rocc and Aderri answered at the same time, the words in Ellys's ears echoing strangely with the ones in her head.

It was necessary.

"Absolutely necessary."

"How in all of Abbad did you pitch me and leave her sitting so, so, perfect?"

Aderri grinned. "You think I'm perfect?"

Ellys growled under her breath. "Not anymore."

Unfortunately for the woman on the ground, Aderri's hearing as a dragon was better than most other shifters. "So, you thought I was perfect before?"

Ellys threw her hands into the air and yelled, scaring dozens of birds from the trees around them. "You're impossible!" Then she started walking down the road toward the keep she could see in the distance.

Rocc began trailing after her bondmate but addressed Aderri. *Walking away in frustration like that is a sure sign she likes you.*

Ellys yelled back. "It is not!"

Aderri called out to her, "Stop eavesdropping." Ellys's only response was to raise her hand over her head, displaying two crossed fingers.

Nearly a quarter candle mark later Rocc caught up to the muttering warrior. *Mount up. We're nearly there, and we need to present a united front to Aderri's kin if we want to make this believable.*

Ellys quickly swung into the saddle. "Who is this 'we' you're talking about? Again, you're a hor—"

Finish that sentence, and I'll buck you again.

"Fine. You don't have to convince anyone of anything. Meanwhile, I have to pretend that we're in a serious romance without actually lying."

Aderri said, "Stop thinking of it as such an extreme. How do couples behave when they're in a romance, having been together for a long time?"

"What do you mean? Physically?"

"Yes, but not in the way you think. One of the biggest things I've noticed about such couples is the level of comfort they display around each other. It's about more than snogging in front of guests. It's about casual touches, looks, all those signs that the two individuals are relaxed in each other's company and care tremendously about the other's well-being."

She's right, Ellys.

Ellys grumbled, "You always agree with her."

She's always right. Adagnitios usually are.

Aderri turned to look at Ellys over her shoulder. "Use our friendship to draw from. That's what I'll be doing. I'm genuinely comfortable with you and feel safe in your presence. Definitely safer than I'll feel in the presence of my kin with the axe of expectation hanging over my head." She turned to face forward again as the entrance to the family keep grew larger ahead of them.

Without even realizing it, Ellys wrapped her arms around Aderri and hugged her from behind. Just knowing that her friend was worried made her want to give comfort in a long-forgotten way. Aderri patted her forearm. "Yes, just like that."

The keep was significantly larger than Ellys had imagined. Tall and defensible, though not necessarily multi-tiered like a castle, it was a massive square structure fronted by a huge door. On closer inspection, Ellys could see that the iron and wood door was also a drawbridge, probably hiding another door behind it as part of the design. She'd seen many like it in all her cycles of travel. The next thing that caught her attention was the reason for the drawbridge. "Your parents have a moat? Who would invade a dragon keep in the middle of Clan lands?"

They dismounted and walked up to a small building on the near side of the anchor point for the bridge. There was no one in the hut so Aderri grabbed the hunting horn that hung on a peg. "One of the promises to those wishing to join Clan Dracona wasn't just for land of their own, but also for protection. The keep needed to be large and secure enough so all the shifters could fit inside in case of attack." She gave Ellys a sad look. "Not everyone is keen to have shifters nearby, and more than one community has hired hunters to clear them out. It matters not if the shifter family is peaceful or even bolstered by the crown, hunters will drive away or kill, depending on the gold paid."

Ellys had never before considered the privilege she held being part human and part elf. Not only were humans one of the more prevalent species across Myth World, but elves were highly respected as an elder race. Even so, she, too, had seen some of the prejudiced comments and actions directed toward shifters. The innkeeper on their first night out of Longoria was a prime example. "I'm sorry your people, all shifters, are treated as such. It's not right and breaks the balance in ways I can't even comprehend."

Aderri nodded but didn't say anything. She lifted the horn to her lips, blew a complicated series of notes, then hung it on the hook and waited while facing the drawbridge.

"Don't they know we're coming?"

"Yes."

Ellys was genuinely curious about the security of Aderri's kin.

"Then why not simply leave the bridge down? I mean, they're not in danger of attack right now or we'd have heard about it."

Rumbling preceded movement of the bridge. "Because they're dramatic old dragons and love theatrical flair."

So typical dragons then, unlike you.

Ellys turned to Rocc. "And just how many dragons have you met?"

Rocc blew a raspberry in Ellys's direction. *I've conversed with plenty and seen even more. I am a nine-hundred-and-forty-two-cycle-old elven mount and thus the majority of my experience is outside your ken.*

"As much as I enjoy your banter," Aderri said, "they're waiting on us."

Ellys and Rocc turned as one to look across the bridge to see a muscular centaur standing in the doorway of the outer wall. He was wearing full armor on his upper and lower halves and sported a plumed helm. Ellys swallowed nervously.

Suddenly the centaur smiled broadly and danced in place before waving them forward. "Come on, Aderri. Everyone is excited for your return. Don't keep them waiting."

Aderri, Ellys, and Rocc crossed the moat, and Aderri walked straight up to hug the grinning centaur. "Hello, Roogie. You're looking quite handsome all grown up."

His mouth dropped open and he sputtered. "How did you know it was me?"

"Because even as a colt you were adamant that you'd become head of keep militia. I'm glad your dream came true."

"Me, too." Then the centaur abruptly straightened and turned his attention to Ellys. "Good evening. I'm Captain Droogus Swifthoof, and I'm here to welcome you into Dracona Keep. Will you"—he turned slightly to glance at Roccotári—"be needing a stable for your mount?"

I won't be needing a stable any more than you will, Captain. My elven heritage has guaranteed only the best of manners when indoors.

Droogus looked momentarily horrified at his breach of etiquette. "My lady! Apologies, but I had no idea you were an advanced creature of light. Please forgive the offense."

The large steed took a step forward and nosed his forearm. *No forgiveness necessary. It was an honest mistake.*

Droogus gave a sigh of relief. "Thank you."

I am Roccotári, and my two-legger bondmate is Ellys DeEnsis.

The centaur turned to Ellys and put out a front hoof before bowing with his upper and lower halves. "It is a pleasure to meet you as well, Ellys. Now, if you will all follow me inside, I'm sure quite a few people will be happy to see Aderri home at last." Droogus spun in place to lead them through the battlements into the keep proper.

Aderri spoke. "Tell me, is everyone in attendance tonight?"

Droogus paused and addressed her. "Not everyone, but more than half of your immediate family are here to welcome our Riki home. Some are on patrol, and others weren't feeling particularly social."

Aderri sighed. "It's going to be a spectacle, isn't it?"

"I'm afraid so."

Ellys looked on in awe as they passed through an incredibly thick stone wall into the small, courtyard-sized bailey beyond. It appeared just large enough for a dragon to take flight or land. Dracona Keep could almost be considered a castle except for the tiny bailey. The building itself took up most of the space. Droogus led them through another door on the right side of the open area twenty paces from where they entered.

Aderri paused. "Why are we going this way? The dining room is in the other direction."

Droogus looked back at her. "Everyone is waiting in Dragon Hall. You are the last to arrive for evening meal."

Aderri groaned and Ellys leaned close and whispered in her ear, "What's the matter?"

Aderri whispered back, "We're eating in Dragon Hall."

"What's the significance?"

"It means that at least one of my kin wants to eat in dragon form tonight."

While the thought made her a bit nervous, Ellys didn't understand Aderri's unhappiness. "Why is that a bad thing? After all, this is their home. It makes sense for them to eat however they please."

Aderri stopped abruptly, causing Ellys to overstep her by a pace before also coming to a halt. "Ellys..."

Ellys looked at her curiously while Rocc and Droogus, deep in conversation, continued walking. Their hooves made a distinctive clip-clop sound on the stone floor. "Yes?"

"What do you think a dragon eats?"

"Uh, big meals?"

Aderri grimaced. "Right, so probably a cow or a few goats."

Ellys tilted her head, considering the issue. "And?"

"Typically, the evening dragon course will be led inside and tied to a post. It's tradition for the dragon to roast their meal before consuming it."

The full notion of what was about to occur finally registered, and Ellys wrinkled her nose in disgust. "That sounds messy."

"Not to mention the fact that the smell of burnt hair will linger in the air long past meal's end. At least, given the heat of dragon fire, death occurs instantly."

Ellys tried to imagine holding her own dinner down while the dining hall reeked of burning meat and hair. "Perhaps I'll just have mead as my dinner."

"To refuse to take meal with kin is considered a grave insult, so I'm afraid you'll have to muddle through." Ellys grew silent and Aderri gestured for them to catch up to the two hooved creatures.

One thing that stood out when walking through the keep was the immense size of the space. From what Ellys could remember of Aderri's form, the halls and doorways could easily fit a dragon and she wondered how often Aderri's parents stayed in beast form. It was on the tip of her tongue to ask, but she was interrupted when they came to a stop in front of a massive wooden door next to Rocc and the centaur captain.

Droogus turned to the trio. "This is where I leave you three. I hope you have a nice meal." He started to walk away when Aderri stopped him.

"Roogie, wait. Aren't you going to eat with us?"

He shifted his weight between the two front hooves. "Well, uh, you see, I'm on duty and really need to get back—"

"You don't get a meal break?"

Finally caught out, Droogus admitted, "I don't really care for the smell of burnt fur. It turns my stomach."

Ellys raised a dark eyebrow. "Really?"

Droogus nodded. "Yes. It will put me off my feed for days, and I'd like to avoid that so I don't get in trouble for not eating my mare's meals at home. Truthfully, I haven't eaten with the dragons since I bonded with my mare a few decades ago."

Speaking of food, what will I eat?

Aderri stroked Rocc's soft neck then patted it affectionately.

"My sister will have given them a full description of both of you. I'm sure there will be something appropriate inside."

Rocc whinnied. *That works for me.* Then she turned to Ellys. *Can you open the door? I seem to have left my hands in the other saddlebags.* Aderri snickered while Ellys just rolled her eyes.

Stalling for a moment, Ellys asked, "Why take meals in your dragon form if you can maintain yourself eating as a smaller creature?"

"Some prefer to take their meals in a more primal manner and others—" Aderri stopped speaking.

"And others what?"

"Others need to practice holding onto their intelligence and control while in dragon form. Some forget who they are when faced with a meal and revert to the primitive beast in thought and deed. So, this would be training."

Ellys paled, remembering the damage Aderri wrought on the soldiers in Carthune. "Isn't that dangerous to those who are a little, uh, softer and more edible than a dragon?"

"Yes, so you may want to stay near me this evening." She gestured toward the door. "When you're ready."

Taking a deep breath, Ellys grabbed onto the pull rope attached to the massive right-side door and shuffled backward to swing it open. Once there was enough space for the three of them to walk through, Aderri held out her hand. "Together?"

Ellys clasped her hand tight and tried to reassure Aderri by the nature of her grip alone. "Of course."

Chapter Sixteen

Dragon Hall was massive. Multiple large hearths were built on three sides of the room, and tables full of people stood off to one side. A mix of races and forms were present. Some chose half-shape, like Aderri's werewolf friend they had met on the way into Clan lands. Ellys's roving gaze saw numerous wolves, a bear, a few satyrs, and an entire tall table of centaurs. There were easily fifty people in attendance, but they barely took up a fraction of the dining hall. Despite all the space available, the grand room felt cramped by, not one or two, but four full-size dragons. Ellys whined quietly under her breath, "So much burnt hair." Aderri squeezed her hand, and together they stepped forward with Roccotári.

The largest of the dragons approached, and Ellys took note that it was nearly identical to Aderri in her other form. "Daughter, you have returned to usss. Come clossser where we can greet you properly."

Aderri led her friends forward until they stood just a few paces from the lowered head of the dragon who had spoken. Ellys wasn't sure which of Aderri's parents it was, not being able to tell male from female of the species, though she assumed it was probably the Drakaina.

Aderri took one more step so she was forward of both Ellys and Rocc. "Mother, my companions are Ellys DeEnsis"—she gestured toward Ellys—"and her lineal bondmate, Lady Roccotári. We have been traveling together outside Clan lands."

Zevieri Dracona, the Drakaina of the Clan, moved her large head until it was less than an arm span in front of Ellys. Then much to Ellys's dismay, the great dragon leaned closer yet and sniffed her right and left sides. She moved over to Rocc, did the same, then backed up a few paces.

"Your mate hasss—"

"Ellys is not my mate."

Zevieri's eyes narrowed as she looked at her daughter, and Aderri rushed to explain. "As I said, we're travelers and have chosen to walk the same path because it suits us, but we are not mates. Ellys is my companion who I've grown quite close to, to both of them really. I want to clarify that because I'm nowhere near ready to think about hatchlings or settling in one place."

Zevieri gave a slight nod and continued. "Asss I wasss sssaying, your *companion* hasss been away from the Ethereal Foressst for a long time. Is she en-eledron?"

Ellys moved to stand next to Aderri. "If I may, Drakaina, I have not returned to the Ethereal Forest by a mutual pact between myself and Queen Ardruel. I was allowed inside the veil exactly once, to pay my respects to the Great Tree where my father's ashes were scattered."

"Why hasss she requesssted you remain outssside her bordersss?"

"Because I'm not pure enough for her, being only half elf." Ellys said the words with such disdain that Roccotári moved closer and nuzzled against her arm while Aderri reached out to clasp her hand again.

"My daughter isss an exssellent judge of character. Clearly the Elven Queen hasss acted in error. Even *she* is not beyond fallibility. You are welcome here, Ellysss DeEnsssisss, for asss long asss the sssun risssesss to grace our world with light." She turned to Rocc and leaned forward to close the gap between them. Then in a display of delicate coordination, she touched the tip of her dragon snout to Roccotári's much smaller muzzle. "You asss well, Lady of Earth."

Roccotári put one hoof out in front of the other and bowed to Zevieri. *Thank you, Drakaina.*

The dragon opened her jaws slightly as the corners of the tooth-filled mouth pulled upward. Ellys wondered if it was her version of a smile. If so, it was more frightening than not. "Call me Zssevieri, both of you." She suddenly shuffled backward, as graceless and ungainly a sight as any, and Ellys struggled not to snicker at the movement. One simply does not laugh at dragons, especially not if they are the ruler of the region.

"You are jusssst in time for lasssst meal." She pointed with a clawed foot toward a table with two empty seats together on one side.

Seeing the layout of the various tables, Rocc parted ways with them. *I think I'll join my hooved brethren at the centaur table. Can you remove my saddle and bags?*

Ellys did as asked and set all Rocc's tack by the door they came in. After a moment to look around, she removed her sword harness and left both swords with the gear. She never traveled anywhere without her blades else she would have simply left them at Aderri's home.

As Rocc was walking away, she gave a swish of her tail and called out, *Don't forget your table manners, Ellys.*

Ellys wasn't going to let the dig pass without a response. "Just remember what happens when your eyes are bigger than your stomach. Colic is no laughing matter."

Maybe not, but your lack of etiquette certainly is.

Aderri whispered out of the side of her mouth as they drew closer to their assigned seats. "The woman on the right is Wyrennia, Cyvrus's mate. He is to the right of her. The one on the left of the empty seats is my sister, Bonvi. The rest I will introduce to you later. Some have mates that I've only read about from Gessy, but I haven't actually met yet."

She paused. "The dragon with orange-and-black coloring is my father, and the red-and-gold dragon is my mother's sister, Grunelde. The blue-and-black one is my sister, Dlemna. Don't go near her. She has always struggled with control. I suspect that's why she's practicing in dragon form tonight."

It was a lot of information to remember, but the part of Ellys's brain responsible for self-preservation forced her to pay attention. Even with what she suspected would be disparate coloring in their dragons due to the hair colors of all the people seated at the dining table where they were headed, Ellys could easily pick out the Dracona sibs. They all had identical dark skin and finely arched brows. Only one didn't have the same slope to their nose as Aderri, and that was Cyvrus.

One of the sibs called out as the pair took their seats. "Long time gone, Addy. We weren't sure you were going to make it."

Ellys whispered, "Addy?" but the comment was lost in the din of voices waiting on the meal.

Aderri said, "You know better, Jorl. No one ignores a summons from the Drakaina."

The one Aderri pointed out as Bonvi leaned forward in her seat to see around Ellys, and Ellys leaned back to accommodate the conversation. "You should have a gathering tomorrow."

"We only just got here, and Ellys isn't used to Clan gatherings."

"Speaking of Ellys, didn't I tell you all that she would make you hungry?" Gessy nudged Jorl's shoulder where they sat farther down the table from Ellys, on the opposite side.

Ellys flushed at being the topic of conversation. She leaned closer to Aderri and whispered quietly enough that no one else could hear, even the shifters. "I don't know how I feel about making a bunch of dragon shifters hungry."

"Relax, it's a compliment."

"Come on, Addy, you know you want to host."

After multiple people along the table of kin called out pleas, Aderri finally gave in. "Okay, enough. My place at sunset tomorrow. Bring your own because I've little left in storage after my travels. We'll supply the usual."

Cheers went down the table, and Ellys couldn't wipe the look of surprise from her face if she tried. She kept her voice low to ask, "Is this normal? You've been gone more than sixty cycles, and half the people in this room are probably unfamiliar, yet your kin just…welcome you back into the fold simple as that?"

Aderri met her gaze, and Ellys's stomach fluttered when she saw the flames within the other woman's pupils. "We are especially long-lived, so extended absences are much like short ones. Celebrate when someone leaves, and rejoice twice as hard when they come back to the Clan."

Ellys glanced to her left and right and across the table. "I have to admit," she said and intently observed Aderri's kin and their mates as they threw back tankards of some unknown brew that Ellys was keen to try, "your kin aren't at all what I expected."

A single dark red brow rose. "No?"

"No. They're so…rambunctious."

"And?"

"And you're—" Ellys didn't finish her sentence, suddenly aware that Aderri could take it in a negative way.

Breath tickled Ellys's ear as Aderri leaned close to whisper, "I'm what exactly?"

Ellys swallowed hard. "You're, um, not."

Aderri bumped against Ellys's left shoulder with her right one. "Oh, I can be. You just haven't seen that side of me."

"I can't wait to explore this bit of uncharted territory then."

Ellys could see the flirtatious remark on the tip of Aderri's tongue, but they were interrupted when a nymph arrived and deposited two tankards in front of her and Aderri. The nymph gave Aderri a little wave. "Good to have you back, Aderri."

Aderri smiled and raised the mead. "Good to be back, Zshee, if only 'til the naming ceremony."

"Heading out again after that, hmm?"

"You know how it is. Too much to see and learn to stay in one place long."

Loud laughter sounded from the centaur table, and as one, Aderri and Ellys turned to see Rocc do a little dance in place, one that was quickly copied by the centaurs. Aderri giggled. "What is she doing?"

Ellys shook her head, perplexed at what was happening two tables over. "I have no clue in six." She looked around. "They said dinner was about to begin, but I don't see anything yet. What will the rest be eating while the dragons are singeing the livestock?"

Wyrennia overheard her. "What has Aderri been telling you about us?"

Bonvi said, "She's been gone a long time, Renny, and we've only had the new dinner routine about ten cycles. Even Droogus hasn't figured it out yet. Most nights, he gallops out of here like his tail is on fire." The group laughed.

Another diner said, "Most likely, his mare has got him on a short rein." A few snorted at the bad joke. The sheer number of people chiming in all at once around Ellys was chaotic and a little dizzying.

Aderri tilted her head and gave her elder brother a curious look. "New routine? Should we be worried?"

Bonvi reached around Ellys's back and patted Aderri's near shoulder. "On the contrary, it's about a hundred times better. Just watch."

Less than a candle drop later, two large iron spits on wheels were rolled out from a door opposite the one they entered. On each spit was an entire skinned low-beast, trussed and ready for roasting. After the rolling spits were placed in the center of the room, a gnome came through the doors leading a bleating goat. "What…" Aderri didn't address a particular sibling. Instead, her voice trailed off as she and Ellys watched intently.

Ellys had picked up her tankard for a drink not long after the goat made an appearance, and she smacked her lips with delight as the brew's flavor hit her tongue. "This is one of the best meads I've ever had. Who brews it?"

"Shh, it's starting!"

A roar sounded through the room, and Ellys's gaze moved from the skinned low-beasts to the blue-and-black dragon. The creature appeared wild with her slavering jaws. She leaned toward the poor gnome and goat only to be reprimanded by the Drakaina. "*Non!* You will not touch the goat." Dlemna roared in response. "You are here to practicsse ressstraint, and that appliesss to all thingsss. Get control of your dragon, Dlemna, or I shall control it for you."

While Zevieri's words were spoken as a promise, Ellys heard it for the threat it was. "What is she doing?"

Aderri whispered, "Teaching."

"Together we will roasssst the ssspitted beassstsss, and you will ignore *zha capra.*"

Smoke curled from Dlemna's nostrils, and she nodded, though her eyes never left the small bleating animal. The gnome looked ready to faint.

Each spit had a large crank at the end, too big for anything other than dragon claws. Both dragons stood in front of their own spit and began turning the cranks, keeping the rotating beasts slow. Then they opened their mouths, and shortened spouts of flame began cooking the meat.

Aderri turned to Bonvi. "I didn't realize we could control the distance of our flame in such a manner."

Gessy called from down the table. "You would if you enjoyed your dragon form more. We've learned a few new tricks since you've been gone."

"I can see the necessity for things, such as cooking a spitted beast, but what would be the use of a shortened flame in any other circumstance?"

Ellys surprised them all by answering. "To minimize same-side casualties. A dragon on the ground in close fighting, or even in the air, would be a liability to both friend and foe. Toroc's third principle states that 'any battle attack that wounds the innocent is unbalanced by nature,' and we are taught to always be aware of our place and actions in any given skirmish."

"Are you a follower of Toroc then, Ellys?"

Ellys looked farther down and across the table to see who spoke. It was a man she hadn't been introduced to, but he appeared quite close to Jorl. "Yes…" She paused so he could supply his name.

"Destain. I am Jorl's mate."

"Thank you, Destain. I have been a follower for one-hundred-and-forty-eight cycles."

Jorl called out, "How old are you?"

Ellys grinned. "One hundred and forty-eight."

Gessy frowned. "How is that even possible?"

"I was born into Toroc's service in the cycle twenty-four fifty and never felt it necessary to leave."

"Like Aderri, an auspicious cycle indeed." Ellys realized quickly that she was going to be the center of the sibs' attention as Bonvi asked the next question. "How did you meet our wayward nest-mate?"

Aderri had told Ellys she feared that things would get tricky if they had to make up some complicated back story. She needn't have worried because despite Ellys's strange way of looking at a situation, she was a fast thinker.

"She," Ellys said and pointed a thumb to her left at Aderri, "tried to hire my swords, and I turned her down." Aderri gasped but Ellys watched her nod as she apparently remembered that her request was turned down, initially.

"Yet you're here together now."

Ellys's attention started to wander toward where she could see the meat roasting nicely. Even so, she did her part and responded to Bonvi's comment. "It turns out, she was just as interested in my face as she was in my blades." She put her arm around Aderri and gestured toward where Rocc stood several paces away, clearly living it up at the centaur table. "And here we are, the three of us a trio unlike any other."

Aderri nudged her side and pointed to where people were bringing in platters of various dishes as well as food suited for all races present. "Looks like the meal is nearly ready."

Suddenly, a loud bleat split the air, followed quickly by a roar. Everyone looked up from their conversations to see the goat get loose from its handler and bolt for the long table where Aderri and Ellys were seated. As the swift prey got away, Dlemna gave chase. Ellys didn't consider the danger, she simply acted. She hopped up on her stool then used it to flip forward over the dining table and the people seated on the other side. After that it was a few short strides to grab the goat and tuck it beneath her left arm so it couldn't get away.

Unfortunately for Ellys, the move left her facing a hungry

dragon whose lizard brain had taken control. Dlemna's head was so close that her roar blew Ellys's hair back from her face. Remembering what she'd learned about predators in her decades of training, instinct kicked in and Ellys tried the same move on Dlemna that she once used on a charging plains cat. She pulled herself up to full height, swatted the snout in front of her, and yelled, "No!"

A collective gasp went through Dragon Hall, and Dlemna reared back to let loose her best weapon. Before the fire could come, she simply froze in place.

Zevieri walked over a few heartbeats later. She was nude and in human form. "You must be very brave or exceedingly foolish, Ellys DeEnsis."

Ellys grimaced. "Roccotári has known me longer than any other, and she'd say a bit of both."

"Either way, there's nothing to fear now. I have stopped her charge, and she will be forced to change form to complete this meal." Zevieri looked up at Dlemna. "Are you ready to be released?"

"Yesss, Mother."

With a wave of Zevieri's hand, the large blue-and-black dragon sagged, then it was surrounded by shimmering light until a woman who looked a lot like Aderri appeared. "What have you to say for yourself?"

Dlemna was clearly embarrassed. She glanced around the hall then brought her attention back to Zevieri. "I'm sorry, Mother. Clearly she got away from me." Then she looked at Ellys. "I apologize to you, too. It was the pinnacle of disrespect to attack a dinner guest."

Ellys gave a slight bow. "It could have been worse."

Dlemna asked the obvious question. "By Cassyn, how could this have been worse?"

Ellys hefted the wiggling goat to get a better grip. "For starters…you could have eaten me. That would have put a damper on the rest of the meal for sure."

The entire room of shifters heard her answer, and they all began laughing. Dlemna clapped her on the shoulder. "I like you, Ellys. You're a good match for our know-it-all sib."

Suddenly everyone froze at the sound of liquid dripping on the stone floor. Ellys felt something wet soak her leg and looked down to see the goat pissing on her left hip. She looked around at the gathering. "Apparently things can still get worse."

Before she could say another word, Aderri was next to her. "Put the goat down. I'll take care of your clothes." The goat was turned loose. Then, with a minor magic spell, Ellys's trousers were good as gold. Aderri clasped her hand, and they made their way back around the table to their seats with the sound of good-natured laughter and cheers ringing throughout the room.

A tall man wearing a robe walked up to Zevieri and handed her a garment matching his own. He gave her a kiss on the cheek then moved to sit at the opposite end of the table from his mate. Zevieri took a seat at the head of the table nearest to where Aderri and Ellys sat.

The meal progressed smoothly from there. The first low-beast was sliced onto platters to be passed around. Ellys noticed that Aderri's aunt chose to stay in dragon form for the meal and she was given half the meat from one spit. Ellys was content to eat her meal and be left alone while Aderri's family caught her up on all the Clan happenings of the past half century.

Ellys's mind had been crammed full of thoughts of late, all centering on the woman at her side. Rocc's suggestion that Ellys felt more for Aderri than she was letting on brought forth a whole host of other notions about the future she truly wanted for her life and her bondmate.

Ellys had just taken a swallow of her mead when she heard her name mentioned.

"Isn't that right, Ellys?"

She took a breath to answer and swallowed at the same time, precipitating a choking fit that resulted in Bonvi and Aderri slapping her on the back with gusto. She finally held up a hand to fend them off. "I'm fine. Just went down the wrong pipe."

Rocc was powerful enough to speak to the entire gathering of fifty plus, and she did just that. Her voice in their heads startled some, but most were used to it. *Ellys has always struggled with multitasking. I'm surprised she's made it this far in life.*

Ellys groaned, much to everyone's delight. "I swear, that…horse will be the death of me." Suddenly laughter swept along the table of centaurs, and Ellys hunched to think of what Rocc could be sharing with them.

Zevieri simultaneously saved her from embarrassment and potentially opened her up for more. "Tell us about yourself, Ellys.

How do you find the ways of Toroc?"

"I quite enjoy bringing balance to the people and places I encounter. It's not something I purposely set out to do, but rather a state I fell into many cycles ago after the death of my mate. Eventually, Rocc and I discovered an affinity for new places, so I registered with the League of Swords and we've been traveling back and forth across the length of six since."

"Your duty to league doesn't interfere with your duty to your Goz?"

"Not so far. It helps that I control what jobs I take so I can turn down any that I feel are unbalanced."

"Are you a monk then?"

She took a careful swallow of her mead. "I'm not a monk, since I never finished my quest, which is necessary in order to take the oath of gender balance. And while I haven't ruled out a return to the monastery should I ever finish—" She paused to glance at Aderri. "It's not calling me either. At least not like other passions in life."

A deep voice from down the table called out, "We can all guess what at least one of those passions is."

Ellys flushed and turned to retort, but Aderri beat her to it.

"Papa, please."

Eyes wide, Ellys first looked at Aderri then turned her gaze toward the other end of the table where Koldaht sat. It was the same tall man that had given Zevieri her clothing. He grinned and raised a tankard into the air, a move quickly followed by everyone at the table. "Lighten up, my dear. I'd wager Ellys knows one end of a joke from the other."

Ellys smiled. "That I do."

"Good then. Now, a toast to new hatchlings and homecomings. Te Zah!" Everyone in the room with capacity for it echoed the call then swiftly drank down their mead.

Thumps sounded around the room as more pitchers were brought out by the kitchen staff to refill mugs and bowls. Ellys shook her head to clear it from the aftereffects of such a potent drink. She leaned over and whispered to Aderri, "Your Clan sure knows how to brew."

Aderri waved a hand. "That is by necessity. You know shifters have a high tolerance, so it was necessary to make something stronger than most could bear. It helps that it's so tasty, too." She took another sip and smacked her lips. "I've certainly missed it."

Ellys watched a pink tongue swipe across Aderri's lower lip and wished more than anything in that moment that she could taste the mead from Aderri's mouth instead of her own mug. She leaned back before doing just that. Clearly the mead was going straight to her head.

They supped for a few candle marks before the dinner broke up. Every able-bodied person helped clear the tables and clean up the remains of the meal afterward. Those that had been working in the kitchen were off taking their own meal, and Aderri had explained that the Clan were trained to pitch in and help when necessary.

It was late by the time all was finished. Many of the guests chose to stay the night at the keep, but Ellys and Aderri had already planned to return to Aderri's home.

Two moons had risen in the sky with the other waning into blackness as they rode Rocc away from the keep. Aderri turned slightly so she could speak to Ellys. "What did you think of your first night with Clan Dracona?"

"Your father was funny, but then most of them were. I thought for certain your sibs would be a lot more high-sounding given how you go on about manners and what not." Ellys waved her right hand to punctuate the 'what not' portion of her answer.

Aderri was silent for a few candle drops. The usual night sounds were all around them: crickets, chirps, wind through the trees, and even the occasional howl in the distance. Aderri was silent long enough that Ellys, in her mead-fogged mind, feared she may have offended her. "I don't mean it in a bad way. It's just that…you're so different from all of them."

"I do know what you mean, and you're right. I guess I've always held myself to high expectation, knowing the fate I was born to, and doing what I could to rebel." Ellys wasn't the only one who'd had too much mead. The drink made Aderri's tongue a lot looser than normal.

"You're telling me that your version of rebelling was to become as knowledgeable and well-mannered as possible to, what, spite your gregarious family?"

Dimples appeared in Aderri's cheeks when she turned and grinned at Ellys. "Maybe."

"Would it be so bad to stay? Surely you've traveled the length and breadth of six many times by now."

"Oh, Ellys…that is a hard question to answer. And I'd wager

that I've not traversed it nearly as often as you. You forget much of my time was spent in study at one place of learning or another. When I consider my life from the view of an outsider, it must seem incredibly selfish. After all, what do I do with all my knowledge? Nothing. I keep it and seek more. I really am as much a hoarder as the rest of my dragon kin."

"Aderri…" Ellys was at a loss for how to help what was clearly an issue that had been brewing in Aderri's mind for a while.

"No, it's true. Do you remember when we first met?"

"How could I ever forget?"

"I accused you of being insouciant, yet I was the one who had been blithely going about life, free from worry or anxiety. It's easy enough to keep on this way. I sell spells for more gold than I really need to live and thrive in the life I've chosen, but who am I helping by living in such a manner?"

"You're not like that at all."

Aderri signaled Rocc that she wanted to get down, and the steed stopped in the middle of the road. Once on the ground, Aderri began pacing. "It's true though. What do I have to offer the world around me? All my life I've been searching for a way out, yet perhaps my best life is one that continues right back where I started, doing what I was born to do."

Ellys dismounted as well and stood next to Rocc, watching helplessly. She wasn't sure how to soothe Aderri but something deep inside her wanted to.

Child, we are born to do a multitude of things. Just because you are slated to rule Clan Dracona someday doesn't mean you're unable to accomplish other things between now and then.

"It still stands that for nearly one hundred cycles I've been living my life only for myself and naught else. What good does all my gathered knowledge do if I don't share it? How could I ever be a good leader if I think so little of others?"

Ellys plucked at that little string of a comment and pulled. "What's stopping you?"

That brought Aderri to a halt. "What do you mean?"

"What's stopping you from sharing all the knowledge you've collected over the cycles?" This time it was Ellys who got excited, skipping a little as she gestured about. "I mean, what if you founded a university of your own? Think on it, you could begin your own library…I'd wager you already have quite a start in your magic travel sack. Let me guess, you've probably copied every one of your favorite tomes in their entirety." Aderri sniffed but didn't answer. "There are so many ways you could use what you've gathered to help others, and unlike your treasure-hoarding brethren, your treasure never runs out no matter how much you share it. On the contrary, shared knowledge grows."

Ellys realized it was the most Aderri had ever heard her speak at once, and the words that poured forth clearly stunned her. Ellys had taken everything Aderri could want and wrapped it into a solid bundle. Perhaps it was that Ellys came to rest right in front of Aderri, or maybe it was the passionate display from both, but Aderri closed the space between them and kissed Ellys.

Ellys's response was immediate. She brought both hands up to thread into Aderri's wild curls and pulled her closer. Their tongues twined together as the fire of passion flared between them. As they stood in the middle of the road mere candle marks before sunrise, Aderri was the first to pull back, leaving Ellys with a little nip to the lower lip.

Ellys took a deep breath and tried to control her pounding heart. "I'm sorry." She didn't expect the laughter.

"By Cassyn, *I* kissed *you*! You have nothing to be sorry for, and I'm not sorry either. You earned that kiss sure as anything."

Ellys told her conscience to take a quick swim and grinned at Aderri. "So, you liked my ideas?" Rather than smile back, her words prompted Aderri to frown. As with many things in life, Ellys assumed it wasn't as easy as she made it sound.

"Starting a university takes many things that knowledge hasn't given me. Immense amounts of gold, land, connections, and a name across the six nations. Who would want to come learn from a place they never heard of?"

Ellys scoffed, "Only the best and brightest. So maybe not a university, but what about work as a historian? There must be something that would allow you to pursue and share knowledge, as well as maintain a closer relationship with your Clan."

Both were silent for a few heartbeats. Ellys stepped near to Aderri and tried to ignore the scent of her, ignore the heat radiating from her body in the cool night air. "Is there even anything of importance left across the six that you haven't already studied aplenty?"

"Of course."

"I challenge you to name a book or collection that you've always wanted to see but never have."

Aderri surprised Ellys with an immediate answer. "The Ancient Tomes of Aeschar."

Ellys shook her head. "I'm sorry, I've never heard of those."

Five of the six were lost not long before the Nothian stronghold was built.

Ellys looked at her bondmate then moved her gaze to Aderri. "Only five? Where is the sixth then?"

"It's the Sky Tome, the great book of prophesy." Aderri looked to Rocc. "You seem knowledgeable on the subject. What do you think happened to them?"

Mount up and I'll tell you during the rest of the trip back to your stead.

A few candle drops later, Ellys grumbled from the back of the saddle, "I feel like I hardly know you anymore, Rocc, with all your secret magical knowledge and mysterious tales."

It's not like that, cara. I promise you've always known the most important part of me.

Ellys didn't like feeling left out or left behind. Too much had happened of late, and she didn't know how to cope with the things that Roccotári never thought to share with her. Ellys took a deep breath, let it out, and analyzed the situation. Rocc was an elven steed who was six times her age. She had lived longer with Ellys's father than Ellys and Aderri had been alive combined. It was logical that she'd have a wealth of experience that even a hundred cycles couldn't touch.

Seeing the truth, Ellys conceded. "You're right. I know you wouldn't keep essential things from me."

I would never.

Aderri said, "I'm glad you've got that sorted out. Now, can you tell us about the Tomes of Aeschar?"

"Wait," Ellys interrupted. "What is Aeschar? Is it a person, beast, or place?"

"I don't know. I've only ever read references to the tomes, but nothing to infer any kind of history, just that they were lost or damaged long ago and that the Sky Tome is the only one left in existence."

Aeschar was an island nation, south of the border between Kuwyth and Muniers.

Ellys tilted her head curiously and tightened her arms around

Aderri. "But everyone knows that there's nothing south, only an uninhabitable wasteland, too cold for people to thrive much of the cycle."

It is now. But those of us magical creatures who are long-lived know of the events that happened ages ago. I wasn't around for the fall, obviously, but I learned of it during my own history lessons in the Sacred Grove.

Aderri asked, "What happened to them?"

According to lore passed down for generations, hubris. The people of Aeschar were incredibly advanced for their time. They had marvels of magical and mechanical creation. They'd unlocked the secrets to make both of the sciences work in tandem. But the rulers, like many across the six, got greedy and wanted more.

They were nearly home, and Aderri made an offer to Rocc. "Will you come inside and tell us more? I'll make a batch of hot mash if you're still hungry, otherwise I know there are some apples that were delivered earlier." She paused. "That is, if you're not too tired."

Rocc slowed when they approached the front entrance to Aderri's home. *I'm not particularly hungry, but I'll never turn down an apple.*

Ellys chuckled. "You're so predictable."

After Aderri and Ellys dismounted, the steed followed them inside. Aderri waved a hand, and the wood she built up in the hearth before they left roared to life. "Ellys, can you get one of the apples from the kitchen pantry while I fetch us something to drink?"

"Sure."

Ellys went into the kitchen to retrieve the fruit and walked out in time to see Aderri pouring two cups of wine from her supply in the cabinet near the edge of the room. Rocc's saddlebags and tack had already been removed. She placed the apple on a low table near the largest lounger, and Rocc's hooves made a clopping sound on the stone floor as she made her way over to it.

Ellys was amused to see a horse in the house. Rather than risk Rocc's wrath to say as much aloud, she opted to take a seat on a nearby lounger instead. Her mind raced with thoughts that were decidedly not about any ancient civilization. For the life of her, she couldn't understand why Aderri had kissed her on the road beneath the light of two moons.

"Here you are." Aderri handed Ellys a cup of wine and took a seat next to her. Both turned their gazes toward where Rocc was crunching away at the red apple.

The island nation of Aeschar sought to harness all the elemental energies of Myth World at once, and it proved to be their downfall.

Aderri shook her head. "You can't do that. The enemy elements will never work well together in magics. The results often prove to be rather…explosive."

True enough. You see, they thought their location would be perfect. The greatest mages spent cycles…nay, lifetimes, putting all their gathered knowledge into the tomes.

Ellys snickered. "She said neigh." Aderri elbowed her and Ellys abruptly quieted again.

Rocc blew a bit of apple in Ellys's direction. *As I was saying, the mages were hoping to harness the magic of the four elements together and use it to make their land better for their people. They wanted to create a magical shield that was powered by a massive spell.*

Aderri said, "Given the rumored state of the land beyond the southern sea, I'd say they failed spectacularly." The idea of so much new knowledge obviously appealed to Aderri, and she leaned forward with excitement.

Yes, as can be expected. It was exactly as you said. You cannot tie elemental enemies together. It's one of the natural laws that should never be broken. The mages were so sure their unique position would help the magic, but that only guaranteed that whatever disaster befell them from the failed spell would destroy the entire island.

Ellys followed the magical discussion by applying what she knew of her Elemental Bones game. As Aderri had mentioned, the game was based on the real magics of their world. "What do you mean when you say their unique position?"

The very heart of their nation was a volcano. It was the source of the island that had formed many millennia ago. Aeschar was far to the south, in the windiest part of the sea, a mass of land surrounded by water.

Aderri's eyes widened. "So, you have earth, besieged by wind, and fire from the volcano assailing the ocean. What happened?"

It worked for a short while, then the elements grew too powerful and broke free of the magical bindings. The earth shook first, giving scant warning to the people of Aeschar. Then great tidal waves struck the island all the way around at the same time a typhoon set them in its sights. And as if that weren't enough to punish the people for their arrogance, the volcano erupted and wiped out the entire northwest section of the massive island. Since that day, nothing has been able to survive there. It's too wild and the magics are out of control.

Something about the story bothered Ellys, a detail that made it seem unfinished. "If all that happened, how did the Sky Tome make it into the six nations to be copied and spread around? For that matter, how does anyone know what happened to this lost civilization?"

In a seeming random change of topic, Rocc addressed Aderri. *Do you know how the nation of Muniers came about?*

"Yes. Thousands of cycles ago, two foreign mages came to the land and saw injustices. They were twins and quite powerful. The two of them pledged to unite the people and protect them from the harm wrought by outsiders. The land of Kuwyth was wild back then, without much law to be found. More so than any other time, people lived and died by the sword daily. It is said that the Twin Regents carved Muniers from neglected portions of Kuwyth and Carthune, and they were strong enough to keep it."

Yes, they were the first and original Twin Regents. Those mages were from Aeschar and stole away with the Sky Tome after reading about their nation's demise within its pages. They knew that tampering with the elements to such extent was naught more than folly, a fact foretold in the very pages they'd saved. They made copies and spread them around the six nations because they believed that people should be able to see the winds of fate and plan accordingly.

Ellys snorted. "Well, fat lot of good that did. I've never made any sense of the blasted thing."

"It's really too bad they couldn't have saved the rest." Aderri stared unseeing into the crackling fire of the hearth.

Rocc wasn't so ideological. *I disagree.*

Both women's mouths opened with surprise but only Ellys got the word out. "What?"

Rocc thumped a hoof on the wood. *Think on it. If people had all six tomes, what would stop them from trying to do the same thing again? There are very few across the six that I'd wager would be wise enough for such knowledge. So, no thank you. I don't care if they're never found.*

Aderri said, "You'd make a terrible adagnitio dragon."

Laughter sounded in their heads. *Maybe so, but I'm an excellent steed. And on that note, I'm tired from hauling your lumps of two-legger flesh around. I'll leave you with that bit of information running through your heads. We can speak on it more tomorrow if you like.*

Aderri and Ellys stood to say their goodbyes. Ellys gave Rocc a soft rub to her muzzle while Aderri caressed her neck. "Good night, Lady Roccotári. We'll see you in the morning."

Rocc lipped at Aderri's hair affectionately then turned and left the house using the specially made rope pulls on the main door.

Chapter Seventeen

Fantastical story aside, once Rocc was gone, Ellys immediately brought up what was really at the forefront of her mind. She sat back onto the lounger, and Aderri copied her action. Ellys didn't look at Aderri, instead fiddling with her empty cup. "Are we going to talk about it?"

"About what, the nation of Aeschar?"

"No…" Ellys looked up, and her gaze landed on Aderri's full lips. "The kiss."

"We've kissed before."

Despite her matter-of-fact words, Ellys could see fear reflected in Aderri's gaze. "True, but that was for practice."

"Was it though?"

Aderri smirked but Ellys wasn't going to be swayed by humor. "It was at the time. And this time there was no one around either, so it wasn't for show."

"No, it wasn't."

"Then why, Aderri? Why did you kiss me?"

"You know why I kissed you. For the same reason you kissed me back."

Ellys leaned forward. "Because you're attracted to me?"

Aderri gave a growl as her brows pulled down. "That's certainly one aspect of it, yes. But you know it goes well beyond that, Ellys. And to be honest, I'm tired of dancing around this subject."

"I don't know what you mean." That time Ellys did look away. The truth was too heavy to bear the weight of Aderri's gaze.

"I think you do."

Ellys abruptly sprung up from the lounger. Her mind raced with thoughts of Aderri and her own lost love, Gwyn. "This isn't possible." She paced the length of the room, spinning and gripping at her own hair in frustration and crazed confusion. "We did everything right. Gwyn's prophesy has no foothold here. I…I cannot feel this way about another. It is betrayal."

"Stop trying to limit yourself."

"What?" Ellys abruptly paused her pacing to stare at Aderri who'd also stood.

"Stop thinking in 'either' and 'or' when it comes to life. There are only two certainties, and those are birth and death. They are the only things that can happen once a lifetime. The rest of our experience is infinite, and love is boundless."

"It betrays her memory."

Aderri walked slowly toward Ellys as their deepest feelings bubbled to the surface. "Does it betray the memory of a favorite wine when you like a new mead?" She took another step. "Would it betray the memory of a close friend if you were to go on and make new friends?"

"No, but—"

Aderri stopped right in front of Ellys. "I don't know your beloved, though I wish I could have met her just based on the stories you and Rocc have shared over the course of our journey. But I will ask this: Would she have wanted you to walk through the world alone?"

Tears shimmered in Ellys's eyes. "Her last words were 'find it again' before she left me in darkness." She looked away and clenched her fists.

"And what did that mean? What were you to find again?"

Ellys swallowed thickly. "She was referring to her foretelling that I'd find love again when I lay with another of the same age. She was telling me to go find that love, but I couldn't." She looked up and met Aderri's gaze. "My love died in my arms, and the possibility that it would happen again hurt too much. I couldn't bear another pain like that." She shook her head. "To lose someone who burned so bright in my heart after so brief a time, just a drop of my life really…even so, it sliced me open worse than any blade."

"Ellys, look at me." Ellys once again trained her wandering gaze on Aderri. "What if you didn't have to?"

"What?"

"What if you didn't have to lose someone like that again? We are well-suited in so many ways, including longevity. Wouldn't you like to see where that could go?"

Ellys sighed and the exhale caused the curls on either side of Aderri's face to dance lightly. "I'm afraid."

Aderri's own tears had come as well. "I'm also afraid. But can't you at least admit what you feel so we can move forward from this point?"

Ellys closed her eyes. Her lies were growing obvious to the person who had gotten to know her so well after nearly two moons together. "There's nothing to admit."

Aderri took her hand and squeezed it, causing Ellys to pay attention. "I'm a dragon, a massive monster of legend who can face armies if needed. You can't lie to me. But beyond that, I also fear. I am afraid of a multitude of things. I'm afraid of the very dragon that I am, I'm afraid of expectation, and I'm afraid of you."

"Me?"

"I've never felt for anyone what I feel for you, and I don't want to spend my life competing with a memory. Yet here I am."

Ellys's eyebrows rose with surprise and she spoke without thinking about her words. "But my love for you doesn't feel the same—" Her sentence cut off at the open admission of her inner truth, and she gazed at Aderri in shock.

"See? Now we can move forward."

Ellys shook her head stubbornly. "There's nothing to move forward from."

Using her grip on Ellys's hands, Aderri slowly drew the two of them together. "What is stopping you, Ellys?"

"Gwyn—"

"Wanted you to be happy, to find exactly what we've found together. Kiss me again and tell me you don't want this." Aderri bit her bottom lip, and the sight of her fangs did something to Ellys's resolve. Between one breath and the next, they crashed together, and those very same fangs had more to work with. Ellys moaned at the explosion of heat between them.

Aderri's arms snaked around Ellys's midsection then moved higher to pull them closer. Nails dug into Ellys's shoulders through her shirt, and she arched her back in response. Aderri dove in to deliver small bites along the length of Ellys's neck. Ellys whined and panted as if she'd been fighting for days, and perhaps she had.

Unfortunately, all good things come to an end, and in a moment of clarity, Ellys gasped as her eyes flew open. She didn't fight the grip but mentally she dug in her heels. "You...you're still m...my patron."

Aderri pulled back and met Ellys's wide-eyed gaze. "Ellys."

Ellys swallowed, afraid of the possibilities. "Yes?"

Using her grip around Ellys as leverage, Aderri pulled them even closer and leaned in to drag a fang along her earlobe and whisper into a pink-tinged, pointed ear, "*Contractus Absol.*"

As if the words alone cut the bindings of Ellys's resolve, she surged forward and captured Aderri in another searing kiss. Her lips trailed down the other woman's neck as she reached behind her to lift Aderri's legs that wrapped around her waist. Ellys walked with her toward the bedroom they shared.

Carrying Aderri would have been an easy enough task but for the distracting way she nipped and bit at Ellys's neck. Ellys nearly dropped her when those blasted fangs grazed along the outer edge of her ear yet again. "Can you—" She whined. "Give me…ung, just a moment—" Ellys suddenly yelped and dropped Aderri onto the bed then stepped back and clasped a hand to her neck. "You *deveel*!"

Aderri was sprawled across the coverlets where she was thrown, eyes dancing with mirth and more as she laughed at Ellys. "You love it." She gave a casual wave toward the bedroom hearth and that too lit with the flames of her fire.

"That hurt."

Aderri crooked a finger, beckoning for Ellys to join her on the bed. "What was it you told Ailith that night? I believe you said that you liked that I was a biter."

"You!" Ellys lowered her hand and closed the distance to the bed. She crawled up to press the full length of her body against Aderri, pinned Aderri's hands in place over her head, and leaned in close. "Your mouth needs to learn some manners." Ellys followed the motion of Aderri's tongue as the woman below her licked her lips in a provocative manner.

"This coming from an uncouth swordswoman with a head for apples and danger."

Offended, Ellys exclaimed "I'm not the one who likes apples."

"And who is going to teach me and my mouth? You?"

"It seems right that I do…if only for the sake of others."

Aderri wrapped her arms around Ellys and pulled her so close that the seams of their trousers pressed in spots that left them both panting. "Ellys…"

"Y…yes?"

"There are no others."

Ellys rolled her hips and leaned down to graze her lips against

Aderri's ear, causing the other woman to shudder with arousal. "Good." She moved her mouth back to Aderri's and kissed her in a way she'd only dreamed possible for many cycles, with a passion she thought she'd lost long ago. Ellys kissed Aderri like her heart was turning inside out and filling them both.

At first, Ellys had worried that any relations between them would be clouded by thoughts of Gwyn. But the emotions pouring from her in the moment convinced her that what she felt was for Aderri alone and not a misplaced love from the past. When they pulled back for air, Aderri met Ellys's eyes with her flaming gaze. "Aren't you supposed to be teaching me a lesson? We can't very well do that with so many layers on."

"Truthfully?"

Aderri nodded.

"I was waiting for the room to warm up more before removing my clothes."

Aderri burst into laughter, and Ellys felt the body below hers grow warmer. It was as if she had a personal heating stone in the bed with her. Granted, it was a warm, breathing, and incredibly alluring heating stone. Ellys sat up and Aderri put the increased space between them to good use. She methodically unbuttoned her shirt, starting from the bottom and working her way up.

Ellys was mesmerized as each sliver of dark flesh was revealed. She groaned in disappointment when the shirt at last parted and revealed a breast band. "You are a tease."

Aderri waved her hand toward Ellys's clothed body. "And what of you? I know what you're keeping from me, and making me wait at this point is unnecessarily cruel. As punishment, I should rip the clothing from your body."

"Erm, could you do that?"

As an answer, Aderri held up her hand and Ellys watched in fascination as the nails morphed and lengthened into short claws. "While I'm not as practiced in the major dragon magics as my kin, I am a master shifter and can morph any part of my body from its natural state for a short time."

Ellys shivered at the thought of those claws trailing down her back in the heat of passion. "And the strength?"

Aderri grabbed the front of Ellys's shirt with one hand and pulled her down. "I'm a dragon. What do you think?" She released Ellys, only to start unfastening the buttons in front of her face. "Now you…are wearing…too…many…clothes." When the last clasp was undone, she spread Ellys's shirt wide and was treated to the sight of a leanly-muscled torso, pale skin, and nearly flat breasts.

Ellys's nipples were hard, and Aderri gazed upon them for a moment before leaning upward to take one into her mouth. Ellys hissed and grabbed the back of Aderri's head to hold her in place. Aderri hummed and caressed the little nub with her tongue.

Ellys panted with pleasure and ground against Aderri, searching for friction in any way possible. When Aderri had Ellys quivering with arousal, she switched to the other breast, a move that finally pulled words from the half-elf's lips. "T…teeth. Use, uh, use your teeth."

Aderri quickly complied by first running one fang along each side of Ellys's left nipple, then she used the other fang. The points dragged against the sensitive flesh, and Ellys nearly tipped over the edge in that moment. Finally, she pulled Aderri's head back. "Enough! I can't take more of that without going insane, a state you should never be in while still in trousers."

"Have you met many trouser-less lunatics then?"

"Cart loads."

They stared at each other for a few moments then burst into laughter. Once Ellys got control of herself, she quickly stood on the bed and stripped off the rest of her clothes. Aderri remained in her reclining position and did the same, kicking her trousers off even as she stripped the shirt and breast band and dropped them over the side onto the stone floor. Then, seeing that Ellys stood above her in all her nude glory, she replied, "Oh look, trouser-less and fully mad." Ellys's smirk quickly turned to a look of shock as Aderri used her legs to trip her and maneuver them so she had Ellys pinned to the bed. "I've got you now."

Ellys grinned. "You like mad. What are you going to do with me?"

"I like *you*, and I'll do whatever I please. Objections?"

"If you start now, no."

Aderri leaned down and kissed Ellys, resuming where they'd left off earlier, only the arousal increased ten-fold while their bare flesh slid together. Ellys found the heat of Aderri a delicious factor while engaged as they were. They writhed together, and Aderri let out a long moan when Ellys lifted her leg to press against the juncture between her thighs.

Almost as a response to the stimulation, Aderri's hands moved up to Ellys's small breasts, and she dragged sharp nails across the hard nipples. Ellys's back arched from the coverlets, and she hissed with pleasure. "Yesss!"

Because she walked the way of balance above all else, Ellys used her strength and training to flip them around again. She held Aderri's gaze as she lowered her own head and took a dark nipple into her mouth. Aderri's breasts were of decent enough size but her nipples were some of the largest Ellys had ever seen. Until that moment, she had no idea that she could derive so much pleasure from the act of sucking alone.

Aderri eventually grabbed onto Ellys's head to hold her closer, those little claws digging in slightly. "I like teeth, too." Ellys fully believed in satisfaction for all. As such, she wasted no time in giving Aderri what she wanted, a mix of pleasure and pain. After a period of maddening torture that left Aderri moaning below her, Ellys pulled back.

"No!" Aderri protested, eyes wide with wildness.

"Yes. Can I taste you?"

"Come here first." Aderri gently tugged at her tousled short hair, pulling the leather band off and dropping it on the floor to join their discarded clothing.

Ellys moved up until her hips rested against Aderri's and she could see into those flaming pupils that burned with more than desire. Aderri gently cupped Ellys's face between her hands. "You know I adore you, right? More than I thought possible after so short a time."

"I've gathered as much."

Aderri took a shuddering breath. "I've had plenty of temporary things, Ellys, and never given my heart to any of them. I don't want this to be a temporary thing."

Ellys considered her words and thought about how she felt deep within her soul. "I've had both and know which I prefer."

"I can feel you here," Aderri said and pointed at her head, "and here," and she pointed at her heart. "But I need you to say it, or it won't be real enough for me. Are you willing to see where this romance leads?"

Ellys's answer was a whisper, "Only with you."

The smile she got in return carried its own heat, and in that moment, Ellys, too, adored. When Aderri spread her legs wider and pushed Ellys's shoulders, the warrior knew she had one land left to conquer. Despite more than a hundred cycles of experience, even Ellys worried about pleasing Aderri because, for the first time in a long time, this bit of sex was serious.

She noticed the heat first as she drew closer to Aderri's treasure. And the scent she associated with Aderri, one of warm fire and smoke, was increased nearest to Aderri's sex. She blew her breath over the moist flesh and Aderri shook.

"Ellys, please."

The words alone sent Ellys into action. She stroked both thumbs along each side of Aderri's folds, carefully avoiding the bundle of pleasure that extended an impossible amount, larger even than Aderri's nipples. She caressed all sides and found every teasing area without touching the two places Aderri wanted her mouth most.

Ellys hissed when she felt those claws prick at her scalp, and she didn't need Aderri's warning of "Ellys" to move into more serious territory. She lowered her mouth again and repeated the actions of her fingers with her tongue. But with her tongue she was much more forward. Ellys dipped down and tasted the nectar flowing straight from Aderri's flower, then moved up and stroked the rest of her sex, still avoiding what they both wanted most.

Sensing Aderri's building frustration and growing nearly too wet herself to function, Ellys finally moved to that last bit of untouched flesh. She took Aderri's clitoral nub straightaway into her mouth and sucked lightly, swirling all around it with her tongue. Aderri cried out and shook from the pleasure of it, increasing her grip on Ellys's head even more. The feeling was such a foreign sensation for Ellys, never before having tupped with someone like Aderri. She was aroused and fascinated by the hard, enlarged clitoris.

She released it with a pop and pulled back. Then she moved her fingers through Aderri's damp curls and stroked until they were soaked, before moving them down to press against the source of all the wetness. "May I?"

Aderri lifted her head, hair and eyes wild with unresolved pleasure. "If you don't, I will."

Permission given, Ellys's action was immediate. She stroked her long fingers into Aderri at the same time she returned her lips to that overeager bit of flesh. When she sensed Aderri was at the end, she curled her fingers upward with each stroke and sucked harder, happy at their species' compatibility.

It had never happened before. Aderri was sure she would have remembered such a thing. But in the moment of her release, possibly the strongest of her life, she gushed into Ellys's hand and saw stars. There was momentary blackness, then swirling pinpricks of light appeared in her vision. Perhaps because Ellys was so knowledgeable in the craft of pleasure, despite Rocc's teasing of the contrary. Or because for the first time she felt someone within her heart at the same time they were within her body. Either way, Aderri was left undone and radiating with pleasure, a heat they both could feel.

It took nearly a candle drop for her eyes to flutter open. "That was...I..." Aderri sighed and her voice trailed off.

Ellys wiped her mouth and moved up to lay next to her. She smiled tenderly and prompted, "That was?"

Aderri licked her lips. "Delicious. Clearly Rocc was wrong. If anyone is ready for slumber, it's me."

"By Toroc, part of me wants you to tell her that, and the other part of me," Ellys said and paused, as if contemplating the very same emotions coursing through her in that moment that Aderri herself felt. "Part of me wants to keep this all to myself right now, to savor the feeling."

Aderri turned onto her side and faced Ellys, running her fingertips up and down Ellys's upper arm. "What other feelings would you like to savor? Because I don't plan on ending the night with one round."

"I thought you said you were ready for slumber."

"That was then, this is now. Shifters recover fast, a fact you should well know." Aderri pushed Ellys onto her back and straddled her pelvis. She leaned closer and grazed Ellys's neck with her fangs.

Ellys shuddered and her pupils dilated with arousal. "Is the big, bad, shifter dragon going to eat me now?"

Aderri licked her lips and slid farther back so she could touch Ellys's mossy mound that glistened with wetness. "You're too trimly-muscled for a proper dragon meal. No, I think I'd much rather savor you like a fine elven wine." She ran her thumb over the small clitoral nub, and Ellys gasped with pleasure. "I'll drink you slowly..." Aderri slid lower yet until she could lean over and face her lover's sex. Ellys's legs parted naturally, and Aderri rested between her thighs. "Thoroughly. I'll taste every bit of nectar you have to offer until you're left empty and both of us are satiated. And then—"

Ellys was panting as if she'd run for leagues, and Aderri had barely touched her. She gazed down the length of her body, straight into Aderri's flaming pupils. "And then?"

Aderri leaned down to swipe her tongue through Ellys's unusual folds and moaned at the flavor. She licked her lips and looked up to find Ellys watching her through half-lidded eyes. "And then I'll lick every bit of you from my lips and begin again."

A shuddering breath followed Aderri's declaration, and Ellys reached out to caress her cheek. Then the caress moved to the back of Aderri's head, and Ellys pulled her closer. "Excellent plan. You should do that. Pretend I'm a fine wine who has only gotten better with age."

Aderri wasted no time in giving what she'd gotten candle drops before. Neither found slumber until long after the sun had risen for the day.

****

Ellys stirred, still in a state of consciousness where she was half-asleep and half-awake. But there was something, intuition perhaps, that made her think she was being watched. She could hear the even breathing of Aderri next to her, an indication that her new lover still slumbered. The smallest of sounds propelled Ellys past the halfway point and into full consciousness. She slowly opened her eyes to see Rocc staring at her from a mere two paces away.

The large steed leaned her head down out of sight from where Ellys lay in bed, then crunching echoed through the room and the head came back into view. *It's about time you left Somna's realm. Did you have a good sleep?*

Ellys groaned quietly, trying not to wake Aderri. Though how the other woman could remain that way with Rocc's noise was beyond her. "You came into the house with an apple, entered our room, then…what, just decided to eat it and watch us sleep?"

That is what I did, yes.

Ellys whispered, "There is something wrong with you."

Rocc snorted then leaned down to crunch another piece of apple. *On the contrary, I feel perfectly fine. Besides, I'm not the one sleeping all day, perhaps it's you who is ill.*

"You're mad!" she whisper-shouted.

At least Aderri isn't the type to make away with your coin purse when you inevitably fall asleep.

Silence reigned for a few heartbeats then Ellys spoke quietly to her best friend. "I don't know what you're talking about."

Unfortunately for her, Rocc was having none of her denial. *You felt unusually happy in my head, so I had to come investigate. That's when I found you nude, smelling of sex, and sharing a bed with Aderri.*

Ellys knew Rocc was going to be impossible if she thought the advice that she'd given to Ellys back in Ailith's stable was correct in any way. "Why exactly are you here? Are you out of food or water? I know that you're smart enough, you could probably work the well crank yourself."

Rocc finished off the last bit of apple and took a step closer. *I got lonely.*

"We are literally in an area rife with shifters and intelligent creatures, as you found out at the dinner last night. You couldn't just go visit one of your new centaur friends?" The steed shifted from foot to foot, scraping along the stones beneath her hooves. It was a sure sign that she was nervous about something, and Ellys grew suspicious. "What did you do?"

I didn't do anything, but one of the farmers, Tyrrox, well...he was a little too feely last night, and I didn't appreciate the way he kept slapping my rump. I know it was in good fun, but still. Just because you have hands doesn't mean you need to use them.

Ellys abruptly sat up. "Did he touch you against your will? I'll kill him."

Rocc closed the distance to the bed and momentarily trapped Ellys's forearm within her big block-toothed bite. The move was gentle but left a fair amount of sticky slobber behind. *Settle down, I handled it. I've had my share of unwanted attention over the cycles. He was in the mead, so I gave him a little kick to sober up. He was actually really nice otherwise and had fine-looking hindquarters.*

"And?"

He was still quite interested at the time we left. He even offered to show me his orchard today.

"Erm...do you want to see it? And are we actually talking about an orchard, or something else involving a trunk and apples?"

Don't be crass. But regarding that, yes. Probably.

"Ellys?" Aderri stirred from her incredibly deep sleep. "Rocc?" Being a shifter, Aderri didn't bother covering her nudity as the coverlet slipped down with her movement. Ellys's gaze was caught by the glorious expanse of dark flesh on display. "Is something wrong?"

Nothing is wrong. I was looking for someone to talk to and came in to see why you were both lazing about so late in the day. I'm glad to see you getting along. Ellys didn't fall asleep on you, did she?

Ellys scowled and pushed Rocc's head away from the bed. "I told you that was under unusual circumstances. I've not made a habit of falling asleep in the middle of tupping a pretty woman."

Rocc lifted her head and turned one liquid dark eye toward Aderri. *You've got first-hand knowledge, is her stamina better than past performance indicates?*

Ellys said, "You're an ass."

Her exclamation drew braying laughter from her bondmate, a sound that was much too big for the two-legger-sized room. *I thought you said I was a donkey.*

"That, too. Now go away and let us cuddle in peace."

You're certainly testy this morning. I thought you'd be in a better mood after all the noise the two of you made last night. I was nearly certain a werewolf had gotten into the house to wreck all Aderri's furniture.

Aderri burst into laughter. Ellys turned to comment on the other woman's betrayal, but the words died on her lips. The sight of Aderri reclining on her elbows in bed, with her head thrown back and breasts in full view, cast Ellys's mind back to the night before. Ellys sucked in a breath when she remembered the passionate display of the previous evening, as Aderri fell over the edge again and again.

Rather than tease, Aderri smiled softly at Ellys. "Roccotári, why don't you give us a little time to clean up then we'll come keep you company. Okay?"

Rocc gave a little swish of her tail. *Sure. I wasn't terribly lonely. I mostly wanted to see if my advice was taken, and embarrass Ellys a bit. Say, you probably didn't hear me talking to Ellys about the centaur, Tyrrox. Do you know who he is, and if so, what's your opinion of him?*

Aderri thought for a moment. "Solid. Why?"

I meant his personality.

"Oh, well I've known his family a long time. He's younger than I am, obviously. I believe the last time I saw him he was naught more than a colt but his herd has always been composed of good stock and great personality. Why do you ask?"

Oh, no reason.

"She totally wants to see his apples."

Rocc rolled a big horse eye, and Ellys had a good view of her disdain. *I spoke with him at length last night. He seemed a bit forward under the influence of your Clan mead, but he was intelligent and expressed interest I rarely see with so much time spent traveling.*

"Did he offer to show you his orchard?"

Ellys nodded vigorously and Rocc took a plodding step forward. *How did you know about that?*

"His uncle used the same line on me cycles ago. And his aunt. I'm pretty sure every member of that gods-be-damned family reuses that terrible line each generation."

Rocc shook her mane, her version of a shrug. *At least they're consistent. I'll be picking flowers on the other side of the lane if you need me.* Then she turned and exited, her hooves clopping all the way to the door at the front of the house.

Aderri collapsed back onto the bed and looked at Ellys through lowered eyelashes. Her dimples were on full display. "She's funny."

"That's one word for it. Roccotári has a habit of making any moment strange."

"Is she really picking flowers?"

Ellys shrugged. "Picking or eating, I never know with her."

"Once a horse, always a—"

Rocc's indignant mental voice filled their heads. *I'm not a horse.*

Ellys cupped her hands and bellowed loudly toward the bedroom shutters that had been opened during the night when Aderri's heat filled the room to near stifling. Clearly the steed wasn't so far away she couldn't hear their conversation. "Stop eavesdropping!"

Chapter Eighteen

Later that afternoon, Aderri had Ellys go into the woods to hunt for a stag to spit in the kitchen hearth. Most of the big shifter species would eat beforehand, and all would bring something to share with the group, but it was common courtesy for the hosting house to provide a large offering, hence the deer.

Aderri and Rocc kept each other company in the open area between the barn and house. There were a few taller tables as well as a large stone circle made to hold a decently-sized fire. Not all creatures liked to stay inside two-legger dwellings during Clan gatherings.

Ogre kills faun. Your move. Rocc used her teeth to lift the carved figurine from the board, placed it on the table at her side, then moved her own ogre figure to take its place.

Aderri studied the board intently, trying to discern a pattern to Rocc's strategy. Ellys had a portable set for their travels with the "board" made from a piece of rolled-up leather. But rather than play with such a small version, Aderri had retrieved her own from inside the house. The Clan had a master carver many cycles before, and she had traded them for it, in exchange for clearing all the rocks from their oversize garden patch. Her set was large enough that all types could use it easily.

Seeing only one possible move, she quickly slid her centaur up and over, so it sat diagonal to the square keep. "'Ware."

Rocc slid the other keep figurine across the board until it knocked over Aderri's centaur. *Keep kills centaur. Beware yourself.*

Aderri groaned and removed the centaur then placed it on Rocc's side of the board. She made another move with a soldier right after, only to have Rocc counter in such a way the game was ended.

Defeat. Do you yield?

"Blast it, I didn't even see that coming. I yield," Aderri grumbled and moved all the pieces back to their starting positions on the board in case some of the guests at the gathering wanted to play later. "I've been playing Knights and Knaves since I was a child. By Cassyn, why can't I beat you?"

The steed brayed at the same time her mental laughter rang in Aderri's head. *Because I've got six times your cycles under my hoof. When your parents were naught more than children themselves, I was learning from elves who were ten times* my *age.*

"Still, experience isn't everything."

Rocc moved close enough to nudge Aderri's shoulder. *Neither is intelligence. A wise creature never depends solely on one or the other.*

"You're full of information today. Do you have any other words of wisdom for me?"

Yes. Quick as a snake strike, Rocc grabbed Aderri's wrist within her bite, very similar to what she had done earlier to Ellys in the bedroom. *Ellys is my lineal bondmate, and I would protect her with my life. I like you, Aderri, and I think you two would make a good match.*

"So—" Aderri stopped speaking when Rocc gave a little shake.

Listen. I support this potential pairing between you, but Ellys will always come first within my heart. And if you are callous with hers, dragon or no, there are things I can do in retribution that are far beyond your understanding.

Aderri swallowed then tilted her head as curiosity got the better of her. "What could—"

Rocc cut her off again. *I've healed you once, so I know how to get inside your defenses. What I give, I can also take, and my spirit is far greater than what you see.*

With those words, Aderri knew what Rocc referred to. In part it was a reference to her healing ability and the way the steed was able to siphon magical energy from the ley lines of the world to direct into another being. The other part acknowledged basic magical conservation theory, and something clicked inside Aderri's mind. "Are you telling me this isn't your natural form?"

The steed released her wrist and stepped back. *I'm telling you nothing. That is knowledge only discovered inside the Sacred Grove, a place you cannot go.*

Aderri took a deep breath to settle her racing heart. Despite Roccotári looking like naught more than an oversize horse, she had a stare that was quite disconcerting. Add that to her words and the knowledge that Ellys's bondmate had always felt larger than life inside her head and Aderri was willing to believe the threat/promise. "You know I would never harm her on purpose. You can read my thoughts a lot better than I can read yours."

I can, but I also know that people are capricious and can be swayed by desires outside their control.

"Well, right now Ellys appears to be my greatest desire."

A joyous whinny sounded, and Rocc shoved her muzzle against Aderri's shoulder. *Do my ears deceive me? Is an adagnitio dragon admitting that something has superseded their desire for knowledge?*

"Laugh all you want, but I've never felt this way." Aderri paused. "I'm not going to lie…her past love frightens me. What if Gwyn remains first within her heart and mind, and she never tells me for fear of causing pain?"

Ellys is many things, but none of them deceitful. She will always be up front with you as long as you are the same. Give her some time to fully accept what she's feeling and to understand that her emotions for you don't take away from her past love.

"I can do that. Thank you for talking to me, even though I know it was more a warning than anything else. I wish I had a friend like you."

Rocc gave a single wink with a big, dark eye. *You do. Now…are you ready to play again?*

An aggrieved sigh passed between Aderri's lips, and she waved toward the board. "Winner's choice. Will you attack first or defend?" She continued mumbling beneath her breath, "Not that it matters, you'll demolish me either way."

Rocc nickered. *Defend, and just remember, winning isn't what's important.*

Aderri gave her a curious look, suspecting more wise horse wisdom. "No?"

No. It's seeing the look on your face as you lose.

"Ellys was right. You really are an ass."

Rocc brayed with laughter, and took Aderri's soldier with her centaur.

****

With Ellys's help, Aderri had placed tall torches around the areas at the front and back of the house, then she lit them along with the central fire using her magic. Rocc did her part and pulled a wagon loaded with deadfall from the forest. They left it near enough to the fire circle to be convenient but not so close that it was in danger of catching a stray spark.

The sun was rapidly sinking below the horizon as Ellys and Aderri cleaned up in the bathing room just off the side of the kitchen. Both were dirty from stacking and hauling wood for the gathering. As it was, they didn't have time to do more than scrub the sweat and grime with cloths and water-filled bowls. Aderri lifted her shirt and took a sniff, then stared intently at a rip in her sleeve and wrinkled her nose. "I don't want to wear the same outfit for the gathering that I've had on all day."

"Why don't you just spell it better?"

"What's the point of being back in my own home if I'm not going to wear something other than the same old thing while I'm here?" Without warning, she finished washing and pulled her top off.

It took only a moment for Ellys's mind to cast back to the night before. She shuddered to see all that dark skin and Aderri's large dusky-pink nipples that had hardened with the chill air in the room. Her breath caught and Aderri turned with concern. "Is something wrong?"

Ellys swallowed and wet her lips before speaking. "You stand in front of me looking like that and ask if something is wrong? By Goz, the only thing wrong is the fact that we're about to have a lot of visitors and I can't take you back to the bedroom and ravage you."

Aderri raised that pesky red eyebrow. "Ravage me? I seem to recall a certain someone calling for their Goz on multiple occasions." She tapped her lip and looked up as if in thought. "Now who could that be?"

"Fair point. Ravage each other then." Ellys's hands twitched with the need to caress Aderri's bare body.

"You're standing too many paces from me, calm as can be. It doesn't appear as though you want to ravage anyone."

Rather than answer, Ellys crossed the room in three long strides and pulled Aderri to her. Her touch was firm, and her lips aggressive. Passion exploded with their kiss and radiated outward and down until Ellys's sex throbbed and her mossy patch grew damp with desire. By the time they pulled apart for air, Ellys had Aderri against the far wall with a knee pressed tight to her lover's sex.

Aderri gasped as Ellys shifted. "By the gods and goddesses, I wouldn't be opposed to a little ravaging right now."

Ellys leaned forward and nibbled at Aderri's neck, which caused Aderri to sag in place and moan before throwing her head back with pleasure. "You said it yourself. We don't have much time. It's nearly sundown."

"Ngh, maybe just a…" Aderri groaned again as Ellys moved her right hand down to slip between her own thigh and Aderri's sex. She pushed her hands into the trousers that Aderri still wore and moved down farther until her fingers found slippery folds.

Aderri moaned. "Yes, right there!" Ellys complied and moved her mouth to the nearest nipple.

Shuddering ran through Aderri's body, and Ellys grasped her tighter with her free arm. She pulled her mouth away from Aderri's breast. "Put your arms around my shoulders if you need to. I can hold you." Then she moved her lips and tongue to the other side, not wanting to neglect one breast or the other.

It seemed as if no time at all had passed before Aderri gave out a cry and came apart beneath Ellys's talented fingers. Ellys herself was on the precipice of desire. While her trousers were too tight for Aderri to fit her hand inside, not to mention the angle wasn't good the way they stood against the wall, Aderri was able to press and rub circles on the front seam. It was enough to send Ellys crashing over the edge heartbeats later.

Rather than attempt to remain standing, as one they pulled apart and turned so they could slide down the wall to recover. After a few heartbeats, they looked at each other and laughed. Ellys pulled herself together first. She sucked the first two fingers of her right hand into her mouth, scouring them of Aderri's desire with her tongue. "Looks like we'll need to clean up again."

The flames of passion burned brightly within Aderri's pupils. "Looks like." She stood then held out a hand to pull Ellys up as well. "Do you think you can control yourself for another washing or must I put my shirt back on."

Ellys gave a slow smile. "I'd say I'm sated well enough for now. Perhaps we can revisit this later when everyone leaves."

"That sounds like a plan."

****

Candle marks later, Ellys found new respect for the stamina of shifters when the gathering was still going strong. She lost sight of both Rocc and Aderri sometime during her conversation with Aderri's nestmate, Bonvi, and Seli, the friend they'd met on the road. Both were quick of wit and humor, and the conversation flowed like water. But soon enough, talk tapered off as one, then the other, was called away to various groups. After so many cycles traveling the six with Rocc, Ellys was unused to the noise of lengthy gatherings, be they indoors or out. She wandered off to the barn in search of a little quiet.

Did you miss me already?

Ellys was pleasantly surprised to find her long-time companion drinking from the trough in her stall. "Why are you hiding away in here instead of admiring Tyrrox's hindquarters by the fire?"

Roccotári pulled her head from the trough, dribbled water across the stones beneath her hooves, and snorted. *Don't be crass.*

"Says the slobbering horse with turds in her fresh stall."

Rocc whipped her head around, barely missing hitting her muzzle against the post. When she turned back to see Ellys laughing, she bared her teeth. *You're as funny as that minstrel in Parelgar, Sorme the Scant. Remember him?*

Ellys was confused. "He wasn't funny at all. As a matter of fact, his bumbling cost him his head halfway through the Festival of Kings."

Yes. It did.

"Well, that's just mean." Ellys put her hands on her hips. "Aderri thinks I'm funny."

Rocc abruptly nipped Ellys's shoulder. It was enough to catch her attention, but it didn't hurt. Much. Ellys tried to swat her away. "Hey!"

I'm sure she does. And on the subject of Aderri, I have something to say.

Ellys's hands stilled as Rocc's words registered. "About Aderri?"

Yes. How serious are you on this, Ellys? I know we've talked about the possibility of you exploring your feelings, but what is your intent here?

Ellys looked at her friend with shock, thinking Rocc was worried about things changing between them. "You're my bondmate. I would never leave you behind, no matter where I wander. You know that."

Rocc tossed her giant head. Silky, silver strands of her mane scattered about, only to lay beautifully against her neck once again. *I'm not worried about me. Where you go, I go. We are unbreakable, cara. My concern is for Aderri. Her heart is not one to be toyed with like one of your conquests of the past. She deserves a lot more. If you can't commit to her fully, if you think your past with Gwyn will interfere with a future with Aderri, you need to tell her.*

Ellys stood in silence, mouth gaped open like a landed fish. Time passed, with heartbeats broken only by the revelry outside as someone with a flute began to play near the fire. "Did you just…defend a dragon's heart from your lineal bondmate?"

Rocc stepped close and lipped at the black hair that lay haphazardly over Ellys's leather headband. *No. I cautioned one friend, who has held a love close to her heart for more than a century, to be careful with another friend's love. A friend who has guarded her own heart for near the same amount of time.*

"I—" Ellys swallowed.

Do you love her?

The half-elf looked at the ground, then traced her gaze back up the strong, dappled legs of her companion. "I…I do." She met Rocc's liquid gaze and saw no judgment for her shifting adoration. "I haven't felt this happy in a very long time."

Someone began singing along with the flute outside, and both creatures of earth in the barn held their breath as the words trickled in.

"All those born in the cycle of gold were kindred souls, kindred souls. Prophesy deep and fools do weep, for a bond like that foretold. Sword of earth and heart of fire, neither old nor timely spent. Cast the bones for destiny, for heart is stronger than element."

Ellys turned to Rocc, her face awash with astonishment. "I know I've heard that song before, but I swear I don't remember those lyrics."

Perhaps you were in your cups…or someone else's moss?

Ellys turned back toward the open barn door and the firelight crackling beyond, observing the two satyrs dancing around the fire. One was playing the flute while the other sang. "Maybe."

Or… Rocc's voice trailed off in Ellys's head, and she turned to give her full regard to her steed. She was curious about what Rocc had to say.

"Or?"

Or the words tonight were always there, and they simply had no meaning all the other times you heard them.

Ellys let out the breath she was holding. "Perhaps."

Rocc gave her a shove forward and took a step to follow. *You should go find Aderri. She's looking for you.*

Ellys glanced back. "What do you mean?"

What do you mean, what do I mean?

"You're being purposely annoying. How do you know that Aderri's looking for me?"

Rocc wuffed. *She told me a few moments ago, of course.*

Sputtering in disbelief, it took Ellys a few heartbeats to organize her thoughts. "How did she tell you when you've been in the barn with me this entire time?"

Ellys, Rocc dropped her head down to eye level, as if she were speaking with a child. *One of a dragon's gifts is that of language. They can speak with any creature that has the capacity to hear. Aderri is both telepathic and empathic. How do you not know this?*

Ellys scowled. "On the contrary, how would I know that? I'm neither of those things. I mean, I knew she was empathic, but…"

Before Ellys could rile up even more, a voice called out from the darkness nearest their side of the house. "There you are. Where have you two been?"

Schooling a two-legger on dragon magic.

"That's not—" Ellys's protest cut off abruptly at the mischievous smile and flaming pupils directed her way. Instead, she gave Aderri a dazed grin. "Uh, you were looking for me?"

Rocc wuffed again and wandered back to the fire where Tyrrox pranced in place as the music began anew. *Have fun,* she called back to them. *I plan to.*

Ellys grimaced and Aderri laughed delightedly. "Cheer up, *callora.* She could do much worse."

Ellys's face twisted into a scowl as the centaur's hand trailed down Rocc's side to her hindquarters, and the steed gave a high whinny. "She could do better, too." Aderri threaded her arm through Ellys's and led her lover back into the house where a competitive game of cups had begun.

****

The next morning was spent in slumber after the gathering ran until nearly sunrise. Aderri woke first, contemplating how fast their dynamic had shifted within a matter of days. A quarter moon ago, she had no hope that Ellys would ever return her favor. Then it was as if a river inside her reversed course and poured forth in the opposite direction. While she wasn't one to complain when events were going her way, Aderri was still leery that Ellys wasn't considering all aspects to their pairing.

Aderri wanted a relationship of length and strength. She'd eventually be called to rule Clan Dracona, to be the Drakaina, and that would require more time in her dragon form. She was desperately afraid that, without being compromised by blood loss, Ellys wouldn't be so enamored with her beast. She was still deep in thought, contemplating the issue, when Ellys spoke from beside her.

"You appear to have troubling thoughts for one on the giving and receiving end of so many moments of passion last night. Is something wrong?" Ellys turned on her side to gaze at Aderri's profile, her smile and wide eyes showing just how much she appreciated the tangle of red hair and smooth, dark skin.

Aderri pressed her teeth into her bottom lip, but this time it wasn't done with seductive intent. Even so, Ellys lifted her hand as though she wanted to caress Aderri's brow where Aderri was sure evidence of her heavy thoughts lay in the wrinkles upon her forehead. Rather than touch, Ellys placed her hand back on the coverlets between them.

Aderri looked into Ellys's silver eyes. "You know I'm a dragon, right?"

"The thought has occurred to me once or twice over the past few moons. What's this about? I thought I made it pretty clear that I've no problem with you as a shifter. I've been with plenty over the cycles."

"Ellys, be serious. What I'm trying to say is that I'm not an ordinary shifter. Dragons are different, we are…" Aderri searched for the words to describe how the world around them saw their species. "I'm a large, carnivorous, and predatory beast…a fact that you've seen with your own eyes. I, um, I would understand if you have second thoughts about our courtship."

"Courtship? Is that what we're calling it?"

Aderri turned onto her side and placed her palm across the back of Ellys's hand. "Ellys, please. You were barely conscious the only time you've been near my dragon. And being nearly eaten by

Dlemna the other night wasn't a good way to gain more exposure. I'm worried that my other form will be…off-putting. Especially if you see it on a regular basis. I'll be the first to admit that I struggle to control her."

"Dlemna?"

"No, my dragon."

"From what I remember, she uh, I mean you, seemed perfectly in control at the time. Well…once all the soldiers were roasted and scattered. Some would say biting off Gahn's head was a bit over the top, but it seemed an act of balance in my eyes."

Aderri scowled with the memory of that day. "That man was repugnant, and I was angry. Just knowing that supporters of blood magic, such as him, oversaw capturing people for their wall left a bad taste in my mouth."

"I'm sure he did." Ellys frowned when Aderri sighed in annoyance. "I'm sorry. So, to sum up, you believe I will be appalled and perhaps disgusted when in the presence of your dragon form, and what, I won't want to continue ravishing your delightful two-legger body?"

"When you put it like that, it seems like a very shallow accusation. But you saw Doonie's reaction in The Stolen Pelt. I can't help a fear I've known my entire life."

"How can I prove to you that your form, any form, won't put me off? I'm only slightly offended that you think the reason you fell into my heart was due to your mischievous smile and strong legs…" Ellys trailed off.

Aderri could only imagine the thoughts going through Ellys's head at the lascivious expression on her face. Aderri remembered how she'd wrapped her legs around her lover's head the night before, or was it morning full by the time they hit their last round of tupping? She shook her thoughts free as Ellys continued.

"Your physical form, while exceedingly lovely, is only part of what makes you, well…you."

Not one to turn away compliments when they're offered on a silver-eyed platter, Aderri prompted, "Go on. What is it you like about me besides my fair form and long fingers?"

Ellys laughed heartily but quickly got control of herself to answer. "For one, I love that you have a curiosity for the world around you. You see all the parts that make a whole in every moment and each situation. It's something followers of Toroc well understand, because only by sensing the whole can you work to promote balance."

"Okay." Aderri thought Ellys would be done, but Ellys continued.

"I love the way you've bonded with Rocc. She is half my life, and for the first time in a long time, our duo has become a trio. Balance doesn't only exist with two halves, but I'll admit it is much harder when you add more sides to any mix. But the three of us…we work."

"We do, don't we?"

"And, by Toroc, you can keep up with me better than anyone I've ever known. I mean, the longevity is a bonus. Of course, it is. But your energy and stamina, and passion…I don't think I've been so well-matched in that regard." She looked both sad and contemplative. "If ever."

"I—"

"And we're not alike. We have different strengths and facets to our minds that complement each other. I enjoy learning new things about you, even when I'm a bit blindsided like I was last night."

Aderri laughed delightedly at the uncharacteristic number of words pouring from her lover's mouth, but she quickly sobered at what Ellys said at the end. "Last night? Did I do something wrong?"

Ellys scowled and lifted a hand to shake her finger at Aderri, then laughed when the woman in question playfully snapped at it. "Yes. Why didn't you mention that you were empathic *and* telepathic? I felt a little…exposed after Rocc told me."

Aderri shifted closer so she could caress the short hairs at the nape of Ellys's neck. "I think you have a misconception about the nature of a dragon's language magic. I can speak whatever language is held by the creature I'm interacting with. If they speak through body language or telepathy, then I can both communicate and listen in such a way. But my empathy is inborn to all dragons and not necessarily part of our language magic. Empathy is not nearly as distinct as the rest. It gives me a vague feeling, but people are complex and they don't usually feel single emotions only. This makes emotions hard to decipher in regard to intent."

"Oh." Ellys let out a sigh of relief. "So, how can I reassure you that I won't be repulsed by the form of your dragon? Wait! You could change, and we can, uh, spend time together?"

"Are you asking or suggesting? And where will we be spending time? My home is large but not enough to fit my dragon."

"The village?"

Aderri shook her head. "Dragon form is limited to the patrol landing area, so we don't scare the livestock. We'd never get milk or eggs again with dragons wandering through the dairy or sidling past the hen yards."

"I guess that makes sense. To do else flies in the face of reason."

Aderri felt a sudden smile blossom across her face. "That's it! I'll take you flying."

"Flying?"

"Yes. I don't know if it was the blood loss talking, but you seemed to really enjoy it. At least until you fell from my back into the sky."

Ellys shivered. "I'm glad I can't really remember that part, but I'm willing to try if you are."

Aderri abruptly sat up on the bed, coverlets pooled near her waist, and spoke with excitement. "That's settled then. After we break our fast, we can head over to the patrol field and I'll fly us up the coast, perhaps to Noth. Maybe we can take dinner at the inn. What say you?"

"Won't we have to be back for last meal with your kin?"

"Not today. We'll get at least one day reprieve after the gathering last night."

Ellys sat up as well and pulled Aderri into a kiss. They broke apart candle drops later, breathing hard from the passion exchanged between them. Ellys smiled. "I like this."

Aderri raised a brow. "Kissing?"

"Not pretending. I like showing you exactly how I feel, touching you freely, and not worrying every heartbeat that one wrong move will trigger Gwyn's prophesy."

Aderri contemplated Ellys's words. The notions only served to bring up her own thoughts on the topic. "Do you think we did something to trigger her prophesy? Or was this thing between us predestined, and she merely foretold of it all those cycles ago."

"Neither of us believes in destiny."

"We don't."

"But I was very careful not to lie with you."

Aderri's gaze became unfocused as she contemplated their situation. "It is a conundrum."

Their conversation was interrupted by the sound of thudding

hooves entering the house. The muffled thumps were followed closely by Rocc's voice in their heads. *It's not that difficult a puzzle to solve. You're just not looking at it from the right direction.*

Aderri called out to be heard through the closed door. "How do you mean?"

Roccotári entered the bedroom and walked right up to the side of the bed. *Why aren't you dressed yet? The day is half gone.*

"Because we didn't get to sleep until night fled the horizon. We are but poor, feeble, creatures…oh mighty steed of light."

Not wanting to get sidetracked into their usual snarky banter, Aderri prompted, "What is the answer?"

Two answers. The first is that, while Ellys didn't lie to others, she certainly lied to herself aplenty.

Ellys immediately swore, "Fenwith's bloody left—" Aderri cleared her throat and made a face, prompting Ellys to finish her usual curse in a slightly different manner. "Uh, ear! She's right."

Of course, I am.

Ellys turned to give Rocc's big head a shove away from where she was leaning over their bed. "Don't gloat."

Aderri asked, "You said two answers. What's the second?"

Rocc stepped backward until she was out of Ellys's reach, then showed them her teeth in her version of a mocking smile. It was frightening. *Destiny, of course. After all, you can't prophesy or foretell something that was never destined to happen. I'd wager both your courses were set before you were born.* Then she turned and walked out of the room with one last comment. *Auspicious cycle, indeed.*

Aderri snorted. "I swear she'd be whistling if she were able. Entirely too full of answers."

Ellys grinned. "I thought you'd appreciate that particular quality, as an adagnitio dragon."

"Even I have my limits."

"Rocc has always been a bit smug when she knows she's right about something. I don't know why I put up with her, sometimes." She looked toward the door where Rocc had disappeared the candle drop before.

Aderri caressed Ellys's cheek. "You two would be lost without each other. Now that the mystery is settled, let's eat and take to the sky." She quickly got out of bed, suddenly excited for their day, and Ellys mirrored her actions on the other side.

Chapter Nineteen

"So how will this work, exactly?"

Aderri led Ellys and Rocc to a weatherproof hutch at the edge of the field. Inside were individual bins where shifters on patrol could store their clothing. She quickly disrobed, but rather than put everything into a bin, she tucked it all into her bottomless satchel. "This is where we would normally store our gear when in flight. However, I will want my clothing when we get to The Stolen Pelt so I'm going to let you carry my satchel."

"Let me, hmm?"

"Just do it."

Ellys slung the offered bag across her shoulders so it would fall at her side without interfering with her sword draw. She'd gotten better about the casual nudity displayed by the shifters since their arrival. The gathering of the previous evening went a long way to desensitize her to the appearance of so much skin, even a body she longed to touch such as Aderri's.

Aderri met Ellys's gaze. "You two stay near the edge of the field until I call for Ellys. Meanwhile I'm going to head to the middle and change."

"Just like that?" Ellys snapped her fingers.

"Yes. Watch and see." She jogged to the center of the small field, her left arm held tight across her chest, probably to prevent uncomfortable bouncing.

Rocc pushed her head against Ellys's shoulder. *You'll want to pay close attention as the transition is fairly fast. But she's beautiful in both forms, if I do say so myself.*

Ellys watched intently as the air around Aderri shimmered under the midday sun. It looked much like a heat mirage often seen in the desert wasteland of northern Legaria. Her focus was so intent she almost missed the moment when Aderri's body caught with flame like the wick of a candle. It rapidly grew and expanded until moments later, a massive black, red, and brown dragon stood in Aderri's place. Ellys's mouth dropped open at the awe-inspiring sight of one creature of magic shifting into another on such a massive scale. Her voice was a whisper as Aderri came closer. "Rocc was right. You're beautiful."

Rocc wuffed from next to her. *Of course I was.*

Aderri lowered her head. Unlike the last time she'd changed, Aderri appeared to have no trouble controlling her beast. "Dragonsss are not beautiful. We are violent and often hungry."

So is Ellys, but at least one or two dim souls over the cycles have called her attractive.

Ellys couldn't even bring herself to be annoyed at Rocc's teasing. Instead, she reached out a hand to touch the warm scales of Aderri's leg. The limb was longer than Ellys was tall, and the rest of her dragon body was easily the size of some of the more modest homes within the village. Ellys found it curious that Aderri was near a match to the Drakaina's size, which was larger than the other three dragons they'd seen on their first night in Clan lands. Ellys stepped back and looked up into the slitted pupils of Aderri's large eyes. Just as with her two-legger shape, flames could be found within their depths.

Aderri tilted her head one way then the other, looking very much like someone's pet canid. A large, sharp-toothed canid that could eat a person in one bite. Her dragon voice was low and rough-sounding, rumbling in a way that Ellys found soothing rather than menacing. "Ellysss, what are you thinking?"

Rather than answer immediately, Ellys made the sign of Toroc toward Aderri, then bowed. When she straightened again, she made her expression hold a fair amount of seriousness. "I'll admit that much of your rescue of me from those soldiers was fuzzy. Blood loss does odd things to one's memory. But now that you're standing in front of me, I think that you're one of the most beautifully-balanced creatures I've ever met. The truth of who you are, inside and out, radiates to those around you, much like your heat."

"I...I don't know what to sssay."

Ellys stepped close again and reached out to rub her hand across Aderri's snout between the two large nostrils. It was a familiar motion that she often made with Roccotári. "You don't have to say anything. It is an honor to know you and call you friend. It is a privilege to receive more than friendship."

Aderri remained silent and Rocc also stepped close. She leaned her neck out and touched her soft muzzle to the tip of Aderri's snout. Ellys watched as the dragon sharply inhaled, and she suspected what Rocc had done. Ellys had been on the receiving end of her steed's energy rush power many times over the cycles.

Rocc moved away again, and Aderri reared her head back, tilting it to and fro in an indication of confusion. "How isss that posssible? Dragonsss have great capacssity, yet you pushed more, asss though it wasss nothing!"

Roccotári struck a hoof to the ground. *Remember my warning of the other night.*

Ellys turned to look at Rocc, suddenly angry on Aderri's behalf. "Warning? What did you say to her?"

While Rocc couldn't smile as a two-legger, she had other ways to make a point of her superiority. *No worries, cara. It was the same thing I said to you.*

A rumbling laugh came from deep within Aderri's chest. "Did she threaten retribution far beyond your undersssstanding for cal-lousssnesss of heart?"

Ellys ducked her head then met the dragon's searing gaze. "She didn't have to." Rather than admit more of her heart in the middle of a field, Ellys moved closer. "Now, how do I mount you?"

I thought all that practicing would have clued you in by now. Rocc brayed even as Aderri rumbled and blew out a waft of smoke from her nostrils in a very dragonish version of laughter.

Ignoring the reaction of her companions, Ellys continued speaking. "I vaguely remember sitting between your plates like it was a war saddle, but I don't remember how I got up there."

Aderri gave a final chuckle and moved her left foreleg back, bending the joint to give Ellys a shorter point to climb.

Candle drops later, Ellys was seated snugly between two large, scaled plates. She wiggled and grinned. "This is warm and tight."

"That'sss not the firsssst time you've sssaid asss much while presssed close againssst my sssskin." The giant head turned one eye toward Ellys, then she winked.

Ellys laughed loudly and slapped at the neck just to the right of the scaled plate. "I'm sure it won't be the last either."

If you two are finished with your interspecies verbal coquetry, I'd like to be on my way.

Both dragon and half-elf turned to stare at the dappled, silver steed. "Where are you going?"

Rocc pranced in place before settling down again. *I've been invited to spend my afternoon at Tyrrox's family orchard.*

Ellys growled. "I don't trust that centaur."

You don't have to. He knows which end of the hoof kicks up. Besides, he's naught more than a bit of distraction, and I told him as much. You need not worry.

Knowing when she was beat, Ellys said, "You're right and I'm sorry. I hope you have fun today."

Rocc whinnied. *At least as much fun as last night.* Then before Ellys could respond, she reared and spun on her hind legs, leaping forward and trotting off down the road that ran alongside the patrol field.

"Are you ready to sssee the sssky?"

Ellys leaned forward excitedly and gave a little kick of her heel against Aderri's side. She paled when Aderri twisted her neck around to meet her gaze. Ellys gave her a contrite smile. "Oops. Sorry."

Without further delay, Aderri unfurled her wings to their fullest extent and leaped into the air with a series of strong downward strokes. They climbed fast, leveling off when she was hundreds of paces above the field below. Then with another snap, Aderri caught a strong breeze and began riding the air current eastward toward the distant coast.

The lack of flapping caught Ellys by surprise, and she yelled to be heard over the buffeting wind. "You're gliding!"

"Yesss. Did you actually think sssomething the sssize of a dragon would continuousssly flap their wingsss like a tiny bird?"

"Maybe."

"Dragonsss are a sssuperior ssspecssiesss. We are sssmart enough to fly with the utmossst efficssiencssy."

Ellys rapidly discovered the key to a dragon's flight was alternating powerful beats of their wings to climb, then diving and gliding to pick up speed. It took less than a quarter candle mark to hit the coast from Clan lands. From there, Aderri headed northeast along the sea. Neither spoke for a while, simply taking in the beautiful view. They'd only gone a short distance when Aderri glided lower and called out to Ellys.

"Sssee that tower?"

Ellys yelled back. "Yes."

"There are sssixss towersss along the coassst, built for dragonsss to ressst and help watch. After all, we can't fly continuousssly."

"How good is your eyesight in dragon form?"

Aderri gradually increased altitude again, ignoring the tower and resting dragon below. She blew a spout of flame off to the side, which she told Ellys was a dragon's way of saying hello, but kept flying toward Noth. "Farther than a two-legger. We can sssee a few leaguesss in good weather, which isss why we alternate between gliding out over the water and resssting atop the lookout tower."

They flew about two candle marks before the city of Noth finally came into view. They had been mostly silent during the journey. Ellys spent her time in awe of the grand view from high above the land. She'd never felt so balanced between the elements of earth and air before.

Aderri was circling the city when she said, "Ellysss, there'sss a long column of sssoldiersss heading along the northern trade road. Doesssn't that road lead to Veniche, the cssity on the border that was bisssected by the blood magic wall?"

Ellys shaded her eyes from the sun so she could see the marching columns of armed and armored soldiers. "It's been many cycles since I've taken it, but yes. It's one of the main roads through Muniers, along with the one leading to Cat's Head, and the other heading directly west, that runs north of Clan lands to Kuwyth beyond."

"Why would the Twin Regentsss send the army north?"

Decades of military and tactical training gave Ellys the answer immediately. "The wall must be down."

"What?" Aderri turned her head to look at Ellys while she was flying, causing a wobble to her glide.

Ellys gripped the armor plate in front of her and screamed, "Eyes front, eyes front!" Flying was fun, but the thought of falling from so high up didn't appeal to Ellys in the slightest. "It makes sense. The logical reason to send the army north would be the threat of imminent aggression from Carthune. That could only happen if the wall comes down."

Aderri began gliding in a circle, slowly tightening it the closer they got to the ground. Just as Ellys thought they were going to crash, Aderri pulled up short with great buffeting strokes of her wings and landed gracefully on the beach near Ailith's inn. Ellys dismounted the same way she had originally climbed upon Aderri's back then moved off to the side.

The transformation back to Aderri's two-legger form was nearly the opposite of changing into a dragon. She shimmered and the flame flickered into existence before reversing course along the dragon's skin and puffing out with a bit of smoke. What remained was a very attractive, very nude woman.

Ellys could barely control her excitement after the exhilaration of experiencing flight via dragonback. "By Toroc, that was amazing!" She suddenly fell silent and watched in fascination as Aderri approached.

"Ellys."

"Yes?" Ellys whispered, more than a little distracted by her lover's attractive form.

Aderri brought Ellys out of her daze. "May I have my satchel please?"

"Oh, right. Sorry."

After quickly dressing, Aderri slung the satchel over her shoulder and looped her arm through Ellys's. "Are you hungry?"

The flame of Ellys's attraction had well and truly caught, and she didn't bother holding back her natural response. She gave Aderri a once-over and whispered, "Starving."

It was early afternoon when they stepped inside the inn, but the chaos within made it seem more like dinnertime. A young server twirled around one patron near the door and stumbled as another stood and knocked into her. The tray and mug that the female dryad had been balancing on her right hand flew into the air. Both were caught handily by Ellys, and the server gave her an appreciative look, one that took in the clothes, elven swords strapped to her back, and the pointed ears.

"Thank ye, Moz—" Her honorific cut off mid syllable as Aderri stepped from around Ellys. "Dracona!" The dryad quickly bowed and backed up a pace, nearly taking out another server.

The exclamation caused a momentary lull in both noise and music as everyone turned in their direction. When patrons and servers alike seemed to realize there was nothing to see, they went back to their business.

The server, naught more than a sapling from what Ellys could tell, swallowed and took another step back. "Uh, um…is there something you need, Dracona?"

Ellys saw a look cross Aderri's face that she'd never witnessed before. The dragon shifter moved closer to the dryad. "Yes. There is." Then she made as if to strike like a snake, clicking her teeth together and showing off her fangs. "I just flew in from the coast and I'm…*famished.*"

Without warning, the dryad's eyes rolled back into her head and she fainted. Ellys quickly dropped the tray so she could catch the woman with a free hand. She was stuck then with an unconscious server and no free hands, so she did the only logical thing she could think of and downed the entire mug of mead. Then she licked her lips and placed the mug on a nearby table so she could lift the dryad with both arms.

Ellys gave Aderri an annoyed look. "Was that necessary?"

"What? I wasn't lying. I'm hungry enough to eat half a low beast and that's in my two-legger form. If she hadn't acted the doe-wit, I wouldn't have—" For the second time in a matter of candle drops, Aderri snapped her mouth shut with an audible click of her teeth. She gave Ellys a contrite look. "My apologies, but it appears as though my hunger has made me extremely volatile."

Ellys snorted. "Volatile, she says."

"Whuh…uh…"

Aderri and Ellys looked at the woman who was slowly rousing in the swordswoman's arms. Seeing both so close and peering down at her, especially Aderri, the server gave a little "eep" and her eyes rolled back again.

A familiar voice called out from a few paces away, "Bring Flora over here out of the way."

Ellys and Aderri made their way to the place along the edge of the room where the selkie had indicated. After Ellys gently lowered the woman, she smiled at Aderri's long-time friend.

"Ailith. Good to see you."

The innkeeper held a hand up in front of Ellys's face. "I'm not speaking with you. You are the reason my Doonie is off studying at the temple, and I've got incompetent tree folk here in their place. Harrumph!" A harried server was passing by when Ailith grabbed the heavy tray from his hands. "I've got this, Del. Go take care of the minstrel so he'll play again tomorrow."

The young man ducked away as Ailith turned and thrust the large, overflowing tray into Ellys's hands. "Make yourself useful and take this to the table of trolls over there." She nodded her head toward a table that was set back from the others. Pointing it out wasn't necessary. Ellys couldn't miss an entire table of trolls if she tried.

"You can't be serious."

Ailith leveled a stern gaze upon Ellys. "Do you want to find out?"

"Uh, no. I'll be back in a candle drop." Without further ado, Ellys made her way across the tavern to the table of ill-mannered brutes.

Aderri laughed quietly. "That was cruel, 'Lith. You know the smell alone at that table would be enough to put anyone off their meal."

"What of it? I am really angry that she encouraged Doonie on their fool's quest."

"Are you though?"

Ailith sighed. "It's complicated."

Aderri put an arm around her friend's shoulders. "Do you have time to sit and take a meal with us?"

Flora came round once again, and Ailith sent her off to the kitchen then turned her attention back to Aderri. "Sure. Let me go retrieve a pin of mead from behind the bar, a mini-barrel should see us through the meal regardless of how much your elf can drink. We can grab some food on the way to my private residence."

Ellys returned a candle drop later, looking a bit green rather than her normal pale. "That was an experience I'd rather forget." She turned and pointed at Aderri. "Never bring this up to Rocc. She knows how much I hate trolls and would never let me live it down."

Curiosity piqued, Aderri asked, "Why do you hate trolls?"

"Well, there was this job about forty cycles ago, and a bridge— you know what? Never mind. It's a tale better left untold."

"I'll just ask Lady Roccotári."

"She won't tell you either."

"Whyever not?"

"She also hates trolls. Same job, different reason."

Ailith reappeared, carrying the small but heavy barrel of mead.

"Do you want me to take that?" Ellys asked.

Rather than a smile, she got another withering glare. "No." They followed Ailith through the kitchen, stopping for a platter of roast meat and vegetables, then continued into Ailith's personal home at the back of the ground floor of the inn.

Ailith placed the pin of mead on a heavy table and removed three mugs from the cabinet below. Ellys wiped a thick coat of dust from the tabletop with her finger. Ailith shrugged and placed the three, newly-filled mugs on the table near the tray. "I rarely have need to eat in here when I have the tavern." The selkie snatched a leg of meat from the tray and took a bite, moaning as the juices hit her tongue. "I should give my cooks a raise."

Apparently, Ellys had gotten over her initial troll-induced nausea and she speared a selection of different vegetables with her eating knife. Aderri really was ravenous and picked up a steaming skewer loaded with meat and vegetables. She too moaned in appreciation. "Perhaps you're right."

"So, you've been gone a seven-day, how goes it with the Clan?" Ailith winked at Ellys. "Have you performed your hired duties with passion and dedication?"

"Erm…" Ellys gave Aderri a helpless look.

"Actually, 'Lith, Ellys hasn't been in my employ for nearly two days."

Ailith thumped the table with her smallish fist. "I knew it! Fired then fucked, hmm?"

Ellys rubbed the point of her right ear, then grimaced and looked at the grease on her finger. "That's, uh, exactly how it happened. How did you know?"

The selkie barked out a laugh and slapped the table again with enough force that the eating knives clattered and the mead sloshed over the side of at least one mug. "Are you kidding me? I'm surprised you made it as far as Clan lands without combusting. I knew neither of you could hold out against that much sexual tension. Well, I was more certain of Aderri."

"Good to know I'm so predictable."

Ailith grinned at her. "One of your best traits, love." She abruptly sobered and turned a hard-eyed gaze back to Ellys and pointed. "Pleased as I am that you two are a'tuppin, I'm still a fair bit mad at you. What did you say to my Doonie?"

"*Your* Doonie? Nothing much, just gave some advice when asked. And provided a letter of sponsorship."

"I didn't care much for your advice or your sea-soaked letter."

Ellys shrugged. "Apologies, Ailith, but it wasn't meant to be liked or disliked. It was intended to bring balance."

The innkeeper scowled. "And just how is Doonie training at the

Temple of Toroc going to bring balance? What it's going to do is get them killed, and I—they're not a fighter."

Obviously, Ailith cared for her fellow selkie. "Doonie will be okay, the temple will thoroughly train them in the style that best suits their strengths and temperament." Ellys leaned across and touched the back of Ailith's clenched fist. "Trust in the balance."

A look of disgust washed across Ailith's face, and she wiped her hand with a rag that had been tucked into her belt. "Seriously? What kind of elf are you? At least clean yourself before touching another in comfort." She paused, then smirked at Aderri. "Unless you need a little grease for the task at hand…" Ellys quickly wiped her hand across her trousers.

Aderri rolled her eyes with exasperation, but she knew her friend too well. "What's really bothering you, 'Lith? You know it will be cycles before Doonie is trained enough to go off in search of your pelt."

Ailith picked up her eating knife and stabbed a piece of broiled shell-tongue with a little too much force. "They've moved into the temple to train. A sacrifice demanded by the head of the Orders, explaining it was law for supplicants to live onsite."

Ellys's fine, dark brow rose. "As a guest?" Ailith nodded. "The abbez should better know the truth, and the truth is, that's not how it's supposed to work. Guests are not the same as a potential follower of Toroc, acolytes. You are only required to live within the temple if you wish to join the order. Is that what Doonie wants? And what of my letter?"

"Abbez?"

"That's the head of the monastery, the Master of Orders. And back to Doonie. They don't want to be an acolyte?"

"No, not at all. But what else could they do but comply? The head of the monastery, Moz Tomvir, told Doonie that they'd not take the word of some 'gender-biased failure' who wasn't even listed in their Book of Orders."

Ellys's brows drew down, and her face twisted with dark anger. Then she took a deep breath. All Aderri and Ailith could do was watch the internal tumult happen. When Ellys's silver eyes opened to look at one, then the other woman again, she was calm. "That is not the way of Toroc. Whoever this Tomvir is, they must be called to task." She shook her head. "Are you sure it's the abbez, and not one of the masters? Because no one with that attitude should be in charge of their own monastery. Even masters don't have to live onsite, just the acolytes. I promise to look into it as soon as possible, after the more immediate events are settled."

"Immediate events, like the naming ceremony? Or are you talking about the fact that the Twin Regents emptied the city's barracks today to join the troops already stationed near the border, after Carthune dropped the wall and attacked four cities along the Vendin River?"

Aderri gave her friend a sharp look. "How did you know that? We saw the columns leaving the city when I circled to land. The news hasn't even traveled down to the Clan yet."

Ellys said, "What about their ships? Are we to believe they're just sitting there, not making any moves of aggression?"

Ailith shrugged at Ellys's question. "I can confirm that both the ships, and their sailors are the very ones that have been sitting there for nearly two moons. It's the same stalemate we've faced since the wall went up. At least on the water. Perhaps Carthune is afraid of the coastal guardians"—she gave Aderri a pointed look—"and chose a land attack where they're more evenly matched."

"It's not just that." Ellys ran a hand through her hair, snagging the leather headband in the process. "I'm afraid the battle won't be a balanced one, as the border is rife with Carthune blood mages. The Regents' soldiers are most likely marching to their deaths. At least those leaving the city now will have a good fourteen days or so before they face such disaster. It will take that long for the troops we saw to reach Veniche."

Ailith frowned. "What do you mean it won't be balanced?"

Aderri, being of a magical mind, caught on immediately. "By Cassyn, it will be a disaster for Muniers. The amount of power it took to hold that wall for so long…if they apply that in an attack capacity…not only that, but the mages will be able to fuel themselves from the battlefield deaths—" She shook her head.

Ailith said, "What can any of us do? I've been here a long time. I'd wager the Regents know all about the mages and will have sent their own to counter. And…well, I'll be the first to admit that I've no want to involve myself in a war. I'm a simple innkeeper who wants to keep my business running and protect my investment. Let's face it, without my pelt…this is all I've got. War does no one good, especially if you ally yourself with the losing side."

"Blood magic…" Ellys muttered, darkly. "This breaks the balance in so many ways, but there isn't much the three of us can do except watch and wait. Balance will prevail, eventually."

Aderri tapped a finger on the table. "Long-lived though I am, I'm not sure I like the thought of *eventually*." She looked back and forth between Ellys and Ailith. "Despite my extended absence, I still have friends and family in Muniers, and I've no wish for them to come to harm."

Ailith brought up another point. "You know you'll be called to defend should Carthune attack by sea."

Aderri was solemn. "Of course. That is the way of Dracona, and I could do no less than my duty as heir to the Mound."

Ellys stole another carrot from the tray and punctuated her statement with it. "Wait, you've never told me why your Clan are only guardians of the coast."

"The pact wasn't always so limited. Lore says that when the pact was first signed, there was no such stipulation and Dracona could be called in any instance of foreign aggression. But many generations ago, the previous king of Carthune, I believe it was Arvol's uncle, decided Muniers would be an easy way to expand his country. Dragons were called to protect, and cities burned on both sides. After that, the people of Muniers went to the Twin Regents and asked for the dragons to be limited to the coast, fearing our power. The pact was changed, and it's been that way since."

"Huh," Ailith remarked, "even I didn't know the original story. I guess I never gave it much thought, but then I've only been landbound for not much longer than I've known you."

Ellys said, "Tactically, it certainly makes sense. Basically, our hands are tied unless Carthune makes a move on the coast."

Aderri looked at Ellys, both brows raised. "*Our* hands? Ellys…you're not Clan, not Dracona. This isn't your fight."

"Did you think my pledge to you was false, or my heart so fickle? Where you go, I will follow. I didn't find you after so long, only to lose you again."

Aderri squeezed Ellys's hand. "You forget that I'm a dragon and more than capable of taking care of myself."

Ellys frowned. "Remind me again of how your great uncle died. Wasn't it an attack from the water, exactly like what you'll be called to defend? And…" She glanced nervously toward Ailith, obviously uncomfortable airing her personal history so openly. "I've already lost one love and I don't think I would survive it again. Please, take me with you if you're called."

Admittedly, the notion of having a partner to take into battle appealed to Aderri's dragon. Even if the battle itself didn't. But there were logistics involved that made it difficult for a dragon to carry a rider while fighting. "Ellys, there are maneuvers I'll need to perform midair, ones that would make it virtually impossible for you to stay on my back. I just don't see how it would work."

Ailith spoke up. "What about a spell? Surely your adagnitio brain can come up with something simple."

Ellys looked from Ailith to Aderri. "Would that work?"

Aderri smiled for the first time since the topic of the coming war began. "I think I do have something I can tailor to this purpose. We can trial it out before heading back to Clan lands later. It will also test how well you can hold your mead with your gut doing tumbles midair."

Ellys scowled. "That sounds a lot less appealing."

"Well and good." Ailith slapped the table. "Now, let's have more mead to celebrate."

Chapter Twenty

It was nearing dusk when Ellys, Aderri, and Ailith stood on the beach across the coastal road from the inn. "Okay," Aderri said, "so I've never tried this before, but it should work. Basic magic theory states—"

"What? You're counting on magical theory to keep my seat while high in the sky?"

Aderri tilted her head. "What else am I supposed to use?"

Ellys waved her arm wildly, more than a little nervous especially after the "holding her mead" comment. "Uh, how about magical certainty or fact? Actual real, proven spells?"

Ailith clapped at her dramatics. "This is a better show than my minstrel puts on."

"'Lith, you're not helping." Aderri turned back to Ellys. "Theory just means that the knowledge of the different parts I'll be using to craft the spell is based on a system of rules and principles. For instance, the spell I'm tailoring is used quite often by earth mages for building. It's a spell of elemental attraction, for binding like-and-like together. Earth mages are often hired by wealthy patrons to perform the elemental attraction spell for any manner of construction projects. Castles, or even something as simple as a brick home." She paused and raised both brows. "You understand so far?"

Ellys grimaced. "I may not be an adagnitio dragon, but despite Rocc's insistence to the contrary, I'm also not...well, a brick. I'm following the explanation just fine. But how will this work for us? While I may be a creature of earth magics, you're not."

"That's true, but I can wrap you in my magic and perform the spell of elemental attraction with the addition of a spell key."

"Spell key?" Ailith looked on in fascination.

"Yes. I'll give Ellys a key word that she can speak aloud to be released. If the worst does happen and I plunge into the sea, I wouldn't want her trapped upon my back." Ellys rubbed her chin in thought and Aderri continued. "You can say nay, and I'll try to come up with an alternative when we return to the Clan."

"No, let's try it this way. If it doesn't work, then you can think of something else later. At least this way we'll know."

"And if you fall from her back?"

"I trust Aderri to catch me. After all, she's done it before."

Ailith chuckled. "More than once from the looks of those heart eyes you two have been throwing all evening."

"Oh, don't be salty just because it's in your nature. After all, you've got your Doonie."

Aderri got a growl for her comment. "*Had* my Doonie, until those blasted monks stole them from me."

Ellys put her hand on Ailith's shoulder. "I'll personally stop in at the temple within a half-moon to sort this out."

Ailith gave a small nod. "Thank you."

"Ready?"

Ellys turned to Aderri. "I suppose."

"At a certain point of the spell I'll begin counting. On three, I want you to stand completely still and hold your breath."

"Why do I have to—"

A dark finger stayed her question. Aderri leaned close enough to ghost her lips across Ellys's after she pulled her finger away. "Trust me."

Ellys sucked in a breath but didn't say any more.

Satchel and clothing were stripped and handed off to Ellys. "I want these with you for the binding, so you don't lose them midair." Ellys accepted the items, stuffed the clothing into the magic sack, and slung it across her chest. She tried her hardest to ignore all the delicious flesh standing in front of her.

Aderri began reciting an incantation while slowly circling Ellys. Her feet stepped sideways, one over the other. When Aderri completed one full circuit, she stopped. Then she counted aloud. "One, two, three—" With no further warning, Aderri inhaled and released a steady stream of smoke as she began circling again. The gray smoke that poured from her mouth shimmered in the fading sun. When she had returned to her spot in front of Ellys, Aderri closed her mouth and swallowed the last bit of dragon vapor.

"Is that it?"

"No, there are two key words. The first *colligo*. It will bind you to the nearest source of fire. Obviously, you should wait until you're firmly on my back to say it. The second is *privo*. That will release you from the binding."

Ellys scrunched her brows as she mulled over the two unfamiliar words. She thought they were some of the many recited during the incantation, but she couldn't be sure.

Ailith said, "Co-leego and preevo? That seems simplistic."

"They can't be difficult to say or remember in case she needs to be released in a hurry. The spell is simple by design, there's no reason it shouldn't work. Now, say a proper goodbye and maybe we'll come visit you another time." Aderri stepped closer, they hugged, then she moved away. "Until we meet again, friend."

Ailith took in Aderri's nude body and winked. "Always a pleasure."

She got an eye roll. "You're such a cad." Aderri was already turned away when she threw the words out, quickly making her way down the beach to where she could safely change.

Ellys and Ailith watched the transformation with awe, taking in the majestic creature standing nearby when she was finished. Ailith called out, "Don't worry about me taking liberties with your nudity, you know our tastes run more the same than dissimilar." She lifted a hand toward Ellys. "I'd much rather fondle your elf here—"

The great dragon swung her head in Ailith's direction almost faster than either of the other two women could follow. The rumbling of warning preceded a single word. "Mine."

Ailith put both her hands in the air and took a step back for good measure. "It was a joke, no need for seared seal today."

"Serves you right," Ellys said, "for provoking a creature that could make you naught more than a snack."

"And you don't mind being claimed in such a manner? You know dragons are not ones to easily let go of what they possess, if at all."

Ellys glanced at Aderri where the massive beast's slitted eyes watched them closely, then she turned back to meet Ailith's curious gaze. "Not if it's Aderri. I don't think I mind in the slightest." She jogged over to the dragon and mounted the way she'd gotten used to. "Talk to you later, Ailith. And don't forget, I'll stop on my way back through to speak with the abbez about Doonie." She gave a jaunty wave then spoke the word of binding. "Colligo!"

Ellys watched Ailith shade her eyes from flying sand as the

dragon's buffeting wings kicked up gusts of wind on the beach. She had to close her own eyes for a few heartbeats when the wind became too strong, opening them again in time to see the innkeeper wave then turn back toward her tavern. She sighed and wondered, not for the first time, if all Ailith's talk of fate had any merit where it concerned her and Aderri's lives. Rocc would probably say yes.

When they were high enough in the air, Aderri snapped her wings out to glide. Her voice was a low rumble, but easily understood after conversing on and off on the way to Noth. "Ready?"

Ellys yelled back, a little chilled with the setting sun. "For what?"

"Thisss." Aderri suddenly dove into a barrel roll, spitting a gout of flame straight out in front of her. Had Ellys been calm and not yelling at top volume, she would have noticed that not only hadn't she flown from her seat, but the fire they flew through had left her completely unsinged. Apparently, a side effect of being wrapped in fire magics meant that flame wouldn't hurt her. Aderri eventually snapped out her wings as they skimmed the treetops below and began pumping once more to gain altitude. "Well?"

Ellys took a shaky breath. "I'm never teasing Rocc about shitting in her stall again."

"Did you really?"

"No, but it was a near enough thing."

Rumbling laughter filled the darkening sky as, one by one, the stars flickered into view above them. "You ssstayed in your ssseat, ssso all isss well."

Ellys thanked Toroc that her elven blades were magically bound into their sheaths to prevent them from coming free when doing flips and tumbles. She groaned aloud as Aderri did a twisting spiral and dove again. "I shouldn't have finished that last mug of mead." A deep chuckle was the only response she got in return, and Ellys suspected Aderri was enjoying herself a little too much.

****

The days passed faster than Ellys would have thought possible. They continued to practice flying maneuvers with Ellys on Aderri's back. The three companions also attended two more gatherings in the evening and numerous events during the day. Even with the typical day-to-day responsibilities for members of the Clan, the upcoming

Cognoment meant there was an almost festival-like mood to the main village. It had been a long time since Ellys had felt as if she were part of something larger than just her and Rocc, part of a group that felt like family. Even Roccotári seemed to be enjoying herself. She mostly stayed with Aderri and Ellys, though occasionally she'd go off to spend time with other members of Clan Dracona.

Rocc was regaling them about one such adventure on their way to Dracona Keep, four days after their visit with Ailith. The ceremony was to be held at sunset, and the stars above them were beginning to fill the sky. *And Gryvet says, 'I'd not suffer that for all the hay at market,' and the entire room flooded with laughter. I don't think I've brayed that hard in ten cycles.*

Aderri looked back at Ellys. "I don't get it."

Ellys shrugged. "Me either."

Rocc suddenly stopped in the middle of the road. *What do you mean, you don't get it? It's one of the funniest things I've ever heard.*

"Perhaps we needed to be there to fully understand," Aderri said.

A loud huff sounded and Rocc stomped the ground with one giant hoof. *Two-leggers. All of you are clueless.*

"But I'm not—"

You are right now.

Ellys leaned closer and whispered in Aderri's ear. "Let her win this one. We'll never hear the end of it if we don't."

Rocc gave a little buck, but not enough to dislodge her riders while they wore nicer garments than their day-to-day gear. *You know I can hear you, right?*

"Absolutely."

There was an indignant whinny, then Rocc began walking again. Her mental voice quietly muttered in their heads, which finally elicited the laughter she'd been looking for with the telling of her story. *Mangy elves and even mangier dragons. I used to like you, Aderri.*

Aderri rubbed Rocc's neck and gave it a little pat. "You love us both a-plenty, and you know it." She sighed. "By Cassyn, I thought Ellys was dramatic."

"Hey!"

They continued bickering for a few more leagues, only dismounting when they crossed the drawbridge and entered the small bailey of the keep. Their conversation was interrupted by Droogus. "The ceremony is to be held in Dragon Hall, but I can't follow you inside because we are expecting more guests that won't know the way. But, before you head in, the Drakaina would like to speak with Aderri in private."

Aderri glanced at Ellys before asking, "Do you know what about?"

"I'm sorry, but I don't. You know your mother, Addy. She keeps her own counsel more often than not...unless it's with Koldaht."

Aderri blinked. "True enough."

Ellys thought perhaps she feared pressure from her mother regarding Clan responsibility. They'd discussed the subject many times over the past handful of days. "If you want, we can wait here until you're finished. Or, Drakaina's orders or not, I'll come with you."

"Your offer is touching but unnecessary. I'll be fine. You both know the way by now. Go ahead and join the others at the main table. I'm sure my mother and I will be along shortly."

"Okay." Ellys took a step closer then hesitated.

But Aderri didn't need her empathy to sense her lover's intention. She closed the distance between them and gave her a gentle kiss. "It's okay, I promise. She'll give me the usual lecture about returning to resume my place as Riki, and I'll explain that I'm not ready to settle down. I'll have to reassert the fact that you and I are not mates, though I've grown quite close with you. Perhaps that will give me the freedom to pursue knowledge for the next one hundred cycles."

Ellys made to speak but was interrupted once again by the captain. Droogus cleared his throat. "I'm sorry, but the Drakaina is waiting."

Aderri disappeared into a smaller door of the keep while Roccotári and Ellys went in the opposite direction toward the large hall where they'd had their first meal with the Clan. As soon as they stepped through the massive doors, a voice called out over the din. "Lady Roccotári!" Another followed from Aderri's family table. "And Ellys!"

Rocc turned liquid dark eyes toward her bondmate after her gear was removed. *I can stay with you until Aderri returns.*

Ellys looked across the room where a tall table of mixed species Clan members who were all on the larger side waved and called to her friend. She smiled. "Go ahead, I'll be fine with Aderri's family."

You're sure?

Ellys shoved Rocc's shoulder. "I'm sure." After Rocc walked away, Ellys made her way to the familiar Dracona table. It was still half empty, but Gessy was there. Ellys knew patrol was soon to change so more would come in just before the ceremony was due to start. Aderri mentioned that some of the distant Dracona kin would take over so her nestmates could attend.

"I saved you and Addy seats by me."

"You mean there aren't assigned seats for these things?"

Gessy was joined by a couple of others at the table. "What do we look like, royalty? That would be such a bore."

The place Gessy indicated happened to be two seats from Aderri's father, Koldaht, and right across from a large cat with a disconcerting stare. She didn't know who it was, since according to Aderri, they hadn't even met a third of the Clan members. Ellys took her seat and gave the cat a curious look. Trying to be polite, she introduced herself. "Hello, I'm Ellys DeEnsis. What's your name?"

The cat continued to stare without answering, which Ellys thought was exceptionally rude. She huffed. "The least you could do is give me a name."

"Ellys." Ellys turned to see that Gessy was barely holding back laughter. "It's just a cat."

Ellys flushed with embarrassment as a bray sounded from the table where Rocc stood. *You can't blame Ellys. She's got the magical sense of a turnstone.*

Ellys yelled back to her. "Stop eavesdropping!" More than a few tables laughed loudly then, and Ellys swore the cat wore a smug look.

Koldaht leaned across the empty seat and patted her arm. "Don't worry, my dear. It happens to the best of us. I'm sure our Aderri will be along soon."

Someone placed a tankard of Clan mead on the table in front of her, and Ellys was quick to quench her thirst, hoping to cool the blush that stained her cheeks. It was then, when Ellys had a mouthful of the strong drink, that Aderri pushed through an adjoining door with Zevieri. While the Drakaina walked to the middle of the hall, Aderri came toward their table. Koldaht's face lit up. Ellys had noticed it was the same expression he wore every time he saw Aderri since her return to the Clan, a look that clearly showed how much he missed his daughter.

"And there is my little phrenic flame now. Isn't she lovely?"

"The quest given to you, on the sixth day of Cervi, is one dictated in the Book of Prophesy and interpreted by Templar Inam. Ellys DeEnsis, you are to warm yourself by the phrenic flame. Only then may you return and have your name entered into the Book of Orders and take the oath of gender balance."

The two words, *phrenic flame*, echoed over and over within Ellys's mind, and she promptly spit her mead all over the cat across the table. It hissed at her, jumped down from the chair, and ran off. Ellys's coughing fit prompted a round of backslaps from Gessy and an extremely concerned look from Aderri when she reached the table.

"Are you okay?"

Ellys, shocked speechless, turned her gaze upon her lover, and Rocc's voice sounded in her head. *Ellys? What is it?*

"I, he…uh—" Ellys's words cut off abruptly because Koldaht's declaration left her reeling, and she didn't know how to process the long-sought-after knowledge. She stood and stepped away from the table, closer to Aderri. She found her voice, and it came out in a whisper. "I've been searching more than a hundred cycles, and it's been right in front of me for moons."

Heartbeats later, Rocc came around the table and stood next to her bondmate. *Tell her, caritas.*

"Tell me what?"

Ellys didn't need any sort of magic to see the concern written across her new love's face. "I was tasked to warm myself by the phrenic flame."

Dark red curls bounced as Aderri tilted her head at Ellys's strange statement. "I don't understand."

"In the cycle twenty-four ninety, I left the monastery on my Quest of Toroc. That was the task given to me one hundred and eight cycles ago."

Aderri covered her mouth in shock. "Ellys…"

"It was you all along."

Rocc blew out a breath through her nostrils then moved her head up to lip at Ellys's hair. *Now who doesn't believe in fate?*

Both women looked at the elven steed, but Aderri was the one who asked, "What do you mean?"

Think on it. Ellys was destined to meet you as far back as that, before Gwyn, before serving Toroc by wandering the land like a nomad in search of balance and coin. Ellys, your quest came from the Book of Prophesy. It was interpreted by the templar and given to the abbez of your monastery for assignment.

Sadness washed across Ellys, and her shoulders drooped. "Does that mean everything between now and then was for naught?"

On the contrary, it's called a quest for a reason, as you should well know. The journey is the most important part, no matter how long it takes.

"Ellys?"

Ellys turned to see a look of worry on Aderri's face. "Yes?"

"What does the discovery that you've completed your quest mean?"

"It means—"

A loud bell tolled through the great hall and cut off their heavy discussion. Two full-sized dragons walked through the large doors with a baby dragon waddling along between them. No other Dracona kin were in dragon form for the ceremony because Cyvrus and Wyrennia, Aderri's brother and his mate, were the only ones that needed to be shifted.

"Oh, my Goz," Ellys said, "that is the cutest thing I've ever seen."

Aderri pulled Ellys into her seat while Rocc wandered back to her own table. "They've kept her in seclusion until this day, waiting to officially introduce her to the Clan. Hey…"

Ellys pulled her gaze away from the baby that had just spat a tiny gout of flame. "Yes?"

"Promise we'll talk after the ceremony?"

"Of course. But, Aderri, you have nothing to worry about. We're balanced." She knew Aderri would understand her words, just as she knew Aderri would fear what the revelation of her completed quest would entail.

Once the small dragon family stood in the center of the chamber, another loud bell sounded. Aderri leaned over and whispered, "The gray, orange, and black dragon is my brother. The girl hatchling is the first Dracona born of her generation. None of my other nestmates have propagated yet."

"Is that why you had to return home for this ceremony?"

"Yes."

Cyvrus gave a great roar, quickly followed by Wyrennia. The baby squawked, and a little puff of smoke came from her tiny snout. Shimmering surrounded both parents as they shifted back to their two-legger form. The tiny dragon remained between, easily as tall as Cyvrus's waist.

Ellys whispered back, "She's so cute. I don't think I've ever wanted to cuddle a creature before, but I would make an exception with her."

"You may want to watch what you wish for as hatchlings are a bit wild and prone to biting." Aderri's words proved prophetic when the little dragon turned to the side, her attention caught by the dangling "worm" that belonged to her papa. She gave a little snap, and Cyvrus twisted his hips away at the last moment.

Ellys laughed then clapped a hand over her mouth when she realized that no one else had.

The Drakaina, in her two-legger form, raised her voice to be heard in the large space. "Clan Dracona and the entirety of the Dracona lineage are honored by the first hatchling born of its generation. Have you chosen a name?"

Cyvrus also raised his voice. "Clan Dracona, you honor us with your presence today, and in return, we'd like to share with you the name of our first born." Another snap had him covering important bits with his hand, and Cyvrus gestured toward his mate to continue. A few snickers and snorts went through the crowd.

Wyrennia placed a steady hand atop the hatchling's head, which seemed to settle her. "To honor both the Drakaina and the Riki, we are calling her Zederri.

"Oh." Aderri touched a hand to her mouth.

Ellys turned her attention to Aderri. "That was really nice of them."

"It is a great honor. I myself was honor-named for my great aunt, Derria."

Noticing movement out of the corner of her eye, Ellys turned her gaze back toward the center of the hall. A large cushion was brought in and placed in front of the baby dragon, then Wyrennia coaxed little Zederri to step up and perch atop the soft pad. Once there, the Drakaina moved closer and placed both hands on either side of the baby dragon's head. The hatchling stood transfixed by her grandam while shimmering surrounded them both. Less than a candle drop later, the hatchling shifted into a small baby, looking to be nearly a cycle old.

Ellys could only imagine that the change was probably both abrupt and startling because little Zederri promptly started crying. Wyrennia quickly picked her up and cuddled her close with Cyvrus.

Zevieri turned to the crowd of onlookers and raised her hands. "It is done. The child has shifted successfully, and Zederri n'ez Dracona will be recorded in the weyr Book of Blood." A cheer went through the crowd, and servers came from side doors bearing food and more mead. Zevieri lowered her hands slightly but held them out in front of her, asking for continued silence. Even the servers stopped in place to comply. "As much as I would love to celebrate this momentous occasion to its fullest, we must continue to keep our wits about us as long as Carthune threatens our nation. Be joyous, but also be aware that all dragons and flighted Dracona kin may be called at any time to fulfil the terms of our pact while war wages on the northeast border."

Ellys wasn't sure what she missed, but the crowd suddenly lifted whatever mugs and cups they had and bellowed, "We will defend!" Even Aderri joined in.

Someone brought robes for Aderri's brother, his mate, and the baby. Then the small family, and Aderri's mother, made their way over to the massive family table.

Ellys frowned. "What was that?"

"What was what?" Aderri glanced toward Ellys.

"The cheer at the end."

Aderri placed her hand on the back of Ellys's. "All Clan are raised to understand that it is our sacred duty to fulfill the terms of the pact from so long ago. It's not just duty though, it is an honor. Dragons earned this land and continue holding it with each new call to defend Muniers. And because of that pact, Dracona has given a home to many shifter families for hundreds of cycles. Everyone that is Clan contributes, but it is common knowledge that my family has the most dangerous job, and we are recognized for that. But one thing my family has always insisted is that all shifters are family within the Clan. Everyone is essential, from satyr to centaur. Dragons may hold the land with wing and flame, but Tyrrox's family holds it with the apples from their orchard. Fayen, the sylph, holds it with her water magic. And the Stonebrow wolf den holds it with their carpentry. The list goes on and on. Understand?"

Ellys was taken aback by Aderri's passionate speech. Despite not wanting to return to Clan duty, Aderri obviously held a lot of love for Clan and kin. "I think your family has the right of it over many other places I've seen. It feels very balanced, and I'm soothed by your home."

While the mead flowed at a significantly slower pace than normal for a Clan gathering, the revelry still lasted quite late. Cyvrus and Wyrennia left not long after the meal, but not before the newly-made baby with light-brown skin was passed around between the various members. Ellys took note that she was an affable child, once she got over the shock of her transformation. She also had a strong grip, a discovery made when she latched on to Ellys's finger and wouldn't let go. Rocc even came to see little Zederri, making the baby giggle and squeal with a soft muzzle to her cheek. Rocc's only comment to Ellys and Aderri was to say how much she missed seeing children as they were quite rare in the Ethereal Forest.

It was an especially dark walk back to Aderri's home since it was the end of a full moon-cycle, with two empty moons and the third was nearly gone over the horizon. Both women followed Rocc to the barn and said their goodnights before heading into the house.

"So…" Ellys said.

Aderri poured water into a wash bowl to wipe her face. When she was finished, she glanced toward Ellys while still holding the rag. "So?"

Rather than answer, Ellys walked up and embraced Aderri from behind. With the front of her body molded to Aderri's back, she caressed her lover's sides, ending just below Aderri's breasts. She leaned closer and spoke quietly in Aderri's ear. "I like your Clan." Her hands moved around to the front, and she began unfastening Aderri's shirt. "I like your family." When she was finished, the shirt was left open and Ellys slowly pulled Aderri's breast band down to have better access to her treasures.

She paused and Aderri whispered, "Don't stop."

With firm, calloused hands, Ellys caressed Aderri's breasts, focusing her attention on the hard nipples pushing against her palms. Aderri gasped and arched back into Ellys's body, pushing into Ellys's strong touch. Ellys ghosted her breath across Aderri's neck then moved her mouth up to nibble on her ear lobe. She pulled back just enough to say what she needed to say. "And I love you."

Aderri spun around within Ellys's arms. "Say it again."

"I love you and nothing changes with the discovery that, all along, *you* were my Quest of Toroc. Nothing changes except that I feel more balanced now than I've ever felt in my life. Knowledge has brought me peace."

"Talking about the benefits of knowledge is the quickest way to my heart."

"Oh yeah? What if it's not your heart I'm looking for tonight?" Ellys moved her hand lower, and Aderri gasped, then she drew her into a passionate kiss. Ellys moaned when Aderri eventually pulled away, dragging fangs across her lower lip as they both fought to catch their breath.

Aderri abruptly stepped back from the intimate touch over her trousers. "We're wearing too many clothes. Strip now."

A dark eyebrow rose with the command. "You're acting very much the demanding patron tonight."

"I'm with my lover, the very same who told me she loves me and is choosing me over becoming a Battling Monk in one of Toroc's many temples. And knowledge is power."

Despite the teasing, both rapidly disrobed. Ellys stepped close again for another kiss, and when it quickly grew heated, she leaned down to pick up Aderri and carry her to the bed. Both knew that Ellys's half-elven heritage gave her strength beyond many, but even so, Ellys could feel how excited Aderri got over the casual display of vigor. The wetness slicking her stomach increased significantly before Ellys could lay her down.

She raised an eyebrow. "You liked that, hmm? Perhaps I should pick you up more often."

Aderri narrowed her eyes. "Ellys?"

"Yes?"

"Shut up and get on the bed, I'm tired of waiting for your touch."

Ellys knew her grin was easily visible in the low light of the hearth fire as she crawled up to sit upon Aderri's hips. "Yes, Riki."

"Oh, you!" They tousled and rolled around on the large bed before Ellys finally found her way back on top again. Her narrow hips settled naturally between Aderri's thighs. Where Ellys was all lean muscle and hard angles, Aderri was curvy with wider hips and soft muscle definition. Pale and dark, earth and flame, they were so different, and yet complementary.

Leaning in for another kiss, Ellys rolled her hips forward to rub her damp moss against Aderri's quim. Aderri's large, distended clitoral nub pushed against her own much smaller one, and they both moaned at the contact. Ellys kept up the motion as the feeling drove them higher.

"Yes, like that!" Aderri's exclamation turned to higher-pitched whines as she rapidly approached her peak. The rocking continued, only stuttering for a few heartbeats when Aderri's hands shifted and long nails dug into Ellys's back. Dragon nails hurt, even in a much smaller form. Lucky for Aderri, Ellys was a quick healer and the mixture of pleasure and pain only drove her into a faster pace.

Ellys held herself up so she could watch Aderri's face while she thrust against her. Suddenly, Aderri's eyes opened and the flames filled her pupils. Aderri pulled her down into a deep kiss, then moved her mouth away, only to bury it in the crook of Ellys's neck as she screamed through her release. Ellys could feel Aderri's teeth dimpling her skin, but she didn't stop moving against her lover, knowing Aderri would ride out her pleasure for an abnormally long time.

Ellys was close as the pressure built inside her head and sex. The hardness of Aderri's nub pressed and dragged against her own with each thrust, but what finally sent her over the edge was when Aderri bit down at the end of her own orgasm. Tiny fangs pierced the flesh of Ellys's neck as a euphoric wash of emotion filled her from Aderri's empathy projection. Ellys's hoarse cry followed her release, and her hips jerked against Aderri's in an uneven rhythm.

When Ellys finally came down from the skies above, collapsing atop her lover, Aderri held her close and licked at the barely bleeding little points on the side of Ellys's neck. Dazed and still riding her wave of satisfaction, Ellys pushed back enough to look Aderri in the eyes. "You bit me."

"You said you liked that about me." Aderri threw back her head and laughed before Ellys could retort.

Ellys rolled to the side so she was no longer atop her lover but cuddled close. "I couldn't lie now, could I?"

Aderri smiled then pushed a lock of dark hair from her eyes. "So, what happens now?"

"Well, I don't know about you, but I'm certainly good for a few more rounds. Maybe this time I'll get a little taste—"

She got a slap to her arm. "That's not what I'm talking about. Though we can discuss that subject again as much as you like, when we're finished with the current conversation."

"Aderri, my heart is yours. Wherever you go, Rocc and I will follow. I mean…I won't sit in a dank library all the day through for you, but Rocc and I can maintain the balance anywhere, be that traveling across the six to expand your knowledge or settling here with Clan Dracona. I know Roccotári would be happy here, and that's what matters most."

"And what about you? What makes you happy?"

"You."

"You make it sound so simple."

"It can be. I've done many things in my life, all the while keeping the mandate of my quest in the back of my mind. It was never about becoming a monk. It was about earning a home and family while continuing to serve my Goz. The last one hundred cycles have shown me that I don't have to join a temple to do that. And the truth revealed by my journey is worth…everything."

"You really mean that?"

"Yes. Where you go, I'll follow."

Aderri's eyes twinkled. "The deserts of Legaria?"

"Rocc will be furious about all the sand, but I'll pack extra water."

"What about the frozen mountains of Menia?"

Ellys pulled her closer. "We're there."

"Being wary of snow foxes, I hope."

They laughed together. "I'm confident you can protect me."

Aderri sucked in a breath and stared directly into Ellys's eyes. "This is real."

"And will be so for as long as I can stand and grasp the blade of my love."

Aderri pulled her close and whispered, "I'm going to hold you to that—" A low and mournful sound echoed through the night, easily heard with the window open, and Aderri stiffened and turned her gaze to the dark sky beyond the sill.

Ellys looked at her with concern. "What is it?"

"The call." Aderri turned wide eyes back to her love. "The coast is under attack."

Chapter Twenty-One

"Where is the sound coming from?"

Both scrambled from the bed, but Aderri didn't bother dressing. She grabbed her usual clothes and boots and stuffed them into her satchel. "Every watchtower has a magical horn that can be heard overland for leagues. One tower will signal the next, which signals the one after that, until warning has gone up and down the entire coast. We also have towers between here and there, to bring the message to Dracona."

"That's convenient." Aderri waited while Ellys went through her pack to pull out the items she needed. Ellys's battle kit wasn't extensive, but for her fighting style it didn't need to be. While her skill often protected her from most of what could cause harm, soft leather pants and vest, greaves and bracers, a relaxed cloth shirt, and magic-imbued elven chainmail went a long way to stop the rest.

Ellys cut a fine figure when she was dressed, a fact proven by Aderri's appreciative gaze. Once Ellys added her sword harness and all her daggers, Aderri asked, "Ready?"

"Let's go."

Roccotári was already waiting for them outside, at the front of the homestead. *You have to leave, don't you?*

The steed's nervous stomping and twitching withers easily telegraphed her worry to the two women in front of her. Aderri said, "We do. You should head up to the keep to wait for us."

I could take you as far as the patrol field, if you like.

Aderri hugged Rocc's neck. "I'm sorry, but there's enough room for me to shift here if I move into the road. It's quicker this way."

Ellys said, "We'll be fine, cara."

Rocc nudged Aderri's shoulder, and her words were for the dragon alone. *Guard her, and return safely.*

I will. You have my word that I'd give my life to ensure Ellys comes back to you.

No! If you don't return with her, I'll have lost you both.

While the topic of Ellys's previous attempt at decumora wasn't mentioned, Rocc's words were a warning that made Aderri's heart race. Aderri nodded at the silence between them, and Ellys stepped forward to caress Rocc's soft muzzle.

"Be safe, my friend. We'll see you on the other side of morning."

Less than a hand span after Aderri took off, Rocc whinnied and raced with unnatural speed through the darkness toward the keep.

The wind whipped around Ellys as they flew faster than they'd ever gone before. She leaned as close to Aderri's body as possible, not only to avoid wind drag but to stay warm. There were no moons to guide them, as the last one had disappeared over the horizon just after midnight. All that was left were the stars in the sky, and the sound of crashing waves once they got to the coast.

Aderri's mighty dragon voice cut through the night like rumbling thunder. "I don't underssstand what happened. Ailith sssaid the shipsss hadn't moved, and the sssupplemental army marching north would ssstill be a quarter moon from the border. It will take usss many candle marksss to fly that far north."

Ellys considered the information they possessed and worked at it with a tactical mind that was honed by more than a century of experience. Suddenly, it all made sense and she cursed herself for not thinking of it sooner. Ellys didn't bother yelling her reply because Aderri confessed that her hearing as a dragon was very acute and she could easily make out what Ellys said while flying.

"Based on what we learned from Captain Kessel last moon, and what Ailith told us the other day, the number of ships that Chancellor Temet ordered to form the sea blockade near the border isn't even a fraction of what Carthune has available. Their nation is infamous for the size and strength of their navy. I'm afraid we won't have to go any farther than Noth. It's not the blockade near the border that has moved. Carthune must have circled their northern fleet around over the past few moons, so they could approach the capital from the southeast. They then dropped the border wall and began attacking with the brunt of their land force, knowing the Regents would draw down the forces within the city to protect the border. Gah! I've been so stupid."

"Not ssstupid, Ellysss. No one predicted thisss."

"Even still."

Aderri continued her lift and glide, getting a good tail wind on their way northeast. "What isss the worssst cassse ssscenario in thisss sssituation?"

"My guess is that they'd have mages and catapults on the ship decks. Didn't Rocc say the Nothian stronghold was protected by magics of earth and fire? They would need mages to break those safeguards, right? I mean, I feel that any spells that can hold against the elements and ravages of time can also hold off something as relatively inconsequential as catapults and flaming arrows."

"You think that'sss it?"

"Hopefully. It seems highly unlikely that Carthune would have been smuggling soldiers through magical doors in the border for the past few moons. I feel as though a lot of extra people would be noticed during a time of imminent war."

They flew along in silence for a bit until Aderri spoke again. "Doesss it need to be many sssoldiersss? I heard rumorsss of elite fightersss while wandering the hallsss of the library and the ssschool of magecraft. Sssomething called the Black Guard."

"Fenwith's bloody balls! I surely hope not. I've heard of the Black Guard of Carthune, rumors mostly. None of them good, I'm afraid. I've never actually come across them in all my cycles of travel, even moving through Carthune itself. With a stripped-down military defending the city from land, and mages battering from sea, this may very well be the end of the stronghold."

Aderri roared and spit a gout of flame ahead of them into the night, easily displaying her frustration and worry to Ellys. "I have to warn you…it hasss been a long time sssincsse I wasss called to defend. Perhapsss I should leave you at the lassst tower."

"I'm not worried in the slightest. We'll defend Muniers together. There's no getting rid of me now."

Aderri was silent for a few candle drops before answering. "Thank you. You should probably ressst if you're able. You'll need your ssstrength when we arrive."

"What about you?"

"They'll have food at the lassst watchtower before Noth, knowing dragonsss will be coming in hungry and in need of energy for the fight. Mossst of the patrol, with the exssseption of the lassst outpossst to the southwessst, will have arrived in Noth before usss. I sssussspect the dragon asssigned to the Carthune border would have been inssstructed to ssstay there in cassse of further aggresssion. The ressst of my kin will come in behind usss asss they mobilizsse."

"Are you faster than the others?"

"I am larger, ssso yesss."

As promised, giant slabs of meat were waiting at the top of the stone tower. The tower was tall enough to look out over the highest trees and had just enough space for a dragon to land atop. Even with only torches to light the surface of the structure, Ellys's impression was that it seemed very block-like and sturdily built. She took the opportunity to stretch her legs and relieve herself while Aderri wolfed down an essential meal. One of the guards on duty handed Ellys a skin of water, a slightly bruised apple, and a hunk of dried meat to take with her. She thanked him, then remounted and settled into place on Aderri's back.

The last short bit of the journey was done in silence. Aderri, with her superior dragon sight, would be able to see the battle well before Ellys. Less than a league out, she called warning to the swordswoman. "Counting flaming projectilesss, there mussst be an entire armada attacking the cssitadel. We don't have enough dragonsss to defend."

"Can you tell who is here already?"

"Two of my nessstmatesss were on duty after the csselebration, Jorl and Dlemna. I'm not sure who of my exsstended kin though, or who wasss ssstationed at which tower."

Within a few candle drops, they drew near enough to watch the flaming balls arc across the sky and explode against some sort of magical barrier. Ellys could see the work of four dragons spitting gouts of flame toward the dark ships that sat in even darker water. The Carthunians had planned their attack perfectly for stealth. Ellys called out to Aderri as they neared the engagement zone. "What can I do to help?"

"Be ready and watch for attacksss outsssside my field of visssion."

Ellys made the sign of Toroc and muttered a prayer to her Goz. "Balance shall prevail."

Aderri used the darkness to her advantage and came in gliding so the nearest ships wouldn't be aware of their approach. When she was nearly upon the vessel, she let loose a great gout of flame that engulfed the mainsail and set fire to the decking below. Another vessel immediately retaliated by swinging the arm of one of its catapults around and pitching a flaming ball to intersect with Aderri's trajectory.

The balls weren't large, and the flames certainly wouldn't hurt them, but they had a thick covering of tar-like pitch that could easily spoil a dragon's flight. Aderri gave a roar and dove into a twisting roll, before snapping out her wings and pumping her way upward to a safer height. The flaming ball of pitch-covered stone just barely missed them.

"How are they so accurate with those things, especially considering their relatively small size and the fact that they're mounted on ships?"

Aderri circled around to begin another attacking run. "It isss sssaid they practicsse hitting the ssstonesss of one catapult with the ssstonesss of another somewhere in the Northern Sssea. Carthune knowsss how to attack flighted creaturesss."

"I didn't see any mages, did you?"

"No. Perhapsss we've gotten lucky today. Hang on!"

The dragon tucked her wings and dove into another pass. Ellys realized why Aderri was bringing her wings in after their first attack. It was to make herself smaller and harder to hit. Even so, it was a near thing each time. They didn't run into trouble until the fourth pass. Two ships had come about in the water, each bringing their catapults to bear. Until that point, Aderri had done a good job at avoiding the projectiles while still doing damage to the ships below. Her main targets were the stockpiles of pitch-covered stones. Unfortunately, despite her advanced eyesight, they were extremely hard to spot in the dark.

Two catapults fired at them as Aderri went into an assault dive. She let out a great blast of flame and didn't see two more flaming stones coming from the side. Ellys called a warning and drew her sword. "Beware the left!" Even with her superior strength and elven-forged blade, she wasn't sure if she'd be able to turn the stone aside. Aderri missed one of the two with a complicated midair twist, but Ellys was forced to swing her sword to prevent the other from striking the dragon's wing. Her strength was only enough to deflect it into Aderri's right front leg. The thick pitch covered the scales from claw to first joint, and Aderri roared in anger and pain. She twisted her serpentine head down to blast the offending substance with dragon fire.

It flared bright enough that Ellys had to cover her eyes before it burned completely away.

They wobbled while Aderri climbed once again and Ellys called out to her. "Are you okay?"

"I'm fine asss long asss they don't get that muck on my wingsss."

More dragon fire lit the night as help arrived from Clan lands. The battled raged above and below for long enough that the sky had begun to brighten into twilight. It would be significantly easier for the ships to hit the dragons when they could see them better. From what Ellys could tell, there were at least two score remaining.

Ellys glanced to her left toward the stronghold and frowned with dismay. "Aderri, the barrier in front of the fortress is shrinking!" Sure enough, they could see some of the stones getting through to strike the imposing structure. Each one made a loud *crack* upon impact.

"The magesss tire. We mussst—" A bright mage blast interrupted whatever Aderri was going to say. As the sparks fell away from the first hit, another flew out from a nearby ship.

"Deveelsss! They *did* bring their own magesss. They merely waited until oursss were worn down before attacking. Watch my sssidesss, I'm going down there."

"Are you sure—by Toroc, you're mad!"

Ellys quickly sheathed her sword, knowing they were going too fast for her to use it. The wind tore at her clothing and caused her lips to flap in an unpleasant manner until she closed her mouth and clenched her teeth. Aderri's dive was fueled by her singular desire to take out the mage, and Ellys recognized the mistake for what it was. Other ships had caught on and were watching for any attack on the ones carrying their magic users. Catapults began lobbing fireballs at them. One hit Aderri's left wing just as her flame reached the mage below, but rather than snap her wings out to begin flapping to a higher altitude, the sticky residue and pain from the strike kept it curled to her side.

Just before plummeting into the waves below, Ellys yelled the word of release. "Privo!" She leaped from Aderri's back and hit the cold water with enough force that she was momentarily shocked. She became aware again as the weight of her armor, weapons, and pack dragged her down. Ellys was a strong swimmer though and had plenty of experience treading water under those exact circumstances.

She was a few hundred paces from the rocky shore below the strong-hold and could easily swim that far, but she could see Aderri strug-gling nearby and quickly realized why. Dragons couldn't swim.

"Ellysss!" Her name was roared into the night, and Ellys pad-dled toward the thrashing dragon, heedless of the danger such an action posed. At least they'd landed far enough away from the near-est ship that she didn't have to worry about attack.

"Aderri, you have to change!" The dragon's head sank below the surface as Ellys got close enough to touch her, and she screamed again under the water. "Change!"

Even as Aderri and her dragon panicked, something within both recognized the one they'd claimed. Ellys's word must have cut through the blinding fear, and Aderri closed her eyes. Heartbeats later she floated as a two-legger in the dark water, and Ellys quickly grabbed her and kicked them toward the surface.

Both gasped when they broke through the waves above. Aderri coughed and Ellys held her tight, kicking furiously to keep them afloat while Aderri was still dazed. "Are you okay?"

Aderri turned to look at her savior. Morning was nearly upon them, and she watched rivulets of water run down Ellys's face, drip-ping from her short dark hair. "Thanks to you."

Ellys began swimming them toward shore. They were jolted when another crack sounded, and a mage blast hit at nearly the same time. A horn sounded right after that, a pattern of rapid notes, fol-lowed by a single long one. Ellys glanced behind them. "What's hap-pening?"

Aderri's eyes widened. "The enemy has breached the bailey. That's never happened in my lifetime."

Ellys kicked harder until she felt sand beneath her soaked boots, then gave a massive shove until they rested on hands and knees in the wet sand. There wasn't much beach, as it was below the cliff face. Ellys panted from the effort of her swim then pulled herself up to stand. "Can you change here?"

Rays of the rising sun gleamed off the dark skin of Aderri's nude body. "I can, but first things first." She reached out to Ellys and pulled her into a tight embrace.

"What are you doing?"

"Shh." Aderri whispered the words of a spell into Ellys's ear, then stood on her tiptoes to kiss the point when she was finished. When she pulled away, Ellys was left feeling clean and wearing dry clothes.

Ellys gave her a grateful smile. "Thanks. Leather chafes worse than a wet saddle."

"After I change, I'm going to drop you off on one of the stronghold balconies and go back to help my kin."

"Not a tower?"

"They'll be sealed tight right now, and you'd never get in. I'll show you where the Twin Regents are located. Try to make your way there and guard them."

Their wish for each other came at the same time. "Be safe!"

Ellys and Aderri smiled, and Ellys gently cupped Aderri's cheeks to lean in for a kiss. Then she pulled back and moved over to stand upon a nearby boulder, to give Aderri as much room to change as possible. As it was, the dragon was left standing half in the water and half on the beach. The gummy tar no longer coated her wing, probably being washed away by the sea.

Ellys quickly remounted and said the word of binding in case any fireballs or mage blasts came their way. With a few great gusts of wind, Aderri rose above the water and sand below. Once high enough that the enemy couldn't reach them, she circled the fortress and called out the location of the Twin Regents, though it was easy enough to see at that point.

The two mage rulers stood side by side on a balcony that overlooked the fleet. With candle marks passed since the battle began, some of Muniers's navy had arrived from their stations up and down the coast. While they were doing good work at whittling down the Carthunian ships, the mages and catapults continued to pummel the stronghold, leaving its defense to the two most powerful mages left standing.

They circled around lower until Aderri called out. "There. We will have but one shot at thisss."

All Ellys could see was a balcony similar to the one the Regents stood upon, quite a few stories below theirs. It was on the opposite side of the stronghold and thankfully away from the attack. "Shot at what?"

"It isss too clossse to the wall. You will have to leap from my back asss I dive by. Oncsse you land, I can turn and exsstend my wingsss again and fly back up."

Ellys's eyes widened at the seemingly suicidal plan. Aderri did another circle before setting up for her dive. Ellys made to voice her skepticism, "I don't think—" but the rapid plummet stole the breath from her lungs, at least until the screaming started. "Fenwith's bloody balls, I didn't know your dragon was so wild!" Ellys hastily yelled, "Privo!" then gripped the armored plate in front of her as tight as possible and pulled her legs up to crouch upon Aderri's back.

Aderri roared and turned her head so Ellys could see her big flame-filled pupil, then winked. "*I* am my dragon. Jump!"

Ellys sprang from her back, hitting the stones of the balcony with enough force to send her tumbling forward. She pushed up with her hands to avoid rolling over the sword pommels that stuck up just over each shoulder. As soon as she got her bearings, she whirled around to see Aderri turn sharply to the left, away from the walls, and gain altitude. Glad her lover was safe, Ellys ran through the balcony doors, ruing the fresh set of bruises the landing had given her.

She dashed toward the back half of the stronghold, hoping to find a way up to the chamber that held the Twin Regents. Apparently, most people had either fled or gone into hiding. Ellys sprinted down a wide stone hallway and around the corner. She pulled up short when she came face-to-face with a smallish man in a fancy uniform, clearly one of the royal servants. He screamed and recoiled at seeing the fighter so close. She quickly fisted the front of his shirt to prevent him from running away. "Stop! I'm with Clan Dracona. The fortress has been breached, and I was sent in to protect the Regents."

The man looked her up and down and made a face. "Just you? What good will you do against an army? Go back the way you came, elf."

"I will serve as Toroc wills. Balance must be maintained." She pulled a dagger from her belt. "Tell me where the Regents are."

He swallowed and his throat bobbed against the point of the blade. "There's a servant's stairwell near the end of this passage." He gestured vaguely toward a door on the right side near the end. "It's narrow but will take you the rest of the way up to their level."

"How many?"

"Four above this one."

She loomed over him. "And then?"

Terrified, he scrunched his eyes shut. "It exits into another main passage. Chamber of Regents is halfway down, through the tall double doors." He shivered and whispered, "Please don't kill me."

Ellys abruptly let the man go and winced as he fell onto his backside on the stone floor. His face twisted with pain, clearly having landed on his tailbone. "Sorry. And I already told you, I'm here to defend Muniers. Run and hide somewhere and hopefully we can bring these brigands to bear sooner rather than later."

He scrambled up painfully and gave a quick bow. "Yes, Moz." Then without looking back, the man took off down the hallway, opposite the way Ellys needed to go.

The sound of fighting had gotten closer, and she assumed the Carthunian soldiers were making their way up one of the main stairways somewhere back the way she'd come from. With no time to spare, she hurried to the door indicated by the servant. If she were lucky, she could come out ahead of the attackers.

She sprinted up the stairs and regretted the energy spent swimming herself and Aderri to shore not long before. She needed all she could get for the fighting to come. Swords and tight spaces didn't go well together, but maybe she could work it to her advantage. She was probably one of the last few defenders remaining and would surely be fighting many.

She exited onto the level that held the Twin Regents' royal chamber and paused to listen. The battle outside seemed unnaturally loud within the stronghold. Both mage blasts and the crack of catapult stones echoed through the open windows and along the high stone hallways. Ellys could hear swordfighters somewhere in the distance. The farther down the passage she sprinted, the louder the ringing of swords became.

Ellys found the source moments later when she rounded another corner. A large group of fighters in black had what appeared to be Muniers royal soldiers on the defensive with a massive set of ornate double doors at their backs. The men in royal blue and white had formed a short line to best defend the opening, but Ellys knew it was only a matter of time before the attackers broke through since the guards were horribly outnumbered.

She charged in from the side, calling out, "I'm with Dracona!" She was able to wound two and kill two more before she made it to the end of the short line. Seeing movement out of the corner of her eye, she yelled to the fighter on the opposite end. "Don't let them flank you!"

Eventually, the defenders were pushed back through the double doors. Ellys took in the room for half a heartbeat and could see the

Twins through the open balcony doors. They didn't move to acknowledge the intrusion, and she could only imagine it was because their sole focus was on maintaining the magical barrier. One man in blue and white cried out and fell to the ground, leaving just Ellys and two others to defend against ten of the black-clad fighters from Carthune.

Ellys called out, "Muniers, move to the right flank and give me space."

One thing could be said about the royal guards, they knew how to take orders. By maneuvering themselves farther to the side, they succeeded in taking six of the ten brigands with them. One Carthunian fell almost immediately to a defender's sword, leaving them with five. The four in front of her eyed Ellys warily, backing away slightly. Not wearing a uniform, she was an unknown element with demonstrated skill, having already killed a handful outside the chamber. Elite soldiers or no, none seemed anxious to taste her blades.

From the corner of her eye, Ellys watched two more of the Carthunian Black Guards fall, as well as one of the Nothian defenders. It was only a matter of time before she would be the sole defender. Considering her options, she sheathed one sword and quick as she could grab them from her holder, sent throwing knives toward two different attackers facing the lone guardsman. One blade struck deep into the joint between upper thigh and hip, an area not covered by the enemy's armor. She must have hit a tendon because the leg wouldn't hold his weight, dropping him to the ground in pain. Ellys got lucky with the other because it stuck in the side of the neck of one of the two men closest to the remaining royal guard.

The throws were fast, something she'd perfected over the cycles, and the attackers seemed especially surprised. Before anyone could respond, she grabbed another and threw it at one of her own attackers who was turned slightly sideways toward her, hitting him in the unprotected side of his thigh. She quickly drew her second sword again as the man cried out in pain. He smartly left the blade in to avoid significant blood loss.

Rather than give them time to regroup, Ellys took the attack to them. She leaped for one, engaging him with one of her swords. Then she spun around him, jumping out of range with a kick to the back of the knee and a slice upon the man's arm. She ducked the swing of the second man then did a spinning kick that hit him in the ribs as his arm was raised. The force was enough to crack a few bones, and she smiled as she crossed the blades in front of her to block the third man's downstroke.

Another cry echoed through the chamber, and she took precious heartbeats to check on the other royal guard. His left arm hung at his side with blood flowing from the shoulder joint, but he still held his sword at the ready. Her distraction cost her, and she just barely missed taking a sword to the neck from the man she'd injured with her throwing knife. The other three were getting ready to advance again, and she made the call to finish off the wounded one rather than leave him at her back.

She attacked him in earnest with a rattling display of swords that left him scrambling backward. His wounded leg gave out, and she slashed his throat as he fell. Without breaking stride, she momentarily clasped her two sword grips in one hand to grab her blade from his thigh and ducked to the left, throwing it at the man nearest to her. He slapped it away with his sword, which opened him up to a quick jab to the knee when she reset her blades for attack. He reeled back in pain, and she flipped to her feet again as the other two advanced.

They circled her like wolves, so she charged one with both blades swinging to push him away. It worked, and she was left with her back facing the Twin Regents' balcony. Seeing the remaining Muniers man flag, she grabbed another throwing knife and aimed it at the back of his opponent. The Black Guard went down, but so, too, did the soldier in blue and white. The man whose knee she stabbed attempted to stand but fell back to the stone floor in pain.

Feeling she would succeed in her defense, Ellys had no qualms about needling the Carthunians. Anger brought imbalance and increased the likelihood of mistakes. "Knee joints hurt like deveel spit, don't they?"

He yelled in pained rage. "Fucking elf-trash!"

"Is it too much to ask for my enemies to think of a better insult? It's no wonder none of you survive my blades. You're all dumb as a low beast at midday." He roared a string of curses at her, but Ellys knew he wasn't a danger unless the other two pushed her into him, so she ignored his vitriol. Instead, she focused on the last two Carthunian Black Guards. "You are out of balance, and I cannot let you pass. If you leave now, you'll at least leave with your life, if not your honor."

The larger man spat upon the floor. "You can take your talk of honor and balance and march straight to Abbad with it. The gold

Temet promised for this job will buy plenty of honor to last me across the six." The other man laughed with him, then their brows drew down as they brought their swords up to bear.

Ellys was exhausted, but she had to finish this because there was no one else to defend the rulers of Muniers. Much like she'd done in the past when she needed to focus beyond the norm, she cleared her mind and moved into the first fundamental stance of secaeli. One blade was held out at an angle at the ready in front of her. The other she raised slightly above her head with the point aimed toward the Black Guards.

They moved as a well-trained unit, one attacking high and the other low. She blocked both blades with her own while delivering a powerful kick to the gut of the smallest attacker. Then she spun away and prepared herself again. She had two throwing knives left and sent one flying toward the man with the injured knee who was attempting, yet again, to stand. With a wet thud, the blade buried itself deep into the man's eye socket, killing him instantly.

She smiled at the other two. "I'm afraid he'll never see the error of his ways now."

They charged again, and rather than engage them both, Ellys ducked to the side and came around behind the smaller man. From there, she swung her ever-sharp elven sword clean through his neck. Not even the notoriously sturdy neck bones could stop her blade. The head was left hanging by a scrap of skin, which promptly ripped the rest of the way through when he fell to the floor, sending the head rolling toward the remaining Carthunian. He stopped the head with a look of disgust and kicked it at Ellys.

It hit her square in the chest, leaving a bloody smear on her leather vest, before dropping to the floor again. Ellys chortled with vicious delight and launched it back at him. "I can do this all day if you like. Though it's a bit of a gruesome game if you ask me."

Seeing the corpse of his fellow soldier treated in such a manner elicited the exact response Ellys was looking for. He roared and charged her, nearly tripping over the very head they'd been kicking around. "I'm going to kill you!"

Her energy nearly spent, Ellys once again engaged the Carthunian. But despite all his skill as an elite fighter, he too was exhausted. As a human, he had a limited range of experience in comparison to her long life. Not only that, but he couldn't hope to keep up with the strength and speed of his half-elven opponent, even on a good day. She locked his blade with both her own and drew in close enough to feel his breath on her face as he panted. She looked him straight in the eye and spoke with the even voice of a master. "Dead men kill nothing." Then she dropped one of her own blades and wrenched the sword from his hand, using it to stab upward through his gut and straight into the heart. She hadn't lied to Aderri; it really was the quickest way.

Ellys panted as she caught her breath and glanced around the chamber to make sure no one was left to challenge the Twin Regents. When all was deemed safe, she picked up her fallen blade then wiped and sheathed both. She turned and made her way onto the balcony. The Regents leaned heavily against the stone rail, nearly at the end of their reserves. Ellys looked out over the water and could see only a couple of ships left flying the Carthunian flag.

The Muniers navy formed a blockade, and it looked as though the catapults had finally run out of ammunition. All at once, the shimmering magical barrier dissolved as both Regents' arms dropped to their sides. They nearly fell to their knees, but Ellys was quick to get an arm around each to help support them. They didn't know her but must have sensed that she was no threat. Rather than pull away, they stood together in mutual exhaustion and looked out over the sea.

Ellys blew a sigh of relief, but her respite was not to last. The events of the next few heartbeats moved almost too fast to see. There was one mage left, and he sent a blast of magical energy toward their balcony. Ellys's eyes widened at the incoming attack, but there was nowhere to go. Suddenly, a black-and-red dragon dove from some-where above and took the blast to the side. The dragon roared in pain and spiraled out of control to the rocky beach far below. With dawning horror, Ellys knew who had taken the hit for them.

She screamed into the wind as she desperately searched over the stone balcony rail, "Aderri!" The dragon sprawled across the rocks didn't move.

Chapter Twenty-Two

"The Riki has fallen."

Startled, Roccotári gazed at the sprite standing near the Drakaina's side. Zevieri looked shocked at the news. "Impossible. My daughter is much too powerful to be taken down so easily."

The sprite's face filled with sorrow. "I'm sorry, but I have seen it. Her life drains away as we speak."

No! Rocc couldn't let Aderri die. Her own bondmate would never survive the loss. Not *this* one. The steed could help, but it meant breaking a vow she'd oathed deep within the Sacred Grove. It meant permanently severing her connection to the Ethereal Forest. It was there she learned that a creature cannot be part of one world and fuse with the magic of another. With no time to spare, Rocc made her decision. She turned to Zevieri. *I can save her.*

"But the cost…" The Clan leader clearly knew something of her kind.

Rocc tossed her head. *I will gladly pay to keep them together.* Very few knew that the natural form of an elven steed was pure earth energy, brought into being within the Sacred Grove and bound to the Ethereal Forest. If she reverted to her natural form outside the Fae kingdom, Rocc would sever her connection to the place of her birth and be unable to cross the veil.

With supreme focus, enough to cut through the terror Rocc felt in knowing Aderri had heartbeats of life left before even she could bring her back, the steed cast her mind down into the earth below her hooves. There she found a strong ley line, perhaps the reason for Dracona Keep's exact location. Less than a heartbeat later, Rocc's body disappeared in a flash of the brightest white, and she plummeted into that line of energy. She followed it straight to Noth and in a blink exited near the base of the stronghold. Reverting to her second form once again, Roccotári galloped over to the unnaturally still dragon. The creature of light hoped she wasn't too late.

Ellys despaired. She could see her love far below, but there was nothing that could be done; Aderri was lost to her. Then, mere heartbeats after Aderri's fall, another form blinked into existence on the sand. "It cannot be…"

"Is that—"

"An earth elemental?"

The Twin Regents seemed just as startled as Ellys. She wanted to question them, wondering why they labeled Roccotári as such, but her attention was riveted on the scene below. Though the distance was great, Ellys watched as Rocc lowered her nose to touch that of the dragon, and a bright glow formed around them. The three on the balcony shielded their eyes as eventually it grew too bright to watch, even from their great height.

Ellys heard a roar above them and looked up to see an orange, black, and gold dragon circling not far from where she stood. She recognized Gessy's coloring and spikes near her head from the day they first met when Aderri's youngest nestmate came off patrol. "Gessy!"

The dragon turned her head away from the scene below to look at Ellys. Gessy roared again with sorrow. "My sssissster…she hasss fallen."

"I need to go down there. Can you take me?"

Even if Gessy wasn't the largest of dragons, her wings were still too big to allow her to get close to the balcony. "I cannot come clossser."

Ellys wracked her brain to come up with a solution. Then she remembered her way in when Aderri had the same problem. "What if I jump? Can you catch me?"

"Yesss, that will work."

Ellys quickly moved inside the balcony doors to get enough room for a proper run up, and the Twin Regents backed out of the way. She sprinted forward, leaped to the rail, then pushed off the sturdy stone and over. For a terrifying moment, she worried that Gessy wouldn't catch her, but the dragon swooped down as soon as Ellys was far enough away that the stronghold wouldn't interfere with the beat of her wings. After seeing the size of Gessy's talons,

Ellys was impressed by the younger creature's skill. The catch was clean, and her talons didn't even puncture Ellys's clothing.

Rather than fly straight down, Gessy glided into a more controlled path of gentle circling. While the slow descent was frustrating, Ellys knew it was probably safer than racing to the bottom then being unable to stop in time.

Gessy's wings created a backdraft over the beach as she was forced to flap the rest of the way. She dropped Ellys a few feet from the ground, and Ellys immediately sprinted to the still forms of Rocc and Aderri. "What can I do?"

Roccotári's voice in her head was faint, as if she were expending most of her energy in the healing. And, considering the size of her patient, she probably was. *She is strong but in much pain. Aderri fights me, not wanting to remain in her body long enough for me to heal it. Convince her to stay.*

Acid rose into Ellys's throat at hearing words so similar to the ones uttered by Rocc on Gwyn's death bed. *"Convince her to stay."* But Gwyn had been at the end of her natural life and refused Ellys's plea. Ellys was determined not to fail again. She fought through the panic and followed her bondmate's orders. Ellys didn't dare touch Rocc or Aderri while in the middle of the energy exchange. Instead, she shielded her eyes and came as close as possible. "Aderri, don't leave us! Please, cara, we have so much time left together. I need your warmth and light. The world needs your knowledge and wisdom." Ellys dropped to her knees in the sand, and her eyes ran with tears she'd only shed two other times in her life. "I'll go wherever you want, but please stay!"

Rocc's front legs gave out, then the back, and she, too, dropped to the sand. *I'm sorry, caritas, but I can go no further. It's up to Aderri now.*

Seeing that the light was gone from both forms, Ellys threw herself toward Aderri and pressed her cheek to the end of Aderri's snout, the flat spot just between her large nostrils. The longer Aderri remained unmoving, the more Ellys anguished. "Stay with me!"

Curls of smoke trailed out of Aderri's nostrils, and her sides moved as a slow breath was indrawn. Ellys heard the low rumble of Aderri's voice and smelled the smoky malodor of her breath as she whispered, "You're getting me wet, and not the fun way that I like."

"Aderri!" Ellys scrambled backward, and Aderri slowly rose to stand on all four feet. The dragon gave her head a shake, and Gessy roared with joy behind them, spitting a gout of fire straight into the air. Rocc whickered softly.

Aderri suddenly changed form and would have collapsed to the sand below if not for Ellys's fast reflexes. The dragon shifter groaned. "Anyone that likes to sleep on surfaces other than soft coverlets is completely mad. Those stones were killer on the back." Ellys looked at her in horror. "Too soon?" Rather than answer, Ellys pulled her close.

Rocc's sides heaved with the energy expended, but she was able to pull herself up to a standing position as well. *I'm glad to see you came back.*

"Yes, well, I couldn't very well leave you two on your own. The three of us balance now, and I'm not going to be the one to upset that."

Ellys finally laughed and swiped at her tear-streaked face. "You great, magnificent, fool-hardy, beautiful, beast. Thank you for saving our lives, but please don't do that again." Ellys wrapped her arms firmly around Aderri, holding her up, and the dragon shifter took full advantage of the situation.

Aderri leaned closer and gave Ellys a single, passionate kiss. When she pulled away, Ellys felt slightly dazed. "Our match was foretold in the Book of Prophesy. I certainly couldn't turn my back on such an auspicious pairing." They laughed quietly, at least until Aderri sobered. "I couldn't leave you, Ellys. *Wouldn't.*"

Ellys placed her palm reverently upon Aderri's left cheek. "Thank you."

A new voice called out to them. "Not that I want to break up your little celebration, but how are you three going to get out of this cove?" They turned to see Gessy walking toward them. She was nude like Aderri, but Ellys had gotten used to it. "While I can lift Ellys and Aderri one at a time and carry them around to the bailey of the stronghold, none of us could lift Lady Roccotári."

"I could lift her." Aderri was significantly larger than Gessy while in dragon form.

Rocc was ever the voice of reason. *You can barely lift yourself right now.*

Ellys huffed. "I'm not sure if any of you noticed, but Aderri isn't lifting herself at all. Thank you very much."

I can leave the same way I arrived. I just needed a few candle drops to get my energy back.

Aderri's obvious exhaustion stooped her shoulders and pulled her eyelids down. "How exactly did you get here? I'm sure we last saw you on Clan lands just a few candle marks ago. That's a many-days-long ride, even at your speed."

So you did. As for the answer to your question, we can discuss it later.

Ellys grumbled, "More secrets."

Roccotári plodded closer and lipped at Ellys's hair. *The last one, I promise.* Her hooves sank into the sand, and she stomped twice and whinnied. *You know how much I hate sand. Ellys, tell your mate to fly over a nice forest the next time she's going to be self-sacrificial to preserve the balance.*

Ellys's eyes grew wide with wonder at Rocc's choice of terms. She smiled and whispered, "My mate," before returning her gaze to Aderri. "I don't care where you go, as long as you always come back."

"Agreed." Aderri kissed her again.

Gessy said, "But seriously though, how are you getting out of here?"

The kiss broke off, and Ellys turned to the younger woman. "If you want to be serious, you're *seriously* ruining our mood here."

Gessy snorted. "If by mood, you mean the atmosphere of you kissing my nestmate while the Twin Regents and a horse look on, then yes I am."

I'm not a horse, you runty wyrm!

Ellys grinned at Aderri. "Oh look, they're acting like family already."

****

Less than a candle mark later, the stronghold was a hive of activity as the bodies of attackers and defenders alike were dragged into the courtyard. The former would be placed on pyres with blessing tokens for each of the six nations, and one more for Moder, the Goddess of Death. The slain of Muniers would get whatever service they indicated when joining royal service, or their families would choose. All would be paid for with crown gold.

Gessy flew back to her kin, to coordinate with those who fought in the battle and assign fresh coastal guardians. That left Aderri to represent Dracona, a role suited to her as Riki of the Clan, though it was a role outside anything she'd previously experienced.

The Twin Regents had offered refreshments to Ellys, Aderri, and Rocc, leading them into a secured meeting chamber on the ground floor of the stronghold. It was easily accessible and large enough to fit all five of them. A bin of hot mash and a plate of apples were placed upon the table for Rocc, while mead and platters full of hearty foods were provided for the other four. Aderri gave the Regents a curious head tilt at the abundance before them.

Regent Devlin smiled and spoke first, but the twins seemed to be nearly symbiotic with their speech, each contributing to the conversation as though they were two halves of a whole. "We recognize that certain prolonged activities require an immense amount of food to recover energy lost."

Regent Dezne said, "We, too, were depleted—"

"—significantly—"

"—during the battle. We can imagine after the events witnessed that you three would feel the same." Regent Dezne finished the statement she shared with her brother. It was something that every set of Twin Regents did for as long as the people of Noth could remember.

Aderri inclined her head. "Thank you."

The three guests waited until Dezne and Devlin took their own food and began eating before they joined. The Regents seemed a little too relaxed given what Ellys last knew of the border, and she said as much between bites of her food. All the fighting had given her quite the appetite.

"Aren't you concerned about your troops heading north?"

"Less so—"

"—now,"

"—than we were."

Aderri took a sip of her mead. "I don't understand. We were near the border last moon, and it was rife with blood mages."

Devlin looked to his sister and nodded, apparently in a silent exchange. Ellys wondered if the Twin Regents shared familial telepathy like Roccotári, or if it was part of their magic as with Aderri. After the quick look, Devlin continued eating while his sister spoke.

"We knew of the Carthunian mages and supplied our troops accordingly. What we didn't expect was for the overreaching Chancellor Temet to pull many of their mages and send them with the king's navy that attacked Noth. We thought we could defend the stronghold from the smaller fleet at the border, not expecting more to come around from so far away. The book said nothing of this."

Ellys said, "About a moon ago, we met Captain Kessel from the Carthunian army. She planned to fetch Princess Ameelia and take her home in time to stop Temet from taking over her country. Did you know of this?"

"We heard rumors—"

"—but she obviously"

"—didn't return before Temet carried out his plans."

Aderri spoke up. "I wonder what happened to her and the princess."

Denze said, "We may never know."

"True," Ellys said. "We can only hope they came to no harm and were just delayed coming back."

After a short pause, she continued. "So, the army you sent to the border will be more than enough to handle what Carthune has in place? Your plan would have been perfect, had you not pulled all the stronghold's defenses to do it. If Noth had fallen, it would have been folly."

"Ellys!" Aderri hissed.

Dezne held up a hand, but it was Devlin who spoke. His voice was a slightly lower tenor than his sister's. "No, she is right. It would have been disaster if not for you three and the rest of Dracona." He inclined his head, his gaze focused on Aderri. "We have never—"

"—met the Clan Riki before. But we know you as such. How—"

"—is that possible?"

Aderri took a breath and glanced at Ellys out of the corner of her eye. Ellys merely shrugged and stuffed another large bite of roast low beast into her mouth. "I have been traveling for many decades, searching for a mate to bring home to the Clan."

Regent Devlin shook his head. "That is a lie. We can—"

"—always tell when we are in the presence of untruth. You are adagnitio—"

"—searching for knowledge."

Ellys moved her hand beneath the table to give Aderri's leg a reassuring squeeze. Aderri confirmed the real answer. "It's true, I left a long time ago to travel the six in search of knowledge. But in the end, I still found the mate I wasn't looking for."

"Prophesy has a way of—"

"—coming true, whether we want it or not."

Aderri swallowed some mead. "A few moons ago, I wouldn't

have believed you." She turned to meet Ellys's silver eyes. Ellys smiled with all the love she felt inside. Then Aderri looked down the table to meet Rocc's dark-eyed stare. "But now," she said and moved her attention back to the Regents, "I've found everything I need with Ellys DeEnsis and Lady Roccotári."

"You no longer seek knowledge?"

"I—" Aderri looked down at her platter then met Dezne's eyes again. "I cannot say that. I still feel the pull. Why do you ask?"

Rather than answer, Regent Devlin turned the subject aside. "You keep the most interesting company, Aderri n'all Dracona."

Before Aderri or Ellys could respond, Dezne continued her brother's thought. "Future leader of Clan Dracona paired with the child of Destier-sen, who is in turn the bondmate to an earth elemental. That is a powerful triad."

"What?" Aderri asked.

Ellys spoke at the same time. "How did you—"

Rocc stomped a hoof loudly and bumped her chest against the long, wood table to get everyone's attention. *How do you know that?*

"It was foretold in two other tomes, the Book of Earth and the Book of Fire."

Those were lost thousands of cycles ago.

Devlin said, "They were—"

"—not. There is a reason the stronghold of Noth has never fallen."

"And can never fall. We preserve the Tomes of Aeschar far below."

No one spoke as the three guests stared at the Twin Regents. Ellys considered whether or not she could take another bite without breaking the heavy silence. She finally gave in to her base need, and the loud crunch of a raw carrot pulled everyone's gaze.

Ellys shrugged. "What? I hate magic and I'm hungry."

Rather than be angry, the Regents seemed amused at her statement. Devlin grinned. "We like you—"

"—Master DeEnsis."

Then, as quick as a snuffed candle wick, their expressions became stern with lowered brows. Dezne placed both her hands, palm down, on the table to each side of her platter. "Today would have ended in disaster, not just for Muniers but the entire six nations. But you three, more than the rest, prevented that."

"We would like to reward you, compensate you with something

you desire."

For the first time in her life, Ellys didn't think of herself or Rocc. She didn't consider gold coin or other compensation. Her thoughts turned to the hope that Aderri would get something to help her achieve her dreams.

In an opposite turn of personality, Aderri was less introspective and more to the point. "Our defense was part of the pact with Dracona, and we need no compensation."

"We know the true motives behind your actions, but we also know that even if your mate had not been on the balcony helping us, you would have defended with your life."

"We are also aware that Ellys is not part of Clan Dracona and owed no such allegiance to the pact, nor to Muniers. She, too, would have defended us from the Carthunian Black Guard, even if Dracona had not been part of this battle. You both shine with the light of goodness that cannot be—"

"—ignored."

Ellys's head swam at the way the Twin Regents' speech jumped back and forth between them, but she understood their intent. Her chair was loud as she slid away from the table and stood to face them. She bowed, and after, she briefly touched her chin, then the left and right sides of her chest with the first two fingers of her right hand. "As a follower of Toroc, it is my duty to preserve the balance, and I need no compensation for that." With those words, she resumed her seat and slid closer to the table again.

"Ellys..."

Ellys moved her gaze from Dezne and Devlin to Aderri. "Yes."

Aderri pointed at her own chin. "You have, uh, gravy on your chin."

Rocc snorted from her end of the table. *Regents Dezne and Devlin, please ignore the lack of manners of my bondmate. She certainly didn't learn anything from me.* Then the steed leaned down and delicately crunched another apple.

Ellys cursed under her breath and quickly wiped her face and fingers with a nearby rag on the table. She also ran it over the leather of her chest for good measure. She felt her pale skin flush as she looked back at the Regents. Their eyes fairly danced with mirth. "My apologies."

"Manners—"

"—or lack thereof aside—"

"—we would like to offer you a place with us. You are a talented fighter and strategist, and have—"

"—well-proven your loyalty." Dezne tilted her head. "Or perhaps, you wish a compensation of gold instead."

Ellys glanced at Rocc, then Aderri, before answering. "I'm afraid I can't choose either of those things without consulting with my companions. Their needs supersede my own in this instance."

"Well enough. Lady Roccotári, what is it you desire for your—"

"—sacrifice—"

"—today?"

It was a sacrifice I was happy to make if it kept me with those I love most.

The word "sacrifice" brought Ellys's thoughts of food and gold to a halt, and she gave Rocc a scrutinizing look. "What do they mean, sacrifice? You never told us how you got here so fast." Rocc shuffled a bit, a sign of her nervousness. "Roccotári, what did you do?"

I broke my Grove oath and reverted to my natural form outside the veil.

Ellys frowned. "Natural form?"

"Grove oath?" Aderri asked.

Rocc remained silent so Regent Devlin answered. "Surely you know that Lady Roccotári is an earth elemental?"

"She is a being of pure earth energy." Dezne looked at Rocc. "Did you travel the ley lines from Dracona Keep?"

I did. I am. Rocc left her place near the opposite end of the table and walked over to where Ellys sat with a dumbfounded look upon her face. *This was the last secret, one that I could not tell even you. It is forbidden, dictated by the oath I took. But now that I've broken it, and can never again cross the veil, it is only fair you know.*

"What do you mean you can't cross the veil? But that—you'll never return to the Ethereal Forest!"

Yes. And I would do it a thousand times over if it meant I didn't lose you or Aderri. By changing form and fusing with the ley line to travel the magic between Dracona Keep and Noth, I severed the connection I held to the magics of the Fae. I am now out of synch with the Ethereal Forest and cannot cross their energy barrier, the veil.

Aderri covered her mouth at hearing the shocking news but didn't speak. Ellys looked at her bondmate with sorrow. Despite the dumb soldier act that she sometimes put on, she wasn't stupid by any definition of the term. Ellys knew exactly why Roccotári gave up her eternal place to save Aderri. "You were afraid I'd leave you if she died."

Rocc rubbed her muzzle against Ellys's cheek. *I was afraid to lose both of you.*

Ellys couldn't speak for a moment, fearing she'd become wrought with emotion. Instead, she stood again and hugged Rocc around the neck. "Just as Aderri promised to me, I'll do my best to always return to you." She stepped back.

Aderri wiped her own tears away. "I couldn't imagine two beings I'd rather spend my life with."

Rocc's next comment returned smiles to all their faces. *I hope you didn't just get gravy on my coat. You know how much I hate being dirty.* Ellys snorted and sat back down. Rocc finally answered the question posed by the Twin Regents. *My desire is to stay with my bondmate and her mate, the location or task matter not. Though I confess a preference to trees over cities.*

As one, the Regents answered, "Very well." They turned their gaze to Aderri, which they all knew was coming. Devlin spoke. "And you, Aderri n'all Dracona, Riki of the Clan. What is it you desire?"

Dezne added, "What is the one thing you've searched for but never found?"

Aderri said, "You already know the last bit of knowledge I seek. Why do you ask?"

"And if we give you that which you wish, how would you use it, and—"

"—why do you want it?"

Aderri paused and her gaze grew unfocused as she contemplated their words. She answered a candle drop later. "I wish to understand the land and people, to make sense of our history and actions across the six nations. I want understanding, but more than that, I wish for peace. I dislike seeing struggle wherever I go. There is also a big part of me that simply wants to know the secrets of the world."

Devlin inclined his head. "As a scholar myself, I can respect that answer."

Dezne smiled. "We are prepared to allow you access to study, provided the information of the five hidden tomes never sees the light of day. It is our belief that this knowledge can only aid you as Drakaina when the time comes, which in turn will benefit all of Muniers."

"Why?"

"Why do we trust you?"

"Yes. As you've mentioned before, you have never met me. Why would you let me study the greatest mysteries our world has never known?"

"We have confidence in all three of you." Aderri looked startled at the simple answer. Dezne elaborated. "We trust you to hold tight to the secrets discovered within the Tomes of Aeschar. We trust Lady Roccotári to keep you from diving further than your spirit can handle. And we trust Ellys DeEnsis to keep you balanced."

"I—" Aderri gave Ellys a helpless look. She was being served her greatest desires upon a golden platter and clearly didn't know what to do with the offer.

Ellys grabbed her hand, interlocking their fingers together. "It's okay to get what you want, Aderri. Just say yes. We'll figure the rest out as necessary."

We will be with you no matter what.

With shining eyes, Aderri gazed upon her companions, and they felt a massive rush of love as she flexed her empathy. Ellys sucked in a breath, and Rocc stepped closer so she could lip at Aderri's flaming red curls. Then Aderri turned back to the Twin Regents. "My answer is yes."

Chapter Twenty-Three

Roccotári and Ellys were fit enough to travel by that evening, but Aderri was still weak and would remain so for a few days, despite Rocc's healing. While her body had been sufficiently repaired, it was Aderri's spirit that needed to rebuild. Rather than subject her to many nights on the road unnecessarily, the Twin Regents offered them all a place at the stronghold until they were ready to travel back to Clan lands. They also sent word with Gessy that the coast was safe, with no Dracona casualties.

They wouldn't know the final outcome of the battle at the border for a few days because the supplemental army hadn't reached Carthune yet. But the Regents had received word from the troops currently stationed there that the tides were already turning, mostly because Carthune had sent more than half their mages with the attacking fleet. And the loss of the northern Carthunian Fleet would severely impact the country's offensive capability for cycles to come, making Muniers safe on at least that front.

Rocc was given a large, open stall and whatever she wanted to eat that evening. Ellys and Aderri were shown to a suite of rooms a few floors below the Chamber of Regents. Because of Aderri's flagging energy, they opted to take last meal in their room. Aderri had been quiet since their meeting with the Twin Regents. Ellys knew she'd eventually speak of her thoughts and did her best to ensure her love's comfort until that time. It didn't take long once they were in their rooms.

"I know you said you didn't care where we went as long as we were together, but what will you do if I stay here in Noth to study the Tomes of Aeschar?"

Ellys poured more wine into their mugs. "Truthfully…I hadn't given it much thought. The meeting was a bit much after such an intense day. I'd love nothing more than a hot soak, in lieu of a round of healing from Rocc."

"You're injured?"

"Not severely, but I've got plenty of cuts and bruises after fending off those Black Guards earlier. I'll give Carthune credit for that. Their elite soldiers were skilled."

Aderri caressed the back of Ellys's hand. The heat of her fingers caused chill bumps to race up Ellys's arm. "Not skilled enough. Thank you for your defense today."

"Shouldn't that be my line?"

"It's as the Regents said, you owe Muniers nothing. Yet you willingly volunteered to defend us with your life. You had no way of knowing how many attackers had come to the stronghold, nor if they were more skilled. Yet you jumped into the fray anyway."

Ellys gave a cocky grin at Aderri's words. "I don't know if you've heard, but I'm no slouch with a sword." She leaned closer and lowered her voice. "I think there's even a song about my exploits somewhere in southern Parelgar." Both women laughed heartily, and it was a healing balm after the day they'd had. "Anyway, to answer your question, I could definitely use a hot soak and scrub. Perhaps even some ointment for the larger cuts. Unfortunately, all my gear is still in your home on Clan lands."

Aderri covered her eyes, and the turn of her lips implied some hidden humor. "Ellys…"

"Yes?"

"Didn't you go into the other room?"

"The one with the large, comfortable-looking bed?"

"No. The other room." Aderri pointed to a door at the far end of the suite, opposite the one they knew led to the sleeping chamber.

Ellys looked from one door to the other, perplexed. "Um, no. I *must* be tired because I would never have missed such a detail otherwise."

Given Ellys's penchant for observation and always having her back to a wall in any unfamiliar place, she spoke the truth.

Aderri said, "The entire stronghold must be imbued with more magic than some will see their entire lifetime. Through the far door is a bathing chamber, as well as a waste closet that disposes matter…who knows where. They've clearly thought of everything a royal guest would need."

"Waste closet? You mean there is no pot to be emptied?"

"No. It's quite handy and certainly better smelling."

The idea of a waste closet intrigued Ellys. "No pot…amazing."

A familiar look of curiosity wrinkled Aderri's brows. Ellys loved that look and awaited the imminent question.

"Elves always act as though they're beyond the mortal races. Do they have something similar within the Ethereal Forest?"

"Elves are very in touch with nature and believe that everything received must have proper return."

"What does that mean, exactly?"

"It means they shit in the woods like an everyday ursine."

Aderri slapped Ellys's arm. "They do not!"

Ellys winced and held her hands up in surrender. "Okay, they probably don't. Honestly, I wasn't there long enough to find out. If you remember, they let me in long enough to attend my father's ceremony then promptly told me to never return."

Rather than continue the current topic, Aderri circled them back around to its beginning point. She reached up to wipe a bit of dirt from Ellys's temple that she had missed earlier. "So, would you like to spend some time in the other chamber?"

Ellys made a face. "I don't think it would be comfortable nor cleanly for both of us to use this waste closet at the same time."

Aderri sighed with exasperation. "Not the closet, you mangy elf! I'm talking about the bathing pool."

"Oh." Then after a beat, Ellys said, "Hey. You've clearly been spending too much time with Rocc."

"Perhaps." Aderri stood. "Come along, darling. A hot bath will do us both good."

"How hot?"

Aderri smirked as they made their way into the other room. "As hot as you can stand…but not *that* hot. We both need to rest for a day or two, healer's orders."

"Your healer is a horse."

"She's not a horse."

"Literally. She actually wasn't a horse all this time. Who knew she was telling the truth?" They both grinned.

"Really." Aderri gestured toward the four wall sconces, and they flickered with flame. She found two levers that appeared to control the flow of water into the pool. "Get the plug, will you?"

Ellys walked down the steps into the waist-deep basin and wedged a nearby stopper into the hole that was perfectly centered in the bottom. She got out again, and Aderri gave one lever a twist. Steaming water splashed across the tile. She must have judged it to be too warm and moved the other lever. Afterward, the water steamed slightly less. "Fascinating."

Ellys explored a cabinet on the opposite side of the chamber. There she found soaps, sea sponges, soft cloths, and much larger drying cloths. "Looks like everything we need here."

Aderri had already stripped and waded into the water with a groan of pleasure. "Why are you still standing over there?"

"Toroc only knows." Ellys quickly gathered up a selection of items and made her way to the edge of the bathing pool. She stripped as quickly as her sore body would allow and joined her lover in the water. It had been a long day, and she was going to soak up as much heat as her bones could handle.

After a few candle drops of bliss, Aderri spoke. "We should talk about our future."

"Weren't we just doing that?"

"To start, we need to decide where to live. What do you prefer, or Roccotári? If I'm to study at the stronghold, we'll need to be close enough for travel to and from our home. Obviously, Clan lands would be too far."

"True. Honestly, I don't have a preference and I suspect Rocc would be amenable to whatever you need. We were both prepared to live within the walls of a monastery, but I know that she prefers the trees over cities. She said as much in front of the Regents."

"It makes sense, given who and what she is. What if we look into someplace on the way out of Noth, farther down the coastal road from Ailith's inn? That's not too far away."

"All right. If I recall, that entire area was heavily forested. It would be a fair bit of luck if the crown held it. Otherwise, we can inquire about purchasing a parcel of land there. Something large enough for a dragon to change, and with enough space to host our kin."

Aderri tilted her head slightly. "*Our* kin?"

"Yes, Dracona. Who else would I be speaking of?" Her lover's face softened when Ellys claimed Clan Dracona as her own. Ellys sucked in a breath at the intense wave of love projected to her via Aderri's empathy.

Aderri grasped her hand under the water. "Thank you." She let the moment settle then continued their discussion. "And where will we get the gold for building our new homestead?"

"The way I see it, the Twin Regents owe us a bit for what we did. If they're extending this privilege to you, they clearly want you to stay. Not only that, but they did actually offer me gold. I can use that to help us create a home."

"But that gold would be your reward."

Ellys moved closer. "My reward is a life with you."

Their kiss was firm and intense, but not full of passion. It wasn't the time and neither had the energy. Aderri pulled away and leaned her shoulder against Ellys's. "And what will you do with yourself as I wile away the candle marks deep within the bowels of the stronghold?"

"Well…I completed my quest. Perhaps I'll spend some time at the Temple of Toroc. I did promise to check in on Doonie's situation. After that, I guess I'll do as Toroc wills. As long as I live in balance, my life is my own."

Aderri blew out a nervous breath. "So, we're doing this?" She turned to gaze into Ellys's eyes.

"We are. Together."

Laughter filled the room. "My mother is sure to be happy that I'm staying close."

Ellys bumped her shoulder against Aderri's. "You'll be happy, too."

"I will." Aderri suddenly moved over on the bench they sat upon and raised her hand out of the water. "Now that our immediate future plans have been settled," she said and moved her pointer finger in a circle, "turn your back to me and I'll scrub it for you. Perhaps we can ask someone for salve when we finish here."

"You have the best ideas."

"Adagnitios usually do."

****

The next day Aderri wanted to go visit with Ailith, to make sure her friend was okay after the coastal attack. The Stolen Pelt was close enough to the stronghold to potentially catch a stray stone from the Carthunian catapults.

Aderri mounted Roccotári once they were on the cobbled road outside the stronghold's inner walls. It was the split where one fork led to the north, one to the south, and the third branch led straight into the heart of Noth and farther beyond, all the way out toward the border crossing at Cat's Head.

Ellys had no plans to go with them. "Rocc, can you take Aderri to the inn?"

"You aren't coming with us?"

"No. As much as I love bearing the brunt of Ailith's biting wit, I have a promise to keep. As long as we're going to be here a few days, I may as well get it out of the way."

"Promise?"

She's going to the temple.

Aderri said, "Is that right?"

"Yes. I plan to visit the Temple of Toroc and have the templar enter my name into the Book of Orders. Then I'm going to speak with the monastery's Master of Orders, their abbez. I promised Ailith I'd see about Doonie's situation, and there is no reason I can't do it now."

"If you're sure…"

"I shouldn't be more than a few candle marks. I'll meet you at The Stolen Pelt after."

"Okay. Be safe, love."

Ellys grinned at her. "Always."

She meant to say, don't be an idiot.

"Hey!"

Rocc ignored her bondmate's offended look and snorted before walking away. Aderri said, "Don't be an idiot, Ellys."

She really can't help herself.

"I suspect you're right."

They were more than a dozen strides down the road, and Ellys called loudly to their retreating backs. "I can still hear you."

Aderri and Rocc's voices came back at the same time.

"Stop eavesdropping!"

Stop eavesdropping!

✳✳✳✳

It didn't take long for Ellys to get directions to the Temple of Toroc from a young errand boy.

"It be right along this road, near where it exits the last set of walls. Be a road there heading to the right when you're going out such. Just take that smaller road, near Joss the baker's place, and it won't be much down the way. You'll see the temple first and the monastery walls be around the back." The boy stood staring at her, clearly expecting a coin for his troubles.

Ellys cursed beneath her breath. "I'm afraid I flew in with Clan Dracona the other day and don't have my pack nor coin purse in Noth right now."

The boy scoffed. "Yeh, right. Be an original excuse, fer sure, but still just an excuse."

Thinking fast, Ellys threw out a suggestion. "You ever hear of The Stolen Pelt?"

"Sure 'nuff, that be the selk's place and the direction I'm headed next. Why?"

"My mate, Aderri, is there visiting with the innkeeper. She can give you a coin for your services. Just tell her Ellys sent you."

The boy raised a single brow, clearly skeptical. "And why would yer mate believe me?"

"She's Dracona. She'll smell if you're lying."

The color washed from the boy's dirty face. "Dr...Dracona? Puh...perhaps I'll just give you a free pass."

Ellys laughed. "She won't eat you. I promise. But watch out for the innkeeper, Ailith. She's a bit dodgy."

After a candle drop of hesitation, the boy finally nodded. "Okay, Moz." Before Ellys could reply, he turned and pelted in the opposite direction with his satchel slapping against his boney hip, perhaps running the next errand that he mentioned. Ellys really hoped he found Aderri because he looked as though he could use a few good meals. She had a feeling Ailith would fill him up for free, dodginess or no.

Scrappy and distrustful though he was, the boy certainly knew the city, and it wasn't long before Ellys stood in front of the temple. Inside she found a few Order of Truth acolytes and the templar. Ellys approached the altar of Toroc. It was nothing more than a tall statue of an armored being with two faces on a single head. The body was muscular, but androgynous. The faces were similar in appearance, much like the Twin Regents', but where one had a broader forehead and square jaw, the other was a bit narrower. Even so, you couldn't point to one over the other and assert a gender. The Goz of War was genderless and sometimes fluid.

"Good morn, traveler. My name is Eenigh, and I am the templar for Toroc in Noth. Are you here to pay homage, Moz, or to learn about walking the path of balance?" Not knowing Ellys's name nor gender, the templar used a common honorific, one that Ellys heard many times since coming to Muniers. Clearly the people of Aderri's homeland were much more familiar with Toroc and those that lived the way of gender balance. Ellys's androgyny meant she was often mistaken for one or the other, even if she didn't take the oath herself.

Ellys bowed to the templar, respecting their place as spiritual leader. "I already follow Toroc's path with every step forward and each new day. If I may, I am here to present myself for entry into the Book of Orders."

The templar raised a brow. "What is your temple of origin?"

Ellys made the sign of Toroc. "I grew up in the Llofgroon Temple. It is located on the southern side of the Galmet Isthmus."

"Kuwythian? You've traveled a long way to record your name."

Ellys smiled. "I've traveled a long time to record my name. You see, I've only just completed my Quest of Toroc. It took me more than a hundred cycles and all six nations to find and warm myself by the phrenic flame."

"Your quest, I assume?" Ellys nodded. "And where is this flame?"

"Aderri n'all Dracona is known as the phrenic flame to her father and family. She is now my informal mate, a bond that was foretold by my previous mate many cycles ago upon her death bed."

The templar stepped aside and waved Ellys up to the dais. "Very well. We shall search the Book of Orders for your quest, then I will write your name next to it. Do you wish to take the oath at this time?"

Ellys was prepared for the question. She'd thought about it many nights while staring at the stars above. Perhaps if she'd completed her quest many cycles before, she would have accepted. But she'd spent too long in her current mindset and found it comforting and familiar. "No." Templar Eenigh gave her a startled look. "It's not required, correct?"

"While unusual, it is not required unless you wish to become a Battling Monk and live permanently within the walls of the monastery." They paused and inclined their head at Ellys, indicating respect for her decision. "Our Goz would never command such. To force against one's nature is to push a creature out of balance, something Toroc finds anathema."

There was an alcove at the back of the dais, behind the giant statue of Toroc. Inside the alcove was the largest tome Ellys had ever seen, with a quill and dry inkwell next to it. The size of the tome made sense, given that every Book of Orders was magically linked.

Each new quest assigned expanded the pages contained within. The only time Ellys had seen one was when she initially received her quest, longer ago than most.

The templar lit two candles, one in each corner of the alcove. "What is the cycle of your unsheathing?"

"Twenty-four ninety. The moon was Podai."

Eenigh pinched a thick selection of pages between their thumb and forefinger and turned them to the side. It took a few more swipes before they found the cycle and moon. The writing was small and precise, neither slanted forward nor backward, as if each word had been pressed into the page whole by an artist with a carved block.

"Here we are." The templar found the reference to the phrenic flame and traced their finger along the entire line. At the end there was Ellys's order and rank. After that, a blank space that was large enough for a name.

Ellys felt the first stirrings of reverence when she whispered, "Ellys DeEnsis." She spelled it out for him with a voice just as quiet.

The templar leaned forward and spat into the inkwell, then used the tip of the quill to mix it around. Once Eenigh was satisfied by the consistency, they gently grasped the flowing sleeves on their right arm with the left hand, then carefully scribed her name on the page. Each letter inked onto the parchment glowed for a heartbeat before fading to resemble the rest of the tome. When Eenigh was finished, they returned the quill to its previous resting place and released the sleeve. Then with a casual wave of their hand, a light draft of air blew into the alcove to simultaneously snuff the candles and finish drying the ink.

The templar took a step back from Ellys and made the sign of Toroc. "Ellys DeEnsis, Master of Sword and Fist, your place in Toroc's Guard is secure for as long as you follow the path of balance. Should you commit reprehensible crimes against our Goz or followers, your name will be stricken from record and you shall only be known to us as '*inaequalis,*' to be cast from the orders with shame."

"Thank you, Templar Eenigh."

Eenigh directed Ellys toward a door off one side of the dais. "Come, it is tradition to share refreshment after induction. Will you join me?"

Ellys nodded and followed. "I have some time. I promised one friend that I'd check on another that I recommended to the monastery for training. I've heard some disturbing things about the abbez, or perhaps it is one of the masters. The details of the *who* were not specific, just the *what*. I wish to see for myself."

The door led to a tiny room with the bare necessities for resting during the day. It contained a small table, a cot near the far wall, and various pitchers and bottles on a nearby shelf. Eenigh waved toward one of the two chairs and stood near the shelf. "Do you have a drink preference between water, mead, or wine?"

"Whatever you're having is fine."

Eenigh removed the stopper from a wine bottle and poured some into two mugs, handed Ellys hers, and sat down across from her. "Tell me of these disturbing things. I haven't been at this post long. I traveled from Carthune before hostilities closed the borders. I was promoted to templar last cycle, and my own monastery got word that Noth was in need."

"What happened to the previous temple head?"

"It remains a mystery. They simply disappeared. Malfeasance was suspected at first, but there is no proof of anything. However," they said and leaned closer to Ellys, "I have been watching since my arrival. I find something about the current abbez's actions…unsettling. Unfortunately, I don't have much to do with the monastery training or direction of the onsite orders. That is why I wish to know of your concerns."

Ellys's mind was already working to unravel the mystery that Eenigh shared with their assignment. "I wrote a sponsorship letter for a young selkie named Doonie. At least that's their nickname. I suspect it's not their proper one. Anyway, I was informed by Doonie's lover that the abbez demanded they move onsite to the monastery for the duration of their two-cycle training."

"By Toroc, that's not how sponsorship works. It's no wonder we can't increase the Order rolls here in Noth if things are mismanaged in such a way. That is how you drive away potential acolytes, not recruit them."

Ellys drank from her mug and contemplated the problem. It would surely make her later than expected to the inn, but she had an idea. "What if you write a similar sponsorship letter, and I pose as someone looking for training? My concern is that if I walk in there as I am now, whoever the abbez is—"

"Their name is Tomvir."

"Tomvir will be wary and defensive, perhaps even not be true to their nature."

Eenigh rubbed their smooth cheek and looked Ellys up and down. "It could work. With your heritage, you certainly look young enough. We would need to get you out of that gear though. It's much too nice for someone seeking training. Your trousers and boots will do, and I should have a shirt here you can borrow." The templar stood and went to the cot and pulled something from beneath the coverlet. They stopped on the way back to the table to grab one of a handful of rolled parchments. "This should do it."

Ellys stripped off her armor and shirt, and replaced it with the templar's. Then she looked down at the small, rolled parchment. "Do what, exactly?"

"I keep a few letters handy in case I meet someone I think would be a good addition to Toroc's Guard. Now, speak your full name when I'm finished reciting the spell. I'll point at you." Eenigh unrolled the parchment, then spoke three words and pointed at Ellys. "*Sonum, nominis scriba.*"

"Ellys DeEnsis."

"There. Done." Sure enough, Ellys's name was written in bold ink at the bottom of the page. They rolled it up again and handed it over to Ellys. "Let me know what you find out. I'll try to watch from a window that overlooks the training yard, but Tomvir seems to have a special sense when I do so and I've yet to see anything untoward."

Ellys bowed and tucked the parchment into the front of her borrowed shirt. "I will." She paused before leaving the small room. "And if they are corrupt? If this Tomvir has left the light of balance, what then?"

Eenigh's face hardened. They may have been recently promoted to templar, but they certainly knew the rules of Toroc. "I will stand as witness. You have my blessing to remove them from their post if it appears as though harm is being done to the acolytes. Refrain from killing if possible, as they will be tried for breaking the balance. If found guilty, they'll be stricken from the Book of Orders, exactly as I warned you."

Eenigh directed Ellys around the side of the temple. There she found large double doors set in a tall wall that surrounded the monastery grounds. It was the way of Toroc for the doors to be open and welcoming from sunup to sundown, just as Ellys remembered from her childhood. She stood off to the side, quietly watching and hoping to remain unnoticed long enough to take in the training techniques of the various masters scattered about.

The courtyard was large and full of sparring acolytes. Some were clearly training with the Order of Swords, and others, the Order of Fist. Acolytes of the Order of Truth became templars, like Eenigh, and were the ones she saw working inside the temple.

Ellys noticed Doonie among a handful of individuals, all swinging dull blades against practice posts, timed by the cadence called out by their instructor. It was an exercise meant to improve strength and stamina, as well as teach them basic strokes.

A harsh voice startled Ellys from the memories such a sight invoked. "You, muzzle-mouthed sea rat! What do you think you're doing?"

A familiar voice answered. "Me, Abbez? I be swingin' me blade as instructed."

"You're doing nothing but wasting our time here. Straighten those shoulders, bend your knees. Do you want to fight for Toroc, Acolyte, or are you naught more than the filth that crawls from Bron's arse?"

Doonie's face darkened. "I fight for meself, Moz. But I believe in the tenets of balance taught as part of Toroc's worship. And I've told ye before I'm not an acolyte. I was given a sponsorship letter fer training—"

The fist to Doonie's gut stole whatever other words were left to be said. At least two masters took a step toward the abbez, but the menacing look on Tomvir's face turned their gazes the other way. For a heartbeat, perhaps more, Ellys felt rage. Then she remembered who she was and took a few deep breaths until she could best walk with balance. She finally spoke up when she saw the abbez's fist draw back again.

"Excuse me? I'm looking for Abbez Tomvir? I was sent here for training." Ellys slouched and schooled her expression to appear humble, something that she had a hard time remembering how to do.

The brutish abbez lowered their hand and stalked across the courtyard toward Ellys. She wasn't afraid, because while they were large and heavily muscled, they were still just a regular human. "And who in the seven levels of Abbad are you? I don't care about letters. We don't accept beggars and street dung at the monastery. If you want to train, you become an acolyte like everyone else." Tomvir sized up Ellys, but her muscles were hidden beneath the templar's baggy shirt. "You don't look like much. Can you even swing a blade, elf?"

Ellys removed her letter from inside her shirt and held it out to Tomvir. "Will you accept my letter of sponsorship?"

Tomvir slapped the letter from Ellys's hand, then faster yet, drew back their arm and backhanded Ellys across the face. She took the blow and didn't react. The abbez grinned at her. "If you can take a hit from me, you just might have potential, slight though you are."

With those words, Ellys drew herself up to her full height and let the weight of her experience wash over her. She stepped back from Tomvir and made the sign of Toroc, much to their confusion. Ellys glanced around and took note that the entire courtyard had fallen silent as everyone watched the interaction between her and the abbez. Doonie still held their stomach, though they sported a wide grin.

"My name is Ellys DeEnsis, Master in the Order of Swords. With the sanction of Templar Eenigh, and by will of Toroc's own laws, I hereby relieve you of your post. I order you to surrender yourself for Toroc's judgment."

Tomvir laughed in her face. "I'll do no such thing. You're not even armed—"

Ellys curled her fingers and struck them in the jaw with the flat of her palm. Then before they could recover, she foot-swept the abbez to the ground. They rolled quickly out of the way and made to run for the rack of swords on the adjacent wall of the courtyard, but Ellys was faster. She ran behind them and gave a flying kick from a position horizontal to the ground. Her feet struck Tomvir in the middle of the back, sending the abbez face first onto the dirt again.

Tomvir groaned but came up raging. Ellys blocked a few more punches, but their movements were getting predictable with their anger, and she easily knocked them down a third time. Before Tomvir could rise again, Ellys dropped a knee onto their ribs, causing them to groan in pain. Then she quickly rolled the abbez over and pinned them with her legs. Before Tomvir could react again, she put them into a headlock. "Stay down or this will get more painful for you."

Their words spat out furiously. "Who are you?"

"I told you already. I'm Ellys DeEnsis, and I don't need to be armed to enforce Toroc's way. I'm a Master of Swords…and oh, I forgot to mention, also a Master of Fist. I just like swords better."

Someone snickered nearby. Ellys looked up to see all the acolytes and the handful of other masters looking on. She nodded to one of the two that initially took a step toward Tomvir when they hit

Doonie. "You, what's your name?"

Their voice was a light tenor but steady. "I'm Master Caze."

"Bring bindings. Tomvir is no longer your abbez."

A voice spoke up from the far side of the courtyard. "You can't do that. You have no authority here."

"On the contrary, Master DeEnsis is following the true path of Toroc, unlike your former abbez."

Ellys recognized Eenigh's voice immediately. "How much did you see?"

"I was watching from the window, so I saw most of it before you started grappling."

Master Caze quickly returned with bindings, and with the help of Ellys's half-elven strength, they were able to immobilize Tomvir.

Eenigh exercised their overarching power. "Acolytes, training is over for the day. Please return to your rooms and study the Book of Toroc until balance can be restored."

"Ellys, you came back!" Doonie walked up and gave her a hearty back slap.

"Easy there, I'm still a bit bruised from the battle at the stronghold. And I promised Ailith I'd look into your situation here. I'm glad I did."

Eenigh said, "Master Caze and Master Fossen, take Tomvir to the solitary meditation room and lock them inside until a determination can be made."

Fossen was the other who looked as though they wanted to defend Doonie, and Ellys thought that Eenigh had made a good choice. She turned to the templar. "What happens now? Who will lead the orders with the abbez gone?"

Eenigh smiled. "It is within my power to nominate a master who I feel exemplifies the qualities needed to lead, teach, and grow the orders. I would look for someone who is trustworthy and dedicated to the way of balance. We need a soldier for Toroc who has experience and skill."

"What about Ellys?" Doonie turned to her. "I know ye be with te Dracona and all, but Ailith sez it's naught but a ruse yet undiscovered. Ye could stay here wit us."

Ellys said, "The ruse is no more. Aderri and I are together now. Besides, I only just entered the Book of Orders, and I've no want to take the vow of gender balance."

Doonie looked at Eenigh. "Does she need ta take that vow so's ta become te abbez?"

"She does not. However, without it," they cautioned, "she would be unable to live in the monastery itself."

"What about it, Ellys? Ye can stay here…unless yer gonna be travelin' wit yer mate. Ailith sez she likes ta wander."

"Ailith clearly says a lot," Ellys muttered under her breath. She rubbed the tip of her left ear as thoughts and futures tumbled before her. "Actually…we will be staying just outside Noth for the foreseeable future." She turned to Eenigh. "Are you serious about offering this?"

"Only if you're serious about accepting and willing to cleanse the monastery of imbalance and corruption."

Ellys remembered decades of fond memories before she left with Roccotári. "No one should have to train through that. It upsets the balance on many levels, and frankly, I'm appalled it got to this point without someone stepping in."

"Begging your pardon, Master DeEnsis, but none of us were strong enough."

Ellys looked over at the new speaker, seeing it was another one of the masters. "What is the first tenet of Toroc, Moz?"

Their eyes widened. "Uh, strength of will is hardened by surety and quenched in the fires of balance."

"And the second?"

"There is strength in numbers, and even a cacophony of voices can make the music of war."

Ellys clasped their shoulder. "Strength is learned as much as it is trained into the body, and none of us are alone when in service to Toroc. I trust you'll remember that next time you see imbalance in its most harmful form."

The master bowed, looking slightly shamed. "I will. Thank you, Moz."

The eyes staring at Ellys shone with the light of respect, and for Doonie, perhaps a bit of hero worship. But Eenigh's eyes held nothing but question.

Ellys said, "I'll need to speak with my mate first."

"I understand."

"But I'll be back tomorrow to let you know yea or nay."

The templar clapped her on the shoulder, causing her to wince at the pain of yet another bruise. "Well then, I expect a positive answer because only horses say nay."

Ellys shook her head and joined their laughter, though her response confused them. "Not mine."

Chapter Twenty-Four

It was late afternoon by the time Ellys made it to The Stolen Pelt. Once Doonie's situation was explained, they were given leave to come back to Ailith's inn with Ellys. The tavern had begun to get busy as last meal neared, but Ellys easily spotted Aderri sitting at a table with Ailith near the far wall.

Doonie was exuberant with their joy. "Ai, 'Lith. Ellys has sprung me free from the monastery. Did ya miss me, lass?"

Ailith stood, pulled Doonie into an embrace, then slapped their arm as she pulled away again. "Just who are you calling lass? I'm old enough to be your grandmer twice over."

"Ah, but still be fine as a deep-sea pearl." Doonie kissed the back of Ailith's hand then danced away from another swat.

"Be good or I'll sic Ellys on you."

Doonie's eyes danced with mischief. "Ellys has been set upon enough by ne'er-do-wells today. Mayhap ye should be givin' her a break."

At Doonie's comment, Aderri gave Ellys a look of consternation. "I thought you were only going to the temple to get your name listed in the Book of Orders."

"Well...you see—"

"It was brilliant! Ellys took down that Tomvir like pow, bam! Then she be all like 'did I forget to mention that I'm also a Master of Fist?' and she pinned the bully like they were naught more than a whelp."

"Doonie!"

The selkie noticed Ellys's stern look and stepped back. "Yeep! Sorry, Ellys. I'll let ye tell it while I go get me a mead." They stopped and looked over their shoulder. "I'll get ye one, too. Ye earned it."

The other two women stared at Ellys. Aderri walked over to Ellys and wiped a bit of dirt from her cheek. At least her shirt and armor were clean, since she'd been wearing the templar's during the scuffle. The same couldn't be said for her trousers. Ellys's gaze was caught and held by twin sparks of flame within Aderri's dark pupils. "Whatever happened sounds like a good story. Do you want to stay for evening meal and tell us about it?"

Aderri looked a bit weary, which concerned Ellys. "Are you sure you're not too tired?"

"I'm fine, cara."

Aderri bit her bottom lip, and Ellys's attention was caught by those two little pointed teeth. She loved those fangs and had fond memories of the few times Aderri had used them on her. Without another thought, she leaned in and caught Aderri's lips in a passionate kiss.

After a few heartbeats they pulled apart, but Aderri didn't release Ellys's left hand. Instead, she pulled her toward the table they'd been sitting at. "Come, tell us your tale."

Doonie returned just as Ellys told them of what she'd learned from the templar and their plan to find out more about the temperament of the abbez. She spoke of the brief scuffle and what would happen to Tomvir now that they were sure to be cast out from the orders as inaequalis.

Ailith tilted her head. "What will happen to the monastery now? Will another master be chosen to lead the orders as the new abbez?"

"Well, it's primarily up to the templar to nominate someone as they have overarching authority when it comes to the temple and monastery. The abbez is in charge of the monastery and training only."

Ailith raised a brow. "And? That didn't answer my question."

Doonie was practically vibrating in their seat. "Can I tell them, Ellys?"

Ellys rubbed her right ear. She had to remind herself that Doonie was relatively young compared to the rest of them, not more than fifty cycles according to Ailith. "I, um—"

"Tell us what?" Aderri leaned closer to Ellys.

"Templar Eenigh offered the position of abbez to me. They are hoping to cleanse the monastery of imbalance and seek an experienced mind to help build Toroc's Guard within Noth."

Aderri leaned back in her seat. "Hmm…"

Ellys's brows drew down. "What?" Suddenly she realized that Rocc never greeted her when she arrived at The Stolen Pelt. It wasn't like her bondmate to not know when she was around. "Where is Roccotári?"

Ailith said, "She's a-ways down shore visiting with Achaius."

Ellys tensed. "Who is this aaykeyus?"

Aderri rested her hand atop Ellys's. "Rest easy. Achaius is a friend of Ailith's." At Ellys's blank look, she added, "He's a kelpie."

"Oh." Ellys blinked.

Ailith grinned. "She said she had an itch that needed scratching."

"Oh." Ellys's lips curled into a disgusted snarl as she turned to look at Ailith. "Fenwith's balls, I didn't need to know that much."

Doonie guffawed but quickly shut their mouth and took a sip of mead at Ellys's dark look. Aderri cleared her throat. "So, what are you going to do?"

"Do? I'm not going to do anything. Roccotári is free to choose her own companionship and needs no guidance from me." That elicited laughter from Doonie and Ailith. "By Toroc, what is so mage-blasted funny?"

She was grounded again when Aderri ran her hand farther up Ellys's forearm. "I meant, what will you do about the offer? What would be required of you if you were to accept?"

"What do you think of it? I know you'll be studying at the stronghold soon, so we'll obviously be in the area for a while given the nature of your task. I would never say yes if you were opposed."

Aderri smiled at her. "And why would I be opposed? Do me a favor and close your eyes."

"But why—"

"Please?"

Ellys closed her eyes and Aderri caressed her cheek. "Look inside yourself and tell me you don't want this."

After a long candle drop of silence, Ellys opened her eyes again. "I cannot."

"Then I think you have your answer, and I'll support you in whatever way you need. I mean…I'm not fond of the idea that you may have to live at the monastery."

Ellys smiled back at her, forgetting that they were in a crowded tavern full of strangers. "I won't. While my path belongs to Toroc, and my spirit to my bondmate, my heart will always belong to you."

"And the oath of gender balance?"

"Also not required. I will remain as you met me. Just Ellys."

Aderri moved closer until her lips were caressing Ellys's. "My love, you've never been 'just Ellys' to me."

"For the love of Cuon," Ailith said, "kiss already. You're putting me off my mead with all this sexual tension."

Ellys pulled Aderri into a kiss with her left hand as she held up two crossed fingers and waved them toward Ailith.

They pulled apart again as Rocc's voice sounded within Ellys's head. *I see you've returned from the temple. What did I miss?*

Ellys spoke aloud at the table because she knew Rocc would hear the words as they formed within her head. "Rocc, how would you feel about me becoming the abbez of the Nothian monastery?"

Ellys imagined Roccotári's eye roll, despite the fact that only the steed's words rang in her head. *It's about time you made something of yourself. I've only been waiting over a century for this day.*

"What?"

What do you mean, what? How many times have I told you that fate wasn't finished with you yet? Your path was set in motion before we even met. The Book of Prophesy clearly foretold the events of your life, if you only had the wherewithal to look.

Aderri merely rolled her eyes at the steed's teasing. "You can't very well blame Ellys. I've been studying the poxing book in all its iterations for ages and still can't make heads nor tails of it sometimes."

Ellys snickered. "Perhaps you need a tail to understand it, like the one worn by the donkey speaking in our heads."

A donkey? Perhaps you can carry your mate to the stronghold on your back while this donkey returns to see if Achaius swims as good as he fu—

"Stop! I'm sorry, and I'll take it back if you please don't finish that statement."

Fine. I'm heading around back to the stable for a drink. Let me know when you're ready to go.

Knowing when she was beaten, but also knowing she had the support of the two most important creatures in her life, Ellys smiled. "Thank you, Rocc."

You will always have my support, caritas.

****

The next day, Ellys returned to the monastery with Aderri and Roccotári. She introduced her love to Eenigh as the Riki of Clan Dracona then introduced Roccotári. The templar's eyes lit as they took in the glorious elven steed. Ellys explained that she would accept the position of abbez but could not begin for another moon, as she had business to wrap up in Dracona. They were very understanding and even offered to regularly play Rocc's favorite strategy game once Ellys started training for her new duties. Even though the position of abbez could only be held by a master of at least one order, which Ellys was, she still needed further training to ensure she knew proper procedure for running a monastery.

After a few days in Noth, Aderri and Ellys had settled the issue of building a new home. The forested land near Ailith's tavern, south of the outer wall of Noth, was indeed owned by the crown. Because Aderri was the Riki of Clan Dracona, the Twin Regents gifted her enough space to be comfortable and provided Ellys enough gold to hire a reputable builder. The builder assured them that her crew could have the entire homestead completed within a few moons because she had an earth mage working for her that was handy with stone blocks.

Ailith agreed to let them stay with her in the meantime, a prospect that pleased Aderri and Rocc a lot more than it pleased Ellys. But in the end, Ellys simply shrugged and thanked Ailith for the offer. The selkie was rubbing off on her. Slowly.

By their fourth day in the city, Aderri was once again in peak health and ready to return to Clan Dracona. It was Rocc who suggested that it would be significantly quicker if they return the same way they all came to Noth.

"You can do that again?" Ellys was referring to whatever it was that Rocc did to travel the ley lines spoken of by the Twin Regents.

Of course. I've slipped my form and tied myself to the earth energies outside the veil. It will be significantly easier now than it was when I initially merged.

"Fascinating," Aderri said.

Ellys looked at Aderri with concern. "Are you strong enough to fly back to Dracona?"

"I'm as strong as I was the last time you rode me."

Would that be before or after the warning horn sounded? Rocc brayed with laughter, and Ellys gave a shove to her large shoulder.

"You're not as funny as you think you are."

I have to agree with you. I'm funnier.

Ellys huffed. "Your humor is as flat as the sea. You don't even laugh at the best jokes."

I laugh at you, don't I?

With those six words, Aderri laughed out loud. "I'm sorry, but that was pretty funny."

Ellys threw her hands into the air. "For the love of tuppery, must you two always join forces against me?"

Aderri stood at Ellys's left side, put an arm around her shoulder, and pulled her close. Rocc plodded over and lipped at her bond-mate's hair with affection. *We do it because…*

"We love you, Ellys."

"I love you both, too. You're the best four-leggers an elf could ask for."

"Hey, I'm not always a four-legger."

No, but Ellys will ride you either way.

Aderri peered around Ellys and scowled at the elven steed. "You are aware that as a dragon, I could eat you in two bites."

Rocc snorted. *Perhaps you should save your appetite for your mate.*

Ellys shook her head and pulled Aderri closer. "You should give up. There is no winning with her when she's like this."

Roccotári bumped against the both of them. *No need to be rude, Ellys. I was merely…*horsing *around.*

Aderri gaped at her. "By Cassyn, did you just make a joke at your own expense?"

*Of course not. You must have mis…*herd *me.*

A calloused hand covered Aderri's mouth before she could say anything else. Ellys grinned. "Are you ready to give me a ride back to Clan lands?"

Aderri spoke in a sultry tone. "And again when we get there if you're good."

"Oh, I'll be good—"

Their banter was interrupted by Roccotári. *Come along, young-lings. That ley line isn't going to travel itself.*

"That's not how magics work—nevermind. I'm ready to get back to my own bed."

What, a royal guest suite in the Nothian stronghold wasn't com-fortable enough? My lodging was exceptionally pleasant.

Ellys burst into laughter. "You stand in a stall. All your lodgings are practically the same when it comes to comfort."

Rocc blew a heavy breath at her, lips flapping with the wind. *To each their own. And on the subject of exceptional pleasantness, I'm going to go visit Tyrrox. Last quarter moon he said he was breeding some early spring apples, a new species, and they were due to come into season any time.*

Ellys said, "I'm sure that's not the only thing he was breeding."

Aderri spoke at the same time. "I'm sure that's not the only thing coming into season."

Ellys and Aderri looked at each other with mouths open. The steed jerked her head around to stare at them but blinked at Aderri. With an aggressive shake of her mane, she intoned, *Traitor!* Then her body glowed bright white as it became a ball of pure energy and disappeared into the ground.

Ellys dissolved into hysterical laughter. "By Toroc, you actually rendered her nearly speechless! That is truly a first. Well done, love. What do you say we follow her back?"

Aderri gave a rueful grin. "Not all of us can be earth elementals. It won't be as easy."

Ellys pulled her love close and kissed her with every bit of passion in her heart. They'd proven that earth and fire could work well together with destiny on their side. "The best things in life rarely are."

Epilogue

The Drakaina watched the gathering within Dragon Hall with Roccotári standing nearby. She'd been on the Mound for nearly two centuries, long enough to understand that, with the newest naming ceremony, it was probably time she found herself a mate. Wanting some hope that she, too, could find love in its purest form, she asked her lineal bondmate for the age-old tale that everyone in Dracona grew up hearing.

"Rocc, will you tell me the tale of my great-grandam, Aderri, and her mate, Ellys?"

Roccotári moved closer and lipped at Adelia n'ak Dracona's flame-red curls. *I would be happy to, caritas.*

About the Author

Award winning author and Michigan native, Kelly Aten-Keilen brings heroines to life in a variety of blended LGBTQ fiction genres. She specializes in speculative fiction, focusing on extraordinary women who are as flawed as they are compelling. She's not afraid of pain or adversity, but loves a happy ending. Kelly's goal with each new novel is to make people #Think, #Feel, and #Discuss.

"Some words end the silence, others begin it."

Email: killerwit68@gmail.com
Website: http://www.katenauthor.com

Books by K. Aten

The Fletcher

Kyri is a fletcher, following in the footsteps of her father, and his father before him. However, fate is a fickle mistress, and six years after the death of her mother, she's faced with the fact that her father is dying as well. Forced to leave her sheltered little homestead in the woods, Kyri discovers that there is more to life than just hunting and making master quality arrows. During her journey to find a new home and happiness, she struggles with the path that seems to take her away from the quiet life of a fletcher. She learns that sometimes the hardest part of growing up is reconciling who we were, with who we will become.

The Archer

Kyri was raised a fletcher but after finding a new home and
family with the Telequire Amazons, she discovers a desire to take on more responsibility within the tribe. She has skills they desperately need and she is called to action to protect those around her. But Kyri's path is ever-changing even as she finds herself altered by love, loyalty, and grief. Far away from home, the new Amazon is forced to decide what to sacrifice and who to become in order to get back to all that she has left behind. And she wonders what is worse, losing everyone she's ever loved or having those people lose her?

The Sagittarius

Kyri has known her share of loss in the two decades that she has been alive. She never expected to find herself a slave in roman lands, nor did she think she had the heart to become a gladiatrix. But with her soul shattered she must fight to see her way back home again. Will she win her freedom and return to all that she has known, or will she become another kind of slave to the killer that has taken over her mind? The only thing that is certain through it all is her love and devotion to Queen Orianna.

Rules of the Road

Jamie is an engineer who keeps humor close to her heart and people at arm's length. Kelsey is a dental assistant who deals with everything from the hilarious to the disgusting on a daily basis. What happens when a driving app brings them together as friends? The nerd car and the rainbow car both know a thing or two about hazard avoidance. When a flat tire brings them together in person, Jamie immediately realizes that Kelsey isn't just another woman on her radar. Both of them have struggled to break free from stereotypes while they navigate the road of life. As their friendship deepens they realize that sometimes you have to break the rules to get where you need to go.

Waking the Dreamer

By the end of the 21st century, the world had become a harsh place. After decades of natural and man-made catastrophes, nations fell, populations shifted, and seventy percent of the continents became uninhabitable without protective suits. Technological advancement strode forward faster than ever and it was the only thing that kept human society steady through it all. No one could have predicted the discovery of the Dream Walkers. They were people born with the ability to leave their bodies at will, unseen by the waking world. Having the potential to become ultimate spies meant the remaining government regimes wanted to study and control them. The North American government, under the leadership of General Rennet, demanded that all Dream Walkers join the military program. For any that refused to comply, they were hunted down and either brainwashed or killed.

The very first Dream Walker discovered was a five year old girl named Julia. And when the soldiers came for her at the age of twenty, she was already hidden away. A decade later found Julia living a new life under the government's radar. As a secure tech courier in the capital city of Chicago, she does her job and the rest of her time avoids other people as much as she is able. The moment she agrees to help another fugitive Walker is when everything changes. Now the government wants them both and they'll stop at nothing to get what they want.

Running From Forever

Sarah Colby has always run from commitment. But after more than a year on the road following her musical dreams, even she yearns for a little stability. Her sister Annie is only too happy to welcome her back home. When she meets Annie's boss, Nobel Keller, she's immediately drawn to the woman's youthful good looks and dangerous charisma. The first night together leaves Sarah aching for more, but the second shows her the true price of passion.

Embracing Forever

Sarah Colby is a musician, teacher, lover, sister, and so much more. In the past year, she learned that sometimes life takes you places you never even knew existed. For Sarah and her sister Annie, they found out that not only were the monsters real but sometimes you loved them. Now the Colby sisters and their friends are being targeted by someone with a grudge. They must discover who is attacking the people of Columbus or risk losing all that they hold dear. Nobel Keller is with them every step of the way but will she bring salvation or merely the end of their lives in Columbus?

Burn It Down

Ash Hayes was failed by the system at the tender age of sixteen and suffered an addiction. As a result she lives her life weighed down by the guilt of her past. To atone for childhood misdeeds, Ash trained as a paramedic after high school and eventually became a firefighter with the Detroit fire department, along with her childhood best friend Derek. Friend, confidant, brother, he has been her light in an otherwise dark life. When tragedy strikes on the job, injury and forced leave from the department are the least of her concerns. Suffering from even more guilt and depression after the loss of her two closest friends Ash is set adrift in a sea of pain.

When Mia Thomas buys the house next door, Ash finds friendship in the most unlikely of places. It's Mia's nature to help and to heal. Many would say she has a knack for finding the broken ones and leading them into the light. But Ash's secret still lives deep inside her. Before the firefighter can even think of a future, she has to amend her past. Like the phoenix of legend, Ash has to burn her fears to the ground before she can be reborn.

Children of the Stars

The world was forever changed when a government genetic experiment created the Chromodecs from a dead alien in 1952. Decades later, when it became apparent that society needed a way to deal with a hybrid humans with unheard of powers, the CORP was created. The Chromodec Office of Restraint and Protection was a special government police agency formed to keep track of the Chromodecs.

This particular tale involves two refugees, young babies who were sent down to Earth to escape being used as pawns in an interplanetary war, despite the fact that Earth itself wasn't so safe. Destined to be Q'sirrahna, or soul mates as the humans called it, Amari Losira Del Rey and Zendara Inyri Baen-Tor would grow to be more powerful than any other beings on the planet, if they could find each other first.

After being forced to hide from the CORP when it's realized their powers could level entire cities, Amari and Zen will have to answer one question. Who will save the world when it all falls apart?

Remember Me, Synthetica

What happens when a woman loses her memory but gains a conscience?

Dr. Alexandra Turing is a roboticist whose intellect is unrivaled in the field of artificial intelligence. While science has always come easy, Alexandra struggles to understand emotional cues and responses. Driven by the legacy of her late great-uncle, she dedicates her life to the Synthetica project at her father's company, Organic Advancement Solutions (OAS).

Her life is rebooted when she wakes from a coma, six months after being struck by a car. Traumatic brain injury altered Alex's senses, her memory, and her personality. Despite the changes, she feels reborn as she navigates her way back into her old life. Part of her new journey includes dating the alluring Doctor of Veterinary Medicine, Emily St. John.

Emily is enamored with the hyper-intelligent scientist, but there are things about Alex and OAS that don't add up. With Emily's prompting, Alex undergoes testing that leaves her with more questions than answers. What she discovers changes more than her life, it will change the world around her.

The Lost Temple of Psiere

As the heir to the throne, Royal Connate Olivienne Dracore cannot escape having a Shield team protecting her wherever she goes. But with the addition of Shield Commander Castellan Tosh, she has a team that doesn't just guard her person but also aids in her job as a historical adventurist. She knows without a doubt that together they can unravel the Divine Mystery of who the Makers were and why they created the great temples.

With the conclusion of their last mission, Olivienne acquired the map needed to find the mysterious third great temple of Psiere. And there is no one better to accompany than her beloved Cmdr. Tosh. But before they can leave to brave the dangers of the unknown, first they must brave their own oathing ceremony. They will need each other for the coming mission because as with all things related to the Makers, mystery often begets mystery and danger is always just a wrong step away. Especially when the prize is something that could change Psiere forever.

Bringing LGBTQAI+ Stories to Life

Visit us at our website: www.flashpointpublications.com